Urza looked out over the vale and shook his head. He thought of Loran's notes, and he thought of Harbin. The boy had seen what the natives of this land could do and had come to believe there were more powerful forces than just artifice and machinery. Perhaps he was right. But it was too late for that.

Perhaps it was always too late, thought Urza.

There was movement to Urza's right, and he turned, expecting to see Tawnos stepping out of the gathering smoke. Instead it was another figure, this one muscular and young, and dressed in the robes of the desert.

"Hello, Brother," said Mishra.

EXPERIENCE THE MAGIC

THE
BROTHERS' WAR
ARTIFACTS CYCLE · BOOK I

Jeff Grubb

THE BROTHERS' WAR

©2001 Wizards of the Coast, Inc.

Distributed in the United States by Holtzbrinck Publishing. Distributed in Canada by Fenn Ltd.

Distributed to the hobby, toy, and comic trade in the United States and Canada by regional distributors.

Distributed worldwide by Wizards of the Coast, Inc. and regional distributors.

Printed in the U.S.A.

Cover art by r.k. post
First Printing: May 1998
Library of Congress Catalog Card Number: 97-062368

9 8 7 6 5 4 3

US ISBN: 0-7869-1170-0
620-08734-001-EN

U.S., CANADA,	EUROPEAN HEADQUARTERS
ASIA, PACIFIC, & LATIN AMERICA	Wizards of the Coast, Belgium
Wizards of the Coast, Inc.	T Hosfveld 6d
P.O. Box 707	1702 Groot-Bijgaarden
Renton, WA 98057-0707	Belgium
+1-800-324-6496	+322 467 3360

Visit our web site at **www.wizards.com**

DEDICATION

To My Own Brother, Scott

who will agree we got along *much* better

than Urza and Mishra

ACKNOWLEDGMENTS

Those stories set in worlds shared by many creative individuals owe their origin to diverse hands, beyond those listed on the cover. As one who has long labored behind (as well as in front of) the scenes, I would like to thank a group of important individuals, many of whom I have never met or spoken with, whose work and creativity formed the basis for this story.

I would like to thank the designers of the MAGIC: THE GATHERING *Antiquities* set: Skaff Elias, Jim Lin, Chris Page, Dave Pettey, and Joel Mick, and the spirit with which they imbued their cards that I have tried to bring forth here, as well as the innumerable talented artists who wrought images out of a few lines of description. I would also like to thank Jeff Gomez, Jerry Prosser, Paul Smith, Tom Ryder, Phil Hester, and Jeof Vita, who have told part of this tale in graphic format.

I would particularly like to recognize a number of individuals who helped bring this book to life. These include, but are not limited to, Peter Venters and the MAGIC: THE GATHERING Team, Chaz Elliot, Mary Kirchoff, and Emily Arons, all of whom have shown brilliance, understanding, and patience in this long process. In particular I'd like to thank Peter Archer and Lynn Abbey, who listened to way too many odd theories and questions.

Last, but by no means least, I would like to thank Richard Garfield, who got the entire ball of wax rolling in the first place. To quote Sir Isaac Newton, "If I have seen further, it is by standing upon the shoulders of giants." I have been most fortunate to work among an esteemed number of giants.

A word about sources and accuracy

The story of Mishra and Urza is the best-known tale in Terisiare and has been carried to all corners of Dominaria. That is not to say that it is a complete or entirely coherent narrative, as there have been several versions of the tale over the years, each reflecting the tenor of its age. During the time known as The Dark, Urza and Mishra were presented as blackhearted villains, responsible for the fallen state of the world they left in their passing. During the long Ice Age, they were reinvented as potential saviors, patron saints of a long-dead technology that could yet save the world. In the present age they have been alternately presented as heroes and villains, savants and fools, exulted to the heavens or condemned to the flaming pits of Phyrexia. This version attempts to portray them as they were, people of their times, both affecting and affected by the world around them.

The version you hold in your hands, like almost all recognized versions, takes as its primary source *The Antiquity Wars*, an epic poem-cycle by Kayla bin-Kroog. It is one of the few complete records to survive from the age of the Brothers' War. In addition, the author has been scrupulous in tracking down what few primary sources exist from that period, and has painstakingly pored through later editions of the tale, removing those parts that were either patently untrue or shaped by the desires and wishes of later scribes.

The result is the most complete and modern account of Urza and Mishra and the conflict that swallowed them and their world. It is a rendition of the classic tale set for the present age. The reader should trust this version and no other.

A word about time

Dates, when provided in the text, are given in Argivian Reckoning (AR), recognized throughout Dominaria as a standard calendric system. The calendar dates from the birth year of Urza and his brother, and only came into common use many years after their passing. The most complete dating record of the time was used by the Argivians, who dated their years from the founding of Penregon, their capital. At the time of Urza's and Mishra's birth the year was 912 PF.

PROLOGUE

Opposites Attract

It was the night before the end of the world.

The two armies had gathered on opposite sides of a blasted vale. Once this had been a verdant valley, its wide plain shaped by a wide, meandering stream, its flanking hills blanketed by thick groves of oak, blanchwood, and ironroot. Now these trees were gone; no more than ragged stumps remained, the grass burned away, and the earth beneath packed hard and barren. The stream was a sluggish flow hidden by a thick film of oil, its surface broken only by the shadowy masses of nameless solids.

Thick, inky clouds concealed the moons and stars from sight. It had been overcast and cold on Argoth, despite unseasonably warmer weather elsewhere on Terisiare. Both sides in the upcoming battle had taken to torching the forests they found, if only to deny their opponents supplies and support. By day the cloud canopy was a dull gray, a sheet of rolled and unfinished steel. By night it was lit only from below, by the thousands of campfires and foundries that now dotted the landscape. Along the opposite rims of the vale the flames lit by both invading forces glimmered like evil eyes in the darkness.

Spanning the shallow stream was a pair of toppled giants, remnants of an earlier battle between one of the invaders and the original inhabitants of this land. One of the fallen giants had been made of living wood, and had been splintered into a thousand shards. Its huge forested head lay on the ground, screaming silently to the uncaring night. It had been the last champion of the natives of Argoth, the avatar of their goddess, and with its death passed away all hope for the island people.

5

The victor in the battle had also been destroyed in the struggle. This huge humanoid monster was made of stone, its joints constructed of massive plates of pitted iron and great brass gears. Its lithic body had been broken and patched a number of times, and great sheets of metal had been bolted to its hide to hold it together. The battle with the living forest beast had overtaxed its pistons and armatures. Its final lunge had splintered its opponent; now it sprawled forward, face-down, a bridge over the tepid stream. One of the stone giant's arms had been ripped loose from the battle and lay a few hundred feet away, its fingers raised to claw the sky.

On the back of the granite giant's silent corpse a lone figure waited. In his youth he had been broad shouldered and handsome, but the years of war and service to his master had exhausted him. His shoulders were slumped now, and his frame carried the additional weight of both his responsibilities and his age. His once-tousled blond hair was worn short, and the first patch of skin was apparent at the crown of his head, herald of eventual baldness. Still, he was taller than most of his fellows, so others did not see it unless he was seated. For the moment he paced along the giant's back.

Tawnos pulled his rough, brown woolen cloak tighter around him, cursing the cold and dark. As he did so his fingers scraped against the metal breastplate beneath. It did not fit him—very little that had not been made specifically for his large frame did, and he had brought it along only as an afterthought. The message had been warm and welcoming, but it came from the enemy camp. Urza would be irritated if his former student let his guard down so easily.

There was motion along the far side of the giant's back, near where its smashed head lay at a twisted angle to the rest of the body. Tawnos did not see her climb up, but suddenly she was there—a flash of red hair surrounded by an ebon cloak. It was as if she wore a piece of the night itself, and wore it very well.

She was alone, as she had promised. As she crossed toward him, Tawnos pulled a small device from his pocket. It was a flattened sphere with a lamp's wick jutting from the top. He pressed a stud along the side of the sphere, and the device sputtered. The wick burst into a brief, yellow flame, which subdued to a soft orange hue as Tawnos manipulated the small stud along the side. Ashnod drew into the light, and he saw that she had that bemused smirk that he had always found attractive. He also saw that there were now silver hairs among the scarlet.

"I'd heard you were dead," he said.

"Don't believe everything you hear, Duck," replied Ashnod the Uncaring with a broad smile. "I've heard I died at least five times in the past ten years." The smile faded and the voice turned solemn. "You came. Thank you."

"You sent a message," said Tawnos.

"It could have been a trap," said Ashnod.

"It could have been," admitted Tawnos and opened his cloak. His breastplate reflected the small light, which glimmered off the two sets of ornate weapons that rode on his hips. Ashnod smiled again.

"Good to know you're still cautious," she said.

"Prepared," observed Tawnos. "That is all. Prepared."

Ashnod slung her pack on the ground and knelt next to it. Tawnos hesitated, then joined her. They sat in relative silence for a long moment. Far off, in the distance on either side of the vale, were the hammers of forges preparing for the bloody business of the next day.

"You sent a message," prompted Tawnos.

"This is the last one, you know," said Ashnod, staring out into a night pierced by red fires. "The last battle. The final conflict. One way or another, the resolution of the war between your master and mine."

"Between Urza and Mishra," said Tawnos with a nod.

"They are both here," Ashnod added. "There are no reinforcements. No retreat is possible for either side. One way or another, it all ends here."

Tawnos shifted uncomfortably. It had been a long time since he had sat cross-legged on hard stone. "It is a good time for an ending," he said. "All this has gone on far too long."

Across from him, Ashnod bowed her head in the light. "And wasted so much."

"Many have lost their lives," agreed Tawnos.

Ashnod giggled, an ill-placed sound that raised the hairs of Tawnos's neck in irritation. "Lives?" she said. "Lives are nothing. Think of all the forests gutted, the lakes drained, the lands plundered to get us to this point. Think what we could have done with those resources. And people: yes, how we could have used them, otherwise."

As she spoke Tawnos could feel his face tighten in disapproval. Even in the dim glow Ashnod could feel his silent irritation. "Sorry," she said at last. "I spoke before I thought."

"Good to know there are universal constants," said Tawnos stonily.

"Sorry." There was another pause, and in the distance something clattered. It sounded like a mechanical demon laughing. "How is he?" she said at last.

"The same, only more so," Tawnos replied. "Yours?"

Ashnod shook her head. "Something's . . . wrong." Tawnos raised an eyebrow and she added quickly, "Mishra's colder than ever. More calculating. I'm worried."

"I always worry," said Tawnos. "Urza has become more withdrawn over the passing years."

"Withdrawn," said Ashnod. "That's the word. As if we aren't even there. Like no one else is." She reached out to touch his shoulder. Tawnos stiffened, leaning away, and she let the gesture drop. "You're right about it being a waste," she said at last. "But it can be avoided even now."

"How?" Tawnos's eyes narrowed.

"Give him what he wants," said Ashnod. "Give Mishra the other half of the stone."

"Surrender?" Tawnos said, his voice too loud. "After all this, surrender? When tomorrow we might carry the field? Before we came to Argoth, it might have been an option, perhaps." He thought a moment and said more to himself than to his companion, "No, not even before."

Ashnod held up both hands in a pacific gesture. "Just a suggestion, Duck."

"He sent you with that message?"

"My words are my own," snapped Ashnod. "He doesn't trust me," she added softly.

"Who would, at this point?" asked Tawnos. The words were out of his mouth before he realized what he said.

"Fine," she snarled, and stood up suddenly. She grabbed the knapsack, and it disappeared again within the shadows of her voluminous cloak. "And I even came bearing gifts."

"Any gift from you would be treated suspiciously," said Tawnos, scrambling to his feet and standing next to her.

They paused for a moment, and a cold wind passed between them. Then Ashnod turned to leave.

"Perhaps . . ." Tawnos began. She hesitated at his words. "Perhaps we could get our two masters together," he continued. "Without their weapons. Without their armies. Perhaps there's a way to make them both understand each other."

Ashnod shook her head. "They are lockstepped into their actions now, as mechanical as their own inventions, as relentless as the phases of the Glimmer Moon." She gave a sad giggle. "You dream of a time when they could understand each other. There was never such a time."

She walked away from him, then paused and turned. "Be careful tomorrow. May you survive the battle." She walked to the far end of the toppled giant, and put her hood up. Her scarlet hair disappeared, and she merged once again with the shadows.

"Be careful yourself," said Tawnos to the unresponsive darkness and turned quietly toward his own camp. As he walked back, one part of his mind noted the condition of the field, seeing pitfalls Urza's troops would have to avoid.

But another segment of his consciousness meditated on Ashnod's words, repeating them over and over.

"There was never such a time. . . ."

PART 1

A Study in Forces

(10 AR – 20 AR)

Chpter 1

Tocasia

The Argivian archaeologist removed her lenses and rubbed her tired eyes. The desert grit was everywhere, all the more so when the stiff breeze blew eastward from the inland wastes. The desert air was warm as forge coals, but Tocasia was glad for the gentle wind. Without the breeze it would be merely unbearably and stiflingly hot at the dig site.

The aged researcher sat at an ornate table, a huge monstrosity with thick, fluted legs and a heavy top inlaid with polished shell. It was a gift from one of the noble families of Argive, a reward for "straightening out" an errant scion of their line. The heirloom looked almost comical perched on the outcropping that Tocasia had claimed as her headquarters, beneath a tarpaulin of pale-gray Tomakul muslin.

The gift had been well intentioned, and she could only imagine the expense incurred in sending the table out to her. The desert had already taken its toll: the hand-rubbed finish had been almost entirely blasted away by the sand-laden wind, and the wood beneath had cracked as the heat boiled away the liquids still locked within. Furniture suitable for an Argivian dressing room was much less acceptable in the desert. Still, it was a flat space, and Tocasia appreciated it.

The tabletop was littered with scrolls half-shoved into their cases and survey maps weighted down by bits of rusted metal, the torn edges of the papers fluttering in the breeze. A particularly large chunk of bluish metal sat directly before Tocasia, damning her with its enigma.

It looked like a parody of a human skull, with a batlike face, and cold, impassive eyes of colored crystal set in the unfamiliar blue-tinted metal. The metal itself seemed as ductile and soft as copper, but

13

bending it only caused it to reform slowly into its original shape. A set of Thran glyphs ran along the underside of the skull, which Tocasia had translated roughly as *su-chi*. Whether this was the name of the creature, its owner, or its manufacturer was a mystery to her.

The skull's lupine lower jaw jutted forward, ending in a handful of fangs. The top of the skull had been peeled away to reveal a tangle of blue metal cables. Set among them was a single large gemstone, the shade of old glass, worn beyond age, and marred by a longitudinal crack along its top.

Tocasia sighed. Even if her diggers could find the rest of this Thran artifact's body, it was unlikely that they would ever get it working again. The damage was too extensive, and even if they could re-create its form, the gemstone that provided its power was shattered. They had found only a double handful of such stones that were whole and functioning. Glowing in rainbow hues, they could power the old Thran devices. The largest of those stones were shipped back to Argive for additional study and in exchange for support and supplies.

A shadow touched the corner of her table, and Tocasia jumped slightly. She had been so involved with the skull that she had not seen anyone approach. She looked up into Loran's dark face and wondered how long the girl had been there.

Loran was a noble's daughter and one of Tocasia's best pupils, though that was not saying much, given the current crop of students. Early in Tocasia's career she had accepted the financial support of many of the noble houses of Penregon. In exchange, the houses would often ship their recalcitrant or rebellious junior members out to the desert for a summer to join the mad archaeologist in her excavation of Thran artifacts.

To be honest, Tocasia thought, most of the youths she received were guilty of nothing more than being typical young people, and their parents were only seeking to get them out of the manor house. Once on the site, their interest in the past varied from minimal to nonexistent. They were glad to be away from the perfumed and protected courts of Penregon, its petty intrigues, and—most important—their parents. Tocasia entrusted them with as much responsibility as they accepted. Some supervised the Fallaji diggers, while others helped glean and catalog the devices they brought to light. Still others were content to man the grapeshot catapults that flanked the camp and served as a deterrent to desert raiders and the scavenging rocs. The young men and women came, served their time, and fled back to the cities with enough tales to impress their friends and enough maturity to mollify their parents.

And a few, such as Loran, had the intelligence, the wisdom, and the presence of mind to come back after their first experience. Loran was on her third season and coming into the full flower of womanhood. Tocasia knew it was only a matter of time before the girl started to care more for ball gowns and dinner parties than for artifacts and dig sites, but for this summer, at least, she was pleased to have her there to help catalog, organize, and coordinate.

Tocasia blinked, pushed her spectacles back up on her nose, and arched an eyebrow at the student. Loran would never speak until spoken to, though Tocasia was trying to break her of that habit.

There was a pause, and then Loran said softly, "The caravan from Argive has arrived."

Tocasia nodded. They had been watching the rising dust cloud from the east all morning, but she'd thought it would be late afternoon before Bly's wagons would reach them. The old wagon master must have finally sprung for new beasts, or else the old aurochs had finally failed him. What Loran meant was that Bly's wagons had finally passed through the stockade gates, and Tocasia had best be there to save her students from the bad-tempered merchant's pique should the mistress of the camp not be there to greet him.

Loran did not move, and Tocasia added, "I will be down as soon as possible. If Bly does not like it, let him stew." Loran's lips compressed in a thin line; then the girl nodded and vanished. Tocasia sighed again. In two or three years Loran would be ordering merchants like Bly around effortlessly, but for now she, and most of the other students, were cowed by the merchant's bluster.

Tocasia watched Loran's retreating form, clad in the cream-colored working shift that most female students labored in. She noted that the girl was already wearing her hair longer, in the fashion favored in the capital. Loran's hair was long, dark, and thick, making her exotic among most of her compatriots. "A touch of the desert" was the saying among the Argivian nobility. It was not a compliment but rather a tacit accusation that some desert barbarian was lurking in the family tree. Perhaps that was why Loran kept coming back for the summers— it could not be family pressure. The last time Tocasia visited Penregon, Loran's mother had made it quite clear that Loran should curb such foolish endeavors as rooting around in the dust for scraps of metal.

Tocasia looked out over the camp, a rough wall built around a collection of hills. The low, rolling hills were incised by dry washes and proved to be extremely productive of Thran artifacts. The stockade was more of a demarcation of territory than a true protection, but it kept what desert bandits that might prove a problem at bay. The barricade of piled stone was flanked by a pair of oversized catapults loaded with loose rubble to keep the rocs away. Within the walls most of the activity of the camp was slow in the summer heat. One particular hill, where they had recovered the *su-chi* skull, proved particularly promising, and was now covered with a grid of string and stakes for further examination. The slow-footed onulets plodded to meet the wagons, steered by noble boys who enjoyed thwacking the great albino beasts with their makeshift goads.

The gate had closed on the last wagon now, and a wide-girthed figure leapt from the lead carriage, waving his arms in an animated fashion. Bly seemed to enjoy terrorizing the students out here, perhaps because he had to kowtow to their parents back in Penregon.

Tocasia smiled at the thought of Bly back in the Argivian capital—hat in hand, head bowed slightly, trying to enunciate his requests without resort to curses. The desert was probably the best place for him as well.

The archaeologist ran her hands through her short graying hair, trying to shake out any nonexistent tangles. When she had been young her hair had been longer and almost as dark and luxuriant as Loran's. There might have been a touch of the desert in her family tree as well. Still, age tended to make all peoples equal, and her shorn locks were easier to care for in the desert.

Tocasia gave the blue-metal skull an affectionate pat and rose from her camp chair. She reached for her walking stick, a shattered fragment of wood and bright steel from some unknown Thran mechanism. She was still spry enough to justify the staff as a walking stick to aid her in navigating the uneven ground and not as a crutch. But aches in her joints in the cool of the early desert morning told a different tale.

Tocasia took her time descending from her perch. Bly would bluster and complain, but that never stopped him from dealing. The artifacts and saleable loot he would bring back from the site was worth the long and arduous trip inland.

It was no surprise, then, that once she reached the wagons there was a wide circle of students and teamsters surrounding the wagon master. The surprise was the pair of young men that Bly was berating.

The two were strangers. One was dark-haired and stocky, and flinched every time Bly bellowed. He was half-hiding behind the other, a lean, tawny-haired boy who stood bolt-upright, taking the full blast of the wagon master's thunder.

"Frauds! Cheats! Liars!" shouted Bly.

The pair were all of ten years old, Tocasia guessed. Twelve at the outside. That was about the age nobles first considered sending their children out to Tocasia's camp. But these were not her students, and no new arrivals were expected until the beginning of the next season. Loran was at one side of the crowd, looking both embarrassed by the scene and relieved that she was not the object of Bly's temper.

"You seek to cheat me! Now get busy unloading, you motherless dogs!" sputtered Bly, a crimson hue crawling through his face.

The dark-haired boy raised his fists and took a step forward. The older blond lad held out an arm to block his companion, but his eyes never left the wagon master.

"Sirrah," he said calmly, though loud enough for the surrounding crowd to hear, "we had a bargain. We would work for you to pay for our passage here. We are now here, so we will work for you no longer."

Wagon master Bly turned an apoplectic purple. "You agreed to serve as hands for the journey. The journey isn't over yet; we still have to get back to Penregon!"

"But then we'll have to get back here on our own!" exploded the stockier boy, leaning forward against the other's restraining arm.

"What's going on here, Bly?" said Tocasia.

The wagon master wheeled on the scholar, blinking as if he had only just then noticed her. "A private matter, Mistress Tocasia. Nothing more."

The leaner of the two youths stepped forward. "You are Tocasia the Scholar?"

"We're not finished," Bly started, but Tocasia held up a hand and replied to the youth.

"I am," she said.

"I am Urza," said the youth. "This is my brother Mishra." The sturdier of the two boys nodded, and the lean youth fished out a battered envelope from within his vest. The seal on the flap, the imprint of a familiar noble household, was intact, but it looked as if the letter had made the entire trip next to the boy's skin. Bly drew in his breath sharply at the sight.

Tocasia looked at the two youths, then at the wagon master. She slid a sandblasted nail beneath the flap and popped the letter open. The script was fluid and well formed, dictated to a scribe, but the signature along the bottom was recognizable, if weak and jerky.

17

There was a silence for a moment as she read, and both Bly and Mishra shifted impatiently, waiting for the opportunity to start the argument again. The youth Urza stood impassively, hands folded in front of him.

Tocasia folded up the letter again and said thoughtfully, "Well, that's that." To the two boys she said, "Get your things, and follow Loran there to your quarters." To Bly she said, "These two are now my responsibility. They are joining as students."

The purplish hue returned to Bly's face. "But they owe me half a trip! You're telling me that I have to let these snipes break an agreement just because of some letter!"

Tocasia let the wagon master complain. She watched the boys pull a pair of slender backpacks from one wagon and lope after the slim form of Loran. Only when they had passed through the crowd and that crowd had dispersed to tend to the immediate business of unloading the supplies did she turn her attention to Bly.

"Your agreement was for them to work their way through their journey," she said sharply. "When they arrived here, that journey ended. They are taking up residence here. Do you understand?"

There was steel in her voice, and even Bly knew he could not push the scholar around when she took this tone. Instead he took a deep breath and forced himself to calm.

Tocasia held up the letter. "This is from their father, from whom I have not heard for many years. What do you know of him?"

Bly stammered for a moment, then said, "He's not well at all. Remarried recently—a virago, a real vixen from a good family with her own children. He was taken seriously ill about a month before we left Penregon. He might be dead by this time."

"He might be," said Tocasia solemnly, "or he might be too ill to see to his sons' well-being. You didn't know about this letter, did you?"

The wagon master looked at his feet, embarrassed. "No, you did not," continued Tocasia. "Because if you had, you wouldn't have tried to lock those children into such a hard bargain. 'Full trip' indeed! Knowing you, you probably worked those two as hard your aurochs, if not harder. Because you knew that without the letter I wouldn't take them in on just their word!"

"The new mother, she's a hellkite," said Bly softly, by way of explanation. "Wanted them gone, but wouldn't spend a groat on their well-being. Didn't want to dip into the family moneys, since they're all probably hers right now."

"So you gave the boys a break, worked them like slaves, and tried to keep them, since no one would notice their fate," said Tocasia. "That's low, even for you, Bly. Now get the supplies unloaded, and yes, I'll do a complete inventory, thank you. And then we'll load the wagons for return. There are some items there that will fetch you a goodly profit, despite your scandalous behavior."

Tocasia wanted to lecture Bly a bit longer, but Loran came running up. "Mistress Tocasia, the new boys!"

Tocasia scowled at the student. The young girl had actually spoken up, so it must be important. "Yes?"

"They're in a fight," said Loran. "With Richlau and a couple of the other boys."

Tocasia uttered a mild curse. Bly chuckled. "I can always take them back if you want, scholar," he said.

The scholar shot the wagon master a look that would skin an ox at fifteen paces. To Loran she said, "Get Ahmahl and a couple of the other diggers to break it up. And bring the boys to my tent." Loran hesitated, and Tocasia practically stamped her foot. "Now!"

The young girl disappeared in a puff of dust, and Bly said, "I think that pair are more trouble than they are worth, if you don't mind me saying."

"I wouldn't be surprised," grunted the scholar. "Their father was always a handful."

"So you're going to keep them?" asked the wagon master, shaking his head.

Tocasia sighed. "Aye. I owe their father that much. For an old favor."

"Must be some favor," said Bly. "What did he give you?"

"Only my freedom," said Tocasia, and turned away from the wagon master without waiting for a reply.

Bly looked at Tocasia's back as she walked back up the hill. Was it his imagination, or did she seem to be older and more fragile than she had been a few moments ago? Then he heard hoarse shouts among the wagons, and the thought was driven from his head.

"You lot!" he bellowed at the teamsters, throwing himself back into the work. "Have you never hauled freight before? That stuff's delicate! Handle it like you would your sister's newborn, or we don't get paid!"

The hill seemed steeper to Tocasia on the way up than it had on way down, and the boys were already waiting for her when she reached the top. Ahmahl and Loran were there as well.

The leader of the desert-tribe diggers nodded sharply at Tocasia. In Fallaji, the desert tongue, he said, "Watch the little one. He was all fists and bites when we pulled him off. So much fire in one so small. The big one bloodied Richlau's nose, but nothing's broken."

Tocasia responded in the same language, "Richlau deserves to have his nose bloodied. Tell him he's on kitchen duty for the rest of the month. And move the boys' gear to Havack's barracks instead." Ahmahl nodded and left the tarp. Loran made no move to leave until Tocasia instructed her to keep an eye on Bly.

The archaeologist strode around her table, sliding the walking cane back into its holder, a drum-shaped basket made from an onulet's foot. She leaned on her palms on the desk and looked at the two boys. Their fine vests had been shredded in the battle, and Urza's pockets had been torn out in the fight. Mishra had acquired a black eye, and both boys showed numerous scratch marks.

Tocasia sighed and lowered herself into her seat. The boys shifted uncomfortably. "Fifteen minutes," she said at last. "Fifteen minutes and you're already in a fight. A new record, even for this place."

Both boys started talking at once. Urza said, "I would like to apologize on behalf of everyone involved—"

Mishra burst out with, "I'm sorry but it really wasn't our fault if—"

"Silence!" Tocasia slapped the table hard, so hard the *su-chi* skull jumped slightly, and a piece of the pearl inlay bounced out of its setting. The two boys quieted immediately and shifted from one foot to another.

Tocasia leaned back in her chair. "What happened?"

The boys looked at each other, as if each were granting the other the chance to explain. By mutual if unspoken consent, Urza won the opportunity.

"One of the older boys picked on my brother. I stopped him," he said primly. "A large boy with red hair and freckles."

"So I see," said Tocasia. To Mishra she said, "And why was Richlau picking on you?"

"No reason," said Mishra. Urza started to say something, but Tocasia held up a hand to silence him. After a long silence, Mishra added, "He said I was on his bunk."

"And were you?" asked the scholar.

Mishra shrugged. "I guess." Then, after a pause, he blurted out, "But he didn't have to be rude about it!"

"Richlau is rude about everything," said Tocasia. "You're going to have to get used to that if you stay here." To Urza she said, "You're the older brother, correct?"

"I am," said Urza, but Mishra made a small coughing noise. Urza made a face and added, "I should say that Mishra and I were born in the same year, I was born on the first day of the year, Mishra was born on the last. So for all days but the last, I am a year older."

"On the last day, we're equal!" piped Mishra, as if pleased that his brother had corrected himself.

Tocasia held up the letter from Urza's vest. "Do you know what this says?"

Again, the two boys looked at each other. Tocasia sensed they were conferring in a secret language, one only they could hear.

"Not exactly," answered Urza at last.

"Your father was a dear friend to whom I owe much," observed Tocasia. "He wants me to look after you, to care for you should something happen to him. That means you're going to be staying here for quite a while. And that means working with me and my students. If you're uncomfortable with this arrangement, I can send you back with Bly, but to be honest I don't know what kind of welcome would await you in Penregon."

Again the boys looked at each other. It was Mishra who spoke this time. "What is it that you do?"

"I dig," said Tocasia. "Or rather, I supervise others who dig. We are searching for artifacts out here. Do you know what I'm talking about?"

"Remnants of the past," said Urza. "Of a civilization that stood here long before Argive or any of the nations of Terisiare. Relics."

"That's right," said Tocasia. "Artifacts that range in power from small toys to great machines, machines that can do the work of many men."

"Like the big white ox-things?" asked Mishra, almost unheard.

Tocasia arched an eyebrow at the younger brother. "Yes, indeed. The onulets that we use as beasts of burden out here are artifacts, ones I created based on the designs we've pieced together of the artifact-creating race, the Thran. The onulets are strong, loyal, unthinking machines that are tireless workers. They require neither food nor water, and when they do at last break down, the fluids from their joints are used to brew a hearty beverage that we then trade with desert tribesmen for information and other artifacts."

"They sound very useful," said Urza.

Tocasia leaned back in her chair. "I'm impressed, Mishra. The framework is covered by stitched hides to protect the workings from the desert sands. I had one student who was quite handy with a needle. Most first-time students assume the onulets are alive, since the only things comparable are the aurochs." She chuckled. "One of the pranks that Richlau and the other boys were probably planning was to assign you to feed an onulet and not to come back until it had finished its meal. How did you guess they weren't living?"

Mishra blinked, then furrowed his brow. "I didn't guess. I just knew."

Urza sniffed and said, "The gait is wrong for something alive. It pitches forward when it takes a step. A real creature would be smoother." He looked at Tocasia and shrugged. "I knew it too, but I didn't think it important enough to mention. The Thran must have been amazing people to have created it."

Tocasia said, "And what do you know of the Thran, young Urza?"

The sandy-haired boy planted his feet apart and put his hands behind his back—a recitation position Tocasia remembered from her own youth.

"The Thran were an ancient race that lived in this land many thousands of years ago. They created a number of wondrous devices, only a few of which have survived to the present day. The great clock of Penregon's Grand Court is said to be a Thran artifact."

Tocasia suppressed a smile; the device at the heart of that clock had been one of her earliest finds. "But who were they?" she asked. "Who were the Thran? Were they human?"

Urza blinked, as if the question were odd. "Of course. Why wouldn't they be?"

"What proof can you offer?" asked Tocasia.

Urza thought for a moment, and Tocasia noticed he dropped his head slightly as if trying to support a thought-filled head with his chest. "I don't remember anything saying they weren't. I assumed they were."

"Most people do," said the scholar. "But the truth of the matter is we don't know. They might be human, yes. Ahmahl, one of the Fallaji, has some folk stories about how the Thran were powerful gods who brought his people into this world, but the stories neglect any specifics. The Thran could have been minotaurs, elves, dwarves—or goblins, for all we know."

"Oh, I hope they were minotaurs!" said Mishra. "Those are neat-looking!"

Urza spread his hands before him and said dryly, "There was a carnival in Penregon when we were younger. Most of what Mishra knows of minotaurs comes from seeing one there."

"But the fact remains we don't know who the Thran were," continued Tocasia. "And so we dig, we examine, and we try to piece together the parts of the past. The onulets are a result of what we have learned. So, to a lesser extent, are the grapeshot catapults that guard the encampment. We do know that many of the Thran devices were powered by crystalline energy sources. We call them power stones. What the Thran called them is anyone's guess. We have a rough idea of their language, though precious little that has been written down. We have not found statuary, art, or pottery—nothing that implies the creative arts. We know they stripped this land bare, but don't know how they died off—whether by internal war, famine, or plague."

She sighed. "We have no idea even of what they look like. They could have looked like us. Or they could have looked like our friend here." She pushed the *su-chi* forward on the desk and patted it.

Mishra reached forward and grabbed the skull. Tocasia was surprised by the speed that only desert predators and small children can manage. He turned it over and over in his hands.

"Stop—" began Tocasia. She wanted to say, "Stop that and put it back down," but she was too late. At the first sound from her Urza leapt on his little brother.

"Put it down!" snapped the sandy-haired boy. "It might be dangerous!"

"Its not dangerous," snarled his darker-haired brother. "If it was dangerous, she'd keep it someplace where we couldn't touch it!"

"Then its fragile!" shouted Urza. "You'll break it!"

"If I break it, it'll be because you made me!" replied Mishra. The pair formed a tight knot, the *su-chi* skull between them.

"Give!" shouted Urza.

"No!" responded Mishra.

"Enough!" roared Tocasia, thundering both hands on top of the table. At once both boys were on their feet again, and the skull was rocking gently against the pearl inlay where it had been a minute before.

The scholar scowled at the boys. "You two talk a good game and seem to have enough energy to burn. Good enough. You're going to spend the rest of the month learning from the ground up. You'll start by working in the kitchen. Alongside Richlau, so I strongly recommend you figure out how to deal with him. If I have any more trouble with the pair of you, I'll send you back with Bly." She glared at them. "Do I make myself clear?"

As one, both boys nodded.

"Good." Tocasia settled her thin frame in the chair. "Now report to the mess tent and start peeling tubers. They're serving a big feast tonight for Bly's men. I trust there will be no more problems?"

Both boys nodded in unison again. Tocasia waved them out, and they vanished from her tarp, leaving trails of dust behind them as they scampered down the hillside.

Despite herself Tocasia smiled. They were so close in age, but their birth order set their attitudes. Urza was ten yet carried himself as if he were much older and felt responsible for his younger brother. Mishra was nearly ten but acted younger and was more exuberant. He would probably always be willing to try new things, thought Tocasia, because big brother would be there to watch out for him.

Still, she mused, a word to Richlau would probably be wise. Let him know she would not appreciate hearing he was making life difficult for the two newest and youngest students. That might create more hard feelings if the "new children" were known to be favorites, but that was a small price, and a temporary one. At the end of this season, this batch of young nobles would head back to Penregon and a new group would take their place. The brothers should be capable of handling themselves by then, she thought, or they would be gone.

Tocasia's smile died as she picked up the metallic skull of the *suchi*. She examined it carefully to see if the boys had damaged it further in their grappling. Somehow, she saw, their fight had jostled the two halves of the power crystal together. The longitudinal crack had vanished, and the crystal now was a solid piece. More interesting, there was a flicker of light deep within the crystal, a weak glow but one that indicated that the crystal still held some of its energy.

Tocasia stared at the skull and its crystalline brain until Loran came to fetch her for dinner with the wagon master's men and her own students. But her eyes and her thoughts strayed often during the meal to the two boys who had so recently arrived in the camp.

Ch**❋**pter 2

Ornithopter

Tocasia did not send the boys back with Bly that trip, or for any other trip to Penregon for the next six summers. Urza came to terms with Richlau, and Mishra was more careful about sitting on others' bunks. Loran went back to Penregon and stayed away for five years. Bly wore out the new oxen and tried to buy one of Tocasia's onulets, to no avail. Tocasia continued to dig and to bring up the two boys put into her care.

At first Tocasia thought of Urza and Mishra as two parts of a single entity. Her inclination was reinforced by the way the two looked at each other before answering a question. Yet they were very different people, and the desert brought out different parts of their personalities.

Urza became more studious, devouring every scrap of information that Tocasia had gathered on the Thran. He pored over the rosters of artifacts from previous seasons and even the scrap heaps of material that had been discarded. In this fashion he found several pieces that belonged with later discoveries but had been discarded at the time.

Urza, Tocasia quickly discovered, was intrigued by the manner in which things worked. At twelve he took apart the front limbs of one of the onulets, reassembling it only after Tocasia threatened dire consequences. He and Mishra rebuilt the beast overnight, and their impromptu redesign stopped the lurching problem the machine had previously experienced.

The elder brother grew lean and wiry in the hot sun. His hair bleached to a straw-colored blond, and he now gathered it in a ponytail across the back of his neck. His knowledge was encyclopedic and his insights keen.

Mishra bloomed in the dry desert air as well. While Urza burrowed through the tattered scrolls and maps, Mishra learned to dig, to sift, and excavate. The younger brother spent more time out in the field than did his sibling. He climbed among the exposed rock faces and dry washes. Soon he could look at a proposed excavation site and hazard a guess on how deep the excavators would have to go to before striking the Thran level of artifacts. More often than not, his guess proved right.

Tocasia noticed that Mishra spent more time with the other students than did his brother, and with Ahmahl's diggers as well. After supper, while Urza was hunched over a ligature of some skeletal artifact, Mishra was to be found at the diggers' camp, listening to the legends of the Fallaji peoples. There were tales of raids and heroes and desert genies; of great cities captured in bottles and hapless souls transformed into donkeys. Mishra learned of the Thran as the desert people knew them—a race of demigods who had used their artifacts to create wonderful, terrible cities.

Tocasia suspected that the diggers let Mishra sample their *nabiz*, the powerful fermented wine spiced with cinnamon favored by the Fallaji, but she said nothing. It seemed good to her that Mishra had moved from beneath his brother's protective wing. Urza, for his part, seemed not to notice that his brother spent more time with the others, so wrapped up was the elder child in his studies.

The work in the desert sun toughened Mishra. He was more muscular, the result of long hours at the dig sites, and his flesh had a deep, worker's tan. His dark hair trailed after him like a banner, ornately braided in the manner of the desert. He had wider shoulders and a stauncher frame than his elder brother and could now handle himself in any scrap without Urza's help.

Both boys were tireless workers, and Tocasia saw why Bly had tried to keep them. But something more than their work bound them to her. Each of the brothers had an enthusiasm for his tasks that was contagious. Tocasia felt no need to talk to them as children; rather she spoke to them as trusted adults, and they returned her trust.

Soon the pair were considered as vital and permanent a part of the encampment as Tocasia herself. Within two years, the young nobles arriving from Penregon were the same age as Urza and Mishra, and the brothers already knew the lay of the land. Remembering their own experiences, the pair always sought out the prospective bullies among the group and made it clear that no persecution of the smaller students would be permitted. Within another two years the brothers were considered the *de facto* leaders of the student contingent, allowing Tocasia more time for her own examination of artifacts and their power stones.

In the fall of the second year word reached the camp via Bly's caravan that Urza and Mishra's father had passed on after a long illness. The word was in a terse note, quickly penned, from the boys' stepmother. The missive said nothing about an inheritance, and Tocasia suspected no mention would be ever be made.

She gave Urza the news first. He was working beneath Tocasia's tarp, clearing the dust from a device found earlier that day, driven by a coiled spring. Tocasia suspected it was merely a clock mechanism, but the young man had found carvings along the length of the spring itself, carvings that seemed to have a relationship to known Thran glyphs. When she told him of his father, Urza set his tools down and stared at the inlaid pearl top for a long moment. He rubbed his eyes and thanked Tocasia for the information, then picked his tools up again, suddenly intent on the device.

Mishra responded very differently. When Tocasia gave him the news he fled the dig site altogether, climbing up the side of the rocky tor above Tocasia's encampment. The old scholar thought to go after him, but Ahmahl counseled against it. Mishra needed to work out his feelings on his own, the Fallaji said. Still, after dinner Tocasia saw Urza climbing the outcropping, and the brothers sat up there a long time, watching the Glimmer Moon rise over the desert. Neither brother mentioned the incident afterward, and Tocasia wondered what they had said to each other on the side of that rocky tor.

In the spring of the sixth year of the boys' arrival Loran returned, this time as an official representative of her house instead of as a mere student. She had grown as well and was now a highborn lady with (Bly informed Tocasia with a wink and an unsubtle nudge) a string of suitors desiring both her hand and her family's moneys. Officially, Loran was to survey the encampment for its recent accomplishments and to recommend if her family should increase their sponsorship of Tocasia's work. In reality that decision could have been made back in Penregon; a growing number of young leaders of the various families had spent at least one summer working for Tocasia, and fond memories now translated into hard currency. The Argivian Crown did not care for Tocasia's work, the archaeologist knew, but the Argivian Crown was weak and treated the matter as it treated everything it did not care for: it ignored the issue.

Loran had made the long and difficult journey out to the encampment primarily to see Tocasia again, and Tocasia knew it. Most of the high manners and debutante softness disappeared by the end of the first evening, and by noon of the second day Loran was prowling alongside Tocasia as she moved from excavation to excavation.

Tocasia had something to show Loran, a story for her to carry back to the other former students in the Argivian capital. There had been a sudden downpour the month before, a hard-hitting desert rain that had threatened several of the dig sites. Rahud, one of Ahmahl's diggers, had heard from a nomadic family member that the rain had hit even harder farther to the north, and flooded out an old dry wash, revealing what looked like a Thran machine. Rahud told Mishra, Mishra reported to Tocasia, and within a day the group had mounted a small expedition north.

It was a device they found, and one definitely of Thran creation. It looked at first like some sort of sailing craft, an impossibility in the desert. Long poles of ancient candlewood jutted from the exposed bank, to which had been attached what looked like sail rigging. Urza examined it and then, to Tocasia's amazement, confidently declared it to be a flying craft, something unseen in Terisiare's skies save only in the oldest of stories.

For the next week the camp activity moved to the new site, seeking to pry loose the birdlike flying machine and haul it back to the main encampment. The diggers had to work quickly to avoid the attention of less-friendly desert Fallaji as well as the predatory sand-colored rocs. The students were pressed into duty hauling dirt and clearing debris, and Urza and Mishra camped on the site to guard the new find.

It took only a few days to pry the device free of the surrounding soil and rock, and Urza was proven right. What Tocasia had thought of as sails were in fact wings. The construction did seem fashioned like a bird, and Tocasia dubbed it an ornithopter. Both wings were intact, though the tail assembly had been crushed. A small maze of wires and tubes at the heart of the craft cradled a now-shattered power stone.

They got the ornithopter back to the camp two days before Loran's arrival, and Tocasia was glad to see the look on the young noblewoman's face when she saw the tattered remains. To any other Argivian it was a mess of fractured poles, smashed metal, and scraps of ancient fabric, but to any former student of Tocasia it was a treasure. To see such a large device after spending a summer trying to pry fragments out of the rock with a small brush made the archaeologist and her students indescribably happy.

Tocasia also noticed that with the passage of time Loran had grown more sure of herself. She no longer hesitated to speak. Nor did she spend all her time with her old mentor. For the first few days she hovered over Urza, who had removed the crystal housing from the ornithopter and was busy disassembling and cleaning the small device. Then, without any warning, she suddenly switched her time and attention to Mishra, who was rebuilding the larger framework of the craft itself. Tocasia did not know what, if anything, had happened to make Loran change her interest; neither young man ever mentioned her in the scholar's presence.

The young woman returned to Penregon with promises of support for Tocasia and an order for light sailcloth, and the brothers returned to their work. Mishra had rebuilt the ornithopter's framework, but the nature of the tail assembly defied him. Almost by unspoken agreement, Urza took over the reconstruction of the glider, discovering what wires went where and how they would function in flight. It was Urza who discovered that the sail-like wings had to be ribbed with thin shoots of candlewood in order to maintain their form in flight. For his part Mishra confirmed that by bringing slender bows of snapped wing ribs back from the dig along with strands of frayed wire. Urza saw that the wire was better for controlling the shape of the wings than mere rope, and another order was placed with Bly. The two young men spent hours together poring over the design, trying to determine how the tail assembly would function.

In all it took eight months for the ornithopter to be rebuilt. The key was the box of wires and disks that served as the craft's engine. Urza, Mishra, and even Tocasia did not know exactly how the small engine could power the large ornithopter; they only knew that it did. Urza used the small, weak crystal that had belonged to the *su-chi* to power the device.

It was the last day of the year, Mishra's birthday, when the craft was ready at last. The day was surprisingly warm, and a soft wind blew from the desert. There was some debate over who would get the honor—and the danger—of the first test flight.

"I should do it," said Urza. "After all, I understand the workings of the power crystal cradle."

"I should do it," countered Mishra. "The flight levers controlling the wings are mulish, and they need a strong hand to keep them in line."

"I'm lighter," said Urza.

"I'm stronger," snapped Mishra.

"I am capable of holding the levers in place," said Urza.

"And I understand the power crystals as well as you do," added Mishra quickly.

"I am the elder," said Urza smugly.

"And it's my birthday!" shouted Mishra, the blood rising to his face. "So we are equal."

Tocasia looked at the two young men and let out a deep sigh. Such disagreements were rare but were severe enough to trouble her. At last she said, "If you cannot decide, then I will have to risk my ancient bones in this device."

The two young men stared at Tocasia, then looked at each other. Each simultaneously pointed to the other and said, "He should fly it."

In the end they flipped a coin. Urza won, and Mishra did a passable job of containing his disappointment as the last of the preparations were made. A wide level place had been cleared outside the stockade gates for the craft. The blond young man climbed into the housing at the front of the ornithopter and slowly depressed the two main levers, engaging the arcane crystal within the maze of gears and wheels that he had lovingly rebuilt over the past months. The entire craft trembled as the last of the slack in the wires was taken up and the wings accordioned out in a pair of great sails.

The wings beat downward: once, twice, and then a third time. The ornithopter gave a small hop on the third beat, and Tocasia saw Mishra start as well. The younger boy said nothing; his eyes seemed transfixed by the sight, and his hands were clenched. Tocasia wondered if he was worried for his brother or worried that his brother would damage the machine before he had a chance to try it.

The device took another short hop, then another, larger leap. Dust from the heavy beating wings blew in all directions, and the students retreated, covering their eyes and mouths from the swirling sand. One last leap, and this time the ornithopter did not come back down.

It was aloft, its wings straining against the warm air. Tocasia and the other students could hear the wires sing from the strain as the small craft, like a fledgling roc leaving the nest, leapt into the air. The ornithopter climbed into the sky, and there was a sharp clatter as Urza threw the locking mechanism into place, fixing the wings into a solid, gliding surface.

Urza was aloft for ten minutes. He circled the encampment twice, and there was a tense second when the craft suddenly dropped ten feet, but it quickly climbed again. Urza circled one last time, then set the ornithopter back down on the pad of level sand. The wings unlocked and beat as he landed. The candlewood supports groaned but held the craft upright.

Urza climbed out. "Hit some colder air," he said briefly to Tocasia. "Apparently that has some effect on its ability to keep aloft."

"Let me try," said Mishra.

Urza did not move away from the device. "We should check all the couplings for wear," he observed, still speaking to Tocasia. "And the struts for fractures. Not to mention the integrity of the power crystal."

Mishra looked at Tocasia, his face clouded.

"Urza," said Tocasia softly, "let your brother use the ornithopter."

Urza opened his mouth to argue, then looked at his brother and silently stepped aside. Mishra piled into the flying device.

Urza leaned into the housing. "The right lever sticks, so you'll have to muscle it," he said.

Mishra only grinned and shouted, "Stand away!" He flung both levers into place, engaging the wings.

Urza backpedaled quickly out of the way of the huge, beating wings. Whatever sand had not been chased away before now was spun in a cyclone of wind.

The ornithopter went almost straight up in a single bounce. The entire encampment could hear the sharp creaking of the candlewood struts and the high-pitched whine of the wires passing through metal loops and pulleys. Urza grimaced as if the sound physically pained him.

"It would have been better had we waited to check out the craft before flying it again," he said to Tocasia through gritted teeth.

"Better, but not wiser," returned the old scholar.

Mishra climbed a hundred feet, locked the wings, then forced the craft into a swooping dive over the encampment. Sheep and goats in their pens below let out frightened bleats as the ornithopter passed only a few feet above them. Mishra pulled back on the levers and reengaged the wings, and the craft climbed again.

"Do you think the craft needs a lighter pilot, now?" said Tocasia.

Urza shrugged. "Actually I think there is enough pull in the wings to take three or four people aloft at once if we expand the housing."

"So the argument that you should have flown it because you were lighter was disproved," pressed the old scholar, smiling as she spoke.

Urza winced but said nothing.

Mishra circled the encampment twice as Urza had before. Tocasia imagined that the lad was searching for the same spot of cold air so he could hiccough the craft as had his brother. She did notice that while Urza had concentrated on keeping the craft level, Mishra continually swooped and dove, banking in one direction, then the other.

Then Mishra flew over the camp once more and headed the craft westward into the deep desert.

The form of the ornithopter became a blur, then a speck on the horizon. Tocasia and Urza looked at each other.

"Perhaps one of the steering wires broke," offered Tocasia.

"Or the little fool wanted to see how far he could go," Urza grumbled, rushing for the rocky tor behind them to get a better view.

Urza had made it only halfway up the hill when the sound of wings cutting through the warm air heralded Mishra's return. The younger brother circled the camp twice and then landed just beyond the stockade gates. By the time Mishra had touched down Urza was waiting, his face as stern as stone.

"What did you think you were doing?" he shouted as Mishra climbed out of the housing. "Bad enough that you probably over-stressed the pulleys with your diving about! But to fly out of sight of the camp! You might have been attacked by rocs. If you had crashed in the desert, we might not have found you!"

Mishra did not seem to be listening. Instead he said, "I saw the drawings. Didn't you?"

Urza was brought up short and looked at his brother, puzzled.

The dark-haired brother turned to Tocasia. "Out in the desert, there are drawings. Mounds of dark earth against the lighter surrounding sand. We've passed them before on foot but never noticed. But from above, you can see that they're pictures! There are dragons, genies, rocs—even minotaurs." He turned to his brother. "You saw them, didn't you?"

Urza blinked at his brother. Then, more cautiously, he replied, "I was more worried about the performance of the craft."

Mishra did not bother to listen. "They surround a large hillock. I'll bet if we checked that out, we'd find it's some sort of old Thran encampment."

"It could be some Fallaji holy place," started Urza, but Mishra shook his head.

"No." He was emphatic. "There's nothing in the old tales about Fallaji settlements in this immediate area. I think it's Thran, and I think we should investigate it."

"We should investigate the damage the flights did to the ornithopter," said Urza, already prowling along the wings, pulling at the sailcloth and running his hands along the struts.

Tocasia spread her hands in a gesture that encompassed both brothers. "We should celebrate," she said. "There will be time enough to do everything else in the morning."

That night students and diggers built a great bonfire in the camp and gathered around the rising flames. There was an air of excitement among the students. The young nobles had new tales to take back to Argive. They had been present when Urza took the first flight and when Mishra found the great drawings in the desert. After long months of backbreaking work in shallow trenches and detailed cleaning of long-dead bits of metal, here at last was something to be proud of. There were songs, and the *nabiz* flowed. Rahud tried to teach several of the noble boys a traditional Fallaji dance. The boys had no concept of the dance's rhythm, but since it involved waving pointed sticks they joined in with the spirit of adventure. Mishra told and retold the story of his flight, and Tocasia knew that every young man and woman in the encampment would be clamoring for their opportunity to fly in the near future.

Urza remained at the edge of the campfire, neither dancing, nor drinking, nor talking.

Tocasia walked over to him. "You are enjoying yourself?"

"Well enough," replied the youth. "But I think we should check the rigging for any wear and tear. And if you want to put a larger housing—"

"Tomorrow," said the old woman. "You are young enough for a lot of tomorrows. Enjoy yourself this evening."

"I enjoy working on the devices," said Urza, watching his brother across the fire pit. The younger boy was surrounded by students as well as a few of the diggers. It seemed to Tocasia that his story grew longer and more exciting with each telling.

"There are other enjoyments," said Tocasia, following Urza's gaze. "Your brother seems to have discovered that."

The two were silent in the flickering firelight for a moment. Then Urza said, "I had nothing against Mishra taking his flight."

"I never said you did," returned Tocasia.

"It's just that there is stress on any object that is put to the test for the first time," continued the older brother. "We should have done a full check before letting him go aloft."

"Of course," said Tocasia in a level tone.

"His own recklessness aside, he could have been hurt," said Urza.

"Yes." Tocasia paused. "But tell that to a young man who wants to be his brother's equal."

"I was only being prudent."

"And would you have been so prudent if you had lost the toss?" asked Tocasia.

Urza did not answer but stood watching his brother across the flames.

Chapter 3

Koilos

Mishra was correct: there were drawings in the sand of the deeper desert to the west of their encampment. They were large figures made from raised mounds of dry earth, darker than their surroundings, and best visible from the air. Tocasia had conducted earlier expeditions in that very area before settling on the present site of the encampment but never guessed their true nature.

The drawings were an odd mixture. There were humanoid figures of every type, any one of which might be the representation of a Thran. There were also all manner of animals: deer, elephants, and camels. There was an odd collection of geometric symbols—curves, spirals, and sharp angles that crossed and recrossed the gathered figures, bisecting some, leaving others untouched. Doodles, thought Tocasia, created by a race of desert titans.

The drawings were of Thran origins, of course, as Mishra had guessed. They were arrayed around a single location, a large mound. This proved to be a rich field of artifacts, including an almost complete *su-chi* skeleton that finally fulfilled Tocasia's dream of putting together one of the enigmatic beasts. There were also the remains of several ornithopters. Yet the discovery of the *su-chi* and ornithopters was secondary to the rich trove of power crystals found in the central mound. Many of the crystals were cracked or expired, but there were among the dross more than enough operational remains: vibrant, lambent jewels that glittered with a rainbow of sparks and patterns within. There were more than enough of the jewels for Tocasia to keep for her own work, with sufficient surplus to send to other scholars and various noble supporters in the capital of Penregon. This in turn supplied enough interest from the nobility to allow her to open a second permanent camp at the site of Mishra's find.

The discovery of the drawings in the deserts was made possible by airborne observation. The same method revealed similar drawing fields, though none as large or intact as the first. An arc of them extended into the desert in a broad sweep outward from the Kher Ridges. Some of the drawings had figures of recognizable races, while others did not. All contained a stylized pattern of curves and zigzagged lines around a central mound containing wrecked artifacts and power stones. During the next two years researchers located almost twenty such mounds.

Still the big questions eluded Tocasia and the brothers. No one found any skeletal remains of the Thran themselves, nor any art. The archaeologist discovered nothing of their language more than a few fragments that seemed little more than labels and an obvious set of numerical symbols. At dinner the scholar, the two brothers, and some of the elder students were accustomed to discuss the Thran's possible nature.

"They had to be human," said Urza in the course of one such talk. "Everything we have found is capable of being used by human-sized individuals. They were probably a successful branch of the early Fallaji people that dominated the others through their advanced science. The surviving Fallaji of today turned their enterprising brethren into godlike beings."

"The fact that we're comfortable with their tools doesn't mean anything," disagreed Mishra. "Dwarves or elves or orcs could have used these items. Or minotaurs."

"Minotaurs are too big," said Urza. "Their hands would be too large to hold most of the devices."

"Minotaurs could be in charge, with humans doing the labor," Mishra returned. Tocasia noted that the younger brother refused to concede to his sibling even the smallest point. "Imagine," he continued. "Minotaurs ruling the Thran nation, and humans as an underclass. Like among the orcs—the big ones are on top, and the little goblins do all the hard work."

"We've found no minotaur remains, Brother," said Urza coolly.

"We've found no human remains, either, Brother," Mishra shot back, raising his glass of *nabiz* in a mock toast to his own logic.

Tocasia leaned back in her chair (recently arrived from the capital—a comfortable, cushioned affair) and let the two brothers spar. This was an old argument, revisited at least once a month. It always ended the same way: in an admission that they did not know enough. That confession always seemed to frustrate both of the young men.

Both of the brothers had changed over the years of discovery. Urza was leaner than ever, though he finally had a good set of shoulders. His face was smooth, and he prided himself on not losing his temper as he had when he was a child. Mishra, for his part, was as impulsive as he had been the day of that first fight. His most obvious change was a sparse dark beard that framed his smiling mouth.

The older students at the table watched the argument as well but did not get involved. Urza and Mishra were older than most of the students now, and in another few years they would be thought of as adults in their own right. The noble students had learned early that voicing a contrary opinion when the two were fighting like this was a sure way to turn both young men against the interloper.

Tocasia was proud of the boys and their achievements, and in turn they were devoted to her. But again and again they returned to this single argument and could not move beyond it. They still had not learned the identity of the Thran.

As the young men's voices rose higher, Tocasia leaned forward, hoping to turn the brothers to a new tack.

"Why haven't we?" she interrupted.

Both young men blinked at the older scholar as she repeated, "Why haven't we found any remains—human or otherwise?"

"Scavengers," said Mishra immediately. Urza made a rude noise.

"Then why haven't we found any scavenger remains?" he asked scornfully. "There are no dead creatures of any type among the wreckage. There should be some, even by accident."

"And you have a theory, Brother?" asked Mishra.

"Plague," said Urza calmly. "Something swept through that not only killed the Thran but destroyed their remains as well. That also explains why the wreckage is so widely scattered."

Mishra shook his head. "Not plague. War. Plague wouldn't explain why there is no art. War would. The victors burned what could burn: paintings, books, bodies. Then they destroyed the rest. We have found ash pits among the various sites."

"Those are the result of manufacture, not battle," observed Urza. "And if you're right, what became of the victors?"

"They became the scavengers," retorted Mishra triumphantly, setting down his glass. "That's what it has to be. A slave race of humans that destroyed the minotaur masters, then fell apart itself without the minotaur science to support them."

Urza chuckled. "A perfect argument. Each point uses as proof another questionable point, which eventually requires you to believe what you are trying to prove in the first place. So, Brother, why didn't these scavenger-survivors create any art after the war?"

Mishra frowned slightly, considering. "They hadn't reached the point of gaining art," he said finally. "So there is no art from the period."

"Except for the drawings in the desert," said Urza.

"Except for the drawings in the desert," agreed his brother.

"Except they aren't, you know," said Urza with a small smile.

Mishra shook his head, looking puzzled. "Those are not drawings in the desert? Nothing natural could produce—"

"Those are not art," interrupted Urza. "Oh, the humanish figures might be, or they may simply be a recognition of other races the Thran had met. But all the lines, angles, and squiggles, those are not art. They are instructions."

Tocasia stared at Urza, intrigued as well. What had he discovered now?

Urza rose from the table and left the tarp without saying another word. He returned with a large map of the area, which he shook open over the table. The other students moved quickly to save the remains of the broiled desert hare and cantaloupe that would otherwise be covered by the sheet. The map showed the arc of ruins they had uncovered.

"Here are the locations of the various Thran outposts we have found," he said, jabbing a thin finger against the map. He followed from one to another, following the curve of wreckage. "At each location, the collection of odd angles and lines seems to point in one direction. From our second encampment, it points slightly west of due north."

Producing a stylus, the blond student sketched a practiced line extending north. "In the next one, farther west, a majority of lines also indicate a particular direction, this one slightly more northerly than the first," he said, drawing another strong, arrow-straight line. "And the next shows yet another line, almost due north in direction; the next points north and slightly east; and so on for each of the discovered sites so far." The stylus scratched out a number of new lines.

Urza stood back from the map so the others could see. The ruins were in an arc, as everyone knew, but the lines Urza had sketched all pointed to one particular location: the center of a circle, of which the ruined mounds were points along the perimeter.

"The Thran were not an artistic people," said Urza, looking at his brother. "Why then leave art in the desert? The answer is, they did not. They left instructions. Instructions about where their larger settlements were. We saw the figures, which we recognized, and ignored the lines, which we did not. But the lines are more important."

Mishra leaned over the map and scowled. "Lines on paper," he snorted. "You saw the arc and calculated the center, then looked for justification in the lines of the various mounds."

"So you disagree with my argument, Brother?" asked Urza quietly.

Mishra smiled, the whiteness of his teeth sharp against the surrounding beard. "But I love your argument, Brother! It's perfect. Each point uses as proof another questionable point, which eventually requires you to believe what you are trying to prove in the first place! The argument I love! It's your conclusions I think are wrong."

Urza rolled up his map slowly. "I suppose that means you don't want to come along tomorrow when I go find out?"

Mishra started, and even Tocasia looked sharply at the elder brother.

"With your permission, Mistress, I would like to take an ornithopter out to check this out," Urza said. "Since my brother does not wish to accompany me, I can manage with one of the smaller craft—"

"I didn't say I wouldn't go," interrupted Mishra sharply. "In fact, I think I should go along, if only to keep you from seeing ruins that are not there."

Urza nodded with a determined smile. Then he ducked from beneath the tarp and strode into the growing dusk. "I have plans to make then," he called over his shoulder. "Evening, all!"

In Urza's wake the dinner table was silent. None of the other students wanted to comment on Urza's theory, and Tocasia needed time to digest what the older brother had said.

Tentatively, the conversation returned to more mundane matters. One student ventured that his area of the dig was producing some interesting disks marked with Thran numerals. Another mentioned that his work was being delayed by a junior student that declared every uprooted rock to be some artifact of the ancient race. That brought a small laugh from the others and from Tocasia a tale of one student, a few years before, who thought that they should dig on mountaintops because if *she* were one of the Thran, that's where *she'd* leave the most valuable items.

Mishra sat quietly just beyond the firelight and stroked his stubbled beard. After a few minutes he excused himself as well and left the table. He did not head for the quarters he shared with Urza, but rather turned down toward where the Fallaji diggers made their camp. Tocasia noticed that the younger brother had a worried look on his face, but at the time she paid it little mind.

That evening, after the dishes had been cleared, Tocasia worked on a *su-chi* leg assembly at her table. The design that they had discovered in the almost complete specimen was different than either Urza or she had anticipated. It was almost, she thought, as if the legs were mounted backward, the knees pointing toward the rear. Was this a design choice of the Thran, she wondered, or was this a model of their real appearance?

A shadow appeared at the entrance of the tarp, and she looked up suddenly as Ahmahl entered. Old Ahmahl as he was known now, she reminded herself; his hair had turned gray in rivulets along either side of his face. Lately he had been complaining that his age was finally catching up with him. Tocasia knew he was a grandfather, and someday soon he would leave the encampment. Tocasia would miss him, for he represented all she felt was admirable among the Fallaji people. He was direct, forthright, and honest.

Now, from the stern look on his face, Tocasia got the feeling she was about get a messy dose of the last quality.

"I hear your young men are flying into the mountains on the morrow," he said, his desert accent still thick after all these years among the Argivians.

"How did . . ." Tocasia started, then realized where Ahmahl got his information. Mishra would have asked him about the ring of ruins and the center point of the arc that Urza had located. And that news had obviously disturbed the elder Fallaji.

She nodded and motioned toward a camp chair. The old leader of the diggers sat himself carefully down upon it, as if either he or the chair would break from the experience.

"Urza has some ideas about finding the wreckage of a large Thran settlement there."

Old Ahmahl looked at the worn, dusty carpeting beneath his feet. "I do not think it is a good idea. The Fallaji would frown on it."

Tocasia knit her brow. Ahmahl and his diggers had never expressed the idea of taboo land before. Indeed, in most of the tribal settlements she had visited the inhabitants were exceedingly proud to show off, if not actively trade, the Thran artifacts they had discovered.

"Not all the Fallaji," Ahmal continued. He looked up quickly at her, as if he could read her thoughts in her eyes. "Most of us are modern enough, are wise enough to know there is nothing in the mountains that is not in the desert. But there are those who are concerned about the spirits of the Thran. About their heart. It is said that their secret heart lies in the mountains, and we Fallaji stay well clear of them."

"Ahmahl," said Tocasia gently, "you have never mentioned anything like this before nor complained about our previous digs."

"That is because it is in the desert, and the desert belongs to all who can endure her," said Ahmahl. "The Fallaji claim all this land but are willing to share it with others who respect it. The high mountains, however, the inner mountains themselves, are dangerous, and not only for the great ruq-birds found there. We claim them as Fallaji territory, but we do not visit them. Nor do we recommend others do so."

Argive claims those mountains as well, thought Tocasia, though she did not voice that opinion. Most of the Argivians were coastal people to begin with, and the broad expanses claimed by the noble factions were just lines on a map.

"If we are violating some taboo—" she began.

Ahmahl held up a hand. "Not a taboo exactly, Mistress. A desire. A concern. Most of the diggers do not believe the stories of their grandmothers, but some do, and they may make things difficult. Hajar, my own assistant, believes in genies, ghouls, and the great dragons, the *mak fawas*, which haunt the night."

"Ahmahl," said Tocasia, smiling slightly, "you know that standing in either brother's way when he has determined to do something is like trying to turn aside the desert wind. They will go looking. And now that you have brought me your concern, I will go with them. My question for you is, should we find something and need to investigate further, will you come along as well to aid us?"

Old Ahmahl sat bolt upright, surprised. Tocasia had phrased the question just right—short of an insulting accusation, but direct enough to demand an answer. He sputtered for a moment, then turned stern again.

"I will be wherever you need me to be," he said coldly. "I have learned more about the ancient days from working with you than I would in a lifetime of roaming the desert. We have moved too much earth, you and I, for us to part ways over a grandmother's story."

Tocasia allowed herself a small grin, then turned a stern face to the old man. "Go, then, and find out among your diggers who believes in grandmothers' stories and who does not. Discover who would go to a dig site in the mountains and who would remain. Do not challenge their pride or their courage, for then even those who think it sacrilege would come along, and feel the worse for it. I do not know if we will find anything, but if we do we will investigate it."

Ahmahl nodded and rose to his feet. "I did not think you would shy away from any challenge, Tocasia. You are like a man in that regard."

Tocasia rose as well in respect. "I did not think you would hide any information I needed to know from me. Thank you."

Ahmahl bowed and was gone. Tocasia shook her head as she watched his shadow join the others of the early evening. You are like a man, he had said, and meant it as a compliment. Typical desert dweller, after all these years. Yet he was still willing to defy old stories and give her a warning.

Tocasia shook her head again and returned to intricacies of the *suchi*'s leg mechanisms.

* * * * *

They left the next morning, packing enough rations for a day and a half's flight out and back. Both of the young men accepted Tocasia's companionship without comment, and neither suggested that she not come along. She left Kantar—one of the more promising older students of that season—in charge while she was gone and told him not to argue with Ahmahl or Hajar and to defer any disputes or major decisions until they returned.

The ornithopter was the original one they had rebuilt years ago. Now the forward housing was enclosed by a larger wooden frame containing more than enough room for the three explorers and their supplies. The control levers remained in the middle of the housing, so either young man could handle them. The power of the stone was nearly inexhaustible, but human flesh was otherwise. After about four hours of flight they would have to change operators.

From the ground the borders of the Great Desert were a low undulating waste of blown dust marred with frequent rocky outcroppings. The region was barren, claimed by the coastal states with intermittent and vague borders far inland. The Fallaji also claimed the wastes, but they enforced that title only when seeking to shake down a few valuables from merchants and explorers in the desert. It seemed an inhospitable and barren world.

From aloft it was transformed. The rocky spires became sentinels, marking the passage of time as their shadows swept beneath them.

The deep and uncrossable canyons turned into rainbows of colored granite and sandstone. The dry lakes were transformed into glittering patches of salt. The desert wind plucked at the ornithopter's control wires as they sailed effortlessly northward.

With Urza at the controls, they flew straight across the sky, fixed on the course that he had set. Occasionally he called out to Mishra to check the coordinates. Inevitably, after checking with map and compass, and taking a reading on the sun, the younger brother declared all was well. Each time Urza nodded, as if he would be surprised by any other result.

When Mishra was piloting, they roamed more, still keeping to the general north and slightly westerly direction but wandering back and forth along that line. If an interesting formation caught Mishra's eye, he steered toward it until Urza warned him they were off course. Then the younger brother sighed and brought the prow of the craft back on track. Occasionally they had to reengage the wings to regain lost altitude. Then Urza would check three times to make sure of their position.

Once they passed over another series of lines. These held no humanoid figures, only spirals and angles juxtaposed against one another. Mishra circled the site as the older brother sketched, then nodded in confirmation. The angles pointed in the direction they should travel.

At the end of the first day they set down on a particularly high mesa. Far from the protection of the stockade and its grapeshot catapults, they camped without a fire and slept within the ornithopter's housing. Though Tocasia had not had to man the control levers during the flight, she was worn by the continual motion. Her head ached from the tinny rush of the wind over the wires. She slept without dreams that evening and awoke stiff from the cramped quarters. The young men were already outside, Urza stretching to elongate his back, Mishra bending at the knees. After a cold breakfast they set out again.

The Thran center, what Ahmahl had referred to as its "secret heart," could not be missed from the air, though it would not be reached easily from the ground. It was at the end of a long, winding canyon leading west, the trail of some ancient long-dead river that had split the low mesa and cradled the ruins.

And ruins they were—long processions of shattered building foundations and tumbled walls. Some of the ruins resembled manor houses from Argive. Others were akin to the onion-domed temples of distant

Tomakul. Still others resembled nothing the three investigators had seen before: a framework of metal that supported nothing at all, a pile of discarded plates, each the size of a man, with serrated edges, or a tangle of what looked like blue metallic worms. Along the far canyon wall was what looked like a nest of broken bronze-colored spiders. The entire cavalcade of wreckage was buried beneath the sands carried out of the desert to the west.

"Do you doubt my calculations now, Brother?" said Urza with a smile.

"Only a fool would doubt his own eyes. Well done, Brother," said Mishra, his grin even wider.

"The Thran's secret heart," murmured Tocasia. Mishra flinched slightly at the phrase and his smile faded, but Urza only nodded.

"The old Argivian word for secret was *koilos*," said Urza. "Let that be the name of this hidden land. Circle around it, Brother. We can best see the lay of the land from up here."

Mishra nodded and was just pulling on the controls when suddenly a shadow passed over the ornithopter housing. It could have been a cloud but for the fact that the desert sky was clear.

Tocasia knew what it meant. She shouted at the same moment that Mishra pitched the flying craft into a steep, banking dive. Urza was taken by surprise and let out a curse as he was flung against the inner side of the craft's housing.

The roc dove through the space that moments ago had been occupied by the ornithopter. The bird was a huge representative of its race, a species reputed in old legends to snatch elephants from the plains for supper. Nearly three times the size of the ornithopter, its passage almost flipped the craft.

The roc recovered as soon as it had passed, gaining altitude quickly to make another dive at the craft.

"Why is it attacking?" shouted Urza.

"We're large, and we're moving!" replied Tocasia, screaming above the wind. "It probably thinks we're another roc."

Mishra cursed and pulled both levers back as far as they would go. "I don't think we can get above it! It's too fast for us!"

The roc was already over them again, making another dive. Mishra reengaged the wings and jinked the craft to the right, but the roc was ready for the maneuver. It shifted slightly; there was a horrendous rip along the right side, and Tocasia saw that one of the wing struts had been ripped loose and was now fluttering in the wind. Better than the entire wing missing, thought Tocasia, but enough to cripple them.

"We can't outfly it!" yelled Mishra. "I'm going to put us down."

"Over there!" shouted Urza, pointing to the nest of broken metal spiders. "I think there's a hole in the cliff wall."

"Won't make it!" shouted Mishra, pulling first one lever, then the other, trying to shake the roc off their tail.

"That's because you're flying like a bird!" snapped Urza, shoving his brother aside and grabbing the control levers himself. "Fly it like a machine and we'll make it."

Under Urza's control, the craft no longer zigzagged across the sky but instead rocketed forward, swooping low over the wrecked landscape of Koilos. The roc, its simple avian brain expecting the craft to act like another flier, expected it to dodge or to turn. The bird hesitated before pursuing. Its indecision was all the time that the three needed.

Urza charged the cliff wall. Mishra shouted in panic. Tocasia suddenly remembered a prayer she had learned as a child back in temple school when temples were still fashionable in Argive. She muttered the words softly as the far wall closed on them.

Suddenly Urza banked, bringing the prow of the craft up. He unlocked the mechanism that held the wings in position, and they automatically began to fold. Without the support, the craft plummeted. Again, the roc passed through empty space that moments ago had housed the flier. Urza dropped about fifty feet, then reengaged the wing locks. The wings spread out immediately, catching the desert air and slowing their fall. Still, they landed with an unceremonious bump on the sand. Had they landed on rock, Tocasia had no doubt they would have broken the supporting struts, not to mention a few bones.

Urza unlatched the wing locks, and the wings folded inward again, the damaged strut sticking out at an odd angle. Tocasia was already at the hatch, scanning the skies.

"It'll be back," she said, scanning the empty heavens. "Let's not be here when it comes."

"Shouldn't take off again immediately anyway," said Urza. "It might be waiting. Besides, we need to get the strut repaired. Let's make for that cavern entrance. Are you all right, Brother?"

"You should care!" said Mishra hotly as Tocasia turned at the hatch, afraid the young man had been hurt. "I knew what I was doing! You didn't need to shove yourself into things!"

Urza blinked and scowled, his concern replaced with irritation. "You were playing its game, flying like another roc. Of course it could outfly you that way. We only lost it because I made for—"

"Shelter now. Argument later," Tocasia broke in sharply. "And bring the torches and water. We might be here until dark."

Neither brother replied, but neither argued with the old scholar. They clambered up the sandy bank behind her, breaking into a full-fledged run as the roc's shadow passed over them.

Tocasia was at the entrance first. She spun and scanned the heavens. Above them, the roc circled the canyon of broken machinery and wrecked buildings.

"We'll have to bring the catapults with us next time," she said.

"Or figure out a way to mount them on an ornithopter," observed Mishra.

"We're going to be here for a while," said Urza. "Should we see where this passage goes?"

The cavern was an entranceway. The first ten feet or so were natural rock, but after that the sandstone gave way to smooth, polished granite. Tocasia ran her hands along the wall. It was constructed of separate blocks, invisible to the eye, detectable as individual stones only by touch. She whistled a low note. Even among the Thran ruins she had excavated, there was no workmanship this precise. Behind her, Mishra lit the candlewood torches. The guttering flames smoked but were better than no light at all.

"It was fortunate you saw this opening," said Tocasia to Urza.

"It was obvious," he returned, taking a torch from his brother. "The wreckage of the buildings indicated roads, all of which radiated from this spot. This is the center of the Thran's supposed 'secret heart.' "

"The heart of the heart," said Tocasia.

They spoke in whispers, as if their words might wake the long dead. Tocasia tried to raise her voice to a normal level, but the very emptiness of the space defeated her.

Mishra examined the corridor before them. "No creatures live here. Look at the dust. No footprints but our own."

Urza held up his torch, the light flaring from the walls. "And no bats, either. Nothing has been here for a long time."

Both young men looked at Tocasia. "Right then," she said at last. "Forward. But stay together and stick to the main path."

There was little worry, for the few openings to either side were mere alcoves, and the cavern ran straight back into the hillside itself. They passed several sets of stairs and one or two large chambers, but nothing that would indicate any occupants, recent or otherwise. Dead crystalline plates dotted the ceiling above them, reflecting the light of the torches but providing none of their own.

The first alcoves were empty, but as they moved forward Tocasia noticed some were filled with the remains of *su-chi* constructs. These were rusted relics, little better than the ones they had pulled from the dig. Several were nothing more than lower torsos, the upper halves lost to time or, perhaps, to tomb robbers. Tocasia noticed with some satisfaction that the knees of the creatures did indeed bend backward.

They had reached another staircase leading down into the darkness when they heard it—or rather, felt it. A deep throbbing came from within the surrounding stone, as if the earth were humming some unknowable ditty. Tocasia looked at the young men. They stared at each other, and the scholar was once again reminded of the silent communication they seemed to share. Then the brothers looked back at Tocasia and nodded.

The three descended toward the noise.

Ahead there was light. No more than a gray smudge against the blackness, it slowly refined itself, growing with each passing step. There were no more *su-chi* alcoves now, only straight walls leading toward the goal.

They entered a chamber as large as any they had passed through. The walls were natural, but supported with ancient steel and pillars of the same closely set blocks that Tocasia had seen earlier. The walls were littered with machines. They were clearly of Thran design but with a difference. These appeared functional. Their cogs were greased and shining, their surfaces polished and mirrorlike in their finish. It was, Tocasia thought, as if the Thran had left only moments before.

There were lights as well. Within this chamber the ceiling-plates were alight with their own ambient glow. Small balls of radiance danced around some of the machinery, orbiting them like small, glowing moons. But this was all outdone by the large crystal in the center.

It was a power stone, unmarred by age and unbroken by accident. Its facets were smooth and reflective, the edges sharp enough to cut the fabric of reality itself. It was about the size of two human fists. Yet it called to Tocasia's mind the image of two hearts, for it pulsed with its own rhythm. A rainbow of colors played across it as it throbbed with life.

The power stone was on a low platform flanked by mirrors, which in turn were attached by wires to various machines around the perimeter. The power stone might be responsible for nothing more than the lights, the archaeologist noted, or it might be a fully operational machine with a greater purpose.

Before the power stone's pedestal was a smooth bank of metal, shaped like an oversized, open book. Its pages were metal and glass, and the glass winked like an evil eye in the night. Never had Tocasia seen a device like this one. She realized this might have come at the end of the cycle of Thran development. Perhaps what they had been excavating so lovingly were nothing more than old scrapyards, where the ancient and unwanted remnants of the Thran's past were discarded.

She stared at the crystal itself, while the two young men moved ahead of her, drawn by its incandescent radiance. They stood before the open metal book, dwarfed by its size and magnificence. Their voices rattled against the walls of the cave, rebounding and gaining strength from the subliminal hum that surrounded them.

"It's beautiful," said Mishra. "Look how it glows."

"It's intact," said Urza. "Think what we can learn."

"These markings," said Mishra, spreading his hands out toward the metal book-glyphs. "They're so much like the Thran writings we've seen, but more detailed. More advanced."

"Don't touch anything!" called Urza sharply, thrusting out his own hand to intercept his brother's. "We don't know what they do!"

Tocasia could not tell which brother was responsible for what happened next. She could not tell which brother touched the particular glyph, or even if either did. Later, neither brother admitted to anything, and each accused the other of causing the disaster.

All Tocasia could say was that as Urza reached out to stop his brother, the glow intensified, suddenly and hotly. There was an explosion, but one without sound, and the huge power stone, the heart of the heart of the secret heart, shattered in a blossom of light.

Chapter 4

Visions

This is what Tocasia saw.

The power stone at the center of the room suddenly began to glow hotter, to consume itself with its own radiance. It shone as if a piece of the sun itself had been detached and set down among them. Instinctively Tocasia flung her arms up in front of her to shield her eyes, but already the two brothers were nothing more than fuzzy silhouettes against the gem's radiance. She shouted out their names but her voice was swallowed by the explosion.

There was an explosion, though its sound was in wavelengths that she could not hear. It resounded through the length of the caverns and rattled every bone in her body.

There was pressure, as if a great hand was pressing down upon her, then pressing *through* her, leaving her standing.

There was heat, as if she had suddenly passed through a furnace. Then the heat was gone as well.

And finally there was a rush of air, from behind her, as if the world was straining to fill the gap of what had been lost. It was the force of the blow from behind, unanticipated and unexpected, that knocked her to her knees.

She stumbled to her feet, her ancient joints complaining, her eyes still seared by the brilliance of the power stone's immolation. The stone was no longer on its pedestal, and the deep humming of the cavern no longer resounded through her bones.

Tocasia blinked back the brilliance. Slowly her sight returned, first at the perimeter of her vision, then slowly returning to the center of her eyes. She blinked back a sheen of new-sprung tears, and with it the last bits of her blindness.

The pedestal was empty. The power stone was gone.

Both of the young men were on the floor, but already stirring. Neither had been hurt physically by the blast as far as she could tell, but they pulled themselves up like old men, careful not to shatter their own bones by rising.

Then she noticed that the power stone was not gone. It had been split in two, and each of the brothers held half in his left hand.

More of the lights came on in the cavern, and she heard the tramp of metal feet against stone.

* * * * *

This is what Urza saw.

He was reaching out to stop Mishra but was too late. There was a brilliant flash that consumed them both. His last clear vision was of his brother's face, his expression surprised, his beard surrounding an open mouth. Shouting a curse or a warning? Urza could not hear him, and suddenly he was surrounded by the whiteness of the blast.

Then he was somewhere else.

He was floating; flying over a landscape that he had never seen before. The earth beneath him was made of cables of corroded metal, crossed and recrossed against themselves until they formed a thick woven mat. Huge gears broke through the metal landscape, turning slowly and straining against the surrounding cables. Copper-colored snakes moved among the mat, but Urza saw that they were instead more cables, blindly seeking their path through the morass of woven wires. There were other great circular plates, gears turned sideways, as thick as Urza was tall and coated with a thick patina of corrosion.

Urza noticed that the entire landscape was undulating slightly, like a living thing, from the motion of cogs and wheels beneath. Hills formed around him, moving slowly, pushing the corroded gears relentlessly to his right. In that direction—west he thought, though in this shifting world it was difficult to be sure—there was a reddish glow.

Urza landed on one of the gears, and it carried him along as it moved. The mat of copper-colored cables snaked around him but did not touch him. The landscape seemed to boil with metal snakes.

There was a storm ahead, ebon clouds building against the darker surrounding. Blue lightning arched between the clouds, giving them definition.

A wave of rain swept over the land. It tasted of oil, but it passed quickly as the shifting hills pushed Urza along. Warm steam leaked from beneath the cables, and there was a brief, grinding noise. Then it too ceased.

Before Urza a great tower erupted in the landscape, ripping metal cables and gears as it did so. It was made of thick plates of heavy metal held together by man-sized bolts, and covered with angular runes. It pistoned upward, and the gear upon which Urza stood rose and orbited it as it shot up above the undulating hills. Then the tower retracted into the earth as quickly as it had appeared, and the heaving landscape carried Urza forward.

There was the sharp sound of insect wings, a thousand in number. The noise was all around, but the creatures were invisible to his eyes. Then this sound faded as well.

Now Urza saw he was no longer alone. There were other beings standing on another moving disk, one larger than his own. These others were carefully building as they were carried along. They looked humanoid, dressed in radiant white robes from head to toe. Their faces were covered by white masks and their heads by white hoods. Urza concentrated, but they grew no more distinct. All he could see was that they were building something.

For the first time Urza became aware that he was dreaming. He should be in a cavern with his brother and Mistress Tocasia, he realized. He held out his hands and counted his fingers. He had always heard that one should do this to determine if one was dreaming. He got the right number of fingers (at least what he thought was the right number), but his flesh was translucent. He judged the experiment inconclusive.

The figures in white were moving more quickly now, and he saw they were assembling pieces of a large device made of bronze. It looked like one of the metal spiders at the foot of the cliff, back in the waking world, where he had left the ornithopter. This device though was no wrecked artifact of another age. It towered over the white figures. If the dream spider was the same size as the wreckage they had seen, Urza determined, then the figures were only slightly shorter than the average human.

The dream spider was tall and made of thick plates of bronze-colored metal. Blue-white lightning sparked at the device's joints, and it was held together by bolts as thick as Urza's forearm. The device had no head, but from the center of its back rose a large prominence topped by a cylinder. Urza thought of the catapults back in his own world, and recognized the cylinder as a weapon.

Looking at the dream spider Urza saw not only its form but its function. He saw the pylonlike legs and knew how they had been fastened together and how they would therefore have to move. He saw the prominence atop the creature's back and knew it had to be fitted to allow it to spin in any direction. He understood the heavy mass of overlapping plates that formed the creature's armor and knew how much power was needed to move a mass of that size.

The figures in white were talking to each other now. They had seen Urza but evidently did not know what to do about the interloper. Suddenly Urza felt something heavy in his chest, pulsing like a second heart. He looked down. All his flesh was transparent now. Almost without conscious thought, he reached inside himself and pulled out a large gemstone, glittering green, blue, red, white, and black. The colors overlapped one another, seeming to coexist in the same space.

The edges of the stone were rough, and Urza knew half of it was missing. He raised the gem and showed it to the figures in white. It seemed sufficient; they immediately forgot about him and returned to their work.

The red glow in the west was growing stronger now as the flying gear approached its destination. Looking around, Urza saw other small white-robed figures on their own sidewise gears, each with his own device. Some of the machines were spiders. Some were titanic statues. Some seemed to be great elephants or oxen. All were made of the heavy plates of reddish-gold metal, and all were armed in the same manner as his spider.

Now he saw the glow ahead came from a great foundry, of the type used to make swords and horseshoes. The furnace was made of rough iron and shaped like a monstrous head. Long, curled horns framed a gaping mouth filled with tongues of flickering flame. Urza knew he was a half-mile away from it, but even so he could feel its heat. It could melt the flesh from his bones, he knew, had he any flesh. A great ramp of red-tinged metal led up to the monster furnace's mouth.

The bronze-colored dream spider and the other bronze spiders were moving now, along with the elephants, oxen, and titans. The disks came to rest at the foot of the long ramp, and the various constructs lurched forward, powered by their own internal engines. Steam and sparks leaked from their joints. The artificial creatures formed a pair of lines, one to either side of the ramp.

Now the figures in white, the builders of these mighty constructs, began to move as well. Slowly, almost reluctantly, they inched up the ramp. As they moved, the cylindrical weapons atop the reddish-gold machines followed them, pacing their approach beneath their barrels.

One of the figures nearest to Urza hesitated for a moment, then turned back. Or rather, it tried to. The nearest machine, the golden dream spider the figure had helped build, fired something from its turret. A beam of incandescent light sprang from the tip of the cylinder and cut down the fleeing figure. Urza saw the creature's yellowish bones clatter to the ground and roll to the foot of the ramp.

The other figures in white paid no attention to the dead defector. Instead they slowly made their way up the ramp, toward the flames, bending beneath the weapons of the gold artifacts. Urza tried to shout a warning, but all he could make was a sound of smithies and ringing hammers.

Some of the figures were melting now, while others burst into flame from the heat. Their companions urged, dragged, and hauled them forward until they reached the monstrous mouth of the furnace itself.

And then they pitched themselves in.

Urza screamed. His cries seemed to throw him back away from the monster furnace, away from the world of golden snakes and moving hillsides and be-weaponed machines. The furnace's mouth diminished to a small reddish dot as he fled, and he felt something warm behind him. He turned toward the new sensation and . . .

. . . woke on the floor of the chamber. He was clutching half of the power stone in his hand. In the distance, Urza heard the tromp of metal feet against stone.

* * * * *

This is what Mishra saw.

Urza lunged forward, and Mishra looked up at him, but by the time he saw his brother's face, stern and angry, the white glow had already consumed them both. All Mishra saw was Urza's scowl. And then he was someplace else.

It was indoors, inside a great hallway. This was unlike the smooth halls bored through the mountain, for the walls seemed to be made of lizard skin, black and pliable. He touched one of the walls, and it flinched. Mishra could see the entire passage ripple, almost as if it were sleeping all around him. The air was thick and moist.

The hallway extended ahead of him forever. He turned around. The hallway extended ahead of him forever. He turned around again.

The hallway extended ahead of him forever. He turned around one last time and headed down the endless hallway.

His foot crunched against something, and he stepped back. Beneath his feet was a small toy made of gold. It was in the shape of a human figure, and irrationally Mishra wondered if Urza was somewhere near. And Tocasia—he remembered Tocasia had been with them just a moment ago. He looked at the figure, but it was no one he recognized. He had inadvertently broken off the figure's arm, and the figure's face was transfixed in a scream.

The floor ahead was littered with small screaming figures. Some were humans, but there were elves and orcs, minotaurs and dwarves among them. He tried to move through them without stepping on them, but there were too many. Then he realized that even those figures that he was not stepping on wore screaming visages as well. Reassured that he was doing no additional damage and that the figurines were probably not alive, he pressed on, scattering the toys in his wake.

Now there were alcoves on either side of him, each set with a dark mirror against the back. Mishra stopped at the first one and saw a human form. No, a humanoid form, naked. It seemed to twist as he looked at it, turning first into one race, then another, then a third. It was a statue, shaped from some dark stone, yet fluid. It reached the end of the series of transformations and began the sequence again.

Mishra passed to the second mirror and saw another figure. This one was wearing armor, or what seemed to be armor. As it shifted from one form to another, Mishra realized the armor was part of the statue as well, perhaps even a part of the creature that the statue represented.

Mishra felt a wave of excitement. Suddenly he *knew* what the machines back in the cavern were about. They could transform shapes of flesh and stone into other things. They could improve themselves. They could build things. He rushed to the next mirror, ignoring the golden toys at his feet.

This was another shapechanging statue, but it had more armor than the one he'd seen previously. It had horns too, splaying backward across the top of its head like an antelope's, not outward like those of a minotaur. It changed shape more slowly, and Mishra saw that the image's flesh had grown leathery, resembling the walls around him. Dark bones jutted from its flesh and into the open air, like dark spires of power.

Mishra passed to the next mirror. Here was but a single unchanging figure. Its flesh was black lizard skin broken by the sharp bones that erupted from its flesh. Its face was narrow and wolflike, and its open mouth was filled with razor-sharp teeth. Its eyes were closed, and atop its head a great pair of antelope horns reached impossibly backward. Around the horns was a nest of wormlike coils buried in the creature's skull; they streamed backward like blood-colored tresses.

Mishra stared at the creature in the dark mirror for a long time, waiting for it to change to another shape. But it remained an inert thing of black stone.

Then the statue opened its eyes, and Mishra took a step back.

They were living eyes—soft, wet, leaking blood at the edges. The eyes blinked, and the brow above them furrowed.

Suddenly Mishra was aware that he was watching not an image but a living thing. And, worse yet, that thing was watching him.

The being raised a hand and touched its chest. Mishra mirrored the action, touching his own chest. His fingers brushed against something smooth, and he looked down. Mounted in the center of his chest was a great gem, radiating a spectrum of colors. Forgetting the creature for a moment, he reached up and pulled the gemstone from his breast. It felt warm to the touch, almost comforting. The great jewel was carved in glittering facets around half of its surface, but along one side a large piece had been broken off, leaving a ragged juncture behind.

The creature reached up and touched its side of the mirror. Despite himself, Mishra felt his own hand rise in response, as if he were the image and the creature now the original. He pressed his hand forward, almost touching the glass itself. The demon of metal, bone, and leather smiled.

Someone called his name. He was sure of it. Someone behind him called his name. He turned away from the mirror, from the dark creature behind it, suddenly caught up in a wave of brilliant white light, and . . .

. . . woke on the floor of the chamber. He was clutching half of the power stone in his hand. In the distance Mishra heard the tromp of metal feet against stone.

* * * * *

Tocasia stumbled toward the two brothers, who were slowly pulling themselves from the ground. Whatever they had done, the huge power stone had split in twain, and each brother held a portion of it. Unlike other cleaved stones Tocasia had found at the dig site, these gems retained their lambence and energy. They flickered with the power that still remained within. Each gem flashed with a range of colors, though Urza's shone most often red, while Mishra's glowed heavily green.

Tocasia blinked and realized it was brighter in the chamber. The crystal plates along the ceiling were lighter now, and there were more flashes along the metal-plated walls.

Urza was already at Mishra's side. The younger brother shrugged off his elder's offer of aid and stood on his own. He rocked slightly as he stood, as if his legs were new things to him.

Urza's face was as pale as a ghost's, the colors of the fractured power stone playing across it. "What happened?" he gasped.

Tocasia looked at the two brothers. They seemed woozy but relatively intact.

"The power gem exploded," she said. "You've got the fragments."

Mishra pointed at his brother. "It was his fault!"

"I was trying to stop you!" Urza snapped.

"Enough!" shouted Tocasia, her voice echoing off the walls. "Listen!"

Both young men stopped for a moment and heard the slow, rhythmic tread of metal feet against stone. Numerous and uniform, the footsteps were heavy and relentless. And they were getting closer.

Shapes appeared at the far end of the chamber. Tocasia did not remember a door being there before the explosion; perhaps there hadn't been. There was an opening now, she realized, and through it came a half-dozen titanic shapes.

Su-chi, the guardians of the Thran, with their lupine faces and backward-mounted knees. For all their hulking, twisted structure, they could move fast, though. They bore down on the trio.

"Flee!" shouted Tocasia.

"No," said Urza. "I think I can handle this." His gem seemed to glow brighter as he spoke, and he held the bauble in front of him. A single beam of ruby light shone from the edges of the stone and lanced across the room, bathing the six oversized mechanisms. They hesitated, drinking in the radiance. Then they moved forward again.

"They're moving faster!" shouted Tocasia. "Whatever you did made them stronger!"

"Then we flee," said Urza.

Mishra raised his own stone, but Urza slapped his brother's arm down. "We tried it, and it doesn't work. Don't make matters worse!" He ran, following Tocasia. Mishra raced behind them.

All the stairs that they had descended were like cliffs now to be climbed again. Tocasia felt her muscles strain and cry out with each flight, and her bones felt as if they were made of stone. By the end of the third set of stairs Tocasia was leaning on Urza's shoulder for support. The *su-chi* were slower on the steps, but the creatures took them two at a time and were untiring.

Tocasia glanced over her shoulder. The *su-chi* were catching up with them.

At the top of the steps Mishra stopped, panting. Urza was in little better shape, and Tocasia felt as if she was going to pass out.

"Perhaps . . . we can find something . . . to push down. Block . . . their path," wheezed Urza.

Mishra held up his stone again, but Urza shook his head, exhausted. "Doesn't work. Makes them . . . stronger. Tried that."

Mishra was panting as well, but he forced his words out. "You tried. With . . . your stone. Let me try . . . mine."

Urza let out a shout, but the younger brother was faster. He raised the stone before him, and its rays arched down the steps. The light from this gem did not pass through the air in straight lines; rather it bent in arching curves tinged with a greenish glow.

The light struck the lead *su-chi* in midstride, as it was climbing a step. The artifact, vigorous and healthy a moment before, now sagged noticeably, as if the vitality had been suddenly leeched from it. It bent forward on the step. The creature behind it was taken by surprise and slipped backward, taking two more with it as it fell. The three collapsed in a pile on the landing, and only two of the figures rose again.

"Didn't stop them," gasped Urza. "Told you."

"Slowed them down," snapped Mishra.

"Fight later," said Tocasia, clutching the front of her robes. "Run now."

Tocasia's chest felt as if it was on fire as they fled back down the corridors. Since there were no side passages, there was little chance of getting lost or of hiding. The crystalline plates along the ceiling were all illuminated, casting odd shadows as the explorers ran. Perhaps that was part of the guarding system for the Thran themselves, thought the old scholar. When someone entered and used the machines, the lights came on and the *su-chi* were roused from their slumber.

In the alcoves they passed, Tocasia glimpsed other Thran artifacts. The machines struggled to mobilize themselves as well, but the passage of time was too great for them. A metal arm rose in mute protest as Urza, Mishra, and Tocasia passed. A lupine head of dark blue metal spun toward them and hissed. At one point, the lower torso of a *su-chi*, backward knees and all, lurched from its alcove, bereft of an upper body. Urza pushed Tocasia behind him, but Mishra brought his stone up. A jade-green lancet of power arced forward, and the remains of the creature exploded, the legs falling in different directions. They ran past the metal corpse; in the back of her mind Tocasia discovered a moment of regret that they had not the time to examine the creature more thoroughly.

The pursuing *su-chi* were out of sight, but the old scholar could still hear their clattering tread, the whir of the mechanisms within their chests, and the clank of their joints. Ahead there was another growing brightness—this one natural. They had reached the entrance and were safe.

Urza held out an arm across the passage, catching both Tocasia and Mishra, who let out a low curse. The older brother pointed with his other hand to the entrance.

A shadow moved across the sand in front of the cavern's mouth. Something large was waiting for them.

Tocasia looked back for a sign of the pursuing *su-chi*, as both brothers crept forward. The roc was perched directly above the lip of the cavern, like an owl waiting above a rodent's hole for its prey to appear. Urza cursed.

"Let me try," said Mishra, holding out his stone. This time Urza did not stop him.

Mishra edged forward to get a clear shot at the roc with his stone. Urza stayed directly behind him. Mishra held his half of the gem aloft, and the greenish arcing light, visible even in the daylight outside, burst forward and streaked up toward the roc. The great bird let out a tremendous shriek. It took to flight, fluttering about a hundred yards away to a large, rocky spur, where it settled again. The greenish rays followed it but did no additional damage.

"Fall, damn you! Fall!" muttered Mishra through clenched teeth.

"You're weakening it," said Urza, "but it's too big to fall. Too tough."

"Company coming," said Tocasia briefly. Far off in the distance was the clatter of the approaching *su-chi*.

"Between the desert and the deep, briny sea." Mishra quoted an old desert saying.

Urza stared at the remains of the metal spider's nest at the foot of the hill. "Mishra, take Tocasia and run for the ornithopter. Don't stop running until you get there."

"But the roc—" began Mishra.

"Let the roc be my problem," said Urza and leapt forward into the sunlight.

Tocasia protested, but Mishra had already grabbed her by the wrist and pulled her after him. Mishra's fingers were like a vise around her arm, and she had little choice but to follow. The lights behind them already reflected off the blue metal of the *su-chi*'s skulls.

The roc was aloft as soon as Urza appeared, swooping back on titanic wings to its perch over the cavern's mouth. Its vulturelike beak snaked down to snare the young man, but Urza was too fast for it. In a moment he was among the remnants of the bronze spider things that littered the base of the cliff.

Tocasia was half-guided, half-dragged by Mishra toward the ornithopter. Halfway there they dodged behind a large boulder for cover. Two pairs of eyes looked around the boulder's edge for any sign of Urza.

"What is that fool doing?" whispered Mishra. They saw Urza dart among the half-buried wreckage of the spiders, then disappear.

Tocasia put her hand to her chest and caught her breath. Urza was among the wrecked bronze metal spiders, she saw. His half of the stone seemed to function differently than Mishra's gem. "He's going . . ." She stopped and gulped. Her mouth felt as if it were lined with metal. "He's going to try to get one of those spiders to work. But why . . .?"

The rest of her statement was lost in a titanic throbbing hum from beneath their feet, and one of the reddish-gold spiders lurched from its sandy tomb. The sand poured away from it like water, and Tocasia saw that the spider's armor was shredded in a half-dozen places and the creature was missing most of its forward legs. Through the peeled side plates she could see Urza frantically pulling levers and pressing buttons. There was a reddish glow around him, giving the steam that poured out of the beast's sides a hellish aura.

"He's powering it with the stone," said Mishra. "He's fitted his stone into the machine. It must make artifacts stronger."

"No. The stone's in his hand," corrected Tocasia. "But you're right. He's using that stone to make the machine more powerful, to enhance whatever power it has."

"Whatever," grunted Mishra, pointing toward the opening. "He's running out of time. Look!" At the entrance to the cavern were the remaining *su-chi*, lurching into the sunlight.

The turret on the spider's back gave a high-pitched metallic rasp as it spun on grit-filled cogs and brought about a long, dangerous-looking barrel. Tocasia knew at once it was a weapon.

The roc screeched and leapt forward to pit the tasty morsel from its shell like a sea gull eating a crab. Tocasia heard Urza shout something unintelligible, and the barrel spat flame. The resounding thunder of the weapon as it fired rattled through the canyon of Koilos.

The flame caught the roc in the center of its chest, igniting its feathers and engulfing its body in flames. The great winged beast tried to fly, but the fire was insidious, creeping along the roc's wings and setting them alight as the creature raised them. For an instant the roc became the phoenix of Fallaji legend, bathed in flame. But instead of rising like the mythical bird, the roc fell, plummeting to the canyon floor below.

The great bird fell directly in front of the cavern mouth where the *su-chi* now stood. The weakened creatures had time to look up, and Tocasia heard a sharp metallic whining noise that might have been a scream. Then the massive body of the flaming roc smashed down on them, crushing them utterly.

There was another screech, this one sharper, more high pitched. It came from the rusted and torn metal spider with which Urza had defeated their opponents. The steam that had surrounded the craft now became black smoke; flames and sparks licked the craft's framework. Urza had climbed loose of the device and was running. Tocasia noticed he cradled the reddish gem against his chest.

The whining noise from the spider became higher. It reached a pitch that almost split Tocasia's brain. Then, with a crescendo of thunder, the metal spider exploded. The noise of the blast reverberated from the cliff sides and was answered a few seconds later by echoes farther up the canyon.

Urza staggered up to the others. Tocasia checked the cavern's entrance, but all that was visible were the smoking remains of the roc.

"That takes care of that," said Urza. His face and hair were streaked with soot, and he smelled of burnt leather and metal.

"You were lucky," said Mishra with a frown.

"We all were lucky," said Tocasia. "Lucky to find this place, lucky to escape the roc. Lucky to escape the caverns without perishing. Now let us be sufficiently lucky to get back home."

"You were lucky," repeated Mishra to his brother.

"Luck had nothing to do with it," replied Urza, a surly note in his voice. "I thought I knew what those spider things did, and I had the power to make a difference. It was fast planning, perhaps, but not luck."

"You had no idea," pressed Mishra. "You accidentally made the guardians stronger with the power of the stone."

"One learns from one's mistakes," said Urza, shrugging. "At least I do. You keep making new mistakes all the time."

"Boys," cautioned Tocasia, "this isn't the time for this."

"I beat the *su-chi* with my stone!" snapped Mishra.

"You blew up the crystal in the first place!" riposted Urza.

"I did not! I didn't touch anything!" yelled Mishra. "That was you!"

"Hold!" shouted Tocasia, stepping between the two young men. "We can argue about this once we get aloft. For the moment we need to repair the ornithopter and get back." She motioned with her head toward the smoldering remains of the roc. "We don't know if that bird was solitary or one of a larger family."

Tocasia turned away from the pair. She wondered if there was something among the debris she could use as a walking stick. In the flight from the caverns she had lost hers, and she could feel the muscles in her legs cramping from overuse. She looked forward to a long rest after this adventure.

Behind her, neither of the brothers moved. Tocasia turned and said, "Today, if you don't mind." Both brothers, she noticed, looked as if steam were going to pour from their ears.

"In a moment," said Urza finally. "But first, give." He held out his right hand. His left still clutched the red-glowing gem.

"What?" asked Mishra, holding his own stone to his chest.

"The stone," returned Urza. "Give it to me. Perhaps we can fit the pieces back together."

Mishra held the stone tighter, and Tocasia could swear she saw the stone flicker, as yellow-green as a cat's eyes, in his hand. "No," he said. His face was set in a deep scowl.

"There is a chance that we can restore it," said Urza crossly.

"Good," snapped Mishra. "Give me yours."

Urza's face grew longer. "I can't. You might break it."

"I don't break things!" said Mishra hotly. His voice was shrill. To Tocasia it seemed on the verge of breaking, as it had done several years before during his adolescence. "You're the one who always thinks you know everything," he continued, "but you always blame me! Well, you're not as smart as you think you are. Everyone knows that!"

"I know better because I'm older," said Urza coldly.

"Then you know I don't want to give up my stone," retorted his brother. "If you want to fit it together, give me yours, Master High-and-Mighty Too-Good-for-the-Rest-of-Us! Show me you're all-wise, Brother. Give me your stone!"

"You want it?" snarled Urza. "Fine. Take it, then! You always take things that aren't yours!"

Tocasia started to shout, but it was too late. Urza's hand lashed out, the stone still gripped tightly in his fist. Mishra stepped forward, directly into Urza's punch. The gem connected with the younger brother's forehead and he went down in a heap.

Urza leapt forward, kneeling over the fallen form of his brother. "I'm sorry, Mishra. I didn't mean to hit you."

Mishra had already pushed himself up on his elbows and was trying to back away. "Get away from me, damn you!"

Tocasia pulled on Urza's shoulder. "Get up. You should know better!" she snarled. Her temper was frayed to the breaking point. "You're always saying you're the older and smarter one," she rapped out. "Well, look what you've done."

Urza started to speak, then looked at his brother. The gem had cut Mishra's face, and crimson blood already welled in the wound at his temple.

Urza looked at Tocasia again. "I—I'm . . . sorry," he stammered. He held out his empty hand to Mishra. "I didn't mean to. I'm sorry."

Mishra lashed out, knocking away Urza's hand. "Go away! I don't need your help!"

Tocasia started to speak. "Now, Mishra, your brother is just trying—"

"And I don't need you to explain things away for him, either," Mishra interrupted. "I'll be fine." He turned to his brother. "The stone is mine. You have one of your own."

Tocasia felt her insides melting with anger. Both young men were stupid, pigheaded fools. She had no time for this. She breathed heavily, controlling her temper by an act of will.

"Fine," she said at last. "Urza, you tend to the strut on the ornithopter. Mishra, check the remains of the roc to see if any of the *suchi* guardians survived. Shout if any do."

Neither brother moved, and Tocasia put steel in her voice. "Now, children!"

Both turned to their tasks, but Tocasia noticed that each glowered at the other as if they were rival dogs.

The trip back to Tocasia's camp was made in moody silence, and they flew into the night to avoid having to camp again. Neither brother spoke more than three words at a time to the other. They confined themselves to practical subjects such as the way the damaged wing was handling, the weather ahead, and the present course of the ornithopter. Neither spoke about the secret heart of the Thran, the roc, or their fight.

Tocasia realized that more than the power stone had been shattered that day.

Chapter 5

Sundering

The world changed after Koilos and became a darker place in the months that followed.

Urza retreated to the quarters he shared with his brother as soon as the three investigators returned to the camp, emerging only for meals. Soon after Mishra moved out of those quarters, taking a tent among the diggers. He could have taken permanent housing among the students, but Tocasia felt the young man was making a statement, both to his brother and to her.

The two brothers sniped at each other continually now. Urza noted publicly that Mishra had instructed the students to dig too deep. Mishra shot back that Urza was demanding more students to clean the artifacts than he truly needed.

Mealtimes were particularly stressful. The arguments were no longer exchanges of wordplay and ideas. An edge of steel, like the blade of a dagger, had slipped into the boys' conversations. Questions now seemed like barbed hooks, and answers held hints of threat and challenge. A few times Mishra blew up at his brother at the table, and after a month Urza stopped attending the communal dinners at all, instead taking his meals in his quarters. He had apparently used Mishra's half of the room to expand his own work space, which irritated his brother all the more. Mishra appeared at dinner for a month beyond that, brooding over the meals. Then he began to dine in the diggers' camp.

Neither brother spoke of personal matters, not to Tocasia nor anyone else. To the old scholar they were polite and tried to keep the conversation focused on the nature of the excavations (for Mishra) or on the latest reassembled marvel (for Urza). When the subject of the caverns came up, however, both young men would turn taciturn and abrupt.

In part, Tocasia felt, it was the stones that had altered their relationship. Urza had fit his to a clawlike clasp of gold and wore it about his neck on a chain. Mishra too wore his around his neck but in a small leather sack dangling from a thong in the manner of the Fallaji talismans. Tocasia did not know if the shattered power stone had created the anger within her two best students or merely unearthed and crystallized resentments that had fermented for years. Soon after Koilos, she went to each and asked to examine the stones themselves, seeking to unlock their mystery.

Urza refused to give up his stone. Instead, he said, he wanted to examine it himself. Surely Tocasia trusted him to make a fair and rational examination? What he did not say, though Tocasia sensed it, was that he was afraid she would turn over the stone to his brother. Mishra would play on the old scholar's feelings. He was the younger brother; therefore Tocasia would give Mishra a chance to examine both halves of the stone.

Mishra in turn would not give up his stone. If Urza kept his half of the stone, he said contemptuously, he would hold his as well. What he did not say, but what Tocasia felt, was that he was afraid she would turn over the stone to his brother. Urza would appeal to her reasoning. Urza was the elder brother; therefore Tocasia would give Urza the chance to examine both halves of the stone.

The archaeologist was thoroughly frustrated. Neither brother would move without the other; neither trusted her sufficiently to let her examine the gems. She turned to the other stones, both the flickering fragments that still held some power and the dull, cracked remains that had lost their energies.

There was nothing there. None of the other power stones they had discovered had similar powers. Mishra's stone seemed to induce weakness in its targets, whether living or artificial. Urza's gem apparently strengthened its targets and in fact allowed the spark of animation to enter the barest of mechanical husks. No other stones, Tocasia noted sadly, seemed to have encouraged such avarice and anger in their possessors.

The nature of the energy itself continued to elude Tocasia. She knew it existed and that it could be harnessed by the devices using the Thran designs they had deciphered. Yet the nature of that energy was beyond her. What was it, and how did it come into being? Was it natural to the crystals, or was it something the Thran had entrapped there? The questions were there, but not the answers, and her own failure to answer darkened Tocasia's mood further.

To be fair, the black mood in the camp was not all the brothers' doing—at least not directly. More Fallaji than Ahmahl had expected were offended by the fact that the archaeologist and her colleagues had found the secret heart of the Thran. Diggers abandoned the camp in droves. Old Ahmahl was clearly embarrassed by this turn of events, since he had assured Tocasia that few of his people would be scared away by ancient legends of the long-dead Thran. Indeed, as word of the discovery of Koilos spread, the flow of artifacts recovered by the desert people, so abundant in previous years, dried up almost entirely.

Part of that drought was caused by an increase in desert raids. A number of tribes such as the Suwwardi, quiet for decades, were more active now. They raided merchant caravans and even struck into Argive itself. The school had not been attacked, owing to its own group of native Fallaji, but it was only a matter of time, Tocasia felt.

Ahmahl agreed. "There are numbers beyond numbers of families, tribes, and clans among the Fallaji," he said one evening, ten months after Koilos. They sat beneath Tocasia's tarp, sipping *nabiz*. Most of the rest of the camp had gone to bed. The only lamps still burning were from Urza's quarters, and those had been dimmed. The brazier between Tocasia and Ahmal crackled low.

The Fallaji spread his fingers and ticked off a roster of tribal names: "The wealthy Muaharin, the once-mighty Ghestos, and my own tribe, the Thaladin," he said. "There are others like the Tomakul, who have the nearest thing you outlander people would think of as a city. The Tomakul claim general rulership over the others. But they are not the true masters of the various tribes either. The clans follow strong leaders; so for one generation everyone followed the Ghestos because they had a wise leader. For the next they followed the Muaharin because the Muaharin had a great warrior as their leader."

"And now the desert people follow a new tribe," said Tocasia bitterly, sipping at her *nabiz*. She took it hot, in the desert style, but never cared for the cinnamon.

"The Suwwardi," agreed Ahmahl. "They moved in from the southwestern lands when I was a boy, from the area bordering the outlander state of Yotia. They have a qadir, a leader who has gained many allies. He talks of the old times when the Fallaji people were powerful. And he fans resentment against the coastal nations, particularly those that are spreading into Fallaji lands."

"Are these Suwwardi your leaders now?" asked Tocasia.

Ahmahl shrugged. "Not like your kings and warlords and nobles are leaders. My people put great value in respect. They respect the Suwwardi for what they have accomplished and therefore listen to their message. Many worry about the coastal nations moving inland, taking land from the traditional Fallaji grounds. Many worry about the discoveries we are making."

"We are discovering things for everyone," said Tocasia flatly.

"That I agree with," returned Ahmahl. "And I thought others would agree as well. But they see the artifacts they bring in to trade, as well as the ones we dig up, move eastward to Argive, southeast to Korlis, or south to Yotia. They worry what great and wondrous things are being lost to them."

"And these Suwwardi play on that worry," concluded Tocasia. "They gather power by creating a common threat, whether one is truly present or not."

Ahmahl nodded and said dryly, "You are familiar with the process."

Tocasia laughed and took a long pull on her *nabiz*. "Basic Argivian politics. The kings of Argive have survived for years on that principle, playing one faction against another. They do things in Penregon that would make your head spin. At least the Fallaji are honest about being someone's enemy."

"That is why we have not moved, and should not move, the base camp to Koilos," said Ahmahl.

"The only way into the canyon where the caverns are found is through the deep desert—" Tocasia began.

"The deep desert is held by the Suwwardi tribe and their allies. Word has gone out that any non-Fallaji found in their lands will be considered Suwwardi property, to be disposed of as they see fit."

Tocasia spread her hands and looked at the wooden surface beneath her wrinkled fingers. The desert had practically won its battle with the great Argivian table. It was wobbly and brittle now; the last of its pearl inlay had surrendered to the differences in temperature and to the dust. Soon she would have to break it up for firewood. Tocasia had not realized how much she would miss the table, both as a level space and as a reminder of distant Penregon.

Would they have had this problem with the tribesmen had Urza not been so brilliant with maps and calculations, or Mishra so close to the desert tribes and their legends? Tocasia shook her head. The past was the past, as inviolate as the rocks from which she and her followers pulled the Thran devices, as solid as the metals they carefully pieced together in the workshops.

A silence grew between her and Ahmal. The only sound was the crackle of the brazier.

"You are not thinking of the desert tribes or your dig site," said Ahmahl at last. "You are thinking of your two young men."

Tocasia let the silence continue, then said, "They have been fighting again."

"Ever since they visited the Secret Heart of the Old Ones," said Ahmahl. Tocasia shot the leader of the diggers a look and he held up a hand. "No, they did not tell me what happened there. No one tells this old digger anything. But it is clear to me and to everyone else that they have had a great falling-out. The kind of battle that brothers do not recover from. Last week they almost came to blows at the dig site." He shot her a sidelong glance. "You know?"

Tocasia nodded. "Urza thought Mishra was digging too deep to find any parts for an onulet. When the diggers found such parts, Urza all but accused Mishra of planting the find there in the trench."

"Mishra found the pieces of that onulet's shoulder mounting fairly," said Ahmahl. "But then he drove the diggers on into the heat of midday, when we normally nap. He would have been happy with nothing less than a complete onulet arising from the earth, fully formed and alive, just to prove his brother wrong."

Tocasia nodded. "Each day they get worse, and neither wants to talk to the other about it. Whenever they are in the same place, the conversation breaks down into argument. Then each continues arguing with me afterward, trying to show me where the other was wrong. And when I try to show them that they may be wrong, each acts as if I've sided with the other. The past few months have been the worst of all the years I have known them."

Ahmahl leaned forward. "The Fallaji believe that man is made of stone and fire, sky and water. The perfect man holds all these elements in balance. The young brother—he had more fire than he needed on the first day I met him, and he has more fire than he needs now. The older brother is consumed by stone: cold and unyielding. Unable to bend, he will shatter or be worn away."

"The Argivians have a similar belief, though few follow it these days," said Tocasia. "The world is divided into reality and dreams. The old temple priests of Argive would say that both those young men have been consumed by their dreams and are forgetting their reality."

Ahmahl grunted. "Does Urza speak of dreams to you?"

Tocasia shook her head. "Urza speaks to no one anymore. Not to me; not his brother." She looked at the leader of the diggers. "Does Mishra?"

Ahmahl nodded. "Not to me, but he does speak. To Hajar, one of my younger assistants, who is closer to him in age and temperament. Hajar has been bitten hard by the fire as well, and he dreams of being a great warrior. I fear we will lose him to the Suwwardi and soon. But Mishra has told Hajar, who has told me and I tell you, that Mishra has dreams."

"Of what?" asked Tocasia, pouring herself more *nabiz*.

"Darkness," said Ahmahl, spreading his fingers out to catch the warmth of the brazier. "He says there is darkness out there, a darkness that sings to him and tries to draw him to it. It tugs at him, like a jackal hanging on to his trouser legs. And he fears it."

"He said that?" prompted Tocasia.

Ahmahl shrugged. "Mishra talks to Hajar. Hajar talks to me. I talk to you. Each time someone talks to another, things are added, other things forgotten. Perhaps you should ask him yourself. He probably would not tell Hajar, 'Hajar, I am afraid of my dreams,' but Mishra does sleep in the digger's camp, and everyone knows he sometimes awakens in the middle of the night shouting at things that are not there."

Tocasia was silent for a moment. She could not say if Mishra had done this before Koilos, when Mishra and Urza were quartered together, but Urza had never said anything about the matter. Nor had Urza spoken of his own dreams, if indeed he had any.

"You know they each took something with them when they left Koilos?" asked Tocasia.

"The gems of power," replied Ahmahl. "They look like the ones that you say move the Old Ones' machines. Each of the Young Masters has one. Yet each man keeps his stone close to himself at all times."

"Could the stones be responsible?" queried Tocasia. "Could their energies be causing the young men to act like this?"

Ahmahl shrugged, and Tocasia added, "Do you know what their stones can do?"

"Mishra has not talked to me of the matter," said Ahmahl flatly. "Perhaps to Hajar, but . . ." He let the words hang in the hot desert air for a long moment.

"Urza's gem makes things stronger," said the scholar. "He called it his Mightstone. Mishra's seems to have the opposite effect. Urza has named it the Weakstone."

Ahmahl chortled. "That probably does not sit well with the younger brother, to have the weaker stone."

"It doesn't," said Tocasia. "Urza knows it, so he calls it that to Mishra's face."

"What does Mishra call it?" asked Ahmahl.

Tocasia thought a moment, "I've never heard him refer to it as one thing or another. Its 'his'—Mishra's—stone. And the other one is 'his,' Urza's, stone."

"That sounds right," observed Ahmahl. "The older brother always had a tendency to name things, to identify them. It makes them his, I suppose."

Tocasia sighed. "All these years they have been with us," she said, "and they remain as great a mystery as the energy within those power crystals. As the Thran themselves."

"The Thran, the Old Ones, you and I will understand, eventually," replied Ahmahl. "For they have the good sense to stay dead. The living, they keep changing as time goes along. It is harder to climb upon a moving mount."

"Old Fallaji saying?" Tocasia raised her cup.

"Old digger saying," said Ahmahl, returning the salute. "From this old digger in particular."

The conversation moved to other subjects, such as the new layer of hard sandstone they had encountered at the second site and whether Bly would need additional outriders for his caravan (and how much he would try to charge Tocasia for them). Finally Ahmahl made farewells and left the tarp. The night was pleasant, and Tocasia knew she would probably sleep sitting up in her camp chair, wrapped in a soft fur from dwarven Sardia.

Ahmahl slowly walked through the camp. The fires had been banked, and the lamps had all been extinguished. Even the lamps from Urza's quarters, usually the last to be doused, were now darkened.

The old digger stood in the center of the camp and looked upward at the stars. The moons had not risen yet, and above the old Fallaji the sky pinwheeled in a heavy scattering of stars. Ahmahl tried to imagine if the sky over the far-off coastal cities looked this beautiful, and decided against it. Fires burned long and wastefully into the night there, obscuring the sky with their smoke. So much like city peoples everywhere.

There was a movement to his left and the sound of a sandal scraping against the dirt. Slowly Ahmahl turned toward the noise, keeping his head raised toward the stars but allowing his eyes to sweep the shadows. The moonless night was dark but not dark enough to foil the sharp eyes of the Fallaji.

There was a rustle along the shadowed side of one of the student barracks. Then came a soft, muffled cough.

"Someone there?" called Ahmahl, suddenly looking directly at the shadow. "Show yourself, shadowy one, or I'll wake the camp!"

A lean form stepped from the shadows, dressed in dark linen. Thin, and wiry; Ahmal recognized Hajar, chief among his assistants. The young Fallaji smiled guiltily, his teeth filling his narrow face.

"It was a beautiful night, and I could not sleep," he said. "I thought I would go for a walk."

Ahmahl smiled. "It is a beautiful night, and I have been walking myself," he said. "Let us stroll back together." The old digger turned away, but Hajar did not move from his position. "Are you coming?" Ahmal asked, then added with a smile, "Or are you not alone?" To the shadows behind Hajar he said, "You can come out now as well."

Ahmahl had expected Hajar's companion to be one of the noble girl students entrusted to Tocasia. Such romances, though officially frowned upon, were common enough, and Ahmahl still remembered his own youth well enough to know all the justifications and excuses one makes in such situations. A stern lecture and a word to Tocasia to keep an eye on the Argivian girl was all that usually resulted from such a discovery.

Ahmahl was thus surprised when the figure who stepped from the shadows was not a young woman but the familiar, broad-shouldered form of Mishra. Ahmahl's smile turned to puzzlement, and the old digger said, "Good evening, young master. Are you enjoying the beautiful night?"

Mishra smiled, and even in the starlight Ahmal could see it was a thin, inconsequential smile. "I needed to fetch something from Urza's—from my old quarters," he said. "I brought Hajar along to help."

"I see," said Ahmahl cautiously, "and this something was so critical that you needed to fetch it now, in the dead of night, when even your brother would be asleep?"

"Yes," said Mishra. The young man seemed to be turning the idea over in his mind a few times; then apparently he decided to stick with it. His back straightened, and he said again, "Yes. Something important. Do you doubt me?"

By this time Ahmahl had closed the distance between himself and the pair. He could smell the odor of desert wine on them. It was more powerful than on himself.

"Not at all, Young Master Mishra," said Ahmahl. "And this something is so heavy you need a second man, or a perhaps a third, to carry it?"

"Yes," said Mishra, then, perhaps feeling he'd given too much away, corrected himself. "No. Not really. Hajar is here more for company."

"Ah," said Ahmahl. "Well, I have a need for Hajar. If you can spare him, he can run an errand for me."

Mishra's face clouded, and Ahmahl wondered if the lad would continue alone or merely abandon his task. It was obvious he was heading for his brother's, and Ahmahl thought it likely the younger brother planned to confront Urza with an argument. The youth had obviously taken his courage from a wineskin, a time-consuming task that accounted for the late hour.

Mishra gave another thin smile. "Of course. If you need Hajar for some matter, I can gladly do without him."

"A small matter," said Ahmahl. "I could use the help. But I tell you again, I don't think your brother is awake. His lamps are out."

Mishra shook his head. "Sometimes my brother lies awake in the darkness and plots into the night. I would be surprised if he were truly asleep."

Ahmahl raised his hands in mock surrender. "As you say. You know him better than I. Come, Hajar. I have work for you."

The wiry Fallaji crossed toward Ahmahl, and the older man turned. The pair started back toward the digger's camp.

Ahmahl looked back. Mishra had already melted back into the shadows. "So why were you there, Hajar?"

The narrow-faced youth scowled in the starlit darkness. "I do not know if I can tell you."

"We are Fallaji," said the older man. "If I cared to find out, I could show that your mother's family and my mother's family shared a common mother. Come out with it. What were you up to, stinking of *nabiz* and slinking through the shadows like jackals?"

The younger Fallaji stopped, as clearly motion and moral thought did not work simultaneously. Ahmahl waited. At last the youth said, "Young Master Mishra was angry."

"Angry at Urza?" asked Ahmahl.

The shadow nodded in the darkness. "About how Master Urza was always picking on him. Was always showing him up. How his brother was trying to trick him out of his stone."

"And finally he got drunk enough and angry enough to do something about it," finished Ahmahl.

The narrow shadow shrugged. Yes, that was it, thought Ahmahl. Wake your brother up in the middle of the night to finish an argument from three days before. Get all your thoughts lined up, soak them with alcohol, and set them on fire.

If he was planning for Urza to be awake when he got there. A nasty thought crystallized in Ahmahl's mind. Perhaps the younger brother was indeed going to Urza's to retrieve something.

The thought sent a small chill up the old digger's spine.

"Quickly, " he said to Hajar. "I have an errand for you after all. Go up to Tocasia's tarp. She should be sleeping there in a chair. Wake her. Tell her what you told me, and tell her to meet me at the brother's . . . at Master Urza's quarters."

Hajar hesitated. "I don't think—" he started.

Ahmahl hissed. "You've had too much to drink to be trusted with thinking, lad! I tell you to fetch Mistress Tocasia, and fetch her you will! Or the next trench you dig will be for the students' privy! Now off with you!"

The sharpness of the words cut like a knife through Hajar's drunken confusion. Very much awake and alert, the lad moved quickly toward the rocky outcropping where Tocasia kept her tent.

Ahmahl shook his head and quickly made for the cabin where Urza and Mishra had grown up. It was a heavy, squat thing made of rough-hewn timbers, with a gray slate roof. An equally stout door and candle-waxed paper windows sealed it against the desert dust. Comfortable for one, thought Ahmahl. Suitable for two young boys, and tight for two young men. Impossibly so for two young man who were angry at each other.

A lamp now glowed through the windows, so if burglary was Mishra's intent it had been foiled. There were voices as well, sharp and argumentative. As Ahmahl approached the cabin, the voices were loud to his hearing, but indistinct. Mishra's voice was a drunken bellow, while that of Urza's had a sharp, nasty twang.

Ahmahl stood across the path from the cabin's doorway. Unless something or someone came flying out the door, he decided, the best course of action would be to wait, at least to wait for Mistress Tocasia.

The sound spread; other lamps were coming on, from the barracks and quarters of the older students. If Young Master Mishra was hoping for a private argument, Ahmahl mused, he had been denied that as well. Now Urza was shouting. All Ahmahl could make out were cries of "Thief!" and "Liar!"

Tocasia arrived, accompanied by Hajar. The young Fallaji took stock of the situation and immediately disappeared in a puff of night air, heading back to the diggers' tents. He would no doubt spread the word that the two brothers were finally having it out.

Tocasia seemed groggy, as if suddenly awakened. She ran her fingers through her short graying hair. "Why haven't you stopped them?" she asked Ahmahl.

"I haven't heard any furniture breaking," returned the older man. "Even then, we should wait a bit longer. This fight has been brewing for months between these two. They need to get it out of their systems."

There was the sound of glass breaking within the quarters. Tocasia took a step toward the cabin's front door, but Ahmahl held out an arm.

"Every time the boys fight, someone breaks up the argument," he said. "Let them go on. They may get some cuts and bruises, but they need to sort things out their way."

The shouting was almost incoherent now, more like barking wild dogs than the sound of human voices. There was another crash, this time of something heavy. Most of the students had gathered out in front of the cabin, and some of the diggers had arrived with Hajar.

Then there was a new glow visible through the windows. The golden radiance of the lamp was joined, then overwhelmed, by beacons of red and green.

Ahmahl lowered his arm. He had never seen such colors before from a lamp. He wondered if the brawl had started a fire. Suddenly the idea of letting the two young men pummel each other into understanding did not seem as wise as it had a moment before.

"The stones," said Tocasia, her voice dry with fear. "They are using the stones against each other."

"The Thran stones?" asked Ahmahl, but he was speaking to empty air. The ancient scholar was already running for the door. A moment later Ahmahl followed her, waving the others to stay back.

Tocasia was through the door first, Ahmahl hot on her heels. The Fallaji smelled smoke and noticed small scorch-marks burned along the interior of the room, though there were no outright fires.

The brothers were at opposite ends of the room. Each clutched his stone. Urza's flickered with red bolts of flame, while Mishra's radiated lances of greenish light. The bolts met in the center, almost as if physical arms grappled with one another, each color trying to overwhelm the other.

The display of power was taking its toll on the brothers. Mishra was sweating like a winded horse; blood streamed from his nostrils. Urza's face was a rictus of concentration and pain, and he too was bleeding from the nose. Mishra was slightly crouched, while his brother stood haughty and erect. Each clung to his power stone with both hands.

The room itself had been affected by the bolts of might and weakness—it was hot in the cabin. The air shimmered with a song of power, a rising, throbbing noise that grew louder each moment. Neither young man would yield, and the space between them glowed brighter by the moment.

Tocasia raised her hands and shouted something Ahmahl did not understand. Neither brother paid the slightest attention, so intent were they on their private duel. Tocasia cried out again and stepped forward into the bands of red and green, her hands raised as if she were trying to physically silence the boys and their gems.

Ahmahl joined her cry himself and leapt forward, but he was too late. Tocasia broke one of the ruby-green, jade-red beams. As one, both brothers stared up at her. Their concentration slipped, their lancing beams suddenly sprayed in all directions. . . .

And the room exploded.

Ahmahl felt himself physically lifted by the blast and thrown backward, out where the door should have been. The blast blew away all four of the walls and most of the roof and showered the observers outside with splinters and flaming chunks of wood.

Ahmahl realized he was looking at the stars again. They spun gently above his upturned face. Slowly he pulled himself to his feet, feeling something soft give in his left knee. The old digger grimaced and pulled himself up.

There were moans around him from the wounded onlookers and shouts from those attending them. He had not heard the noise a moment before and wondered if he had gone deaf for a moment from the blast. There were more torches now, he saw, and someone had lit a bonfire. Ahmahl staggered to his feet and saw the remains of the old cabin.

It was almost entirely destroyed, only one corner still standing. The entire perimeter was smoking, framing the forms within. There were two, kneeling over a third.

Ahmahl limped into the wreckage of the cabin. Tocasia's form lay on Urza's lap, while Mishra knelt at her side. She lay like a broken doll, her neck canted at an odd angle to her body. Mishra held his fingers to her neck, then looked up at Ahmahl. The younger brother shook his head.

Urza looked up as well, ignoring Ahmahl and glaring at his younger brother. It was a hate-filled stare that blazed through the tears streaming down his cheeks. Ahmahl could not remember Urza ever crying in all the time the young man had been in the camp. But beneath the tears, the digger saw accusing fury in Urza's eyes.

Mishra fell back from his brother as if he had been struck. He rose and staggered a few paces away from Tocasia's body. Urza did not move; nor did he say anything. Mishra took a step away, then a second, and then the younger brother was running, away from the shattered house and into the night.

No one stopped him in his flight.

* * * * *

Ahmahl laid the last of the cairnstones in place. The students had paid their respects, as well as the diggers, and Hajar had volunteered to make a marker stone to commemorate her resting place. In an area littered with holes and ditches, they buried her in the rocky soil of the outcropping where her tarp had been pitched.

Urza remained beside her through the entire day as the body was dressed, the prayers spoken (old Argivian invocations and Fallaji chants), and the last of the stones were laid over her. Of Mishra there had been no sign, and everyone assumed he would not be seen again.

Urza's face was gaunt from grief, and Ahmahl for a moment thought the young man could be taken for older than Tocasia had been. The digger started to say something to him, but Urza held up a hand, silencing him. Ahmahl nodded and retreated, limping on his injured knee, leaning on one of Tocasia's old staves for support. It was the afternoon of the first day after Tocasia's death.

At dawn of the second day Ahmahl returned to find Urza in the same position, as if he had been turned to stone to serve as a statue commemorating Tocasia's passing.

"Master Urza, we must talk," said Ahmahl softly.

Urza nodded. "I know. There is much to do. There is still a school to run, diggings to continue. Things to take out of the ground." He said the last in a flat, toneless voice as if it were the last thing he wanted to do.

"We have things we must discuss," said Ahmahl. "Most of the other students and diggers are all right, though a handful were injured in the blast. Nothing serious."

Urza nodded, and Ahmahl wondered if Urza had even thought of the others in the camp. Or of his own minor injuries. The scrapes and burns along his arms and neck already had nasty, dark scabs on them.

Ahmahl shook his head and forced out the words. "It would be best to send the students back to Penregon as soon as possible."

Urza looked up at Ahmahl, surprised. Awareness flickered behind the eyes, dead a few moments before.

"We need to continue Tocasia's work," the young man said, stammering in his intensity. "We need to keep going."

Ahmahl sighed. "The Fallaji follow people more than ideas. The Fallaji respected Tocasia, and so they followed her. They might have followed your brother, who lived among them. But you they do not know. You rarely spent time with them. They will not stay."

"We can get other diggers," protested Urza, "and there are the students. We can use them."

"Without Fallaji present here, you would be more of a target for desert raiders," Ahmahl said. "There are increasing numbers of Fallaji who do not like Argivians in what they think of as their land. You would have to bring in more men from Argive itself. Soldiers. Diggers. It is not a place for students anymore."

Urza's mouth was a thin line. "I see." Ahmahl could almost see the young man's thoughts, as one conclusion led to another. "Tell me," he said finally, "am I safe here now?"

Ahmahl looked at the cairn. He had once assured Tocasia that there would be no trouble and had been wrong. He would not make a similar mistake again. "I do not think you are. The students will be safe, but there are those among my people who blame you for Tocasia's death. For Mishra's disappearance."

Urza looked down. "I don't know where he is," he said softly, then added, "I wish he'd come back."

Ahmahl nodded. "I wish he would as well." He put his hand on the young man's shoulder. Urza shuddered for a moment, unused to the touch, and shied away. The digger dropped his arm and left the young man at the cairn.

A message about the disaster was sent to Penregon by ornithopter, and the craft returned with Loran and—to Ahmahl's surprise—Richlau. The young noblewoman was to take stock of Tocasia's works and writing, while the older nobleman was to oversee the striking of

77

the camp. A caravan was already being sent out from Penregon by worried parents, fearful that savage desert riders were about to swoop down and slay their now-unprotected children.

Urza was gone by the time the evacuation caravan arrived. He had spent two days with Loran summarizing Tocasia's notes, then left with another, smaller caravan heading south. The young man told Loran he had no desire to return to Penregon. To Ahmahl he made clear he had no desire to remain and watch his beloved camp abandoned.

Of Mishra there was no sign, though Richlau ordered ornithopter patrols to try to find him from the air. If he ever returned to the camp none saw him, or admitted to seeing him.

Ahmahl was the last to see Urza off. None of the other Fallaji wanted to be near him, and as there was no real work to do now, the diggers themselves were drifting off in twos and threes. The camp felt like a town of ghosts: still occupied but missing its own secret heart. That heart had died with Tocasia.

Ahmahl watched from beside Tocasia's cairn as the caravan, made up of "friendly" Fallaji, wound its way out of the camp. Urza was on foot, using one of his mentor's staves as a hiking staff. That and a few drained and cracked power stones were the only things he took from the camp. Those things and his knowledge, thought the Fallaji digger.

Urza turned, looking up at where Ahmahl stood. No, corrected the old man. He was looking at where Tocasia lay. Ahmahl was too far away to see the young man's face clearly, but he saw Urza's shoulders, dejected and defeated.

Ahmahl thought he understood. The young man had lost his mentor, his home, and his brother, all because of the actions of a single night.

What Ahmahl did not understand—and what would take years for him to understand—was which of the three losses was the hardest for the young scholar to bear.

PART 2

Objects In Motion

(21-28 AR)

Chapter 6

Kroog

Kayla bin-Kroog, daughter of the warlord of the city of Kroog, princess of the nation of Yotia, and the most beautiful woman east of the mighty Mardun River, was shopping when she met the strange Argivian.

She had sampled the new shipment of plums from the Yotian coastal provinces and been shown the sheerest and most colorful of fabrics from Zegon. She had been offered the freshest of spices from far-off Almaaz and the largest of the great-clawed river prawns of the Upper Mardun. A group of Sardian dwarves offered to sell her golden earrings, which they swore once belonged to their greatest empress. A nomad woman dressed in scarves offered to predict the princess's fortune from the lines on her palms. And all of this was done with great ceremony and respect, which Kayla found extremely pleasing. There were, after all, advantages to being a princess.

She examined handfuls of the lustrous ice-stones of Sarinth, gems crystal clear, and hard as steel. She ran her fingers over the thick weaves of Fallaji rugs imported from Tomakul. A minstrel serenaded her with verses that he swore he made up on the spot to honor her. A group of street jesters built a human pyramid on her behalf. Storekeepers left their stores with samples of food, linen, or crafts they wanted to show to the most important woman in the city of Kroog.

But Kayla bin-Kroog had a purpose to her journey through the merchants' quarter. This was no whimsical spree (though if it was, none would dare to question it—except perhaps her father, who was a bit of a grump about such things). She held that purpose in a small clasp purse clutched close to her breast. She had not told her father

81

the reason for her journey; nor had she informed the guards assigned to protect her person nor even the redoubtable matron who served as her official chaperone on such larks. But she had a purpose, and that goal brought a spring to her step.

At each stop during her itinerary she asked about the other shops nearby. There were taverns, clothing shops, hat makers, gem crafters, bead stringers, and all manner of shops, large and small. But only when someone mentioned a clockmaker did her dark brown eyes light up. That would be her next stop, she informed the matron, who in turn told the guards, who in turn asked for directions and cleared a path through the rabble for her royal highness's visit.

The clockmaker's shop was a small one, even by the crowded standards of the crowded merchant district of Kroog. It was a narrow, two-story building tucked between a blacksmith's forge and a jeweler. The first floor was made smaller still by a low counter that ran most of the way across the width of the room, separating the clockmaker's workshop from the display and customers.

The guards remained outside, but only an act of the gods would keep the matron from her place, glued securely to the princess's side. Kayla's nose wrinkled as she entered the shop—it smelled of wood and oil and other things she could not put a name to and would rather not try.

There was noise. One clock ticking was an amusing distraction. Ten was an irritation, and here there were no fewer than twenty mounted along the right and left walls. Great pendulums swung back and forth in smooth rhythms, while other timepieces chimed softly to indicate the passage of each fleeting instant. It was both charming and overwhelming.

The clockmaker was typical of his breed: well fed, as her father would say, turning the reference from one concerning another's health to an endorsement of his own farming policies. Actually this fellow was a bit more than well fed, verging on stout. He could give the matron a run for her money in the heft department, and Kayla wondered for a moment if all three of them could stand to be in the same building.

In addition to being stout, the clockmaker was balding, with gray hair showing at the temples. He wore a set of Argivian spectacles common to those crafts requiring detailed work. He was dressed in an oil-spattered shirt covered only partially by a heavy leather vest. The vest either belonged to a younger relation, or had been purchased when the clockmaker was thinner.

"Your Most Esteemed Highness," burbled the clockmaker. Grovelling was a typical greeting for the princess in Kroog. Entire workshops and stores came to a screeching halt at her entrance, as the staffs bowed, scraped, and fawned.

The clockmaker twittered with the best of them. "I cannot believe how fortunate we are to have your illustrious presence gracing my humble shop," he murmured in rapid cadence. "I am honored, truly honored."

"You make clocks," she said sweetly, and the clockmaker's eyes lit up as if she had just announced the arrival of the gods.

"Yes, yes," he said emphatically. "This is the House of Rusko, home of the Clocks of Rusko, and we bid you welcome. Is our most Radiant Majesty interested in a time-keeping mechanism?"

"No," said Kayla shortly. Indeed, she could imagine few things more irritating than clocks. They were necessary, she realized, for those poor, sad people who had to be at a certain place at a certain time, but that did not apply to her. Events began when she arrived, and everyone else was ready for her.

She set down the clasp bag on the counter and opened it. "I have an item here in need of repair. It belonged to my mother, but it has not worked in years."

She produced a small silver box from her bag. It was so brightly polished that it seemed to suck sunlight from outside the store in order to add to its luster. Kayla caught sight of her own reflection in the lid—clear eyes of deepest brown; lustrous, raven-dark hair; soft lips that just verged on pouting. She liked to think that everyone would make a fuss over her even if she were not the daughter of the most powerful man in Yotia.

She handed it to the clockmaker, who turned it over in his hands as if it was a live mouse. Carefully he placed a thumb against the latch, and the top sprang open soundlessly. "Ah!" he said, then repeated for emphasis, "Ah!"

Kayla was suddenly sure that the clockmaker had never seen such a device in all his days. "It is supposed to play music when it is opened," she said.

"Yes!" said the clockmaker quickly. "Yes, of course it does!" He closed the box and turned it over in his hands a few times. Then he touched his fingers to his lips, his brow pursed, and set it down on the counter. He looked up at Kayla and smiled, a kind of greasy leer. "Let me call my assistant for this one. Young eyes and deft hands and all that." Without waiting for her response, he turned and shouted toward the back of the shop, "Assistant! Counter!"

Kayla looked in the direction of the shout and saw the clockmaker was addressing a slender, blond man who had been working at a bench toward the back. She had not noticed him because he had not risen and come forward when she entered. That fact struck her as odd. Everyone rose and came forward when she entered.

The young man was tall but not too tall, lean but not too lean, and handsome but not in an obvious way. His hair was the color of white gold, pulled into a simple ponytail. He ambled toward the front counter, raised an eyebrow, and said, "How can I help, Good-lady?"

Upon hearing his accent Kayla was doubly reassured. The clipped tone of his words indicated he was an Argivian, and as such unlearned in how to treat true royalty. The king was weak in Argive, and she had heard the nobles did as they pleased. Second, and more important, she thought, he was an Argivian, and young Argivians knew how to handle artifacts and old mechanisms.

The clockmaker presented the silver box. "Her *majesty* has an item in need of repairs," he said, stressing the introduction enough so there would be no question as to station with the stranger. "It's a *music* box."

The Argivian picked up the box and turned it over in his hands a few times. To Kayla's eyes he was much more sure of himself than the clockmaker had been. "And the problem is?" he asked.

"It doesn't *work*," hissed the clockmaker. "It's supposed to play *music*."

"Oh," said the stranger calmly. "Well, let's see what the problem is." He flipped the box over and pressed both thumbs against the base. The box gave a sharp, distinct snap.

Kayla bin-Kroog jumped at the sound, and the clockmaker looked as if he was going to faint dead away. Had the apprentice just destroyed a priceless heirloom? Kayla wondered. Then she saw that in reality all the young man had done was slip a panel from the box's base. Within the case was a maze of gears and metal. It did not seem to belong inside a container so delicate and precious.

"Here's the problem," said the Argivian. His quick fingers were delicately probing and poking the apparatus. "The mainspring is knocked out of its socket. Hold on." He left the box on the counter and retreated to his own bench, returning with a thin tool with a crooked tip. "This should do it it," he murmured. There was a soft click, and the stranger smiled. "There you go." He slipped the bottom panel into place with another loud snap and handed it back to the princess. Their fingers brushed as he did so.

Kayla bin-Kroog took the box and opened it. Nothing happened.

The matron scowled deeply. Kayla regarded the stranger coldly and lifted an immaculate eyebrow. The clockmaker suddenly looked apoplectic. "If you've *broken* the princess's music box —"

"Well, you have to wind it," said the Argivian, and Kayla was sure there was a hint of smugness in his voice. "You have the key, don't you?"

"Key?" said Kayla.

"Let me see," said the Argivian, holding his hand out. The princess handed the box back, their fingers touching again. The young stranger took the music box back behind the counter and rummaged through several drawers. Finally he lifted his head and returned to the front of the shop.

"Key," he said. "Found one that fit the winding peg." He held up a thick, inelegant key made of some dull, common metal, rusted along one side. He inserted the key, gave it a few quick turns, pulled it out, and then handed the box back to the princess. "Try it now."

Kayla opened the box, and a soft, tinny music filled the shop. For a moment she forgot the incessant ticking that surrounded them. It sounded like small pixies playing crystalline bells. There seemed to be one tune, and a second, softer one playing underneath the first.

She held the box to her ear and said, "I hear two songs."

The Argivian nodded. "It's a contra tempo. Two distinct melodies in different times weave in and out. I remember having a music box like that as a child, though, of course, one not so elegant and well crafted."

Kayla smiled, taking the compliment as a reflection on her. She closed the box, and the music stopped.

"Thank you," she said.

The Argivian held out the thick key. "Take this with you to wind it."

The clockmaker lashed out an arm with a speed that belied his girth, then held the key aloft, presenting it formally to the princess. "The *music box* of *Kroog* with the *key* of *Rusko!*" he said, laying the key in Kayla's dainty hand.

The princess looked at the Argivian. "You are Rusko?"

The Argivian smirked, and it was definite smirk. "He is Rusko. I am Urza. And you'll be able to have a better-looking key made at any jeweler's."

"Thank you, Goodsir Urza," she said, with a gracious smile aimed directly at the young man. That smile had melted courtiers and dashing young captains.

The Argivian named Urza smiled back, apparently unmoved, and said, "Be sure not to overwind it. That's probably what knocked the spring out in the first place. Just turn the key until you get some resistance." He spoke to the matron, whom he apparently assumed would take care of such tasks as music box winding.

Kayla smiled again but did not offer her hand. She glided out of the shop, her matron in tow. The fat woman was scowling, as if she had not understood what had just happened.

Out on the street, the matron said to Kayla, "The jeweler, then, milady?"

Kayla put the silver box back into her clutch purse, but held on to the thick, slightly rusted key. "Eventually," she said thoughtfully, "but not today. I've had enough shopping for one excursion."

With that the entire procession—guards, matron, princess, hangers-on, and well-wishers—steered their way back to the imperial quarter and daddy's palace.

* * * * *

Inside the clockmaker's shop, Rusko remained glued to the window until the last of the princess's procession had disappeared and the street returned to a semblance of normalcy.

"The princess!" he said half to himself, rubbing his hands together. His voice had returned to normal, "The princess of Kroog was here! In my shop!"

"With an overwound music box." Urza shook his head. "Don't they have a flunky in charge of such things?"

"Mind your tongue, lad," said Rusko sharply. "When news gets out that she was in my shop, admiring my clocks, we'll have more business than we know what to do with."

"I didn't notice her admiring any clocks," said Urza.

"That's because you weren't paying attention!" said Rusko with a chuckle. "Which is a tragedy for two reasons. One, she is royalty, and you should always pay attention to royalty; they can hurt you if you don't. And two, even if she wasn't royalty, she's incredibly beautiful."

"I suppose. I hadn't noticed," said Urza, retiring to his workbench.

"Not noticed?" spat Rusko. A wide smile crossed his face. "You must have ice water coursing through your veins, lad. That or such beauties are ten for a copper in Penregon."

Urza did not reply, and Rusko shook his head. The young man was a hard worker, but seemed to Rusko that he had no interests beyond his own bench.

Three months earlier, the youth had appeared seeking employment. He had arrived on some Fallaji caravan out of the desert, but his accent marked him as an Argivian, and probably well born as well. Rusko guessed he was some errant scion of a noble family. Probably got in trouble with his elders for using the wrong soup spoon or something, the clockmaker thought.

Rusko had heard the youth had approached the temple schools first, seeking employment as a scholar. Of course, his lack of religious training counted against him. He then sought employment among the guilds. His Argivian heritage told against him there, too, for most of the guilds took native Yotians first. Rusko was a minor member of the clockmakers and jewelers guild (but poised to expand, he always reminded others) and was in need of an extra hand. And the Argivian would work for little more than room and board.

Of course, Rusko appreciated the dedicated nature of his new assistant. But he worried that as an Argivian Urza was missing the finer things in life. A dour and pragmatic people the Argivians were, in Rusko's opinion, and his new assistant confirmed that view.

"I think she took an interest in you," he said after a moment. "I noticed the way she looked at you when I presented her the key."

"The Key of Rusko," said Urza, looking up from his work. "Why did you make such a fuss when you gave her that key?"

"Ah," said the clockmaker with a fatherly smile. "Let me expand your education, young man. Rule number one: always sign your work. I don't just sell clocks, I sell the Clocks of Rusko!" He waved at the assorted timepieces lining the walls. "Always attach your name to your work. That way others know what you did, and your fame spreads as a result. A hundred years from now, people will remember Rusko and his clocks."

"Only if they are good clocks," returned Urza.

"Aye, and ours are the finest!" Rusko beamed. "How do they know? Because we *tell* them so! Always show what you can do. And always sign your work!"

Urza had returned to the partially built clock on his bench, and now fiddled with the lever arm of a particularly recalcitrant timepiece. "Are you listening to me?" Rusko asked.

"We tell them," said Urza calmly. "Show what you can do. Sign your work. I am listening to you." He did not look up.

Three months. Three months the Argivian had been working for him, sleeping in the shop at nights, and Rusko still knew almost nothing about him. He had employed an enigma; a hard-working enigma, but an enigma nonetheless.

Someone needed to show the young man there was more to life than his work. Rusko sighed. Failing anyone else suddenly appearing, that person would have to be he.

The older clockmaker observed, "You Argivians are such dull children. So proper and practical. Why does it hurt to admit that you've just seen a lovely vision?"

Urza set down the lever arm. "Fine. She was very pretty. Can I get back to work?"

"I think it's a lack of gods," said Rusko, holding up both fingers to frame his point. "The people of Argive don't worship that much, do they?"

"Once," returned Urza. "Not much these days."

"That's the problem," said Rusko, placing a palm flat against the worktable. "No gods, no life. You've reduced your gods to sayings and psalms, parables and dry scriptures. Yotia's gods are alive and well! We have an overflowing pantheon and bring more in from the hinterlands! Bok, Mabok, Horiel the swift, Gaea the earthpower, Thindar, Rindar, Melan—"

"A god for every occasion," said Urza dryly.

"Exactly!" cried Rusko. "Whatever you do, some deity approves of it, or disapproves of it, or has some dire warning about it. It's much more exciting that way."

"Seems like a waste of energy," said Urza. "Unless, of course, you're in charge of the temples that benefit from all this veneration."

Rusko waved at hand at his assistant in frustration. "You miss the point. A Yotian would at least admit that he saw a very pretty and powerful young lady. He'd enjoy that revelation. You are just denying it, and in the process you stunt your soul."

Urza set down his tools and took a deep breath, then smiled deeply and shook his head. "I admit it, Goodsir Rusko! She was lovely. Radiant. And now that I have admitted it, what can you or I do about it? The warlord probably has her already promised to some powerful noble or faction leader to seal an alliance."

Rusko looked hard at the young man, trying to determine if the Argivian was merely making fun of him. Then the clockmaker smiled. "There you would be wrong, my lad. Oh yes. The warlord had a wedding all arranged, but the young man in question drowned. His ship reefed in a storm en route to Korlis. And they call it the Shielded Sea, by Bok and Mabok! No love lost, of course." He snorted. "You saw how deeply she was in mourning. She is free for a moment, free to pursue her own interests."

"But only for a moment," said Urza, "for your warlord probably has some other plan for his daughter. And then neither you nor I will ever see her again."

Rusko sighed. The lad had all the romantic spirit of a box of nails.

Urza turned once again to his workbench. "Now, if you would like to get back to business, I've found why this old caisson clock you have is losing time."

* * * * *

The warlord did have a plan for his daughter, though not one that Rusko would have thought of. The warlord had spent his early days in battle, married late, and fathered still later. Kayla was the apple of his eye and the prize of his kingdom. She was not a gift he gave away lightly.

Around him the warlord saw a nation at peace. His last major campaign, in which he had seized and held the Sword Marches and incorporated them into Yotia, was decades in the past. An entire generation, including his daughter, had been brought up in a land without war.

The warlord hated it.

He was surrounded by soft men and women: courtiers who used words instead of daggers; old generals content to spend their declining years playing with their grandchildren; dashing young captains who had earned their commendations by keeping clean uniforms, not by fighting an enemy.

Soft, all of them, he thought. Kayla's betrothed had been the best of a bad lot, and the warlord had agreed to that one only after his own counselors made noises about a successor to the throne. And then the damned fool ran aground off Korlis and died.

He did not want to see his line diminished, as had been the blood of the weak kings of Argive. His line needed strength. Kayla, his angel, was a strong young woman, and deserved an equally firm mate.

He made the announcement the month after the official mourning period for Kayla's intended had passed. His daughter was to marry the strongest man in the kingdom. And to find this man, the warlord had established a test.

In the central court before the palace, he erected a great statue. It was made entirely of a single piece of jade, twenty feet in height, crafted with the warlord's face. It took a team of fifteen men to winch it into place. His daughter's hand, he decreed, would go to the man who could move the statue from one end of the court to the other.

When the first day of the contest arrived, Urza said that it was the stupidest thing he had ever heard of, which statement set Rusko off again on a comparative study of Argive and Yotia.

"That is because you have no romance," argued Rusko, locking the shop behind them. Closing the shop seemed to be the only way to get the young man to leave its confines, and Rusko saw the contest as an excellent chance to expose Urza to the finer things that Kroog offered.

"The idea of mighty quests and impossible tasks is in all our folklore, " he continued. "Look at the saga of Bish and Kana, or how Alorian vied for Titania's love."

Urza stopped in the center of the street. "But the legends say Bish and Kana died on their wedding day, and Alorian was torn to pieces by Titania's hounds after she rejected him."

Rusko made a harrumphing noise. "I didn't say it was an *exact* comparison." He headed off down the street to the court. Urza followed, shaking his head.

The competition was set for the first of every month, when the warlord and Kayla would attend. Most of the city closed down for those five hours while sturdy men tried to win the princess's hand. Servants cleared the court between the statue and the opposite end and set out lines of benches on each side as a makeshift stadium.

Urza and Rusko looked down and saw that a group of thick, stalwart men had already gathered in a rough line. The smallest was twice Urza's size, and several looked as if they could take on an elephant bare-handed. From the scars on a few exposed torsos, it appeared some apparently had. At the far end of the court was a low riser. Seated on a padded bench were the warlord and his daughter.

As Urza and Rusko pressed into the court, a gong sounded. The first suitor strode forward to meet his jade foe. He wrapped his massive arms around the statue's knees and gave a mighty heft. The towering figure did not so much as sway under his assault. The strong man grunted, regained his grip, then tried to lift again. The statue was immobile. The gong sounded again, declaring the attempt over.

Another burly individual waddled forward, this one so muscular that he was wider than he was tall. He tried to pry his fingers beneath the edge of the statue but was rewarded only with crushed digits. Another gong, and a third individual locked his arms around the statue's legs, bending at his knees for better support. This contestant gave a mighty bellow as he attempted to pull the jade figure from its moorings. The bellow became a scream as the muscular man suddenly let go of the statue and dropped to the court's floor, gripping another part of his anatomy. The gong sounded and a group of temple healers rushed forward to attend to the fallen champion.

"Come, let's pay our respects," said Rusko, nodding his head toward the royal bench.

There was a moving line in front of the warlord and princess. The Yotians passed before the pair, quickly bowing and touching their fingers to their lips in the fashion of that city. Rusko joined the throng, dragging Urza behind him. The clockmaker made a full bow and finger-kiss, but Urza merely gave a respectful head bob. And then they were past the royal couple.

"She looked at you," said Rusko as soon as they were past.

"She did not," said Urza, shaking his head. "She's seen a thousand people this day alone."

"She smiled," countered Rusko.

"She is a princess," said Urza. "Smiling is automatic for such people. Were I she, I would be seriously worried that one of those muscle-bound warriors will actually succeed in lugging the statue around. I don't think his majesty is breeding for intelligence in future generations."

Rusko shook his head. "You're being too logical, again, too pragmatic. Probably she is sure that no one *will* succeed. Sooner or later her father will come up with a more reasonable task. What's wrong?"

Urza was staring intently, at the pile of treasure to one side of the dais. "What is that?" he asked.

Rusko blinked. Urza was pointing toward a large pile of gifts laid out over a luxurious swath of gold cloth. There were great swords, mirrored shields, and armor of the type that no one had worn in generations. Bins of rubies, diamonds, and sapphires glittered in the sunlight, accompanied by red-velvet boxes holding crowns and diadems.

"That's the dowry," answered Rusko, and quickly added, "I know what you are thinking with your logical mind: 'Why does the daughter of the most powerful man in Yotia need a dowry?' Well, it's a tradition. Those are all old items belonging to the previous warlords. Some date back to the dawn of the nation. Some were made before Kroog was even founded.

"What of the book?" said Urza.

Rusko had not seen the young man this excited in all the time he had been in Kroog. He squinted to see the object to which Urza was referring to. "You mean the one next to the ivory shield?"

"Yes, the large one," said the young man, "What is it?"

Rusko leaned forward. "It's a book," he confirmed. "Definitely a book."

"Yes, of course it's a book. But look. On the binding are Thran glyphs!" snapped Urza.

Rusko blinked again. The young man was positively thrilled by the discovery.

Rusko removed his lenses, rubbed them on his shirt, and put them on his face again. He shrugged. "If you say so. Can you read them from this distance?"

Urza was silent a long moment, apparently puzzling out the geometric writing. Then he said, "'Ja-lum.' Was there a Jalum in Yotia's history?"

"Hmmm," considered Rusko. "I think there was an advisor or scholar. Or a philosopher. Long ago, before the temple schools. Is it important?"

Urza looked at the table laden with treasure, then back at the princess. As he looked, she was just turning away from him, apparently intent on the latest attempt to lift the statue. Her face was smooth and impassive and very lovely in the noonday sun.

Urza chewed on his lip, then said, "Goodsir Rusko, I think I want to move a statue."

Rusko could hardly contain his disbelief. "And I want to fly to the moon, and kidnap the harim of the Pasha of Sumifa. I'll even settle for my head to hurt less after a night of drinking brandy. But I don't expect it to happen. That's rule one in life—don't expect the impossible, and you won't be disappointed."

"I do expect it to happen," said Urza, staring intently at the huge jade statue. Another contestant was trying to manhandle it to no avail. "But I will need supplies." He turned to the clockmaker, his voice hard and decisive. "Metal bolts, ironroot spurs, and other things. Will you help?"

Rusko stammered for a moment. He was all for romance, but suddenly this posed a threat to his own pocketbook.

"Well, I could give you an advance," he said reluctantly, "but you're talking about a sizable outlay."

Urza nodded, then said, "Have you heard about ornithopters? The Argivian flying machines?"

Rusko nodded. "I've heard traveler's tales." He paused, then hissed a question at the young man. "You know how they work?"

Urza nodded again and said, "I . . . helped build the first ones. I could give you the plans. If I did, would you provide supplies for my work?"

Rusko felt both his heart and his pocketbook opening to the young man. He smiled.

* * * * *

"These are wonderful!" said Rusko, thumbing through the plans. The first purchase the clockmaker had made was a supply of parchment and quills, and the young Argivian spent the night sketching out the ornithopters. First was a general description in neat lettering. Then page after page of details, showing how the levers in the pilot's housing functioned, how the wiring operated, of what materials the wings and struts needed to be made, and to what dimensions they had to be machined for perfect performance.

Rusko was astounded. All this from the quiet scholar who had been repairing his clocks. A trained ape could build ornithopters from these plans. No, even *Rusko* could build an ornithopter from these plans.

"Marvelous," he muttered, leafing through the loose parchment pages. "Amazing. A work of art." The clockmaker could scarcely contain himself, for the machine practically leapt off the page, fully realized.

Urza smiled, but Rusko could not tell if the smile was in response to his compliments or for his current work. They had curtained off the back of the shop, and Urza had begun constructing a new machine there.

Actually it looked as if he were building a statue of his own to counter the jade one of the warlord. It looked like a beast of curved metal spars, fashioned in the upright form of a man. Its limbs were metal frames, cross-bolted in a thick latticework. Its upper torso was thinner metal and ironroot, and it pivoted at the base of the spine. One inelegantly long arm drooped at either side, each looking like that of a gorilla. A roughly hewn helmet, with a faceplate that flipped up or down, served as the head. The face guard was open now, revealing a tangle of cables and gears set around a single, dull gem.

It suddenly occurred to Rusko that Urza had smiled more in the past few weeks than in all the time the clockmaker had known him. They had not been the polite, for-the-customer smiles or smug Argivian-scholar smiles or even put-up-with-old-Rusko smiles. The young man seemed more alive as he tinkered with his creation.

Rusko had only made one suggestion during the entire process. "You've got the knees on backward," he said.

"Supposed to be that way," muttered Urza, not waiting for a reply. He burrowed back into the creature's chest with a spanner.

In two months the creation had blossomed from a mixed collection of parts that Rusko had gathered, cadged, or "borrowed" from other shops into a towering giant. It was vaguely humanoid, and Rusko wondered if it was based on any living creature. It was not a question he wanted answered.

Instead, late at night, as Urza was checking connections and splicing wires, he asked another question.

"Who is Mishra?"

Urza's rapidly moving fingers almost dropped the splicing tool he was holding.

"Someone important to you, I assume," continued the clockmaker.

Urza stared at Rusko, and for a moment there was a flicker of coldness on the youth's face. Just for a moment, the quiet, solemn man of the past months was back, and Rusko was afraid he had lost the smiling Urza forever. Then Urza sighed and the moment passed. He turned back to his machine. "How do you know of Mishra?"

Rusko fought a temptation to laugh. "You rarely sleep, Urza, but when you do, you talk. You mention Mishra a lot. And another. Tacashia."

"Tocasia," corrected Urza. "Tocasia . . . was my teacher. She's dead now."

"Hmmm," said Rusko. "And Mishra?"

"My brother," said Urza quietly. He peered more intently into the creature's interior.

"Alive?"

"I suppose." Urza shrugged. He gazed up with the pretense of working on the wiring and leaned back. "I don't know. We parted on less than friendly terms."

"Ah," said Rusko. There was a lot going on beneath the surface there, and he felt resistance to his questions. "And you feel badly about it," he persisted.

"I wish there was something that could have been done to change things," said Urza. Rusko thought the youth's statement was probably true, as far as it went, but there seemed to be something more, something yet unsaid.

A silence grew between the two men. Finally Rusko broke it. "In Yotia, we believe a man has many souls. Did you know that?"

Urza shook his head, but a small smile appeared at the corners of his mouth. A put-up-with-old-Rusko smile, the clockmaker thought.

"You don't wear the same clothes as you did when you were a boy, and you won't wear the same clothes when you're older," Rusko continued. "The same applies to souls. You have one soul as a child, another as a youth, and several as an adult."

Urza shrugged. "I wear different clothes. I don't know about souls, though."

Rusko stroked his chin. "Most Yotian faiths believe that when you die each of your souls is judged individually. Let us say your first three souls were basically good. Then you became a robber and a thief and grew a fourth, evil soul. Then you repented and lived a virtuous life, growing a fifth, more kindly soul. When you die, your souls are judged independently. The first three souls, and the fifth, will be rewarded for their virtue. The fourth soul will be sent to hell, destroyed, or sent back, depending on what gods you venerate."

"You are going somewhere with this?" asked Urza. His eyes strayed toward his machine.

Rusko smiled. "Only that you may be feeling guilty about what happened with your brother. Or your late mentor. Don't. You have a new soul since you've arrived here: a Yotian soul. Let that be your guide."

Urza stood for a moment, untangling Rusko's advice. Then he shook his head. "Until I talk again with my brother, I will carry my regrets with me. But thank you for your advice. It's very . . ." He paused, then broke into a wide smile. "Much like Kroog itself."

Rusko smiled back, taking the young man's words as a compliment. "So," he said, looking up at the titanic figure, "does it work?"

"Not yet." Urza pulled a chain from around his neck. Rusko saw that the chain was attached to a large gem, a dark ruby flecked with streaks of multicolored fire. Urza climbed the stepladder until he was level with the great creature's head, and pushed the gem inside.

Standing on tiptoe, Rusko could see the young man touching the ruby stone to the dead, inert gem in the creature's head.

The gem in the creature's head began to glow, slowly, erratically at first, then with a stronger beacon, until it was as strong as the stone Urza held. It radiated with a sapphire light shot through with sparks of white.

It was, thought the clockmaker, like watching someone set a fire by placing a burning stick against another.

As the new gem glowed, the creature began to move. It raised one arm, then lowered it, then raised it again. The gears and pulleys at the machine's arm and shoulder whined softly as they moved. Urza lowered the creature's visor. The light of the gem shone through its eye-holes.

"There," said Urza. "Now the machine has a new soul as well."

* * * * *

It was the third month of the competition, and for Kayla it was proceeding much the same way as the first two. A cavalcade of horns and gongs sounded. A throng of well-wishers passed before her and her father (though there were fewer with each passing month, she noticed). A gathering of overly muscled warriors waited their turn to attempt the impossible. Again, there were fewer than previously.

On the first day of competition it had all been a great celebration. A month later, at the second trial, it was merely interesting. Now, two months after the first day of competition for her hand, Kayla felt the whole affair was becoming tedious.

She reviewed the candidates and suppressed a shudder. This lot might look well behind a plow (or pulling one, she thought wickedly), but as far as leadership material went, they were sorely lacking. Some part of Kayla's mind gave a mental shrug. What did it matter? After the wedding, she would make all the important decisions.

At first, as each took his turn, she imagined what life would be like with each of the hulking brutes. That proved to be less than appealing, so she soon settled on guessing the nature of their injuries after they had failed to move the statue. She had counted so far that day ten pulled muscles (three in the groin), two burst intestines, seven cases of exhaustion, and a head injury. The last was from a young man from the Sword Marches of the far north, who grew so frustrated that he head-butted the statue. The temple healers hauled him off the field by his feet.

The current contestant was a grunter, gripping the statue and trying to pull it down on top of himself. Kayla did not care for grunters. She liked the bellowers better. They made more noise, and tended to give up more quickly.

The lists had thinned out quickly, and there were now bare spots among the benches for the loyal subjects. She wondered how much longer her father was going to continue this exercise in futility. Probably, she decided, until one of the lesser noble families made a better offer for her hand. Daddy was always doing things in secret.

Kayla was resigned to her fate. She had always been a dutiful daughter, and if her father arranged for her to marry a Fallaji, she would live in some desert tent beyond civilization. She was no stranger to court politics. For years, she knew, she had been groomed to eventually marry in a fashion that would make Kroog stronger. The fact that the original target of that marriage had the misfortune to die before getting the chance to wed her did not change the process in the least.

She looked at her father as he watched the proceedings. He had on his solemn face now: cool, thoughtful, and regal. Would the common people think less of him if they knew that after the first day he had cursed like a sailor at the failure of the contestants, storming around the royal suites for a good hour? Probably not, Kayla decided. Her father was a great war hero, a valiant warlord, and she suspected this farce being played out before her represented one last attempt to prove to himself that there were still warriors in Yotia.

And, she was sure, her father felt he could have lifted the jade statue by himself when he was young.

Another bellowing titan pulled a groin muscle, and Kayla saw the lists were empty. No, there were three figures left. One slender, one fat, and one shrouded in a great cape and hood, who towered over the other two.

The seneschal walked over to the trio, and there was a quick consultation among the two smaller figures and the ruler's advisor. The seneschal moved to the warlord's side and spoke in a low voice.

"We have one more candidate," said the seneschal, a quaking, nervous man who both loved and feared his warlord, "but it's a bit unusual."

The warlord grunted. "The big one?"

"No, milord," said the seneschal. "The thin one. He says he can move your statue by the strength of his mind, if you will but permit it."

A smile crossed the warlord's face, and Kayla knew that it was not one of his more pleasant expressions. "Let him. But tell him the penalty for wasting the warlord's time."

The seneschal bowed and retreated. Kayla stared at the newcomers. The slender one was attractive, but it was only in proximity to the fat one that she remembered where she had seen him before. He was the Argivian clockmaker, the stranger with the wry smile and clipped accent.

For a fleeting moment, Kayla allowed herself to think about life with this one. The prospect was not totally unpleasant. She also wondered if he could truly move the statue with his mind, or if he would sprain his brain in the process.

Kayla's memory spun for a moment. Urza—that was the young man's name. She still had his key next to her mother's music box. And his companion, the fat one. She knew she had heard his name at the shop, but nothing came to her now.

Urza stepped directly before the statue. Behind him strode the fat man, helping along the titanic cloaked figure. There was a smell in the air, like the air before a storm. The Argivian bowed deeply.

"I thank the crown for the chance to succeed in a task that has defeated so many others," said Urza. The warlord waved his hand, urging the young man to speed up his speech. Kayla was sure that after today Daddy would abandon this method of choosing a suitor.

"I will now move the statue by the strength of my mind," declared Urza. Reaching back, he pulled the cape from the large figure behind him. There was a collective gasp from the crowd as the cloth fell away to reveal the figure beneath.

It was made of metal, and was human in form. At first Kayla thought it was a living being, but immediately she saw that she had been mistaken. It was a machine. Of course, she thought. He is a clockmaker, after all, and an Argivian. The Argivians were always poking around the old ruins, trying to find powerful devices for their own use.

"I built this, using my mind," said Urza, and the fat man made a harrumphing noise. "That and using the services of Goodsir Rusko, maker of fine clocks," the youth added. "Let what I have built with my mind move your statue."

The large humanoid machine lumbered forward, and for a moment Kayla expected it to pitch over onto the stonework. As it walked, the Argivian stayed next to it, speaking to it, guiding each of its motions.

The pair reached the statue. Urza pointed to one side of the statue, and the machine placed a hand, metal with fingers of polished wood, on that location. He pointed to the other side, and the machine placed its other hand there.

Urza patted the side of the creature, and it began to lift. After the bellowers, screamers, and grunters, the silence that surrounded the artifact was eerie. There was a slight humming, like the space between the notes of Kayla's music box. The metal humanoid bent at the knees (which seemed, from the princess's vantage point, to be constructed backward) and slowly lifted the figure from the ground.

There was a collective gasp from the crowd as daylight appeared beneath the jade statue. The construct pulled the statue straight up, holding it about a foot off the ground. Slowly the great machine spun on its hips, its spine rotating all the way around, so that its knees were pointing forward. Then slowly, the machine started to walk toward the opposite side of the court.

It was slow going. The machine could hold the statue, but the courtyard had difficulty supporting both the machine and the statue. Paving stones crushed beneath the giant's feet, and at one point, the great metal creature pitched precipitously to the right as the stones turned to dust beneath the weight of its tread. There was a whining noise as wires spooled through pulleys, and Kayla was sure she was about to see the mechanical equivalent of a groin pull.

Urza was at the machine's side at once, examining the problem and shouting orders. The great metal thing responded, tipped the other way, and at last reached its final destination. Urza gave one last command, and the machine set down the jade megalith so that it faced the royal dais.

The crowd applauded. Some fled the stands to tell their friends the king's statue had been defeated by a metal creature made by an Argivian.

Kayla found herself on her feet applauding as well, but one glance at her father stopped her. His face was a storm cloud, and veins throbbed at his temples. Wordlessly he rose and turned away from the dais, thundering back into the palace. Ever dutiful, Kayla rose as well, but allowed herself the opportunity to look once more at the talented Argivian.

He stood there in the center of the court, his machine next to him, the clockmaker on the other side. The common people were already spilling into the courtyard to congratulate him. On his face was a wide, beaming smile.

She decided it was a pleasant smile, and smiled back at him. She did not stop to see if he saw her mark of favor, but instead turned and followed her father through the palace doors. She only hoped the warlord would reach a room with thick walls before he exploded.

* * * * *

It took fifteen minutes for the warlord to stop cursing, and another fifteen before he was using coherent sentences. Kayla, the seneschal, Kayla's matron, and a brace of nervous courtiers waited for the storm to abate before even venturing an opinion.

"The temerity!" he shouted at the rafters. "The insult! How dare that . . . that . . ." His mouth opened and closed for a moment until he found the proper word. "Weed! That weed thinks he deserves my daughter's hand in exchange for some parlor trick!"

"Well," said the trembling seneschal, "you did say her hand would go to whoever could move the statue."

The warlord grunted harshly.

"And you did allow him to try," said the seneschal, gathering strength as he spoke. "He said he would move the statue with his mind."

"But he didn't!" bellowed the warlord. "That wind-up machine did all the moving!"

"Well," said the seneschal, "your daughter could marry the machine."

Kayla stifled a giggle, but the joke prompted another cascade of war-camp obscenities from the warlord. The seneschal fled under the assault, and, Kayla thought at the time, out of the discussion entirely.

"And you!" roared the warlord, turning to his daughter, "what have you to say of all this?"

"Say?" cried Kayla. She was suddenly indignant at being the target of his yelling. "I had no *say* when you wanted me to marry that hapless mariner." She charged, stalking toward her father. "I had no *say* when you decided to award me to the strongest ox in the kingdom. So now, when someone has finally beaten you at one of your little games, I suddenly have a say?"

The warlord stared at Kayla, stunned by her outburst. His shoulders sagged with defeat. "I just want what's best for you. But to have to give you to this . . . foreigner. This . . . Argivian. This . . . *weed*!"

"You are the warlord of Kroog," said Kayla coldly. "You can do whatever you want. You can banish him if you want. But if you want my opinion, here it is. He has a pleasant face, a good shape, and seems rather bright. I would not mind being his bride."

The warlord's brows furrowed, and Kayla wondered which part her father was thinking about—the fact that she would not mind marrying Urza, or the fact he could have the Argivian banished. Behind her came the squeak of the heavy-timbered door, and the seneschal poked his head back in.

"What?" snapped the warlord. Kayla thought that the seneschal might evaporate entirely. To her surprise the nervous bureaucrat stood his ground and managed a convincing mewl. "A visitor requests an audience, milord."

"The weed?" snarled the warlord. "Tell him we have not yet ruled as to the legitimacy of his little trick."

"Not the . . ." The seneschal gulped and continued, "Argivian. His, uh, sponsor."

The warlord looked at Kayla, and the princess nodded vigorously. Her father could bully most of the staff. Perhaps the little clockmaker had a better chance of making Urza's case.

At first it seemed a vain hope. The clockmaker bowed three times before reaching the warlord. Each bow being a deep, knee-buckling affair that consumed time and further shredded her father's patience. As Rusko rose from the third bow Kayla walked to his side and helped the overweight merchant to his feet, escorting him to the warlord.

"Your Grace and Your Highness," gasped the fat little man. "Conqueror of the Sword Marches, Bearer of Prosperity, Master of our Fates."

The warlord flapped his hand impatiently, while Kayla wondered if the clockmaker talked that way in real life.

"I bring *two* messages," said Rusko. "The first is from my boon assistant and companion, Goodsir Urza, the Argivian." He paused and waited for a response.

"Go on," snapped the warlord, biting off his words as if they were bits of meat.

The clockmaker cleared his voice. "Sir, Urza says that he understands if you choose to rescind your challenge, though he would be very disappointed in losing the companionship of your lovely daughter." He bowed to Kayla, and the princess returned it with a nod. She wondered if what the clockmaker said about Urza's disappointment was true.

"Is that it?" asked the warlord.

"The *first* message, yes," replied Rusko.

"And the second?" inquired the warlord.

"The *second* is from me," said the clockmaker. He lowered his voice somewhat. "And this is it." He reached into his vest, pulling out a sheaf of papers. He handed them to the seneschal, who in turn handed them to the warlord.

The ruler flipped through the pages and grunted, "And these are?"

"Plans, my grace," said Rusko. "Plans for a flying machine, an *Argivian* flying machine, designed by the talented young Goodsir Urza."

The warlord looked from the clockmaker, to the plans, to the clockmaker. "The Argivian knows how to build flying machines? Do they work?"

The clockmaker bowed deeply. "I do not know for certain. Two months ago, I could not tell you that his mechanical man would work. But it has."

The warlord looked through the papers a third time. "And the Argivian might have other secrets locked up in his mind," he said, almost to himself.

"I would presume so," said Rusko. "He is a private man, closed to *all* but those closest to him. Definitely in need of a woman's touch to bring out his best." Again he bowed to Kayla.

The warlord grew silent, and Kayla knew he was weighing the alternatives. Finally he said, "Daughter, did you mean it when you said you would not mind marrying this . . . talented . . . weed?"

Kayla gave a small nod and said, "I spoke truly when I say he is the best candidate you have found so far."

The ruler gave out a deep sigh and rubbed his eyes. Handing the plans back to the fat clockmaker, he spoke. "Very well. Then let us go back out and congratulate my future son-in-law."

* * * * *

The ceremony was ornate, even by Yotian standards. Kroog had more than thirty major temples and a host of smaller ones with important patrons, and every one wanted to have a say in the wedding. Kayla tried to count the number of officiating priests but gave up after the fifteenth or sixteenth.

It was tediously long. Sermons were read. Prayers were chanted. Spirits were banished. Gods were invoked. More sermons. More prayers. The couple kissed icons. They placed hands on scriptures. They danced around a ceremonial pyre. They were doused with blessed water and drank sanctified wine. They freed a dove and burned a scroll of regrets. They paraded beneath unsheathed blades. They received benedictions, blessings, and well-wishes. In deference to Urza's Argivian heritage, each wore a gold circlet on his or her brow, each of the circlets joined by a single silver chain.

Kayla could not say at what point during the day she was officially married to Urza, scholar of Argive, new Chief Artificer of Kroog. All she could say was that by the end of the day there was no question that she was well and truly married.

And through it all Urza was understanding, not impatient in the way most men were about such things (Daddy was visibly uncomfortable after the seventh responsive reading). Nor was the young man visibly bored, or apparently making a show of being tolerant. He seemed to be taking mental notes on everything he saw and commenting on nothing. She expected to see that smug Argivian smile during some of the more rustic and traditional parts of the ceremony, but he took those with good grace as well.

And after the interminable ceremonies was an equally long procession through the streets, as the people waved and cast multicolored streamers and waved colored torches. And then a long feast of several dozen courses, each course broken by long toasts from anyone who felt he had something good to say about the princess and her surprising (if still generally mysterious) groom.

And when at last the ceremonies and the processions and the feasts were done, long after the midnight bell had sounded, the couple was escorted to their own wing of the palace, into the bridal chamber. The dowry had been placed there, along with some of more tasteful gifts of various powerful well-wishers. The bed was made with sheets of Almaaz silk and dusted with rose petals. Incense burned from a dozen small braziers, and the room was lit with candles.

The servants left the newlyweds there, closing the doors behind them as they departed.

Kayla took a deep breath and reached out to her new husband. Urza slowly took her hand, and the princess realized that the slender young man was trembling slightly and almost flinched at the touch. She wondered if he even knew he was shouting his nervousness to her.

Instead she said, "You have strong hands."

"Working with artifacts," he said, his voice rasping a bit, "you need strong fingers."

"And a strong mind as well," she said, and drew herself closer to him. His body felt as tight as the spring in her music box.

"Kayla," Urza spoke into her hair, "there's something I need to tell you."

Kayla froze, but only for a moment. Levelly, she said, "You can tell me anything."

"I—" said Urza, then backed away from her and looked into her eyes. "I've been told I talk in my sleep."

She smiled and pressed two fingers against her husband's lips. "It's all right," she said in a throaty whisper. "I'm a very good listener." And she kissed him.

Afterward, Kayla's breathing was long and deep, She slept on her side, nestled against Urza's lanky frame. He touched her brow, softly. She squirmed in bed, rolled over, and fell in still-deeper slumber.

Quietly, Urza rose from his wedding bed. The sky was still an hour from lightening, and the city of Yotia was quiet beneath his window. Beyond his sight, a city exhausted by its own celebration lay wreathed in sleep, and only a few lights still shone between the castle and the Mardun River.

Slowly, Urza crossed the room. He extinguished each of the guttering candles in the room, save one. This he took to the accumulated dowry. He looked over the pile of treasure, then carefully knelt down and extricated a heavy book, marked with Thran glyphs on the spine. The Tome of Jalum.

Urza took the book to the writing desk on the far side of the bedroom. He set the candle in its holder and looked at his new wife, lying in the darkness, for a long time. Then he opened the ancient book and began to read.

Chapter 7

Mak Fawa

"Up, slave!" snarled the taskmaster, prodding Mishra's side with his goad. The stocky young man groaned and tried to turn over, earning another sharp prod. In Fallaji the taskmaster repeated the order. "*Rakiq! Qayim!*"

Mishra coughed through a dust-filled throat that he was awake, and he hauled himself to his elbows to prove it. The taskmaster moved on to the next slave as Mishra blinked the dust from his eyes.

His dreams had been wrapped in darkness, utter and black. He was alone, all alone, without Tocasia, Urza, or any of the others. They had abandoned him. And in that darkness of his dream there was singing. Lovely singing, that issued from his green stone. But he had lost the stone as surely as he had lost the rest of his life.

Mishra blinked back the last of the darkness and knew that his waking world was little better than that of his dreams. He was in the camp of the Suwwardi. He had been captured and claimed by them. He was property now. He was a slave. He was *rakiq*.

After Tocasia's death he had fled northward, toward the cavern at Koilos. He didn't mean to at first, he had just fled. But his feet found their way into the desert and along the long shelf of the mountains, inevitably leading toward the lost canyon. The scrubby, succulent plants that etched out their lives along the desert's borders provided him with life-giving water during the trek. Still, he was thin and weak when the Suwwardi outriders found him.

At first Mishra thought they were rescuers, friends from among the Fallaji diggers who had come looking for him, sent by Ahmahl or Hajar. But the riders who found him were tougher and crueler men

105

than the diggers at camp, hard men with wind-carved faces and no patience for outlanders found in their desert. They wore broad-brimmed, flat helmets that marked them as Suwwardi, each bronze helmet inscribed along the brim with the vows of courage in battle.

The warriors dragged him back to their camp, but only because it was nearby. Otherwise they would have simply killed him and stripped his body. They took his glittering stone as treasure as well, but they did not treat it as anything more than an attractive bauble. Mishra had the strength to let out a weak shout as they pulled the bag containing the gem from his neck. That earned him an elbow to the face, a cuff intended both to silence and to train.

The Suwwardi set Mishra to work with the other slaves. Most were Fallaji, captured from other tribes and held until proper ransom was established or proper loyalties to the Suwwardi were ensured. These captives were treated fairly well, as slaves go. There were a few other outlanders as well—hardscrabble survivors of caravans that did not pay the demanded tolls for traversing Suwwardi land. These slaves the tribe worked to death. Of the seven other outlanders who had been among the slaves when he was first brought there three months earlier, Mishra was the sole survivor. There were a few later additions, but they had died quickly.

There had been no additional outlander slaves since then. The Suwwardi had apparently stopped taking them.

So Mishra worked as a slave. He built. He dug. He dragged heavy things. He did not ask questions. Another outlander had asked questions and his teeth were removed with a chisel. Mishra slept when he was allowed. He ate what he was given, which was less than the qadir's hounds received.

And he dreamed. He dreamed of the darkness and the fractured power crystal singing to him. He tried to look for it but found he was too exhausted to move, held captive in the prison of his own flesh.

During the day, when he laid stone upon stone, or dug a new cooking pit, midden, or grave, he thought of the dreams. This day he was digging a trench, for some unknown reason. Occasionally his spade struck a bit of old metal from the age of the Thran, and he tossed it on the pile of churned earth with the other garbage.

As he dug and thought, Mishra did not hear his name being called, not the first time, or the second. Only when a hand was laid on his shoulder did the stocky man react. Mishra started and raised an arm to protect himself. No one touched an outlander with good intent in the Suwwardi camp.

"Master Mishra, it is you!" cried Hajar.

Mishra looked up at the one addressing him and saw the young, lean-faced digger from Tocasia's camp. The one who had accompanied him the night that everything fell apart. But this Hajar was wearing a Suwwardi helmet, a pair of swords mounted on a harness across his back. And he was smiling.

"Are you all right?" asked Hajar, in Fallaji.

Mishra waited a moment, then nodded. He had no use for words for the past few months, and few spoke to him beyond simple orders.

A shadow appeared on Mishra's right. It was the taskmaster, who had fewer slaves to deal with over time and kept his hold on his remaining treasures that much tighter.

"Do not speak with the *rakiq*," said the taskmaster sharply.

Hajar laughed, and Mishra realized that the former digger was taller than the one who ordered him about. "Do you know who you have digging holes for you?"

Mishra wanted to say that he enjoyed digging the holes, and Hajar should not take that one pleasure away from him. But the words were lost on the way to his mouth.

"This man is a great scholar," continued Hajar. "He knows things no one other man knows. He has discovered secrets of the Old Ones. And you have him digging ditches!" Hajar laughed again.

"Scholar!" the taskmaster spat into the dust. "That explains why he digs ditches so poorly. Now go away."

Hajar shook his head. "He should not be digging ditches at all!"

"You're right," the taskmaster exploded. "I expected him to die months ago. He is an outlander and a slave. He works for me, Maurik the Taskmaster, for the moment. You want him to work for you, go to the qadir!"

Hajar paused for a moment, then said, "I shall. Try not to kill him before I return." And Hajar was gone, head held high, heading for the center of camp.

Mishra dug energetically, but the taskmaster was displeased with his work. A sharp jab in the side with the butt-end of the goad reminded the former scholar that he should not have talkative friends. Mishra groaned under the blow and slowed only slightly as the ache spread through his body. He let the pain pass through him, and resumed his digging.

* * * * *

At the end of the day, the Suwwardi held their communal dinner. The qadir's tent was fed first, then the warriors, then the women and children, then the qadir's dogs, and finally the slaves. And the Fallaji slaves were fed before the outlanders, for there was a reason to keep the Fallaji alive.

Mishra was chewing a piece of stale, mold-spotted bread when they came for him; men in direct service to the qadir, with their broad helmets and ornate necklaces of heavy gold. Ceremonial guards, the young man realized. The qadir of the Suwwardi must be doing very well, to thus equip his warriors.

The guards spoke a few words, unheard by Mishra, to Maurik the Taskmaster, and the brawny master of slaves retired, grumbling, to his own quarters. Then the guards half-marched, half-dragged Mishra to the qadir's tent, a broad, wax-colored pavilion lit from within. The soldiers stopped outside only long enough to remove the heavy hobbles that bound Mishra's feet. Then they pushed him inside.

The tent was soft and smoky. Braziers were lit around the perimeter, and Mishra caught the scent of sandalwood and desert cedar wafting up from them, mixed with other pungent spices. The scent hurt his nose and made his eyes water, but it succeeded in dampening the stench of the Suwwardi themselves in these close quarters.

The ground was covered with thick rugs woven from the wool of mountain sheep, and stained with food and, in some places, blood. Great reclining pillows were scattered about. To either side of the room were the immediate relations of the qadir, the hangers-on, the courtiers, and the ambassadors from the other tribes. At the center of the tent was a platform, raised and covered with slightly cleaner carpets. This was the qadir's place.

The qadir was a massive man, thick-shouldered, thick-necked, and thick-headed. He was beginning to give in to the results of his own success—his belly spilled slightly over the belt holding his robes shut. As Mishra entered the tent the qadir was helping himself to a great bowl of shelled nuts. At one side of the Fallaji leader was seated a similarly built, similarly dressed younger version of the qadir. On the other side, standing, was Hajar.

Mishra dropped to both knees, in the Fallaji custom, and waited for whatever would come next.

The qadir snorted down a handful of nuts. "This slave-dog of the desert is the one you speak of, Hajar?" he asked, in Fallaji. His voice poured out the words like thick coffee.

"That he is, most eminent one," replied Hajar in the same language.

"And he is a scholar, you say?" said the qadir.

"A most respected one," said Hajar, and Mishra noticed that the young version of the qadir was not smiling. In fact, he looked bored.

The qadir leaned forward and stared at Mishra. "Doesn't look like much of anything. Even for an outlander." Laughter rippled among the courtiers, relations, and ambassadors.

"Do you judge your horses by their bridles," asked Mishra, "or by how hard they serve?"

He said it in a low voice, barely more than a whisper. It was a desert saying he had learned from Ahmahl, and the young man said it in perfect Fallaji. He did not look up as he said it. He did not say it proudly, or angrily. But he did say it.

The room grew quiet immediately. The qadir shot Hajar a venomous look that seemed to melt the young man in place. "And the *rakiq* speaks our language as well," the qadir observed.

Hajar bowed nervously. "I said he was most learned in a number of fields." When the thin Fallaji looked up, the qadir no longer looked at him. Instead he regarded the outlander through heavy-lidded eyes.

"You know the legends?" asked the qadir. "Of the Old Ones?"

"I know of the Thran," replied Mishra. "An ancient race they were, which predated all other living races in the land of Terisiare. They left no bones of themselves, but they left the bones of their machines across the deserts."

"Bones you outlanders pick at like vultures!" snapped the qadir.

Hajar saw Mishra hesitate for a moment. When he spoke, the scholar chose his words carefully. "Those nations of the eastern coast seek to understand that which has come before, the better to understand what is to be."

The qadir made a grumbling noise that sounded like an unsettled stomach. "There are some things that are best not known. The Old Ones may discover you picking through their garbage and punish you for your effrontery. And punish us for not stopping you."

Another silence from Mishra, then the Argivian said, "As you say, most eminent one." He did not look down now, and his face was an impassive mask. Hajar could detect not a trace of sarcasm.

Neither could the qadir. He leaned back on his pillows and snatched a huge metal wine cup from its tray. "So. You are a scholar?" he inquired.

"I am but a student," returned Mishra. "But I have much knowledge."

"You know your Fallaji well," said the chieftain.

Mishra shrugged. "I had good teachers. It was one more tool in learning the past."

The qadir rumbled again. Hajar had already surmised that the leader of the Suwwardi had little time for, or interest in, the past. "You know the outlander languages? Argive, Korlis, and Yotian?" He spat the last name like a curse.

"They are one and the same language," said Mishra calmly, "though there are differences in dialect and accent. The dialects diverged over centuries due to—"

The qadir held up a hand, and the young man was immediately silenced. "You know your calculations?"

"I do."

"I have nine patrols of eight men each. How many men do I have?" asked the qadir.

"Seventy-two," replied Mishra immediately.

"Four of those patrols are mounted on horseback. How many legs are there?" said the qadir with a harsh smile.

"Two hundred and seventy-two," returned the Argivian smoothly, apparently without thinking.

The qadir's face darkened again, and he looked at Hajar. The younger Fallaji thought for a long moment, his fingers twitching as he sorted mounted and unmounted troops, and number of legs of each. Then he nodded.

The qadir regarded the stocky slave with stony eyes. "You will do." To the guards he said, "Take him out and bathe him." To Mishra he said, "*Rakiq*, you will be my son's tutor. Teach him to speak your language and master his calculations. Do this, and you will be treated well. Fail me, and you will be killed."

Mishra rose and bowed deeply. "As your will is merciful, Eminent One." The two guards flanked Mishra again. One of them still carried the hobbles. The other put a hand on Mishra's shoulder. The stocky Argivian turned and left without saying a word.

Hajar noted that throughout the entire conversation, the young qadir, the smaller version of his father, had said nothing and seemed no more interested in his new tutor than in anything else in the tent.

* * * * *

Hajar had left the Argivians' camp when the last of the outlander students had fled back to their coastal lowlands and the bits of metal they had excavated had been carefully shipped away on ox-drawn carts. He wanted Ahmahl to come with him, but the old digger chose to remain in the area.

Hajar joined one band of nomads, and then another, finally finding his way to the qadir's camp. A distant relation on each one's mother's side gave him tentative entrance, and his hard work and bravery in a raid against a merchant caravan cemented the young Fallaji's position within the camp hierarchy.

But now he had taken a risk, recommending one of Tocasia's students as the young qadir's tutor. His own fortunes would be tied to those of the the Argivian now, and Mishra's failure would be considered his own.

Hajar visited Mishra's new quarters, a small open-sided tarp near the cook's, whenever he could. When Mishra was not teaching he was expected to aid in the preparation of meals—simple, lumpish tasks such as fetching wood, tending the fire, and butchering meat for smoking.

At first things did not seem to go well. At ten years old the young qadir had no more interest in language and calculations than did his father. Worse, he seemed utterly repelled by the idea of being taught by anyone, particularly an outlander.

Mishra, for his part, was desolate. "I will be back digging ditches within a fortnight," he said one evening to Hajar, as he hobbled to gather more brush to tuck into the fire pit.

Hajar knew better. To fail the qadir did not result in demotion, but in death. Neither he nor Mishra had asked if there had been previous tutors, but the implication was that there had been; there were Argivian books in the young qadir's quarters, as well as an abacus. Both books and abacus had been apparently untouched by the chieftain's son's hands.

"He does not want to learn," said Mishra firmly, "and I will not spend my days speaking to a wall." The Argivian let out a deep sigh. "All he cares about is battle and the great things his father has done and what he will do when he becomes qadir."

"Perhaps I could speak with the qadir," said Hajar, then shook his head at the foolishness of his own idea. The father cared even less about knowledge than his son, except he demanded that his son know what he did not. It was a demand with the steel edge of a sword master's blade.

"At best, he fidgets," resumed Mishra. "At worst, he sleeps. I once prodded him awake, and he had his guards beat me." The stocky scholar rubbed his shoulder. "It is not something I want to do again."

"I am sorry it is not working out the way I had hoped," said Hajar.

"I as well," returned the scholar. "And it just seems so . . . hopeless. I feel empty inside. Empty, and useless." Indeed the Argivian looked as if he had not slept for some time. It could not be the work, thought Hajar, for his life was slightly easier in that regard. It had to be something else. Perhaps his own sense of failure gnawed at him.

Hajar was silent for a moment, then said, "Why did you learn Fallaji?"

Mishra looked up at the younger man. "What?"

Hajar continued, "The Argivian woman knew our language, but she had to deal with Ahmahl and the other diggers. None of the outlander students seemed particularly interested in learning more than the curse words. Your brother never learned, as far as I know. But you did. Why?"

"My brother was interested in devices, in things," said Mishra wearily. "I have always found people more interesting."

"There were 'people' among the Argivian students," said Hajar. "Why did you learn our language?"

Mishra shrugged his shoulders. "I suppose I wanted to hear the old legends of your people. The genie nations, the heroes, and the princesses. The dragons you call *mak fawa* and the warriors. When they were put in my language the stories always seemed dry, shriveled things, bloodless and lifeless. They meant more in their original tongue."

"And don't you outlanders have your own legends?" asked Hajar. "Old battles and legends."

"Well, of course," said Mishra. "There was the tale of the Gray Pirate who raided the Korlis coast, and of the warrior-queen of Argive who lived five hundred years ago. There are all manner of old god stories that they only believe in Yotia and other backward nations."

Hajar smiled. "Perhaps your young charge would rather hear about those stories instead. And that might encourage him to learn the language as well."

Mishra thought for a moment, then nodded.

"And put your calculations lessons in terms of things he understands," continued Hajar. "Remember the question the qadir put to you? Probably that was how he learned his ciphers and fractions."

Mishra did not say anything for a moment but stared into the cook fire. "You might be right," he said at last. "It's worth a try at least."

"Worth a try for both our sakes," said Hajar. He added, "Also, you can teach him how to curse in Argivian. I'm sure the boy would like that as well."

* * * * *

Several months passed. Things seemed to go better for the Argivian scholar, and Hajar allowed himself to relax. If anything went wrong at this late date, it was unlikely that he would now be remembered and blamed for recommending the young man's tutor.

Indeed, Mishra's lessons, now couched in Argivian history and Yotian mythology, seemed to have more than their desired effect on the young qadir. He had gathered a basic feel for the outlanders' language, and had professed even an interest in Argivian customs beyond the battlefield.

The youth's temper toward his slave tutor had improved as well, and the beatings became less frequent, then disappeared entirely. Nor, according to Mishra, did the youth sleep in class anymore. Indeed, the young qadir seemed almost to warm to the Argivian scholar, and ofttimes now Mishra was spared from his cleaning duties in order to finish a tale begun earlier in the afternoon.

One evening Mishra had asked Hajar to attend as the young qadir recited the tale of the Gray Pirate and the Last of the Sea Dragons. There were about a dozen attending, but only Hajar and Mishra understood what the boy was saying fully. He would tell part of the tale in Argivian, then speak again in Fallaji. The Fallaji versions were much more florid, obscene, and bloody in their descriptions, but Mishra did not correct the youth.

Soon afterward Mishra's hobbles were removed, though he still was expected to tend the cooking fires when not in the young qadir's company.

Hajar's own life went well. Many of the local tribes swore fealty to the Suwwardi. The clan's raids had become more effective and the tribes more prosperous. Merchant caravans were held for tolls and in some cases outright ransom. Several Argivian settlements on Fallaji land were removed by fire and sword. When the Argivians sent their slow, heavy-armored patrols into Suwwardi lands seeking retribution, the more nimble Fallaji had evaded them.

So it was with some surprise when Hajar, following one such raid, was summoned to the qadir's tent. Save for the ceremonial guards, no one else was present. The qadir leaned back on his pillows, turning something large and green in his fingers. Hajar entered, knelt in respect, and waited.

"You know the *rakiq* tutor," said the qadir presently. He did not look in Hajar's direction,

"I do," said Hajar, rising after being addressed. He suddenly wondered how much he should admit regarding Mishra.

"He has done well," said the qadir. "The boy knows his additions and subtractions, his ciphers and fractions. And he speaks outlander passingly well, I am told."

"Very well, indeed," said Hajar. "I have heard him speak, and his words are well formed and proper."

"The boy is doing well," said the qadir. "Perhaps too well."

The qadir let the statement fall into silence. Finally Hajar said cautiously, "How so, Most Eminent One?"

The qadir held up the green object to his eye, regarding it as a merchant inspects his stock. "Do you know what this is?"

Hajar had never seen it before, but he knew at once what it was: one of the power stones that Tocasia and the brothers had always made a fuss over. It still held its energy, for it glowed with a bright jade sheen. This one glowed even though it had been broken, sheared along one side.

Hajar thought of one of the stories around the diggers' fires after the brothers returned from the Secret Heart. Of the pouch that Mishra had kept around his neck. Carefully he chose his words.

"It looks like an Eye of the Old Ones," he said, using the Fallaji word for the power stone.

The qadir grumbled, making that low, camel-about-to-spit sound that so unsettled Hajar. "Indeed. There are Argivians, and Yotians as well, trespassing into the desert looking for trinkets such as this. What do you know about this particular one?"

Hajar was silent, attempting to gather his thoughts, but the qadir pressed on. "This one was taken from the *rakiq* tutor when he was captured. It was put among my treasures and forgotten. But my son asked about it the other day, and I had it brought out. Why does my son request it?"

Hajar was silent for a moment, hoping that this was another rhetorical question. It was not. At last he ventured, "Probably the tutor mentioned it to him, and he was curious."

The qadir gave a low harrumph and said, "And perhaps he wants it back, eh? Now why would the *rakiq* want this particular stone?"

"Perhaps it has special meaning to him," replied Hajar quickly. "Look at the way it is cut along one side."

"Shattered, not cut," returned the qadir shrewdly. "And shattered Eyes are often useless and dull. This one still holds whatever fire the Old Ones imbued it with. So this may be special. The question is, how special is it?"

Hajar thought of that last night in the Argivian camp, and the unearthly lights that had shown from the brothers' cabin. The stones, Tocasia had said; she had said something about the stones. Then there had been the blast and the fire, and Mishra had disappeared into the desert until Hajar had found him digging a ditch in the qadir's camp.

He had never asked what had really happened that night. He had assumed it was something that Mishra's older brother, the lean, spooky one, had done.

Hajar gulped for a moment, then said, "I cannot say, Respected One."

The qadir made that low gurgling noise again and said, "Neither can I. And for that reason I will deny it to my son, so he is not tempted to pass it into the hands of the *rakiq*. I will keep it myself and see if it carries any power of the Old Ones."

He slipped the gem into a voluminous pocket of his vest and shifted position, facing Hajar fully, now. He laced his fingers before his face and said, "The question now is, why would the boy ask for something on behalf of a *rakiq*?"

Hajar stammered, then said, "It could be that your son heard of the stone from the *rakiq* and wanted it for his own."

The qadir tilted his head for a moment, as if considering that option for the first time. "Perhaps," he said, shaking his head. "Or perhaps he wanted to retrieve it for his friend and tutor."

Hajar searched for the proper words. "A qadir's son would never be friends with an outlander *rakiq*."

"Agreed," replied the qadir. "My fear, though, is that he listens to the outlander too much. He leans on him, as a man leans on a crutch. And if one leans too often, one forgets how to walk on one's own."

Hajar said softly, "I do not think you need to fear that occurring."

"I fear nothing," said the qadir quickly. "But now the boy will ride on our raids as well. He is young but not too young to learn a man's craft of battle. He will be taught when he is in camp, but otherwise the *rakiq* will have only the cook fires to worry about. Tell me, if he spends his time on our raids, will the boy still know enough by the end of next year to be considered educated?"

Hajar thought for a moment. The qadir's son was now more knowledgeable than most of the other Suwwardi in camp. But somehow he felt that was the wrong answer. Instead he spoke most of the truth. "By the end of next year. Yes, he would."

The qadir leaned back on his pillows. "Excellent. When the boy comes of his majority, he will no longer need the crutch. And when that time comes, that crutch will be broken and cast aside. Do I make myself clear?"

Hajar looked into the qadir's porcine eyes. It was very clear indeed. The qadir worried about his son's loyalties. When the time came, Mishra would be taken out into the desert and killed quietly. Hajar would oversee that slaying on the qadir's command.

Hajar heard himself say, "As you wish, Respected One. Your words are as law." The qadir waved him off, and Hajar knelt briefly, then fled the tent.

Hajar's mouth felt as if it had been filled with dust. He had heard the qadir's death warrant, and he knew if he disobeyed he would be signing his own. And for what? A pack of fatherly fears and half a stone.

Hajar walked past the prince's tent and saw, through the opening, Mishra and the young qadir talking. Their voices were low, but they frequently broke apart and laughed, sharing private jokes. The qadir's son motioned, and Mishra poured drinks. He lifted his cup and joined the young qadir in a toast of *nabiz*.

Hajar frowned. Perhaps the old qadir was not wrong in his worries about his son. Perhaps as a youth the qadir himself had had a friend upon whom he depended, and who mysteriously disappeared one day. Perhaps, thought Hajar, that was the nature of being a leader: one relies on others, but one does not depend utterly on them.

Hajar decided to walk back to his own quarters the long way around. He would not tell Mishra and could not tell the qadir's son. He would hope that once the lad had more battle experience he would be less interested in the scholar's teachings. With that diminished interest, the qadir's fears and the death sentence would vanish. Unlikely, thought Hajar, but possible.

After all, a lot could happen before the end of the next year.

* * * * *

Mishra dreamed.

As his body healed from its beatings and his spirit recovered from its daily exhaustion, Mishra's dreams grew stronger. Sometimes he dreamed of Tocasia, sometimes of his brother. But most often he dreamed of the stone, as it sang to him out of the darkness.

He had told the qadir's son of the stone, and the boy had discovered that, yes, his father still had it in his possession. Mishra knew this already, for the stone held him to the camp as no hobbles ever could.

So he dreamed of the stone, imagined it spinning in space, singing its plaintive dirge, crying out to him. He wanted it back. He wanted to go to it.

And in his dreams he went.

In the dream he awoke and realized he was somewhere else, far from the Suwwardi encampment, far from the desert itself. Far from the world.

The sky above him was not filled with the familiar Fallaji stars, the thick light-dotted soup of the night sky. Instead it was overcast and dark, flickering with diffused pulses of lightning. He could see in the darkness, and he realized he was atop a low, bare tor, surrounded by thick vegetation.

He heard the singing of his gem in the distance, and he moved toward it.

The vegetation around the bare hillock was thick and tangled, but he moved through it as if he were a wraith. It was a riot of bright yellows and oranges against darker leaves. He paused and saw the leaves themselves had a strange sheen, as if they had been stamped from steel plates. The flowers as well were metallic and dripped foul-smelling ether instead of nectar.

He touched one of the leaves, and it reverberated to his touch. Its keening matched that of the stone, and he ignored the leaf, following the heart-tugging wail of his gem.

He made a detour around a great pool with an oily film dancing across the surface. He looked away for moment, and something large and black surfaced in the pond, then dived again. When he looked back he saw only slowly spreading rings rippling out toward the borders. The water moved oddly, as if it were made of something thicker and more syrupy than ordinary water.

He found a clear-shelled egg and for a moment thought it was his missing gem. On closer inspection, he saw that the hand-sized egg had a translucent shell, and within that shell a small, gold-colored creature was growing. No, not growing, he realized; being assembled. Smaller golden creatures were moving spans and joints around within the shell, assembling it like one of Urza's devices. As he watched, the

117

thin form of a lizard's skin and skull appeared in the murky darkness of the egg.

Then the singing began again. He set the egg down and followed the siren call.

It began to rain, and the rain tasted like tears, leaving oil-streaked patches on his clothing.

He followed the song.

Finally he reached a building, a pyramid among the jungle of metal plants. The building's architecture seemed familiar. It was made of ropy roots and metallic cables. There were markings along the side of the building, but in his dream he could not decipher them.

The plants had pulled their trailing roots away from the base of the pyramid, and Mishra saw a set of stairs leading upward to a small alcove. Within that cave shown the greenish light of the power stone.

Yes, he had seen this type of building before. He had been inside one, once, in a hallway lined with mirrors when he had first gained the stone—the stone that now waited for him.

There was a loud metallic crash to his right among the thick, serrated leaves. A huge brass head erupted from the surrounding vegetation. At first Mishra thought it was a giant serpent, for it had a huge triangular head mounted at the end of a looping metallic neck. Then the beast emerged fully, and Mishra saw the neck was moored to a huge, elephantine body, with leonine paws ending in sharp, steel claws.

It was a dragon, but a mechanical one, crafted by unknown hands and granted inhuman life. Its eyes were dull, flickering blue gems; steam vented from its nostrils and leaked from its joints. It was an engine built in the shape of a great wyrm.

The dragon engine saw Mishra and let out a low, challenging bellow. Then it began to move forward, half-loping, half-slithering from its jungle hiding place.

Mishra froze for a moment, but only for a moment. Then he fled up the stairs, toward his lost gem. His dream logic told him that if he reached the gem, everything would be fine.

The stairs seemed to elongate endlessly, and his feet were suddenly mired in tar. Still he pressed upward, feeling the hot breath of the dragon engine behind him. Finally he reached the top of the steps, and his fingers closed around the green gem.

At the first touch of the gem a wave of peace washed over Mishra, and he forgot the steam-dripping engine behind him. When he did turn, the creature was no longer trying to scale the stairs to reach him.

Instead it lay along the length of the steps. Its ears were laid back along its head, and its eyes flickered not with rage but with obedience. Steam dribbled weakly from its nostrils.

It was waiting for him to tell it what to do.

Mishra held up the gem, and its light bathed the creature fully. It was truly a mechanical engine in dragon form. Its forelegs were like that of a dragon, but instead of rear limbs it possessed a set of linked plates curled over a collection of smaller wheels. Treads, thought Mishra. The device carried with it a continual road that could be laid down before it and picked up afterward. It made perfect sense.

"Interesting."

Someone said the word, and Mishra wheeled around. No one spoke again, but Mishra heard the word echoing in his mind. There above the alcove was perched the mirror figure from his earlier vision, a creature of bones, armor, horns, and tendrils. Somehow Mishra knew this was more than just another construct, with its exposed muscles of ropelike cables and its backward-pointing horns. It was a living thing, a powerful one, and unlike the engine it would not be cowed by the power of the stone.

The creature perched over the alcove regarded Mishra for a long moment. The young man was dimly aware that the long tresses along the creature's horns were more like draped tentacles and moved of their own volition.

Then the creature laughed at Mishra, a dry, hollow laugh, the laugh of a skeleton. "Give me the stone!" shouted the creature and leapt down on top of him.

Mishra screamed. He tried to wake himself up, tried to force himself to run, tried to force the dragon engine to defend him. But the horned creature laughed, and Mishra felt its clawlike grip close around his own hand, the one holding the gem. There was a wrenching pain along his arm as the creature pulled the gem away, taking Mishra's arm with it.

Mishra screamed again and woke. He was in his tent, the open-sided tarp pitched near the cooking fire. One of the guards was by the fire, looking at him but not moving either to help or to punish.

Mishra looked at his left arm. It was still there, though there were streaks of red along its length, as if a briar had worn its way along its length. Or as if claws had grabbed it.

His fist was clenched tightly; slowly Mishra opened his fingers. There was no green gem at the center of his hand. There was nothing at all.

Mishra took a deep breath. It was a dream, more savage and life-like than before, but still a dream. He exhaled slowly.

Then the ground beneath him began to shake.

* * * * *

Hajar was on guard duty that night, but at the far perimeter of the camp. One of the survivors later said he heard the young qadir's *rakiq* cry out a curse before the abyss yawned open and released its hell-creature, but that could have been something added after the fact. So much of what happened that night was later embellished.

At first Hajar thought it was nothing more than a night tremor, a shifting of the sands cooling after the hot summer heat. Sometimes a ripple like that traveled thousands of miles from the Sardian Mountains all the way to Zegon. Some said such tremors were omens, but then, in the desert, anything the least bit unusual was assumed to be an omen.

But a night tremor lasted for a moment, perhaps two, then subsided. This one persisted for a full ten seconds. Then it grew stronger.

Already the camp was reacting to the assault. The goats rushed from one end of their pen to the other, looking for some means of escape. Several of the horses, tethered for the evening, pulled at the reins, trying to escape. There were shouts among the camp as guards called to each other and sleeping Fallaji awoke to find the earth rippling about them.

Hajar shouted but did not know if he made any noise. Already the roar of the earth was more than his ears could take.

Tents came loose from their moorings and collapsed. The low fence around the goat pen was shaken free, and the goats, a flurry of white and gray, bounded to freedom. The horses pulled their pegs loose from the ground and fled into the night.

Then the *mak fawa* escaped from its earthen prison and bored up through the center of the camp.

It was a dragon of the old legends, its head a wedge-shaped spike that effortlessly plowed from the ground, followed by a chainlike neck, and finally a great body made of metal ribs. It took a moment for that to sink in on Hajar. The *mak fawa* was made entirely of metal, its brass hide shining in the moonlight.

Several of the guards were already fleeing, but more were rushing toward the monstrosity. The creature had appeared from below, near the center of the camp, near the qadir's tent. In some Fallaji, that inspired loyalty, in others, fear. Hajar felt nothing more than life-saving caution. Gripping his spear, he spiraled around the perimeter of the camp, hoping to pick up some reinforcements before charging the beast.

Some of his brethren would not wait to gain allies and were already attacking the creature. In response, it snaked its head down in a leisurely gesture and snagged one of the attacking men. Its jaws closed on the head and shoulders of the attacker, and the warrior screamed. The scream continued as the dragon snapped its head up like a whip, opening its jaws as its head reached its highest point of the arc and releasing its attacker. The scream sailed over Hajar's head and was suddenly cut short when the warrior landed in the darkness beyond the camp.

Other warriors were attacking now, but their curved swords and barbed Suwwardi spears had no more effect than if they were trying to hack through a stone wall. The dragon's head darted forward again and came up with the struggling form of another warrior. This one it shook back and forth, like one of the qadir's dogs tormenting a hare. It flung that man away as well and slowly climbed the rest of the way out of its pit.

Hajar wanted to charge as well, as many of the warriors were doing, to protect their qadir and their camp, to gain revenge against the creature. But the part of him that had worked for Ahmahl in the Argivian woman's camp knew what the thing had to be and who would best know how to handle it.

He found Mishra huddled beneath his tarp, curled into a small ball. "The dream," he muttered, his eyes welded shut. "The dream." It seemed to Hajar as if the youth were trying to wish the creature away.

"It's real," snapped Hajar, adding in Argivian, "It is a device. An artifact. You know about such devices. How do we defeat it?"

The outlander's words seemed to pull the scholar from his panic. "Of course," he said slowly. "It has to be a device. Perhaps not Thran, but still a device. I must have the stone!"

"Stone?" said Hajar, a sick feeling growing in the pit of his stomach.

"A green gem, cut in half," said Mishra quickly. "They took it from me when I first came here. With it I can weaken the dragon engine."

"I've seen it," said Hajar, turning toward the battle. Quietly he added, "The qadir has it."

Hajar looked across the devastation that the dragon engine had already created. Women, children, and elderly were already fleeing the camp, while the warriors had regrouped for another assault. The Fallaji youth saw the broad figure of the qadir among them. There was a flash of green against the qadir's broad chest.

"There!" Hajar pointed to the large figure of the Suwwardi chieftain. "He has it!" He did not wait to see if Mishra was following but leapt forward into the fray.

Hajar was about two hundred paces behind the main mass of men led by the qadir. His position saved his life.

The dragon engine leaned forward and opened its mouth in front of the charging concentration of men. There was the sound of a whirlwind within the great beast's body, and it breathed a gout of red-tinged steam.

Hajar heard screams ahead of him as the billowing cloud enfolded the warriors. He felt the heat and staggered back a few paces, then charged forward again into the quickly dissipating cloud.

The men had been cooked where they stood, their flesh peeled back and charred by the heat. Hajar felt bile rising in his throat, but he looked around for a large form; a form that had to be the qadir.

Hajar found him facedown in the dirt, a growing pool of blood beneath his body from where the steam had disintegrated the qadir's skin down to the bone. Cursing the task, Hajar knelt next to the old man's corpse and began rifling his pockets. Hajar looked up only once, to see an assault led by the qadir's son make a minimal impact on the creature's armored hide.

The qadir had been true to his word and had kept the stone close to him. It glowed now, reflecting the embers of the charred flesh around it.

Hajar grabbed the stone and made the mistake of looking up again. He stared directly into the eyes and maw of the *mak fawa*.

There was thought behind those eyes, Hajar realized. This was not like the *su-chi* or the plodding onulets of the Argivian camp. There was an intelligence within those eyes and a malignancy behind that intelligence. The *mak fawa* looked at Hajar and knew in an instant who he was, what he was holding in his hands, and why he could not use it.

The dragon opened its mouth, and there was the sound of desert wind again. Hajar knew what to expect next and bolted for the perimeter of the camp.

His back blazed as the passing cloud of steam dissipated around him. Then he was free of it and saw Mishra approaching from the other direction.

Hajar looked back. The *mak fawa* was already breaking loose of its bank of steam. It lumbered forward toward them.

Hajar turned and tossed the half-stone at Mishra. Then he jumped aside, covering his face with his arms on the chance that Mishra did not truly know what to do to defeat the dragon engine. Maybe, he thought desperately, the dragon would think him dead and pass him by.

For a long moment Hajar held his position. At any moment he expected to feel the dragon's wrath. When it did not come he slowly moved his hands away from his face.

The *mak fawa* was supine, looking for all the world like one of the qadir's (no, Hajar reminded himself, the *late* qadir's) dogs. Its steel-taloned paws were drawn up under its forward haunches, and Hajar noted that instead of rear feet it had a curious set of wheels and plates. The dragon engine's neck was bolt-straight and lying flat on the ground, an arrow with the beast's metallic snout as its head. Streamlets of reddish steam hissed from the corners of its closed mouth.

At the point of the arrow stood Mishra, holding the green half-gem aloft. In his hands the power stone was shining brightly, a beacon in the night.

Hajar stood and staggered over to the scholar. "Did you kill it?" he asked.

Mishra shook his head, and his voice sounded distant. "No. This is different. It is not weakened by me. I think it obeys me."

There were shouts, and Hajar saw the young qadir approaching. He was bleeding from a nasty cut along one arm, and his reddened face looked as if he had caught part of the steam cloud. "Is it dead?" he shouted at Mishra.

"Subdued," replied the scholar. "I think I think I can control it now."

The young qadir nodded and said, "My father will be pleased."

Hajar started, then spoke. "I am sorry, young one, but your father is . . ." He let his voice trail off. "You are qadir now."

As he spoke, he saw a veil come down over the young qadir's face. It was as if the news had turned the youth to stone, had petrified his features. His face suddenly seemed harder than it had moments before when he was just the son of the qadir.

The new qadir nodded and turned to Mishra. "You can control this thing?" It was a blunt question.

"I believe I can," said Mishra.

"Can anyone else?" asked the young chieftain.

Mishra thought for a moment, than shook his head. "I believe that if your father could have, he would." Then another pause. "We can check later."

"Agreed," said the young qadir. "Take this thing away from the camp for the moment and remain with it until morning." To Hajar he said, "Take me to my father's body. We must inspect the wounded and see how much damage has been done. We have lost much this night." He looked at the dragon engine thoughtfully and said as much to himself as to Hajar, "But perhaps we have gained much as well."

Hajar and Mishra hesitated for only a moment, but it was enough to earn the reproach from the new Qadir of the Suwwardi, chiefmost of the Fallaji tribes. "Get moving!"

Mishra said softly, "As you wish, Most Revered One. I remain your *rakiq*."

"No," said the young man, holding up a hand in the same manner as his father had months before. His face softened for a moment. "You are no longer *rakiq*, a slave. I make you now *raki*, my wizard. I will need you at my side, with this amazing device. With it we can maintain our hold over the other tribes and gain new ones as well. Will you serve me willingly?"

Mishra dropped to one knee and said, "Of course."

Hajar was impressed as well. The boy acted as if he had been preparing for this moment and knew exactly what had to be done.

"Thank you," said the youth to Mishra. "Truly your mother and my mother must have shared a common mother. But right now, let's hurry! We have much yet to do this night!"

Chapter 8

Tawnos

The newcomer arrived unannounced at the Palace of Artifice in Kroog, capital of Yotia. It had been a long journey from the southern coast, and he was bone weary from his travels. Had he been sensible he would have bedded down for a day or ten, paid for a suitably tailored gown, and then called for an official appointment through established channels. However the newcomer was unschooled in the ways and practices of High Yotian society and presented himself directly to the palace, his letter of introduction in the vest pocket of his traveling cloak and his gift in a satchel slung over his arm.

The Palace of Artifice was a separate wing of the royal palace itself, flung off from the main buildings in an eruption of new construction. There was no one to receive the traveler at the main doors, which surprised him slightly, but there was no one to block his entry either. Indeed there seemed to be a steady flow of clerks, librarians, and petty officials milling about, but nothing that looked like an armed guard or even a helpful guide.

He stopped one of the clerks, a round, friendly-looking fellow with an armload of scrolls and vials. This individual explained that the Chief Artificer could be found in the central domed workshop at the back of the palace, and that the visitor could reach it by going up the stairs toward the rear, right at the first intersection, left at the second, rightish-but-not-too-right at the star-shaped one, down one more flight, and there he would be. The clerk never asked why the tall, blond-haired man was looking for the Chief Artificer in the first place.

The friendly clerk's instructions also left something to be desired;

it took another fifteen minutes (and two more helpful clerks) for the traveler to finally locate the orniary, which was, as promised, a large dome-shaped structure mounted on the back of the main building. The newcomer noticed that the circular roof of the building was built on a sliding pivot so that it might be unbolted and moved to one side.

Within the orniary was a form of controlled madness. Along the far wall was the frame of one of the fabled ornithopters, frozen in mid-explosion. Each of the pieces was mounted separately, with inscribed lines showing what piece fit where. A group of young students stood along one side with trundle-operated lathes, gently shaping candle-wood spars. Along the other side an ornithopter was in the midst of construction, as another group of young people stretched canvas over the wings.

In the center, standing over a huge table littered with plans, was the Chief Artificer. His hair was pale blond, almost white. While shorter than the newcomer, he commanded a presence that made him seem much taller.

"Three point four inches to the first flange," shouted the Chief Artificer to the lathe workers, who dutifully pulled out their calipers and began measuring. "No, no!" He stalked over to the crew assembling the ornithopter. "Place the skin over the lead grommets along the wing first! That will allow the wing to unfurl naturally."

As the newcomer watched, another clerk elbowed his way past and handed a scroll to the Chief Artificer. Urza scanned the paper for a moment, shook his head, and made the clerk wait as he returned to his paper-covered work desk. He pulled out a stylus and quickly edited the message. "And tell him I need the supplies by noon tomorrow," he snapped impatiently. "No later!" The clerk pushed his way past the newcomer and back into the main building.

Suddenly the visitor noticed the woman standing alongside one wall. She stood so still among the pandemonium that the traveler at first thought her a statue. She was dressed in a simple blue gown, and her lustrous dark brown hair spilled over her shoulders. Her arms were folded in front of her, and she wore an expression on her face that hinted she disapproved of the entire scene around her.

"Excuse me, miss," said the newcomer. "I was wondering if—"

The woman turned, and the newcomer choked on his words as he recognized the full lips, the dark, fiery eyes, and the fine lines of her face. At once he realized whom he was addressing and managed a gargle. "Your Majesty, forgive me." He was well on his way to the floor.

His knee had just touched the hardwood when a soft hand touched his shoulder.

"Arise, young man," said Kayla bin-Kroog, Princess of Yotia and wife of the Chief Artificer. When he looked up she was smiling slightly, as if his manner amused her. He felt the blood rush to his face.

"I'm sorry," he said. "I had no idea who you were."

"We don't stand on much ceremony here in the lair of the Chief Artificer," returned the princess.

Out on the main floor of the dome, Urza was bellowing at the lathe workers. "I said three point four, not three point two! I need a tolerance no more than oh point two for these struts!"

"Is your husb—" The newcomer stopped and began again. "Is the Chief Artificer free at the moment?"

"I can't tell," said the princess, with a catch in her voice. "I've been standing here for ten minutes waiting for him to notice me. If I have to wait fifteen, I usually assume that he's too busy."

The newcomer looked at her face more closely and nodded. "Perhaps it would be better to come back tomorrow," he ventured.

The princess laughed a tired laugh. "This is about as un-busy as he ever gets. Is it important?"

The visitor reached in his coat pocket and pulled the envelope from its hiding place. "I'm his new apprentice."

Kayla opened the letter and scanned it quickly. The newcomer held his breath as she did so, fearful she might find some impropriety within the letter of introduction that would prevent him from even talking to the mighty Urza. "A toy maker?" she said at last.

"From Jorilin, on the coast," said the young man quickly.

She nodded. "We summered there when I was girl, and it got too hot even for Kroog."

"Well," said the traveler, "I've been making toys there for the past few years, full journeyman and everything. People thought my work was fairly impressive, and they suggested that I apply to be one of his apprentices . . ." He let the statement trail off with a embarrassed shrug. It had sounded so logical back in Jorilin, much more logical than it did now explaining to the most powerful (and beautiful) woman in Kroog.

"I see," the princess said, and that amused look returned to her face. "His apprentice."

"One of them, anyway," said the traveler.

"Please," said the princess. "All these are not apprentices. They're drones, toiling around the king bee that is Urza. Assistants, students, extra sets of hands, that's all. Apprentices have higher demands put on them than this lot. They usually don't last more than a month at the outside. He's a hard man to keep pace with and a very demanding man to work for."

As if to prove her point, Urza let out another shout. "I said I needed oh point two tolerance here, lathe number one! Are you using some number system I'm not familiar with?" There was laughter among the younger lathe workers as one blushing youth returned to his machine.

"Perhaps I should come back later," repeated the newcomer.

"No time like the present," Kayla responded. "He'll be just as bad tomorrow, and I won't be here to help. Urza! Husband! A moment, please!"

The Chief Artificer responded to his wife's call by holding up a single hand. With the other he held a stylus, checking a long column of figures. He did not look up.

"Of all the . . ." muttered the princess, several decidedly unregal lines appearing on her forehead. "I swear, he spends every living moment working until he is exhausted. Then he wakes in the morning feeling he's fallen six hours behind schedule because of sleep. Urza!"

The hand stayed up, and, as if to show he was listening, waved back and forth a little.

"Perhaps this will help," said the visitor, reaching into the satchel and pulling out his gift. What he produced looked like nothing more than an inanimate hunk of rope of chain. He flicked a switch at one end of the chain, and it suddenly stiffened and struck forward. It was a snake, suddenly come to life in his hands. Kayla jumped at the transformation.

The snake leapt across the open space as if on invisible wings, landing among the papers littering Urza's table. It burrowed among them, emerging directly beneath the Chief Artificer's notepad. It raised its head, rattled its tail, and rasped a hissed warning at the Argivian scholar.

The entire orniary went dead silent. The lathes stopped, the students wrestling with the wing tarps froze, and Urza paused, stylus in hand, regarding the snake's fang-filled mouth.

Then he leaned forward and tapped the snake's snout with the end of his stylus. It rang out with a hollow sound, and the serpent immediately curled into a small coil. The Chief Artificer looked up, a broad smile on his face. "Who did this?"

The newcomer blushed. "That would be me."

Kayla stepped forward with the letter of introduction. "This is Tawnos, a toy maker from Jorilin. He wants to become your appren—"

Urza did not let her finish but took the letter from her hand and said, "Toy maker? And that is one of yours?"

"One of them," replied Tawnos.

"Why wood?" asked Urza. "Metal would be a lot more long-lasting."

"Wood's lighter," answer the younger man. "And yarrow wood produces a more natural sound for the snake when it moves. Metal versions tended to clatter."

"So you tried it," said Urza, his eyebrows raised. "Good. That's very good. Spring-driven, I suppose."

"Clock mechanism," said Tawnos. "I was told you worked as a clockmaker."

"For a time," said Urza abstractedly. His hands were busy examining the snake, probing, bending, pushing. "Then I retired to join the government. Less heavy lifting."

Kayla began, "Darling husband, my father is expecting—" but was silenced with by an upraised hand.

"It's very lifelike," the artificer observed. "Did you study snakes to make it?"

"We have a lot of coastal snakes," said Tawnos. "That one was based on a kind of viper found along the coast. I made it for my own amusement, as a kind of practical joke."

"Urza," Kayla began again but was completely forgotten by the Chief Artificer.

"What about birds?" asked Urza. "I've been trying to improve the lift ratio of the ornithopters."

"It depends what you want," said Tawnos. "Soaring birds like gulls or even vultures might be inappropriate as models for ornithopters. I should think you want ones that can launch quickly from a perch, like predatory owls and other raptors."

Urza's face brightened, and at that precise moment Tawnos knew he had secured his position. "I had not considered that," said the blond-haired artificer. "I always considered a bird to be a bird, regardless. But you are correct: form follows function, and function determines form. Here, take a look at these plans, and tell me if I have a soarer or a fast launcher."

Tawnos looked over the papers littering the desk and inhaled deeply. There were all manner of ornithopter plans, showing different wing configurations and positions. Some of the machines resembled things he had seen in nature, while some looked as if they would never fly under any circumstances.

Suddenly he remembered the princess, who had been trying to get two words in edgewise as he and Urza talked. But when he looked up from the plans, she was gone, and Urza was shouting at the lathe workers again for greater precision.

* * * * *

The princess's heels were shod with metal and always sent a message as she moved across the palace's polished marble floors. Sometimes it was a leisurely tapping, reassuring the staff that her majesty was thinking as she walked. Sometimes it was a slow, methodical clack, which usually meant she was walking with someone else, usually some official from the hinterland who was getting a local tour. And occasionally it was a skipping staccato produced by her run, much less common now than in the times before she was married.

The message being tapped out at the moment was a warning. She had just been to see her husband, the Argivian artificer, and was not happy with the results. The stern rapping of metal on stone was enough to send the most hardened courtiers fleeing in terror, and to cause even the most experienced servants to reverse their directions and quietly back up the way they came.

As a result, Kayla had empty halls and full thoughts as she stalked along the way leading to the drawing room. She fumed as she walked.

He was busy. He was always busy. Given sufficient resources, he would devote all his time to his projects. The ornithopters. The metal statues. The great plodding beasts that had suddenly appeared one morning in the rose garden. He would work until exhausted, and he would work everyone around him to the same state. If she did not send a guard for him, he would sleep in that orniary of his. Sometimes she did let him sleep there, but that did not slow him down.

Of course her husband was not the only guilty party here, she realized. Her dear father was just as much a cause of her husband's neglect. Always asking for something new. Some special favor for this baron. Some particular device for that temple. Something to make one guild or another's life easier. A new way to haul water. A new way to harvest crops. And of course the Chief Artificer could not refuse his warlord anything, particularly if it was excuse to develop some new device.

It was a perfect match. Urza liked to build things, and Daddy liked the things Urza built. It didn't matter to the warlord how Urza created his wondrous devices, and Urza never thought about what her father wanted the devices for. All of their scheming left Kayla alone.

She stopped and stamped a foot hard on the stone floor, causing several of the hiding servants to wince and wonder if the mark she left could be polished out or would require replacement of the stone. She took a deep breath and tried to calm down.

Actually, she told herself, things were not as bad as they might be. The Yotian people, after a brief period of concern about the warlord's new son-in-law, quickly warmed to Urza. The wedding helped win over the common people and most of the merchants. The minor nobility was vastly relieved to see that Urza did not care for political power beyond the limits of his worktable. And the temples . . .

Well, the temples were a small problem at first, despite their supposed enthusiasm at the wedding itself. Argivians were nastily irreligious, and the devotion of various gods, real and otherwise, was a major political consideration in Kroog. Not to mention the fact that all the assembled religions were keenly aware that they themselves had had the chance to admit this Urza the Argivian into their temple schools but had turned him away because of his heritage.

Things were a little problematic for the first few years, what with the churches all waiting for some misstep or announcement from Urza that would trample on one group or another's beliefs. Urza himself provided the solution to that potential problem. First, by staying in his workshop he provided little provocation to the temples. Second, he managed to wrangle from the Jalum Tome a small bit of old Thran science on the temples' behalf.

It was a simple device, a small amulet with a sliver of active power stone mounted on its back. It emitted a low-pitched hum that served to keep the wearer calm, and in doing so provided a modicum of protection. Naturally anything that smacked of the healing arts was snatched up by the temples, who immediately pronounced Urza to be a wonderfully fine fellow, even for an Argivian.

So the temples were happy. The merchants were happy when more people flocked to Kroog, hearing of their "magical" amulets. And the common folk were made happy by merchants hiring more help, and by the ornithopters that were now seen flitting among the towers, attracting still more people to Yotia. And, Kayla told herself, Daddy was happy because he had metal statues, ornithopters, and wonders others did not have, and a son-in-law who delighted in making more.

In fact, Chief Artificer Urza was making everyone happy in Yotia except its princess, his wife. To make matters worse, Daddy had mentioned to her that he did not have a grandson yet, an heir to carry on the title. Was it *her* fault that the warlord kept her husband continually occupied with other matters?

Kayla knew there were other options for intimate companionship, of course, but she had always found them distasteful. When she was growing up, the matron had all manner of stories of queens and princesses who dallied with some handsome young courtier or kindhearted commoner. But most of those stories were cautionary tales that usually ended with one or both of the two people involved dead or in exile. Somehow it did not seem like a good set of choices to her.

But she was still young, and beautiful, and there were those who looked at her in a fashion that her husband did not have time for. It was nice to know that one could turn heads, she reflected. Kayla was sure that the tall, brawny toy maker from the coast had almost swallowed his tongue when he finally recognized her. It was little things such as that that made her feel good.

She thought about the newcomer, Tawnos. He was tall and broad-shouldered; she had no doubt he had drifted into craft work after spending his youth hauling in the sardine catch off Jorilin Point. His blond hair was in continual disarray, giving him a lost, puppy-dog look. There was a man, she thought with a smile, who was in need of a good young woman to put his life in order. And his manners! Pure hinterland; you could even hear the gulls when he talked. Under court tutelage, that would change soon enough.

Of course, from the start Tawnos seemed to have developed a rapport with her husband. If her husband was sometimes unreachable by her, he might listen to a man who spoke in the language of inventions, devices, and science.

Kayla shook her head. Part of her wanted to see the handsome young newcomer survive the grind of working with her husband—Tawnos seemed like a nice young man. But part of the princess knew that if he was to fit into her husband's world he would have to alter to fit Urza's needs. She had learned that if one did not fit into his plans, one was simply ignored.

She was walking slowly now, her heels a soft tap against the marble. The courtiers knew that the storm was over, whatever its cause, and she passed several of the servants, who bowed briefly as they carted fresh linens, silverware, more of the inevitable scrolls about the palace.

Finally she reached the drawing room, took a deep breath, and entered. The privy council was already meeting.

Her father the warlord was already there, hunched over one end of the long table. On his left hand was Rusko, who had arrived at the palace with Urza and showed no sign of ever decamping. Indeed, the clockmaker had become the semiofficial liaison with the merchant guilds in Kroog and would only part with that title (and the perquisites included) when either he or Kroog was no more.

On the right side were the Captain of the Guard and the seneschal. The captain had been the warlord's squire back at the dawn of time but had aged less gracefully than her father, and in fact spent most of his time napping. The seneschal looked much as he had on her betrothal day. Probably his own frantic nervousness prevented any illness or misfortune from getting within twenty feet of him.

The three men were Daddy's closest advisors. And herself, of course—always welcome and always paid attention to. The four of them formed the warlord's privy council.

"Is he coming?" asked the warlord sternly.

"Is he ever?" replied the princess, trying to keep a bright tone in her voice. "No, he's wrapped up, breaking in his new apprentice."

The warlord looked a question at Rusko, who merely shrugged. "A new one to me. I'd bet this one lasts a month at the outside."

The princess took a seat next to Rusko. The clockmaker used to burble in the royal presence, but that had diminished and finally stopped some years before. Kayla realized she missed the fawning, just a little.

"What is the situation along the Sword Marches?" asked the warlord.

The Captain of the Guard sniffed and stifled a sneeze. Kayla always noticed that direct questions caused the old man to sneeze. "Steady," he mumbled. "The Fallaji are getting more and more brazen with each month. There's talk that one of the tribes is gaining control over the others."

"Another tribe besides the Tomakul?" asked the seneschal nervously.

The captain fought off another sneeze, then replied, "The city Fallaji are token heads, and I've heard that even they have agreed to go along with this new desert clan. Usually the tribes of the deep desert spend most of their time raiding each other."

"Except now," said the warlord. "They're raiding more caravans now."

"Or demanding exorbitant 'tolls,' " added Rusko, "or, in some cases, 'caretaker fees' for additional caravan guards they provide. It's extortion, sucking the lifeblood out of the merchant class!"

"And our patrols?" inquired the warlord.

The captain pinched his nose. "We have three companies along the marches. Once a caravan reaches Yotian territory, it is safe. There have been no raids into Yotia proper at all. But we don't have enough men to accompany every caravan across the desert."

"What about the ornithopters?" asked Kayla.

That question evoked a full-fledged sneeze, followed by a handkerchief produced with a flourish and a loud blast of the nose. "We could send them along with the caravans," the captain said at last, supporting Kayla's suggestion.

The warlord shook his head. "I wouldn't want anything like that falling into the Fallaji hands. How about using them to patrol the marches?"

The captain blinked hard. "We could. We don't have enough of them right now."

"Why not?" demanded the warlord.

The captain looked as if this query would produce another sneezing fit, so Rusko came to his aid. "The limit is not in raw machines, or even in young men and women foolhardy enough to want to fly them. The problem is power. The ornithopters run off an old Thran device, a power stone. The metal statues do the same. There aren't a lot of them in Yotia. Urza has been working to try to mend broken power stones, but it's an iffy job. We can build all manner of ornithopters, but they're just pretty kites without the proper stones. That's problem number one."

The warlord grunted. "Any place else we can get more stones?"

The seneschal spoke up in a meek voice. "The Argivians have collected a large number of stones over the years, but they use them for their own devices. And they are scouring the desert for more, I understand."

There was a pause. Kayla could see the wheels turn in her father's head. Whenever he started thinking like this, the result was normally trouble for someone.

"Captain," he said finally, "I want you to send exploration parties into the desert. They will carry descriptions of the stones so they know what to look for. We'll ask Urza about the most likely places to find them."

This last was not a question, so the captain nodded in agreement.

"But what if our parties meet Argivians looking for the same stones?" squeaked the seneschal.

"They'll probably be relieved to meet other civilized men in the desert, as opposed to those Fallaji fanatics," snapped the warlord. "But just to be sure, I want you to frame a letter to the Argivian king. Tell him what we're doing, but frame it in terms of mutual defense: All of us against the savages in the heartlands. That should calm him down enough. Anything else?"

Rusko spoke up. "One thing, Your Majesty." He produced from beneath the voluminous folds of his vest a small dish and a bottle of black powder. "With the Chief Artificer's successes, you have decreed that we keep our eyes open for other devices, either in old books or the marketplace, that could be used by Kroog to better protect itself. I think I have something that may be useful."

The former clockmaker laid the dish on the table; into it he poured a small amount of the black powder. The powder was crystallized into small spheres and reminded Kayla of shriveled peas. Rusko then rose and lit a taper from a nearby oil lamp. He touched the lit taper to the crystals, and they popped and burned brightly, setting up a cloud of noxious smoke that hung over the table.

That was too much for the old Captain of the Guard, who already had his kerchief over his face. The seneschal looked as if he was about to bolt for the door. The warlord waved a hand through the cloud. "Goblin powder," he grumbled. "What of it?"

"Goblin powder," agreed Rusko. "Also called dwarven fireblack, or black dust, or burningbright. It's a chemical concoction that the goblins and dwarves of the north use."

"And usually blow themselves up in the process," commented the warlord. Kayla leaned away from the table, in search of clean air.

"Because it is volatile, tricky, and temperamental," replied Rusko. "It's hard to use because you have to be close to it in order to light it, and if you are too close when the fuse burns down, you get blown up."

"It is used in small amounts for children's poppers, and other noisemakers," the seneschal ventured, "but it has no practical use."

"Ah," said Rusko, holding a hand up. "What if you could set a fuse and throw the powder at an enemy before it explodes? Or, better yet, if you could fit the container with a flint that causes a spark when it strikes the earth?"

"Sounds temperamental as ever," said the warlord. "You'd have to drop it from a great height to create such a spark. If you drop it from a wall, you blow up your support in the process."

Rusko nodded. "And if you dropped it, say, from an ornithopter?"

There was silence around the table. Then the warlord started to chuckle. "And the enemy could not throw it back. Yes, I like that idea."

"I have your permission to investigate further, then?" asked Rusko.

"Yes," said the warlord, still chuckling. "Yes, you do. Oh, and don't tell Urza about it, at least not yet. If he can't show up for the meetings, it serves him right."

The seneschal sniffed. "At least it will show him that *others* have good ideas."

"Agreed," said the warlord, slapping the tabletop with his hand. "Then we're adjourned. We have a lot to do, and we should get to it!"

But by that time Kayla was already halfway to the door, seeking to escape the stench of the burning powder, her heels clicking rapidly against the stone.

Chapter 9

Ashnod

The invasion party was stalled outside the walls of Zegon, and Hajar knew Mishra well enough to realize he was worried. But Mishra would not tell the qadir about his concerns. Nor, for that matter, would Hajar.

In the last few years the qadir had grown to manhood, and not all his development had been good. The eager young man who was interested in Argivian folktales had blossomed into an overweight tyrant. He was pampered by his tribe and supporters and appeased by the tribes that now followed the Suwwardi. No one said no to him. At least no one survived to say no a second time.

What was once petulance had now transformed into foul-tempered rants. What once was eager bravery was now foolhardiness. He had become fatter than his father ever had been but was still convinced he could lead battles himself. His moods were mercurial, his responses violent.

As the qadir grew more tyrannical, Mishra grew more popular among the Suwwardi. The former slave knew how to speak to the qadir in such a way that he could present the most unpalatable options and escape with his head still attached to his body. The qadir's war captains noticed this first, then the courtiers, and lastly the chiefs of other tribes. Soon those with bad news or new plans visited Mishra first for his advice and aid before speaking directly to the qadir.

For his part Mishra was open and welcoming to a people that had held him as a slave so recently. He was well versed in desert lore and legend and always had the correct analogy, the right words, and a ewer of *nabiz* handy. But he always made clear his advice was based

137

upon what was best for the Qadir of the Suwwardi; he crossed the qadir directly only with greatest reluctance.

Early on there was little need to argue with the qadir at all. There was a moment of wavering among some of the tribes, the Thaladin in particular, when word spread that the old qadir was dead. But such rumblings of independence were drowned by the greater rumblings of the dragon engine now possessed by the Suwwardi. Early on the young qadir made it a point to visit the main clans of each of his allies, strong or weak. Each was in turn impressed by the power of the great metal beast.

Some preached that it was a sign from the Old Ones themselves, a demonstration that they favored the Fallaji in their attempts to keep the desert free of such invaders as the Argivians and the Yotians. This despite the fact that the old qadir and a number of good Fallaji warriors had all perished in the dragon engine's initial attack.

Similarly, tribes now regarded the young qadir as the ruler of the *mak fawa*, handily ignoring the fact that it was really the qadir's wizard, his Argivian *raki*, who controlled the beast. But Fallaji logic was simple in this regard as well. The outlander wizard might control the beast, but the qadir controlled the wizard.

The Suwwardi soon discovered that only the *raki* could control the great dragon engine. As soon as he passed the power stone to another (with great reservations and only on the qadir's direct orders), the dragon engine reared up on its hind treads and threatened to run amok. After a few such experiments the gem was put permanently in Mishra's hands, and those in the tribe who knew of it were informed the gem would stay there. Mishra could put the beast to sleep while he rested and make it respond to his slightest whim. Indeed, Hajar noticed that soon no real words were spoken between the *raki* and his mechanical servant. A gesture or a nod was enough.

The Suwwardi conquest of the deep desert was not entirely without incident. A group of hotheads from the Thaladin clan tried to ambush the qadir's procession. The main part of the caravan retreated before their assault, and Mishra unleashed his dragon engine among the young riders. Fifteen died, including the Thaladin chieftain's son, without loss of a single Suwwardi. The Thaladin submitted soon afterward.

After solidifying his position in the eastern desert, the qadir looked west. Onion-domed Tomakul was the center of Fallaji power, its greatest and oldest city. Mishra said he was more concerned about Argivian patrols along the eastern borders and the increased activities of the Yotians to the south. In reality, Hajar knew he wanted more time to study his marvelous creature, but the qadir would not be dissuaded. The party headed west toward the capital. Time was of the essence, the qadir said, in order to counter any plans made in the halls of Tomakul's many palaces.

He need not have worried. Tomakul was as rotten as an old fruit, waiting for the slightest tap to split apart. In many ways the city dwellers were more like Yotians than Fallaji. They were preoccupied with wealth, money, and caravans. As long as the qadir promised to not interfere with their daily lives, they were quite content to open their gates to him. The qadir accepted their tribute but would not enter the city. Instead he camped beyond their walls in the shadow of his great beast and made the city folk come to him.

Hajar and Mishra had gone into the city. They found it beautiful and corrupt, wondrous and diseased. Here trade routes from the Sarinth to Kroog converged with those from the eastern coastal nations to Terisia City farther west. The last was no more than a legend to Hajar, a city of scholars far to the west, who traded with the desert folk for artifacts and old tales much as the Argivians had.

The city was a brightly colored cavalcade of different peoples: dwarves from Sardia, holy men of distant Gix, and minotaur mariners from some far-off islands. There were warriors in zebra-hide capes from Zegon and furred traders from the Yumok nation in the shadow of its great glacier. Yotian merchants trod the city streets as well, visibly nervous among the celebratory Fallaji. And there were other folk wandering the narrow byways who defied identification of homeland or race.

But in the end Hajar and Mishra retreated to the desert to confer with their qadir. Though Mishra strongly urged his chieftain to push on toward the west to this reputed city of scholars, the qadir determined they would move south instead. To Zegon they would go, he said, to the place that shared its heritage with the Fallaji and was rightfully part of their shared empire. Mishra argued, but in the end the qadir made it clear the matter was closed.

And now, mused Hajar, they were stalled outside the capital city of Zegon, with five hundred men and a mechanical dragon. Worse, the dragon was misbehaving.

It was a simple matter. When they got within a half-mile of the capital, the *mak fawa* stalled. It simply refused to proceed any farther toward the city. It could move to the east or west or back up, but it would not come any closer to Zegon, and no amount of mental commands, hand motions, shouting, or hitting it could convince the mechanical beast otherwise.

The qadir, not one to be denied, was apoplectic. He wanted the beast looming before Zegon's front gates when the city surrendered. Instead his armies were within sight of the city's whitewashed walls but could advance no farther. Hajar could see the city guard lined up on the battlements of the outer wall, spears in hand, almost taunting the qadir's armies. Some of the spears had skulls on their points, no doubt some additional Zegoni taunt Hajar was unfamiliar with.

The only thing the qadir's forces could do was make the best of a bad situation. The dragon engine began a long, slow patrol around the perimeter of the city, keeping the half-mile distance that seemed to hold it at bay like a physical wall. A message was sent to the leaders of Zegon, calling to their attention the power of the dragon engine and demanding the city's immediate capitulation.

The Zegoni sent back a terse note that they would consider the qadir's offer and he was welcome to wait while they made up their minds.

That defiance did not improve the qadir's mood. That evening in his tent he railed against his captains and in particular against his *raki*.

"Why can't you move it any closer?" he thundered.

"We don't know why," answered Mishra calmly.

"Why don't you know?" cried the qadir.

Because you have demanded we run all over the continent impressing the other tribes, thought Hajar. Because we have not had the time or the resources to study the beast, other than what hurried sketches we can make while moving from place to place. Because it has not been a priority for you until now. Hajar wondered if Mishra was thinking the same thing.

Instead the qadir's *raki* said, "It could be many things. Possibly there is something about the city itself that keeps us at bay. Or it may be something about the nature of the *mak fawa*. There may be some item the Zegoni have that's affecting the engine. We don't have enough information to be sure. Right now the question is, do we press on or do we fold our tents and abandon Zegon, contenting ourselves with the riches of a united desert nation?"

The qadir slumped back into his pillows, and a serving girl bathed his head with a damp cloth. He ignored her and said, "You have traveled through this land. It is rich in timber and metals. It is properly part of our empire. Its people are Fallaji in origin."

As much as the Tomakul were, thought Hajar. Indeed, from what he had seen of the Zegoni, they were much like the city-dwelling Fallaji in their mercantile outlook. He wondered idly if all the coastal nations had some unknown means of stopping the dragon engine and how the qadir would react if that were indeed the case.

The qadir was still talking. "We go on. We patrol with the dragon engine. We start leveling the smaller towns, beyond the half-mile radius. We drive people into the capital: panicked people, who tell of the monster that lies waiting beyond the gates. In the meantime we send messengers back to Tomakul to gather more warriors. We'll assemble enough to break down the walls if need be."

Hajar thought the plan represented the waste of a better part of a year, but if any of the war captains agreed with him they remained silent. A few advisors had argued loudly with the qadir in the past. They had disappeared soon afterward. The only one who seemed to get away with it was Mishra, and he had several tons of dragon to support his argument.

But Mishra only nodded and said, "We will need siege machinery. Nothing complex. Simple battering rams to assault their gates from all sides. That, in addition to a large amount of troops, should be enough."

Hajar wondered, not for the first or last time, why Mishra did not simply use the power of the dragon engine to escape from the qadir's petty tyranny or to establish himself as qadir. The former digger thought he knew the answer to that question, though. The *raki* could overturn the qadir and even maintain a core group of tribes to support him. But to what end? He had no apparent desire to rule over an empire or even over a small part of one. He would rather be the power behind the throne.

Hajar was still turning these matters over in his mind as he and Mishra walked back to the *raki*'s tent, located on the outskirts of the encampment on the off-chance that the *raki* might summon more dragons in the dead of night. Mishra was quiet, as he always was after one of the qadir's explosions.

A guard stood outside of the *raki*'s tent, which was unusual. More unusual, the brazier within was already lit, and the tent issued a warm, inviting glow.

"Visitor," said the guard. His accent was atrocious, and Hajar immediately pegged him as one of the westerners from the tribes around Tomakul.

"It is late," said Mishra.

The guard shrugged.

"Does the qadir know?" asked Mishra, earning another shrug.

Hajar felt his irritation rise at the guard. What good is a guard who doesn't guard anything? Is this the kind of man to whom we are trusting our empire?

"I see," said Mishra without apparent anger. "Go back to your duties."

The man gave a gold-toothed smile and faded back into the darkness.

Mishra stepped into his tent, regarding the interloper. "I've been expecting you," he said, much to Hajar's surprise. "I'm glad you made yourself at home in my absence."

The visitor was a woman, among the most cruelly beautiful women Hajar had ever seen. Red hair was rare in the desert and was taken as an evil omen among the Suwwardi. Hers was the red of a flickering camp flame. It rolled over her shoulders in thick, wavy curls. Her eyes were the gray-green of the sea that lapped Zegon's shores, and just as stormy. She was dressed in mannish armor of the outlander style, but the armor had been cut and shaped more to favor her figure than to offer any real protection.

Hajar realized he had stopped breathing. He inhaled deeply and wondered if she had noticed.

She was reclining on Mishra's pillows, and she stretched as he entered. "I was expected?" she asked. Her voice was soft but carried a razor's edge with it.

"You or someone like you," replied Mishra calmly. "You represent Zegon's rulers, and you're going to propose a deal to save your city."

"I don't remember telling anyone that but the guard I bribed," said the woman. "If he told you, I'll have to have him killed."

"Not to worry," returned Mishra. "He will be punished enough for letting an outlander into camp, regardless of the bribe. He will be made an example of, and in the end he will wish you had killed him. May I offer you some *nabiz*?"

"Please," said the woman, and Mishra motioned for Hajar to put a ewer of wine on the brazier. He sat down opposite the woman and waited for her to begin.

Instead she stared at Hajar. "Your manservant," she said coldly. Hajar bridled at the insult.

"He is my bodyguard," said Mishra.

"He should not be here," said the woman shortly.

"Go," said Mishra to Hajar, still staring intently at the woman.

Hajar began to protest, but Mishra cut him off. "Go to your tent. Tell no one. If I need anything, I will shout."

Hajar wavered a moment and looked at Mishra. The Argivian

revealed nothing but merely watched the woman sitting among his pillows. He seemed as he was with the qadir, thought Hajar: closed and unapproachable.

The Fallaji sighed deeply and bowed, then backed out of the tent. His face marked his disapproval.

"You are right, of course," said the woman as soon as Hajar had left. "I have been empowered by the rulers of Zegon to negotiate on their behalf with the Fallaji invaders."

"But you are not Zegoni," observed Mishra.

A small smile played across the woman's face. "And you are not Fallaji."

"I am Mishra, *raki* of the Suwwardi," returned Mishra.

"I am Ashnod," said the woman, "of nothing in particular."

"Is Zegon your home?" asked Mishra, running a hand over the rim of the metal ewer. The *nabiz* was almost ready.

"I did not say that," answered Ashnod.

"And you are loyal to them?" inquired the *raki*.

"I did not say that either," responded Ashnod. "I merely told you they empowered me to speak on their behalf. They agreed quite readily. I'm afraid some of them feel that if I make a muck of things and get myself killed, they can forswear me and will breathe more easily."

"And the offer you are presenting is . . . ?" inquired the Argivian, reaching for the heavy metal cups.

Ashnod cocked her head for a moment, then said, "Just a moment."

She reached down to the floor at the base of the pillows and brought up a long staff. It was made of black thunderwood and was topped by a tangle of copper wires and the narrow skull of some sea creature. She raised the staff quickly and pointed it at the doorway.

Ashnod barked a string of words, and the tangle of copper wires sang a discordant song. Wisps of lightning raced along the tracery of wires and into the skull itself. The staff lurched a fraction in her hand, but Mishra saw no obvious beam or other discharge.

He did see the effect. Just outside the tent entrance, Hajar gave a choked scream and fell into view, clutching his chest.

Mishra was on his feet at once, crossing the tent and kneeling beside his bodyguard. Hajar twitched as he stooped beside him.

"So cold," managed the Fallaji. "It feels so cold."

"We were to be left alone," said Ashnod stonily. She lowered the staff. Her forehead was damp with perspiration. "I hate it when underlings cannot follow orders."

The chill wave of nausea passed through Hajar, and slowly the world righted itself. "She . . ." he gasped, "she did . . . this."

"She did," agreed Mishra, helping his bodyguard to his feet. "Because you disobeyed an order. I told you to go to your tent."

"But—"

"Go now, old friend," said Mishra. Hajar looked at the young man, and there was nothing. No, there was the faint trace of a smile on his face. Mishra was pleased. By Hajar's loyalty? No, thought the bodyguard, there was more to it than that. He was pleased by something the woman had done? He was pleased Ashnod had attacked the bodyguard with her witch staff?

Hajar pulled himself to his feet.

"And Hajar . . ." said Mishra.

Hajar turned.

"Thank you for not screaming too loudly," said the Argivian. Again the ghost of a smile. "I want to talk to our guest before any guards arrive," he said. "Now go."

Hajar stumbled into the night. Mishra watched him disappear in the darkness before turning back.

Ashnod had taken the opportunity to pour the *nabiz* into its brass cups and was reclining on the pillows again, looking as if nothing out of the ordinary had occurred. The skull-tipped staff was back at the base of the pillows.

Mishra took his own cup and sat down opposite her. Then he laughed.

It started as a small chuckle, descended into a chortle, then moved into a full-fledged belly laugh. At length he offered his cup in a toast and said, "That was *very* foolish."

Ashnod looked indignant and did not raise her cup in response. "He was spying on us and disobeyed your order."

Mishra took a long pull on the *nabiz* and chuckled again. "No, not attacking Hajar. But by attacking him the way you did, you tipped your hand."

Ashnod gave him a cross look, and Mishra smiled. The woman noted it was a warm grin, without malice, and relaxed for the moment.

"That staff," Mishra said. "You made it?"

"Yes," she replied.

Mishra nodded to himself and smiled again. "That's what is keeping the dragon engine at bay, isn't it? The guards along Zegon's walls held similar staves. You made the staves and told the Zegoni rulers they could keep the great, evil Fallaji away from their city."

Slowly Ashnod nodded. "Your engine is a big target."

Mishra continued, "But your staves have a flaw. They take a lot out of the user."

Ashnod was silent.

"After using it only briefly, you are sweating," added Mishra.

Ashnod grunted. "Men sweat. Women glow."

"You were glowing like a horse after a hard race then," Mishra chuckled. "And if the city guards were similarly affected, they would be debilitated. The rulers of Zegon would not be pleased by that."

Ashnod snorted. "The rulers were all too quick to adopt my staves for their defense," she said. "Once the guards started to weaken from their use, those same rulers panicked."

"And sent you into the desert to sue for peace," added Mishra. "They probably said it was your idea that encouraged them to resist, so it was your fault."

"You've met the Zegoni before," said Ashnod, a small smile crossing her lips as well.

"I've dealt with their type in many forms," said Mishra, leaning back. "So tell me, what do they want? Bare minimum."

Ashnod took a deep breath. "Tomakul's deal. They surrender, pay some tribute, recognize your boy as ultimate leader, and get back to their lives."

Mishra considered. "Sounds reasonable. Not to say that the qadir will be reasonable. After all, you did stop us in our tracks, if only temporarily. I'll see what I can do."

The Argivian set his cup down. "Now let me see your toy."

Ashnod leaned forward and hefted the staff. She looked into Mishra's eyes for a moment, as if trying to determine what malice, if any, lay within. Then she handed the staff to him.

The Fallaji *raki* turned the staff over in his hands. "I see some Thran influences, but this is new. How does it work?"

"It affects the nerves of the body," replied Ashnod. "The lightning in the staff upsets the body's mechanism that allows one to feel and distinguish pain. Too much upset, and the target is incapacitated. At the range of your dragon engine, it was not severely affected, but it would come no closer."

"Nerves," said Mishra, nodding and tapping the small power crystal that had been set within the staff's skull.

"Right," agreed Ashnod, setting her cup down and leaning forward. "The body has all manner of systems within it. Living tubes for blood, soft wires for nerves, strands of cable for muscle." She reached out, touching Mishra's arm. He did not flinch or pull away. "You are no book scholar. Your arms are like spun steel."

"Life in the desert is hard," said Mishra softly. "I never thought of the body as a machine."

"It is the best machine!" said Ashnod, releasing his arm. "Tested in the field, continually growing, and self-replicating! Once we understand the mysteries of our own bodies, we understand the world. Everything else will fall into place. Your dragon engine is a wonder, but it is a crude imitation of living things."

Mishra chuckled. "This is the first *real* conversation I've had in a long while."

Ashnod curled up amongst the pillows. "There is a lack of intellectual companionship among the Fallaji?"

Mishra laughed and leaned forward. "Most of the conversations I've had with the Suwwardi are along the lines of, 'You give me that' in various forms, followed closely by, 'You and what army.' " The young man chuckled again and set down the staff. "I hadn't considered the body as a machine, but it makes sense. After all, we create things in our own image. Perhaps the Thran did as well." He moved over and sat next to Ashnod.

Ashnod leaned close; Mishra could smell her musky perfume, accented with the tang of drying sweat. It was a pleasant combination.

"I think I can convince the qadir to accept your ruler's request," he said softly.

"I thought you could," said Ashnod. "You seem very capable."

"There's that."

Ashnod wondered if Mishra smiled at anyone else in that fashion. The *raki* added, "And the fact that our most revered one is still as impatient as a child. If he had to wait for reinforcements from Tomakul he would explode from the delay. Of course, there is one other thing."

Ashnod pulled away from him. "One other thing?"

Mishra said, "The Zegoni must be seen to pay for their token resistance. They must suffer more than Tomakul, which threw open its gates to us. We will need an additional guarantee."

"Guarantee?" asked Ashnod.

"The Fallaji take hostages to encourage obedience," said Mishra, "Surely taking their premier artificer would be sufficient?"

Ashnod's eyes became slits. "And would I be a Fallaji hostage, or yours?"

Mishra smiled again, and there was a touch of maliciousness in the expression. "The Fallaji have little use for women," he said, "beyond the basics."

"The basics do not include intelligent conversation, correct?" inquired Ashnod.

"You have the general idea," returned her companion. "You would be viewed more as something we are denying the Zegoni, as opposed to something to benefit the tribe."

Ashnod leaned forward and touched Mishra's cheek. "Hostage is such a nasty word. How does 'assistant' sound?"

Mishra's eyebrows raised for a moment, then settled again. "Is that really what you came here for?"

"Am I so transparent?" she asked, coy once again.

"As glass," said Mishra and laughed. "When would you like to begin your lessons?"

"Lessons in the morning," said Ashnod in a throaty whisper. "This evening we are alone. I don't think your bodyguard is coming back anytime soon."

Mishra smiled and closed the grate on the brazier. There were no more words that evening.

In the morning it was announced that the City of Zegon, fearful of the great dragon engine, had joined the Fallaji Empire. Tribute would be paid, and obeisance made to the great and revered Qadir of the Suwwardi, ever the first among equals.

As terms of their surrender, the Zegoni agreed to remove the gates of their city so they could never stand in opposition to the Fallaji again. And they gave up their best artificer, who joined the Fallaji camp as the *raki's* apprentice. If any of the warriors felt uncomfortable about the presence of the cold-eyed woman with the cursed hair in their midst, they did not say so, at least not where the *raki* could overhear.

Soon afterward, word arrived that the outlanders along the coast were making heavy raids into Fallaji lands, and the invasion force turned east again.

Chapter 10

Korlis

The Chief Artificer had missed so many meetings of the privy council that his absence was no longer even commented upon. Rusko was there as his official representative, but Kayla knew that Urza hardly spent any time talking to Rusko anymore either. The Chief Artificer spent most of his time working with the new apprentice, Tawnos, who had lasted much longer than Rusko had predicted, much to the clockmaker's chagrin.

There was a new Captain of the Guard; the old one had finally retired to spend time with his horses and grandchildren. The warlord chose this one himself, and the new captain mirrored many of the ruler's qualities—he was impulsive, decisive, and active. Patrolling the borders was not enough, this new captain said when he first rose to the position. The Yotians must secure a corridor to Tomakul itself in order to protect the caravans.

Now the privy council picked through the rubble of that plan. Armed patrols to Tomakul encouraged even larger attacks from the desert nomads. Fallaji tribesmen were now raiding into the Sword Marches, which had been relatively free of such incursions since the warlord had driven the native tribes out in his youth. Yotia did not have the manpower to both maintain its borders and guarantee safe passage to the desert capital.

"We need to pull the plants out by the roots," said the new captain. "Go into the desert, find the Fallaji base, and crush it!"

"If you can show me where it is and guarantee that it would still be there when we get there, I will gladly try," grumbled the warlord. "But the desert is like an ocean. Most of it is empty, and we do more damage to our own forces than to the Fallaji by taking the battle there. They are at home in the desert. We are not."

"There are the ornithopters," said the captain. "We can scout the desert with them."

"Still few in number," said Rusko. "There are no more than two dozen in all, and the Chief Artificer is wary of exposing them to the risk. We practically had to break his arm to convince him to allow them as scouts along the border."

"And what of the search for more Thran stones?" asked the warlord.

"Slow and tedious," said Rusko. "There are raiders everywhere, and they seem to be able to smell out our exploration parties. Bok and Mabok preserve us!"

"T-th-the Argivians have the same problem," stammered the seneschal. "They have been attempting to find more stones as well, but have met heavy resistance."

The warlord stroked his chin. "Perhaps it is time to provide a unified front."

"With the Argivians?" hiccoughed the seneschal.

"And the Korlisians as well," returned the warlord. "Perhaps it is time to bring the coastal nations together. Do you think a combined front, offering peace, could lure these savages out of their desert?"

The captain sputtered for a moment, then said, "You think we should *talk* with those savages? After all the men we have lost?"

"You're not listening," said the warlord patiently. "I asked if a combined front, offering peace, could lure their leaders into one place."

The captain cocked his head to one side, then said, "Yes. Yes, I think it would." An ugly smile passed over his face.

"They would be more likely to accept the invitation," added the seneschal, "if it were extended by the merchants of Korlis—"

"—Who do not share a border with the Fallaji," finished the captain, "and as such pose no immediate threat."

"And the Korlisians," added the warlord thoughtfully, "want to get their own ornithopters, which both we and the Argivians have. This would be an excellent opportunity for them to gain them, should they get the Fallaji leaders to the table."

The warlord chuckled and the captain joined his merriment. For Kayla, entirely too much was unsaid. The men masked their thoughts with a cover of words.

"So we are talking peace with the Fallaji?" she asked.

"Yes," replied her father, his face suddenly somber. "We are *talking* peace. But we will also make sure we talk from a position of strength." He thumped the table with the flat of his hand. "Meeting adjourned. Goodsir Rusko, I want you to stay and update me on your"—he glanced at Kayla—"special project."

The captain and seneschal left, speaking animatedly about the diplomatic requirements for the proposed gathering. Kayla departed as well, her metal heels sliding softly against the marble floor. Something else had happened at the table, something she was present for but not privy to. Previous conversations had been enigmatically concluded in her presence.

It boiled down to one thing, she thought: Daddy was up to something. Even though she was a grown woman, he still sought to spare her certain harsh facts about the world: Her mother's death; the plans for her marriage; anything that smacked of secrets, battle, or hardship for others.

He was up to something now. Of that Kayla had no doubt. And it involved Rusko but not her husband.

Despite herself, her footsteps took her toward the orniary. She found her husband and the broad-shouldered Tawnos alone in the domed room. They had dismissed the remainder of the students for the day. Tawnos was stripped to the waist and bending a thick spar of candlewood along a graceful line chalked against one wall. Kayla knew enough to recognize it as a wing support for one of the ornithopters. The tall toy maker grunted with the effort, and his muscles bulged as he bent the spar to match the chalk line exactly.

"Hold it!" said Urza, dropping beneath Tawnos's grip and wiring the newly curved section back to the ornithopter's main spine. "Now bend it the other way."

Tawnos gasped and twisted the beam in the other direction, forming an **S**-shaped curve. Kayla was impressed. Candlewood was light, but the spar the young man was manhandling was the thickness of her wrist. And, she thought, Tawnos looked very good stripped to the waist.

"Husband, we need to talk," Kayla said.

Urza quickly held up a hand and waved it slightly, but Kayla would not be dissuaded. "No, we need to talk."

Urza looked up at his assistant. "Go ahead. I'll wait," said Tawnos through clenched teeth.

Urza turned toward his wife. His hair had gone entirely white, probably, thought Kayla, due to the amount of work he'd been doing. He was dressed in the heavy leather smock that had practically become his second skin over the years. "I'm sorry, dear," he said, "but I am very busy."

"You are always very busy," snapped Kayla, "except when you are sleeping. And even then you seem restless." She relented and held out a hand to stroke his cheek.

Urza flinched slightly at the touch. He reached up and gently took her hand. "It's just that we may have a way to improve the diving speed of the ornithopters. Tawnos has suggested that if we truly shape the spar to resemble a predatory bird's wing, then it would be more maneuverable as well."

Kayla nodded and pushed his words aside unconsidered. "I think Father is planning something."

Urza sighed, and looked at his assistant. Tawnos gave a good-natured nod, but his veins were standing out at his neck from holding the candlewood spar in its twisted position. To Kayla Urza said, "Your father is always planning something. That's what he does best."

The princess sighed and shook her head. "It's not that. He wants to negotiate with the Fallaji leaders and to get the Argivians and Korlisians involved as well."

"That's good," said Urza abstractedly, watching the way the wing spur lined up against the chalk mark on the wall. "Most of the Fallaji I've known have been rational men, even if there are problems with the caravans and a few hotheaded leaders. And your father is too sharp to let Argivians get away with anything. What's the problem?"

"He never wanted to talk to the Fallaji before," Kayla said.

"People change." Urza shrugged, his eyes never leaving the line of the wing.

You don't, thought Kayla, but instead she said, "I don't know. I just think something is wrong with this situation."

Urza looked at Kayla and sighed deeply. "Your father is a reasonable man. An old war-horse, but a reasonable man. There are reasonable men among the Fallaji. Even among the Argivians. I'm sure things will work out."

"Uh, Master Urza?" called Tawnos. "It's beginning to slip a little."

"I have to go," said Urza. He turned back to the spar.

"But what about—" began his wife.

Urza held up a hand as he walked away. "Your father wants peace. Sounds good, though a little odd. Argivians involved. Probably he'll tell you what's going on eventually."

There was the sound of a metal-heeled foot stomping the floor behind him, and the brisk clatter of heels storming out of the room. It ended in a resounding slam of the orniary doors.

"What was that about?" asked Tawnos, sweat streaming down his face.

"I'm not quite sure," returned Urza. "Kayla worries about her father too much. Bend the wing spar a little more convex there. That's it. Now, hold it. . . . "

* * * * *

The announcement was made the following month. Representatives of Argive, Yotia, and Korlis were to meet in Korlis to discuss the problems with the desert raiders. Runners were sent under a flag of truce to Tomakul, Zegon, and other Fallaji towns to invite the qadir of the Suwwardi to attend as well. Safe conduct was promised to all attendees.

The coastal nations selected not Korlis's main city itself as the site for the meeting, but rather an outpost town, Korlinda, located farther up the Kor River, on the haunches of the Kher Ridges themselves. Should the Fallaji appear, the warlord said, they would have less distance to travel. Kayla thought there was another purpose behind the location. The Fallaji would be far from their traditionally claimed land, and the civilized nations would have ample warning of how large their party was before it arrived.

Urza was pried loose from his orniary only by the announcement that two of his older ornithopters would be provided as a gift to the people of Korlis. A full force of a dozen winged machines would appear at the meeting, and two would be left behind. After Urza complained that he would have to be present to tell the Korlisian how to maintain the ornithopters, the warlord graciously extended an invitation to the artificer.

Knowing he had been outmaneuvered, Urza protested no further but instead worked out a schedule that provided for a minimum amount of time away from his shop. The warlord and his entourage would leave early; he would follow with the ornithopters five days before the session began. He also left detailed instructions for Tawnos and the students to follow while he was gone. Tawnos thought at the time that Urza spent more time detailing the tasks that needed to be done in his absence than the tasks themselves would take, but he merely nodded when the Chief Artificer handed over the ream of parchment.

Urza's metal humanoid would also be sent out to the meeting, but would go by wagon. Rusko was in charge of this move and used one of the spring-axled wagons Urza had developed the previous year. The clockmaker was particularly interested in a vehicle that would not rock excessively, though Urza pointed out that his metal creation could walk to Korlis and probably make better time than Rusko would. Rusko, for his part, invoked a number of Yotian and non-Yotian deities and insisted he did not want to have to come back and tell the artificer that his great creation had been lost due to a broken limb assembly or had been spotted by farmers while walking through eastern Korlis and accidentally dismantled.

In the end Tawnos was left behind with the school; Kayla remained behind as well. The warlord cited the dangers of travel, even through friendly lands. He needed her and the seneschal, he said, to remain behind and run the country in his absence. He did, however, take the Captain of the Guard with him. The royal party left at midsummer's day, and Urza left twenty days later with his flight of ornithopters.

The natives of Kroog threw celebrations at the drop of a plumed hat, and both departures were filled with much pomp and cheering. The warlord rode out at the head of his royal caravan, mounted on a powerful horse, the descendant of ones he had ridden in his great war triumphs. For many of the natives of Kroog, that was how he would always be remembered: astride his stallion in full armor, cantering at the head of his forces.

Yet even that departure paled before the celebration when Urza and the ornithopters took off.

They had cleared the palace's great court for the departure, and for the week before Urza camped on the site with his craft. He double-checked every strut and spar and made sure there were sufficient spare parts to cover every eventuality. Tawnos mentioned to Kayla that they were carrying enough components to knit an additional ornithopter if need be.

The crowds started gathering as the week progressed, watching Urza move between the machines, checking figures with Tawnos, testing and retesting wires, and going over charts and schedules. An electric thrill mounted as the crowd swelled. All had seen the ornithopters before; they were a common sight in the skies over Kroog. Yet never had the citizens seen so many together at once.

On the morning of the departure Kayla appeared to wish her husband well. The crowds watched the couple embrace and imagined quiet, tender words spoken between them. Then Urza gave the signal to Tawnos. Tawnos in turn waved to the rest of the flight to prepare their crafts as Urza climbed into his ornithopter's white housing.

As one the ornithopter pilots engaged their power stones, and the great winged devices came to life. Slowly they pumped the air, limbering up the wings that had been carefully prepared and preened for days previously. A wave of applause swept through the gathered crowd. A few of the pilots waved from the windows, bringing another, louder round of clapping.

Then the beating of the wings intensified. Urza's craft, the one with the double-curved wings, took a little hop, and then suddenly was airborne, as effortlessly as a bird in flight. The two ornithopters behind it took similar hops, and they were aloft as well. Then the two behind those joined in the flight. In turn each pair of ornithopters arose from the courtyard like a flock of startled doves. The assembled citizens of Kroog cheered as they took to the sky.

The ornithopters took a long, leisurely arc around the palace of Kroog, beating wings to gain altitude, and the crowd yelled itself raw as they did so. The people waved pennants and threw the small smoke-poppers that had become popular of late. Some climbed the higher spires and waved great flags. The ornithopters locked their wings and gave a wing dip in response to the shouting populace. Then they were gone, dancing into the morning sun.

The people watched them until they were lost from sight, until other buildings or the low hills to the east blocked the view or, for those who had climbed the spires, when the ornithopter fleet had become small, indistinct dots on the horizon. A few watched the princess, however, and some claimed that her eyes were wet and that she dabbed them with her kerchief as she turned back to her palace, the seneschal at her side.

In the days and months that followed, some would say she had wept because her husband was leaving her. Some would say it was because she had dreamed what was about to happen and knew she could not change it. And some would say that she knew that the end of her small part of the world and the destruction of Kroog would begin at the Council of Korlis.

* * * * *

The machines performed remarkably well, and took only four days to make the trip to Korlinda. Urza had ordered Rusko to set up a series of base camps between Kroog and Korlinda as the clockmaker pushed eastward with the wagons. All the camps were in Yotian territory and in clear terrain. Each was fully operational by the time Urza's ships reached it, ready with soft beds and hot meals for the pilots after they had completed their day's flying.

The weather was clear and pristine, and even the storms that regularly lashed the southeastern coast of Terisiare seemed to have gone on holiday. Urza had allowed for an extra day of flying time in case of heavy thunderstorms, which normally roosted in the southern Khers, but there was not so much as a heavy ground fog for the entire trip.

Indeed the most difficult problem the pilots faced was the Yotians themselves. At every base camp a collection of spectators assembled, all curious about the Chief Artificer and his mighty machines. They clustered around the fields, waiting for the craft, and on occasion the ornithopters would be forced to pass close over the crowd in order to disperse them and create a large enough site on which to land. One of the pilots observed it was like herding sheep, but he said it too close to the Chief Artificer. That pilot spent the rest of the flight in the rear of the formation and did not speak again for the rest of the trip.

And once they had landed, there were requests for favors—in particular, for rides. Urza at first refused, but the pilots, even after a full day at the controls, were willing to volunteer the time to take young children and teenagers aloft. Finally Urza gave his assent but made clear he was not going to provide rides himself or allow anyone to fly his white craft with the double-curved wings.

The pilots had all been chosen by Rusko, who said he had done so to save Urza time. They were at least five years Urza's junior and had an enthusiasm the artificer did not remember having possessed at the same age. The majority were known for stunt flying, for pushing their crafts as far as they could go, and several had walked away from nasty crack-ups. Urza would have chosen those with a better technical background and a higher safety rating, but he knew anyone properly vetted and trained could be a suitable pilot for the ornithopters. Indeed during this trip even the most cavalier of the young men flew dead level and kept in formation with Urza's ornithopter for the entire journey.

The site that had been chosen for the council was near the meeting point of the three "civilized" nations of eastern Terisiare. Where the River Kor tumbled from the Khers into the first of several level plateaus stepping down to the Shielded Sea was a suitable spot. It was also connected at the point with an anomalous sliver of no-man's-land, an undulating strip that followed the inhospitable peaks of the Kher Ridges, as yet unofficially claimed by any side in the dispute.

The site was a huge, level field with a great, open-air pavilion erected in the center over a raised platform. Four other camp areas surrounded the central pavilion, one for each of the attendees. When Urza arrived, three sides of the square had been complete. The warlord's Yotians formed the western side of the square, the mercantile Korlisians were to the south, and the Argivians occupied the eastern side. The space to the north of the pavilion was empty. That had been reserved for the Fallaji, though none knew if they would appear.

Urza set down his ornithopter to the west, near the Yotian camp. The other pilots followed with military precision. Each ornithopter swooped, hovered for moment on back-pushing wings, then settled in place. There were no crowds here, no rush of commoners hoping to catch a glimpse of the Chief Artificer and his pilots. The Yotians were familiar with ornithopters, and the representatives of the two other nations feigned disinterest for purely political reasons.

If Urza had hoped to meet any of Tocasia's former students among the Argivian delegation, he was disappointed. The Argivians were, to a man, bureaucrats and diplomats with strong connections to the Argivian king. Argivian politicians considered that the artifact-hunting scholars and their supporting nobles held radical views in the matter of the Fallaji, namely that the desert should be free and open for Argivian exploration. The Crown, though weak, felt otherwise: Argive should end where the hills grew rough and waterless, and the Fallaji should be left to their desert ways. Since the Crown chose who went to Korlinda, all the Argivians sent were isolationist in nature, hoping to obtain a quick treaty, recognized borders, and a safe retreat back home. The warlord was visibly irritated by their presence.

The Argivians did bring their own ornithopters, but these were primitive in design, little advanced beyond the constructs that Urza, his brother, and Tocasia had pulled from the embankment of the dry wash many years before. Urza learned from the Argivian pilots that the Crown had put a claim on all salvage from the desert and had appropriated most of Tocasia's legacy. The noble houses continued to dig and explore the desert, but many no longer told the Crown what they found there.

The Korlisians were pure merchants; the ruling council of that nation had rested in the hands of the guilds for generations. The current lord of the council was a portly woman. Her opinion, and the opinion of the well-dressed merchants in attendance, was that they would negotiate dearly but without a doubt would secure unmolested trade routes to Tomakul. The warlord seemed to tolerate them only slightly more than he did the Argivians.

Each of the civilized countries brought its own honor guards. Yotia's force was the largest, Argive's was the most ornately armored, and Korlis's was the best equipped, as benefited mercenaries in the merchants' employ.

Urza retreated to his own tent, where Rusko already had uncrated his metal humanoid. The transit had not been kind to the metallic titan, and something had jarred loose in one of its ankles. Urza spent the first night and part of the next day fixing it so the mechanical creature would be fit to operate in time for the opening ceremonies.

The opening came and passed without the Fallaji's presence. Official introductions were made and professional courtesies established. There was much talk of cooperation, most of it over the course of a large feast in the pavilion the first night. The Fallaji did not appear during the day, nor did any of the outriders report signs of them.

Urza spent most of that day dressed in the high-collared, stiff-necked gowns of office, which he had worn previously only once: at his official appointment as Chief Artificer. The robes were fire-red with white piping and covered his body from neck to ankles. In the summer warmth of the highlands they were unbearable, and Urza's only consolation was that the official dress of most of the rest of the assemblage looked even more uncomfortable.

The second day came and went in similar fashion, though by the day's end the alliance of the three coastal nations was already starting to fray. The representatives of the Argivian king refused to admit there were any incursions from Argive into the Fallaji territory. The king did, however, have a surplus of functional power stones, which he was willing to use as bargaining chips to buy agreement from the Korlisians and Yotians. The warlord was insulted by such a blatant bribe but knew both his country and the merchants could use the Thran stones. The Korlisians were already on the verge of self-destruction since only two ornithopters were to be left behind and no fewer than five major guilds felt they had the rights to them. Tense words threatened to break into open squabbles, and by the end of the second day all parties took their evening meals in their own camps.

There was still no word from the Fallaji, and many were starting to say the conference would disband without them appearing. The warlord spoke of insults to the Yotian people by their absence, and the Argivian diplomats spoke of patience. The Korlisians seemed visibly worried they would not get their ornithopters if the Fallaji did not appear, since the warlord had thrown an armed guard around the flying craft.

The Fallaji appeared on the morning of the third day, without warning. There was a low mountain fog that day, and as it slowly burned off, the desert people were suddenly . . . there.

None had seen them arrive, but as the mist lifted there appeared lines of tents clustered around a large, white central tent. The desert people outnumbered any two of the other groups combined, and all apparently were warriors.

A path had been cleared from the Fallaji tents to the main pavilion, and down this pathway came a strange procession. First marched an honor guard of warriors with gold, broad-brimmed helmets. Then came a litter carrying the qadir of the Fallaji's self-styled empire. But it was at the object behind the qadir that most of the assembled personages gawked in a way they had not done when the Yotian ornithopters had arrived.

It was a huge device made of brass, fashioned in the shape of a dragon. The morning sun glittered off the condensation along its flanks, and its head twisted slowly from side to side. Its front legs were like those of a legendary dragon, but its rear quarters were a collection of cogs and treads, and it churned the earth as it moved.

The procession moved forward with slow, stately grace, in part to give the other members of the council time to prepare for the official meeting. The warlord assembled his staff on the pavilion first, including Urza and his mechanical man. The device that had won Kayla's hand seemed woefully insufficient to deal with the titanic monster that approached. Urza followed his father-in-law's pitying look at his creation, and his own countenance grew stern.

The Korlisians gathered as well, their lord patiently waiting alongside the warlord as the Fallaji approached. The Argivians were late; its representatives pulled on their ceremonial jackets just as the procession reached the base of the pavilion.

The honor guard parted, and the litter carrying the qadir came forward. Urza noted that the ruler of the Fallaji Empire, though younger than he, was already running to fat, and his flesh strained at his ceremonial robes.

A stocky individual stepped out from behind the litter and Urza's jaw dropped in shock. Mishra stood among the Fallaji.

He was dressed in jade green robes, cut in the desert fashion with high slits along both legs to allow the wearer to ride and fight easily. He wore a cloth around his forehead, this also of green, embroidered with gold lettering in the Fallaji tongue.

In his amazement Urza did not notice for a moment the female accompanying his brother, a stunning red-haired woman bearing an ornate staff, one tipped with a dolphin's skull.

Mishra halted next to the qadir's litter, as if listening to last-minute instructions. His eyes flicked across the assembled group and stopped when they reached Urza. It could have been a trick of the morning light, but to Urza it seemed as if Mishra nodded at him.

Urza returned the greeting with a slight bob of the head. Mishra stepped forward and addressed the gathered representatives of the other nations.

"Greetings, most respected authorities and agents of the Eastern Nations. I am Mishra, the chief advisor of the qadir of the Suwwardi, first among equals of the Fallaji peoples. His most wise and respected excellency gives you his greetings, his apologies, and asks for your indulgence.

"He gives you his greetings, for he hopes that matters will be resolved here to avoid further bloodshed on all sides. He makes his apologies for being so tardy in his arrival. We came here by mountain paths that many had thought lost, and had to proceed carefully. And last, he begs your indulgence, for his has been a long journey, and he would appreciate an opportunity to rest before attending to the task at hand. He would like to return to this pavilion after the noon meal to formally begin his work. He and I thank you for both the invitation and for your patience in this matter."

Mishra made a deep bow. The qadir did not wait for a response from the other council members. Instead he silently raised his hand. As one, the Fallaji procession reversed course. The dragon engine backed toward the Fallaji camp, followed by the litter and the honor guard. Mishra and the woman took up the rear, but the dark-haired young man lingered just long enough to look over his shoulder.

Urza shouted, "Brother!" and stepped forward, away from the rest of his delegation. He could hear the other delegates suddenly burst into a buzz of gossip. He looked back and saw the warlord look stern. Rusko was at the warlord's side and whispered something in the ruler's ear. The warlord nodded, and Urza turned back to his brother.

Mishra turned around entirely now. The woman next to him

tightened her grip on her staff, but the younger brother raised a hand and dismissed her as well. She hesitated a moment, then turned and followed the rest of the retreating Fallaji.

Mishra stood statue-stiff as Urza descended from the pavilion. The younger brother did not extend his hand, but rather stood calmly, hands folded before him. Urza stopped a few feet away and assumed an identical position, hands folded in front of him.

"Brother," repeated Urza.

"Brother," replied Mishra.

A long silence grew between them, and each studied the other. To Urza, Mishra looked more weather-beaten, tanned, and muscular than the last time he had seen him. To Mishra, Urza looked leaner and older than before. The younger brother noticed small lines were already growing around his older sibling's eyes. Urza's flesh was the pasty color of the city dwellers.

Finally Urza said, "It is good to see you are well."

Mishra replied, "I am well enough. And you?"

Urza nodded briefly, then added, "I am surprised to see you among the Fallaji delegation."

"I must confess that I am not surprised to see you among the Argivians," returned Mishra.

"Yotians, actually," corrected his brother.

Mishra nodded smoothly. "Ah. Of course. That would explain why the Yotians are suddenly so interested in raiding for power stones and Thran devices."

"Exploring," said Urza. "Yotians do not raid."

"Of course," repeated Mishra, a tight smile appearing on his face. "It must be as you say. We shall let the diplomats parse the words for us."

Urza gave a stiff nod. "I had heard that the Fallaji had unified with surprising speed. But I had not heard your name mentioned."

Mishra gave a pronounced bow. "I am but a simple *raki*, a servant of the qadir, his name be most revered, his thoughts be most wise." Another silence followed his words.

Urza let the pause play out, as if unsure what to say next. "I am the Chief Artificer of Kroog," he said finally.

Mishra allowed himself another smile. "How very nice. I thought I recognized a metal soldier among your ranks. One of yours?"

Urza nodded, and Mishra added, "Clearly influenced by the *su-chi* you studied as a lad. It shows in the knees."

Urza said, "I built it as a challenge," but did not elaborate.

Another uncomfortable silence grew. This time Mishra broke it. "I trust you have been well?"

"Very well," said Urza; then his eyebrows shot up. "I am married, you know."

"I did not know," returned his brother. "I am surprised to find there exists a woman who could tear you away from your books and researches."

"Her name is Kayla. She is the warlord's daughter," said Urza.

"Ah," said Mishra quietly, but said nothing else.

Another silence. Behind Urza, most of the delegates had dissolved into tight little groups. The warlord remained in the pavilion, watching the two brothers talk.

Finally Urza said, "That young woman who was with you. Is she . . . ?"

"Ashnod?" Mishra shifted as if uneasy. "She is my apprentice. She is very talented."

"Most likely," replied his older brother. "I too have an apprentice. Tawnos. Another Yotian. And a school with about twenty students."

"Ah," repeated Mishra, his face very cold. "Very good for you. It sounds as if you are thriving."

"And you," asked Urza, "do you have a school?"

Mishra shook his head. "The desert does not allow such luxuries. We must fight to stay alive. Learning is what you pick up as you go along."

"You seem to have picked up an interesting device as well," remarked Urza.

"Yes," said Mishra, and this time the smile was genuine.

"It does not look like any Thran device we ever uncovered," said Urza. "Where did you find it?"

"Beneath the sand," returned his brother. "I had a hunch. It just came to me."

"You always had a talent for such things," said Urza. A tentative smile shaped itself on his lips. "Perhaps later you'll tell me the full story and favor me with a chance to look at it." He added quickly, "I've made some changes to Tocasia's original ornithopter. I'd like to show them to you as well."

Mishra was silent for a moment. Then he said, "I would like that very much. Later, perhaps, when this conference is resolved." He bowed deeply and backed away a step, lowering his head to indicate the conversation was over.

Urza half-turned away. The Mightstone around his neck felt heavy. He touched the stone, then turned back. "Mishra?"

Mishra looked up. His hand was touching the pouch resting on his chest. "Yes, Brother?"

Urza's face twisted for a moment, and his next words were halting, "It . . . is . . . good to see you again."

"And you," said Mishra smoothly.

"After this is all finished," said the older brother, "we need to talk. You and I. About what we have been doing. About the past."

"The past exists all around us," said the younger brother calmly. "The only question is whether we choose to dig it up or not."

* * * * *

The warlord summoned Urza at once when he returned to the Argivian camp. As the artificer entered the warlord's tent, the ruler was seated in his camp chair, flanked by the Captain of the Guard and Rusko.

"Your brother is Fallaji?" spat the warlord.

Urza shook his head. "My brother is not Fallaji, but he serves their qadir, as I serve you."

"Why did you not tell me?" demanded the sovereign.

"Until today, I didn't even know he was still alive," returned Urza.

"I see," said the warlord, leaning back in his camp chair, Rusko, watching quietly from his side, thought the ruler did see, though not necessarily what Urza intended. The warlord's enemies had an ally obviously every bit as talented as his son-in-law. The taste of that revelation was sour.

"What has he been doing with them?" asked the warlord.

"I do not know," returned Urza, shrugging expressively.

"How did he end up with them?" continued the warlord. His feet kicked restlessly at the stool in front of him.

"I do not know," repeated the Chief Artificer.

"What can that mechanical behemoth do?" demanded the warlord. His voice was rising in volume, and Rusko felt the temperature in the tent growing hotter.

Urza held up his hands before him to show his lack of knowledge. "We spoke of it only briefly."

The warlord rubbed his lower lip; his fingers came away stained with blood. "Here's one I hope you can answer. Can you build one like it?"

Urza thought for a moment. "Probably. If I get a chance to examine it. Mishra says that he found it in the desert. But it is much more advanced than any Thran device I've ever seen. I do not think it is Thran at all."

The warlord muttered half to himself, half to the captain and Rusko, "We have patrols scouring the sand for stones, and his brother finds an ancient mechanical behemoth, fully functional."

"He says he found it," said Urza stoically. "I don't know if that's the truth."

"You don't know if your brother is truthful?" said the warlord quickly, raising an eyebrow.

"I didn't say that, either," said Urza, hotly. "We . . . we did not part on the best of terms."

"So Rusko has told me," said the warlord.

"Later, we will talk, he and I," offered Urza.

"If there is a later," said the chieftain, shaking his head. "These Fallaji played a trick on us, with their behemoth. We were prepared to show them our power, demonstrating our ornithopters and the mechanical man. Instead they roll up with a legendary beast the size of a ship. The Argivians are all ready to bolt, and the Korlisians want to thank everyone for coming, take their ornithopters, and go home. No, those desert raiders aided by your brother pulled a fast one on us. And we have to respond."

Urza did not question the warlord's words, even when he was dismissed and Rusko and the young captain remained behind. He did not even visit the ornithopters, which were the hub of much additional activity. Instead he went to his own quarters and lay in his hammock, waiting for the meetings to begin and for a chance to see his brother again.

* * * * *

A table had been set up beneath the pavilion, four-sided, with great chairs on three of the sides. The one on the west was occupied by the warlord, flanked by Urza and the mechanical man. The Yotian ruler's mood had not improved since his talk with Urza, and the old man seemed on the verge of exploding.

The chair on the south was occupied by the lord of Korlis, flanked by two mercenary guards from different units. The eastern chair was occupied by a nervous Argivian diplomat, with two equally nervous bureaucrats at his side.

The northern seat was a low bench, desert style, set for the Fallaji qadir. He arrived in his litter and half rolled, half waddled onto his seat. He was supported by Mishra on one side, and the red-haired staff-wielder, Ashnod, on the other. The Fallaji had left their brass behemoth back at their camp, though its serpentine neck was clearly visible behind them.

The Korlisian lord began the meeting softly. "We welcome the representatives of the Fallaji to the conference. I hope we may be able to resolve matters that have vexed us all individually and to come to a mutually beneficial compromise."

"With your kind permission," interrupted Mishra, "on behalf of His Most Eminent Qadir I have a statement to read."

The Korlisian lord's mouth flapped open for a moment. Then she nodded. The warlord sputtered a protest.

Mishra began without further encouragement, his words louder than the complaining warlord. "We, the Fallaji people, welcome the opportunity to speak with the men of the eastern coastlands. Know that we are a unified people under our qadir, and our empire stretches from Tomakul to the Argivian border, from ice-fed Ronom Lake to the warm Zegoni coast. We are many gathered together, and as such we are mighty.

"Whatever else may be decided by this conference, we must make clear that it is our ultimate goal to regain all the land of the Fallaji people and to protect that land and the resources that it contains from all invaders, raiders, and would-be conquerors."

The warlord started at the words, and interrupted with a snarl. "Not a bad little speech for a race of invaders, raiders, and would-be conquerors. Do the people of Tomakul and Zegon agree with your statements, or are they just waiting for someone to strike your young puppy of a qadir across the snout on their behalf?"

Mishra raised an eyebrow at the interruption, and even Urza was surprised by the heat of the warlord's words. He put a hand on the ruler's shoulder to calm him.

However, it was the qadir who answered, in the clipped accent of an Argivian. "Have a care, old man. You do not wish to cross me."

Urza looked at Mishra, and Mishra nodded back at his brother. The qadir had learned Argivian from his *raki* and knew enough to realize when he was being insulted and to respond in kind.

The warlord would not be dissuaded. "Have a care yourself, child warrior. Do not trifle with those who possess more experience and wisdom than you."

Urza started to speak. "Perhaps now would be a good time to adjourn and think about—," but the qadir was already talking again.

"Do you know who I am?" demanded the young Fallaji. "I am the Qadir of the Suwwardi tribe. Once, long ago, we lived in the Suwwardi lands north of Yotia. You called them the Suwwardi Marches."

"The *Sword* Marches," shot back the warlord. "When I was a younger man, we cleaned that land of raiders and brought true civilization to it."

"It is Suwwardi land and belongs to the Fallaji people," snapped the qadir.

"There have not been any Suwwardi there since your great-grandfather's age," rejoined the warlord hotly.

"Yes," hissed the qadir. "You drove my great-grandfather from our land. My grandfather wandered the empty wastes. My father gathered the tribes. And now I come to you with my empire at my back and demand the return of my family's land."

Urza looked at Mishra, but his brother had a blank expression on his face. Could it be he had not known about the qadir's demands? The Korlisians and the Argivians were talking as well now, as chaos erupted at the table.

"You are an old fool," continued the qadir, with a contemptuous sneer, "to hope to prevail in the face of our obvious power."

"I'll show you what I know of power," replied the warlord. "Take a lesson, child!"

The warlord made a gesture. The Captain of the Guard, waiting outside the pavilion, turned, raised his hand, and then dropped it. Out by the Yotian camp Rusko turned and waved to the ornithopter crews, already at their machines.

In a matter of moments the sky around the pavilion was heavy with the beating of great canvas wings.

The flight of eleven ornithopters (lacking only Urza's new one with its double-bent wings) came in low over the pavilion. The qadir looked up in shock, but Mishra was already next to him, shouting something in Fallaji. Urza was yelling at the warlord as well.

"What is this?" the artificer roared. "Why are my ornithopters in the air? Why wasn't I told?"

"It's a lesson in power!" the warlord shouted in return, his teeth bright like a shark's. "You would do well to pay attention to it as well."

The ornithopters banked over the pavilion and made a beeline toward the Fallaji camp. Three of the craft banked right, and three veered left. The remaining five headed straight for the dragon engine.

Small objects fell from the ornithopters, jettisoned by their pilots. They were black bits of shadow that plummeted into the Fallaji camp.

Where they landed the ground erupted in explosions of flames and smoke. There were screams as the flames spread, and more bombs dropped.

Urza shouted, but his voice was drowned in another round of explosions. The five ornithopters that bore down on the dragon engine glided in low, trying to fling their bombs along the base of the great metallic creature. A string of eruptions blossomed beneath the beast, and it wheeled and gave a metallic scream but seemed otherwise unhurt.

The dragon engine exhaled a huge gout of reddish mist directly in the path of one of the ornithopters. As the craft passed through it, the ornithopter came apart in mid-air. Its wings folded upon itself, and it crashed among the tents, releasing a larger gout of flame as the rest of its deadly cargo exploded.

Within the pavilion reaction among the delegates was instantaneous. The Argivians flung themselves under the table. The Korlisian mercenaries grabbed their lord by each arm and dragged her backward, away from the table, while she shouted orders and obscenities at them. The warlord was laughing now, taunting the young qadir.

The Fallaji ruler rose from his bench with a speed that surprised Urza. His hand lashed out. The warlord saw the blow coming and tried to lean away from it, but the youth was too quick. Before either brother could react, a curved blade jutted from the old man's chest, blood spouting from the wound like a fountain.

"No!" shouted Urza, and felt his Mightstone heavy on his chest. He laid one hand upon it, and with the other activated his mechanical humanoid. "Stop him!" Urza shouted.

The mechanical man lurched forward and grabbed the qadir by the front of his robes. The young man let out a choked cry as inhumanly long arms reached across the table and snared him with fingers of ironroot and metal. Simultaneously the red-haired woman lowered her staff and pointed it at Urza's metallic creation. Lightning danced along the dolphin's skull, and Urza felt a wave of nausea pass over him. It felt as if every part of his skin had become acutely sensitive. The movement of the breeze inflicted horrible pain. Gritting his teeth, Urza barked another command, and the mechanical being pulled the qadir toward itself across the corner of the table.

Out on the battlefield, the Fallaji were attempting to regroup. Mishra had signaled his dragon engine, and now the beast's serpentine neck dodged and darted among the diving ornithopters. It caught one and flung it to the ground, the canvas wings catching fire as it did so. On the ground, the Yotian troops charged, trying to kill any Fallaji who escaped the bombing. Some of the Korlisian mercenaries joined them in the assault.

Ashnod shouted, and Mishra turned to see the qadir in the grip of the metal man. He spun toward the dragon engine to signal one last command, then wheeled to face Urza and his mechanical creation. Mishra gripped a thin hide pouch around his own neck, and green lambent power leaked out between his fingers. He concentrated that power on Urza's machine.

Urza caught the backwash of the energies and staggered. The mechanical creation was more greatly affected. Sparks danced at its joints, and steam began to seep from beneath its helmeted face. Its fingers loosened, and the qadir dropped free, clutching his throat and gasping for breath.

Ashnod shouted something, and Mishra nodded. Suddenly the northern side of the pavilion was shattered as the dragon engine smashed its way onto the raised platform. Ashnod let her staff down, and its fires died. She tucked the staff under one arm, grabbing the qadir with the other, and dragged the ruler toward the engine as if he were no more than a puppet.

Urza felt the pain subside. He focused his Mightstone at his metal creation. "Mishra," he shouted, his head still spinning, "we have to stop this!"

Dimly he heard his brother's voice snarl back, "So you can betray us again, Brother?"

Urza started to reply, "I didn't know—" but the stress of the Mightstone and Weakstone proved to be too much for the mechanical beast between the brothers. It exploded at the waist, its torso spinning around its central pivot and its head jutting flames. Urza screamed as the flames arched around him. The last thing he saw was Mishra, running back toward his dragon engine, his creation framed by a wreath of smoke from the ornithopter bombs.

* * * * *

The searchers found Urza in the shattered pavilion, cradling the dead body of the warlord. The blasted legs and hips of his mechanical humanoid still stood next to him, the fragments of its head and torso scattered around the lopsided platform.

The Captain of the Guard arrived and saluted. "The enemy is in full retreat, sir."

Urza said nothing, and the captain continued. "We inflicted heavy casualties on the Fallaji troops with minimum losses to our own. We lost four ornithopters in the attack. Several of the Korlisian mercenaries joined in the assault and want to be paid for their contribution. The Argivians have already fled without drawing a sword."

Urza looked in the pale, quiet face of the captain as the soldier continued. "The enemy leader and"—he paused—"your brother have escaped with their engine into the mountains. We will scout for them with the remaining ornithopters."

Urza said something softly that the captain could not hear.

"Beg pardon, sir?" he asked.

"I just asked why," said Urza sadly, looking at the warlord's face. "Why did he do this?"

"You heard the Fallaji devil," the captain said. "They wanted to invade Yotia. To regain land they lost generations ago. It's the desert way, carrying grudges for generations—"

"No," said Urza, his voice now filled with steel. "He was ready for this. This ambush. The ornithopters. The bombs. Goblin powder, wasn't it? The warlord was preparing for an attack all the time. It should have been a massacre. If not for my brother's engine, it would have been."

The Captain of the Guard shifted uneasily but said nothing.

"And why did he not tell me?" asked Urza bitterly. "Why not tell me he was going to use my machines like this?"

The captain stammered, "I-I couldn't say, sir."

Urza laid the body of the warlord on the shattered floor of the pavilion and turned toward the captain. "Yes, you *can* say," Urza said icily. "You can say everything you know. Who knew about this? What were the full plans? What did you hope to accomplish? Why did you not tell me? Why did you not tell the princess? You can, and will answer those questions."

The captain shifted his feet uneasily.

"Because," Urza continued, turning back to the body, "because I have to go back to Kroog now and tell my wife her father is dead. And I will need all the reasons I can muster to make her understand. Because I don't understand it myself."

Chapter 11

Affairs of State

Tawnos moved softly through the halls of the palace, with a subtle grace that belied his large frame. In the months since the death of the warlord, everyone had learned to move more quietly through the marble halls of the palace of Kroog.

The news of the warlord's death struck the Yotians like a cold wave of seawater. It was sudden, unexpected, and decisive. For most of the Yotians, the warlord had been the only leader they had ever known, and he had seemed immortal.

Now he was dead. Cut down by a Fallaji blade, said one story. No, said another, his heart was burst by Fallaji magic. No, contended a third, he was boiled alive by the steaming breath of a diabolic machine, a machine controlled by the Chief Artificer's evil brother. No, the ruler was wearing one of the Chief Artificer's amulets, and it exploded. The warlord saved the Chief Artificer from a red-haired demoness summoned by the Chief Artificer's evil brother. Even when the truth was finally determined and circulated, the other tales survived and grew in the telling.

One tale both true and widely popular was that Urza returned from Korlinda late one evening, piloting his distinctive ornithopter and bearing the body of the warlord. It was said he flew without rest from Korlinda. Others noted he did stop briefly, but the flight took him only two days. He laid the body to rest in the palace shrine and sent word to the temples of the news. Then he visited the new queen with the sad tidings.

The state funeral was lavish and lasted ten days. People came from the farthest reaches of Yotia to pass before the warlord one last time and pay their final respects. Guards had to be mounted along the funeral bier, not to protect the body but to help move those who collapsed alongside, fainting from despair. The most notable casualty during this procession was Kayla's matron, who flung herself in tears onto the bier and eventually had to be dispatched to relatives in the country to recover.

Queen Kayla and her royal consort, Chief Artificer Urza, appeared only on the last day. Their faces were drawn and tired, and they neither spoke nor smiled during their grim vigil.

After the body was interred within its great shrine, the queen retired to her quarters, and the Chief Artificer went to his orniary. A calm settled over Kroog, but it was a false peace as the merchants returned to their stores, the guildsmen to their crafts, and the scholars to their temple classes. The calm only barely hid the anger of the people. The Fallaji had killed their beloved warlord, and the desert people would pay.

There were incidents. Fallaji traders (and in one case a Zegon jeweler) were lynched in the streets. Bands of young adventurers rode into Fallaji territory seeking revenge, and when they did not return, additional bands set out to seek revenge for them. In order to prevent further foolhardiness, the army swung its doors wide open to anyone who wished to join. Recruitment tripled in a month.

Eventually the queen appeared in public, but she looked worn by her ordeal. Some noted that the warlord had protected her for too long from the duties of her position, and now she was feeling the strain. Others said she was meeting with the nobles and the guild leaders, assembling her own response to the Fallaji. Many, including Tawnos, noticed that when she appeared, she appeared alone.

The Chief Artificer, it was whispered, had retreated to his lab to prepare a secret weapon with which to defeat the desert tribesmen. Some said that it was a new version of ornithopter, a more powerful bomb, or a gigantic version of his metal soldier, which had now gained the sobriquet of "Urza's Avenger" for its attempt to seek revenge against the warlord's murderer. When the machine's fragments were returned from Korlinda with the returning army, it was interred alongside the warlord, like a faithful dog with its master.

Rusko had not returned, and Tawnos learned that while the clockmaker had survived the attack, he would not be coming back to Kroog any time soon. The Captain of the Guard had been reassigned to a patrol unit to the west along the Fallaji frontier and replaced in his duties within the palace. Over the course of the month every pilot who had gone to Korlinda was transferred as well, also to units along the long frontier with the desert tribesmen. The seneschal remained, but seemed to be on a short leash, with Queen Kayla holding the other end.

Every other official, courtier, and servant in the palace was made suddenly aware that if the new queen noticed something she did not care for, that something was removed. Everyone moved around the palace on tiptoe and spoke in whispers.

The Fallaji were, for their part, surprisingly quiet. They launched a brief raid into the Sword Marches, which provoked a counterraid deep into the desert before it ran out of both supplies and enemies. Soon after the order came down, signed both by the queen and the Chief Artificer: Every inch of Yotian ground would be held, but no one would raid Fallaji territories without explicit orders. Many took this as a sign that the queen's consort was working on something very deadly and decisive for the Fallaji.

Of all the people in the city of Kroog, only Tawnos knew what the Chief Artificer had been doing for the month following the warlord's death. Urza had stayed in the orniary night and day. He had dismissed the students for the moment, sending them to mourn the warlord and never calling them back. He allowed Tawnos to remain, though, and his chief apprentice worked hard, keeping the machines oiled and the canvas supple. Mostly, however, Tawnos stayed out of Urza's way.

Once or twice a day Urza would emerge from his lair to meet with the newest Captain of the Guard or to send a terse message to some bureaucrat or other. Then he retreated again to his lair.

And in his study, he stared at a piece of blank paper mounted on his drawing board. He stared at it for hours. At first Tawnos wondered at what marvels Urza was dreaming up. But after the fifth day, the young toy maker became convinced that his master was simply overwhelmed by the responsibility that awaited him outside the orniary.

Tawnos had ventured his opinion on the current situation to Urza just once. He had heard others note that the Chief Artificer would not strike against the Fallaji because the desert tribesmen were led by his evil brother, whom Urza had not seen since they were both children. Some argued that Urza hesitated because he wanted to kill his brother himself. Others argued that he was afraid of the brother and did not want to fight. Tawnos cut away the implications of cowardice and put the question to his master. Why had he not struck back?

Urza almost exploded. "War is a waste of resources!" he shouted. "We lost four ornithopters in that fruitless assault, and I cannot replace them until I get more power stones! Why should I waste time, gold, and precious lives in battle? To chase ghosts in the desert? Why don't I just burn down the city and save my brother the bother?"

The outburst was as surprising as it was sudden. Afterward Tawnos moved more quietly in the orniary as well.

Messages arrived, and Tawnos received them at the door. To those sent by the Captain of the Guard, Urza responded in a short note delivered by Tawnos. Sometimes the message was from some merchant or craftsmen. Half the time the artificer would respond; other times he crumpled the letter and tossed it away.

Some messages were marked with the signet ring of the queen. These Urza left unopened by his drafting table. A flurry of them appeared for a while, and then they gradually tapered off.

Finally such a note arrived for Tawnos, demanding his presence in the queen's quarters that evening. A meeting at midnight, the missive said, and no one, not even Urza, should be told.

Tawnos moved quietly through the corridors. There were no guards in the private wing of the building, and had not been since the warlord's funeral. It was late, and even the servants had abandoned their continual fussing and retired for the evening.

He reached the doors to the royal household. In the distance he heard the temple bells sounding the midnight hour. He knocked softly.

For a moment there was nothing, and Tawnos feared his rapping had not been heard. Then a weak voice said "Enter."

Tawnos pushed the door open gently. "Your Majesty?"

Queen Kayla was seated by the window looking out at the city of Kroog spread below. She was dressed in a sheer gown covered by a crimson robe. She held a large brandy snifter in her hand, and even from across the room Tawnos could see it was filled higher than it should have been.

The queen said nothing, and Tawnos entered, closing the door behind him. "Your Majesty?" he repeated.

Kayla sighed deeply. "No," she said. "Don't call me that. I have been 'Your Majesty'd' to tears today. Today and every other day." She took a sip of the brandy. "Call me Kayla. Can you do that, Tawnos Toy Maker?"

Tawnos opened his mouth and tried to form his lips around the words, but they refused to cooperate. Finally, he said, "I'm afraid I can't, Ma'am."

Kayla snorted, a pretty, ladylike sound. "Ma'am will have to do, then—at least for the moment." She spun in place on the window seat and set her slippered feet to the floor. "Would you like something to eat? I had the kitchen send up some chilled meat and cheeses."

She waved an arm at a nearby table. It had been set with fine crystal and silverware and a pair of elegantly twisted candles. Porcelain plates as translucent as the wings of an ornithopter were laden with food. There were meats, both chopped and shaved, cheeses, fruits, and several pickled items that Tawnos could not immediately identify.

"If you wish, Your . . Ma'am," said Tawnos, moving toward the tables.

Kayla crossed paths with him, *en route* to her own seat. As she passed, she stumbled, spilling a bit of her drink and brushing against the apprentice.

"Sorry," she murmured, holding a hand out against his chest to steady herself.

"Not to worry," replied Tawnos. He inhaled a heady lungful of her perfume mixed with the fumes of brandy. If forced to guess, he would say that the brandy was older than the warlord had been.

Tawnos tried to recall the last time the queen drank more than a single glass of wine with dinner. He came up empty but surmised that Kayla had already refilled her goblet at least once before he had arrived.

Carefully, Tawnos sat down, unsure what to do next. He thought of himself as a simple coastal boy, lacking the sophistication of High Yotian society, but he was fairly certain of how the evening was shaping up.

Kayla stabbed a morsel of cheese with her knife and waved the cheddar-tipped utensil at the apprentice.

"So," she said. "How is he?"

"He who, Ma'am?" parried Tawnos, looking over the pickled things, trying to determine what exactly they had been in life.

His answer amused Kayla. " 'He who?' he asks. He who is my loving and dedicated husband, that is who. He who you see more regularly than I these days." She bit off the last words neatly, and leaned back, evidently pleased she had managed to say them without tangling her tongue.

Tawnos grasped at words. "He . . . He is well, Your Majesty."

"Kayla," said the queen.

"Kay . . . Kayla. Ma'am." Tawnos blushed as he said it.

"I write to him, but he does not respond," she sighed, popping the bit of cheese in her mouth and looking for another target.

"I know," said Tawnos quietly. "But he has been busy. With patrols and things. His designs."

"Ah yes." The queen raised her hands toward the ceiling. "Urza's wonderful designs! How I envy him! He can lock himself up in his room and not talk to anyone, least of all his wife, because he is always working on his wonderful designs!"

Tawnos suddenly realized he had answered her original question wrong from the start. But how was he to know that she wanted to hear Master Urza was miserable?

The queen seemed deeply interested in her brandy glass; then she suddenly looked up. "I didn't expect much from the marriage, you know. I hoped for someone to talk to. Or a least someone to listen. An heir or two to make Daddy happy. And now, no heirs, no Daddy, and not even a husband anymore." She looked over at Tawnos. "So, are you?"

Tawnos blinked. His head was swimming from the perfume. "Am I what?"

"Are you someone I can talk to?" asked the queen. "Because I've had it with people whom I can talk *at*. Who make all the right noises but really don't engage in conversation *at all*." She was motioning with both arms now, the ancient brandy slopping over the sides of the glass. "I can talk *at* the seneschal, and I can talk *at* the matron, or I could when she was here. But there's no one I can talk *to*."

"I mean, I felt I could talk *to* Urza," she added softly. "Not often. If there was daylight, he worked on his plans, his wondrous devices. But often enough. And I always liked listening to him, even if I didn't understand what he was talking about. And now. . . now . . ." She let her voice trail off.

When Tawnos had been a very young man, he had worked on his uncle's fishing rig. One morning, when he was not paying sufficient attention, the boat had been breached by a large wave, and he had been knocked overboard. The young Tawnos panicked, floundered, and found himself struggling underwater. He was saved by his uncle, who pulled him aboard and suggested gently that the young man find another line of work.

At this moment Tawnos felt much the same way, though no helpful uncle was in sight.

"I am sooooo jealous of you, you know," Kayla said, her eyes becoming hooded slits as she charged off on a new tack. "I mean, he spends all his time with you, and when he talks about lift and drag and pulley ratios and snail-gears, you honestly understand what he's talking about. I'm not dumb, but on my best day I couldn't venture a guess about ideal pulley ratios."

Tawnos started to speak. "Everybody has their own strengths and weakne—"

"Am I so horrible?" she demanded, leaning across the table and grabbing his hand. "Am I so repulsive?" As she leaned forward her robe fell open, the gown beneath almost transparent in the candlelight.

Tawnos closed his eyes tightly. "No," he said, "you're not horrible at all."

"Then why won't he come home?" she said, drawing back. Her hand still clutched him, and her voice was filled with unwept tears. "He sleeps at his work. You know that. That's what I need to know. Why won't he come back to me?"

Carefully, Tawnos pried the queen's fingers from around his wrists. As he spoke, he was aware that Kayla was listening for the first time that evening. "I think," he said calmly, "he's in pain himself."

"Him?" said Kayla, leaning back. "The great thinking machine? The paragon of logic? The chief artifact of Kroog?"

"All that," replied Tawnos. "And the man who stood next to your father when he was killed. The man who could not save him from dying. Have you talked to him about what happened at Korlinda? I mean, really talked?"

Kayla looked at him and blinked.

"I'll take that as a no, then," said Tawnos.

"But he didn't know what Daddy was planning," she said. "I didn't realize it myself."

"Right," answered Tawnos. "But that doesn't make it any easier. Urza came back, and everyone treated him like a hero because he survived and your father didn't. And he has to come back to you. . . ." He motioned with his hands.

"So he doesn't come back," finished Kayla, softly. The fuzziness of the alcohol seemed banished for the moment. "He's punishing himself because he thinks I blame him. Or I should blame him, even if I don't. Which I don't."

"Uh-huh," grunted Tawnos.

"So I should march down to his workshop and we should talk about this?" she asked.

Tawnos held up both hands, remembering his own experience at being direct. "Perhaps it would be better to start with something else. Something not directly connected with the past few months. Do you two have any happy moments together?"

"Wait," said Kayla, and Tawnos thought of an overworked engine, leaking steam and straining to function. "Yes. Yes I do."

"Start with that," said Tawnos.

The queen's face brightened visibly. "Yes. Yes, I know what will work." She crossed over to the writing desk and penned a short note, then handed it to Tawnos. "Here. Give this to Urza. Make sure he reads it. Tell him it is urgent."

"Of course," said Tawnos, rising from his chair. "He'll still be awake at this hour."

"And, Tawnos," she said. The apprentice turned, and Kayla leaned forward, pressing her lips against his cheeks. "Thank you."

Tawnos blushed, the blood in his face clear even in the candle-light. "It is my pleasure. The kingdom can't take much more of every-one walking on eggshells around you two."

"Not that," she said. "That was for being a better person than I might be."

Tawnos made sure Urza read the message, and fifteen minutes later, the Chief Artificer poked his head into his own living quarters. "My queen?" he said. "Kayla?"

Queen Kayla bin-Kroog was seated at a table set with fine crystal and laden with meats and cheeses.

"Ah, my Chief Artificer. Thank you for coming on such short notice."

"Your note said there was an emergency," said Urza, his eyes ad-justing to the candlelight. "A technical emergency?"

"Yes," responded the queen. "I have a small music box. An heir-loom. I think it's broken."

She motioned to the place setting opposite her. On the plate was a small silver box.

Carefully Urza opened the box, then turned it over slowly in his hands. "I think that all is wrong with it is that the spring has wound down again." he said at last.

Kayla opened her eyes wide. "Wound down?"

Urza nodded and cleared his throat. "Yes. I would need a key for it."

"A key," she said, and opened her robe. The sheer gown she wore was almost translucent in the candlelight. Around her neck she wore a pink ribbon, and hanging from that ribbon was a battered metal key, red with rust along one edge. "Would this one do, Lord Artificer?"

Urza looked at the key and at the music box. He stared long and deep into the queen's eyes. "Yes," he said at last. "I think that will do indeed."

And for the first time in a month, Urza smiled.

The Chief Artificer did not come to the orniary the next day, nor the day after that. On the third day, Tawnos arrived to find a sheaf of parchment marked with detailed instructions, starting with recalling the students and quickly moving on to a list of improvements to ornithopter design and plans for building new avenger-style mechanical men. There was no sign of Urza, and a marginal note to Tawnos indicated that he should not be expected until mid-afternoon. If then.

Tawnos allowed himself a healthy grin and quickly began to fulfill Master Urza's list of demands.

Chapter 12

Phyrexia

The winter dust storm boiled out of the south, a major sirocco that reached from horizon to horizon and climbed almost to the zenith of the sky. It was a grandfather storm, one that the old people spoke of, a storm that blotted the sun with its shadow. The storm breathed dust-laden winds capable of flaying the living flesh from those caught in the open. Along its leading edge great tornadoes spawned and danced, only to be sucked back within the advancing wall of churning black dust.

The storm overtook the lumbering form of the *mak fawa* and swallowed it whole, disturbing neither the storm nor the dragon engine. The *mak fawa* continued to roll forward, unfazed by the swirling winds and pounding sand that assailed it. Though one could no longer see across the width of the creature's body, the engine plodded forward with the resolute and absolute confidence of a machine.

Mishra and Ashnod huddled in a cramped space beneath the creature's back plates. The dragon engine had not been designed to carry passengers within, but there was a low-roofed hollow along the beast's spine, and the *raki* and his apprentice crouched there, listening to the sand rasp against the metal flesh around them.

"How can it see where it's going?" shouted Ashnod over the clatter of blowing sand.

"It does not need to see," replied Mishra. "It knows, as surely as I know, what direction it needs to go. It seeks out the Secret Heart of the Thran. I can feel Koilos's call, and because the machine responds to me, so can it feel the pull, like a raptor returning to the same nest with each passing season."

Ashnod stared at the stocky man huddled next to her. Mishra's tendency to cloak his words in allusions and mysticism bothered her. Did he truly believe what he said, or was it all just verbal play to cover the fact that he did not know?

Ashnod wanted to believe the former, because otherwise they were charging blindly through a Grandfather Storm, navigated only by a vague feeling in Mishra's heart.

It was in the winter of the year of the Korlinda massacre, the year that the warlord of Kroog perished at the hands of the young qadir, that Mishra and Ashnod set out for Koilos, the Secret Heart of the Thran. They told no one among the Suwwardi of their plans or of their destination, not even Hajar and particularly not the qadir. The idea that the tribe's *raki* was seeking out the Secret Heart of the Thran once more would not have been a comforting thought to the leader of the Fallaji.

The retreat from Korlinda had been harrowing, and only one of every five men who entered Korlis returned to Fallaji lands. The survivors had traveled by night, cowering in mountain passes, constantly seeking places to hide the huge *mak fawa* from the pursuing ornithopters. The qadir had at first wanted to turn around and launch an immediate counterattack. Cooler heads, and the fact that they were a mere fraction of their initial numbers, convinced him to withdraw and take comfort in the apparent death of the warlord.

Ultimately the qadir blamed his *raki* for the ambush. Mishra should have known that his talented and treacherous brother was among the enemy. Mishra should have told the qadir immediately upon discovering that fact. Mishra should have concentrated on protecting him, the qadir, instead of giving commands to his dragon engine during the attack.

And of course, Ashnod thought ironically, Mishra was at fault for coming out of this debacle more popular among the Fallaji than ever. The other tribal chieftains made sure that the *raki* was all right and asked about the health of the qadir as a secondary matter. While the qadir had slain the ancient warlord, it was Mishra and his engine who were credited with saving those who made it back to the Fallaji lands. No one blamed Mishra for the ambush save the qadir, but the chieftain made his complaints well known to anyone who was nearby, and no one would disagree with the corpulent young man.

The qadir had other complaints upon their return. Mishra should have found more machines by now similar to his *mak fawa*. A single dragon engine was too big a target and too vulnerable. He reminded

Mishra of the difficulties they had experienced at Zegon. If the Yotians could field dozens of their machines, the qadir should be able to do the same.

Of course no one doubted Mishra's loyalty, the qadir said, or his talent, though in mentioning them the young chieftain managed to bring both into doubt. It had been many years since the *raki* had first conjured the *mak fawa*, and now his people needed more. There were whispers, which the qadir assured Mishra were completely disbelieved by anyone who truly counted, that the *raki* was afraid of his brother's flying machines and his brother's power.

Ashnod had watched the entire dressing-down, silent as a woman among the Fallaji was expected to be. After the qadir had dismissed them, she snarled quietly to Mishra, "But what have you done for me lately?" Mishra merely returned to his own tent and began to issue orders.

They needed to locate more finds of Old One artifacts, preferably ones that were nearly operational. Scouts were sent out with orders describing what to look for. Within the month they had returned with news of a large device located near the banks of the Mardun River. The qadir, busy reconfirming his power over the other tribes, allowed his *raki* and the *raki's* woman to investigate.

The site was large, and the remains were generally complete. The machine was evidently some sort of transport used by the Thran to haul unknown equipment. It appeared to be a great wagon or wain and had been overturned in whatever accident that had claimed it. Rust blossomed along both sides of its skeleton, and its spoked wheels were twisted and shattered. The wire-laden framework that held the power crystals was missing, if it had existed at all.

Mishra shook his head. It would require time and effort to put this monstrosity back together, and even then it would be but a fraction of the grandeur of the *mak fawa*. The qadir would not be pleased.

The morning after surveying the find, Mishra left Hajar in charge of the excavation and departed, taking both the dragon engine and Ashnod with him. They headed east, and traveled night and day, the dragon engine a tireless mount. They slept within the creature's metal carapace and now hid there while the great storm blossomed out of the southern horizon.

They were trapped within the beast's body for ten days and nights while the storm whirled around them. They had sufficient supplies and light, but the protected hollow was barely comfortable for one and tight for two. To pass the time, Mishra told Ashnod the story of his first visit to Koilos. He also took the opportunity to inform her how she might better conduct herself among the Fallaji. Soon Ashnod was willing to consider braving the storms outside to avoid listening further to Mishra point out her foibles, great and small.

"I did nothing wrong," she finally said in frustration on the tenth day of the storm, after Mishra mentioned (for the fifth time that day) a recent incident in the qadir's camp.

"The warrior you struck down would disagree," replied Mishra.

"He *said* I thought like a man," she said, exasperated.

"It is an old desert saying," replied Mishra. "It is *meant* to be a compliment."

"Trust me," said Ashnod, "it isn't."

"You did not need to cripple him," said Mishra sternly.

Ashnod forcefully placed a hand against Mishra's broad chest. "Would you prefer if I said I turned my staff on him because he insulted my gentle, feminine ears with lewd and guttural suggestions?" she asked. "Because he did that, too."

Mishra did not respond immediately. Instead he pointed to the outer hull and said, "Listen."

Ashnod paused. "I don't hear anything."

"Exactly," said Mishra. "I think we have passed through the storm at last. Check outside."

Ashnod blinked at the man. "And if this is only a momentary lull in the winds? What happens if they kick up again while I'm outside?"

Mishra leaned against the inner wall. "You're the apprentice. That means if a task is dangerous or unpleasant, it's your job."

Muttering, Ashnod inched toward the access plates and carefully peeled them back and peered outside. There was a wall of blackness along the north, but the sky above was bright blue, and the sands had already settled in the wake of the great storm.

"It's over," said Mishra, following her out from their hiding place within the mechanical beast. "We can ride on the outside for a while."

"And not a moment too soon," muttered Ashnod, not caring if Mishra heard her or not.

In the wake of the storm, they saw no other living thing. The desert had been wiped clean, and old rock formations had been buried as new ones were exposed. At last, after another week of travel, they reached the canyon of Koilos.

The site was untouched by the storm and apparently undisturbed since Mishra was last there. The bleached bones of the roc were still scattered in front of the cave entrance, mixed with the wreckage of other ancient Thran machines.

As they moved through the valley, Mishra grew quiet and somber. Ashnod thought the man was reliving old memories, some apparently painful.

They pawed through the wreckage and the ruins immediately around the cavern's mouth, but after several days work the two had come up with nothing that could be immediately pressed into the qadir's service.

"Those metal spiders might have been useful, once," said Ashnod that evening. "But your brother definitely did a number on them when that machine exploded. They weren't in the best condition before, and now they're little more than scrap."

In the firelight Mishra flinched just a bit at the mention of his brother. Ashnod had discovered that the subject of Urza was off-limits around the younger brother, a fact that made her all the more curious about their relationship. Mishra did not respond to her comment, and Ashnod saw him staring at the roc bones at the base of the plateau and the cavern they partially concealed.

Whatever answer was at Koilos lay within the caverns.

That night Mishra slept badly and awoke screaming. Ashnod calmed him as best as she was able.

"I dreamed of the wind, of a great dark wind," was all he said, the night sweat evaporating in the still air. "It swept around me, it spoke to me, and it carried horrible secrets it wanted to tell me."

"It will be all right," murmured Ashnod. "It's just a dream. Dreams aren't important."

"They are to me," said Mishra, staring into the darkness.

In the morning they entered the caverns. The long corridor had been brightly lit once, Mishra had said, but it was now dark again, and they brought oil lamps with them. Ashnod ran a hand over the inner walls of the tunnel. There were bricks there, but she could not see the joints.

They passed the wreckage of the *su-chi* guardians. Mishra picked up one blackened, narrow-headed skull and smashed it against the wall. It cracked like a walnut, but instead of meat inside there was a power stone, an Eye of the Old Ones. It was slightly chipped but still held the fire of the Thran energies. He grunted approval, and they continued.

They reached an interminable set of stairs and came at last to the great cavern, the lair of the Thran machines. It was bathed in a flickering light of inconstant crystalline plates along the ceiling. The centermost machine was made up of a great series of plates and mirrors surrounding an empty spot.

Mishra placed the stone from the *su-chi's* head in the void of the machine. Immediately there came a low humming, a throbbing that seemed to issue from the walls itself. The flickering stopped, and the entire cavern was bathed in a soft light.

"How did you know to do that?" asked Ashnod.

"I just knew," replied Mishra. He sounded as if he were a thousand miles away. Then the *raki* shrugged, apparently shaking off an old memory.

Ashnod examined the bank of glyphs and lights before the great machine, set into a podium that looked like a huge, open-faced book. She did not touch the glyphs but studied each in turn.

Somewhere among the signs was a mechanism that opened other doors, doors that had held the mechanical humanoids whose remains littered the entrance. If they could find them, she and Mishra reasoned, they could bring back new wonders for the qadir. Working wonders.

After a short while, Mishra asked, "Well?"

Ashnod shook her head. The glyphs were simple geometric shapes and could be labels, instructions, or dire warnings. They provided no clue as to the purpose of the machines. She pointed. "This one might be the symbol of a doorway."

Mishra looked over her shoulder, and assented. "Press it," he said.

"Is this something else you just know?" asked Ashnod.

Mishra frowned. "I'm guessing as much as you. But press it anyway. It feels like the right thing to do."

Ashnod brushed the glyph with her long fingertips, and somewhere in the depths of the mountain there was a low chime, more felt than heard. Something deep within the Thran machine had engaged, and Ashnod hoped that it was connected with other, working mechanisms.

She held her breath.

A light appeared in the air to their right. First a mote, hanging in space, it soon expanded, twisting the air around it until it formed a thin, glowing disk, positioned perpendicular to the ground, hanging unsupported. Slowly Ashnod walked around it. It seemed as thin as the qadir's temper and had a soft, almost enticing radiance to it. Along the surface of the disk Ashnod could almost see a set of scribed hairlines, forming the shape of a child's star.

Ashnod looked at Mishra, but he did nothing. The disk grew until it was twice the size of a man.

Ashnod leaned her black thunderwood staff forward and pressed its butt end against the disk. The light offered no resistance, nor did it dissipate at the touch. She leaned forward, and the staff passed easily through the disk.

But the staff did not come out the other side. Ashnod had shoved three feet of wood into a wafer-thin glowing disk, and nothing came out the other side.

Ashnod withdrew the staff. The immersed end seemed unharmed.

Ashnod looked at Mishra again. "We've found our doorway," said Mishra calmly.

"Who goes in first?" asked Ashnod. Mishra looked at her. After a moment, she nodded. "Right," she said. "If it's dangerous or unpleasant, it's the apprentice's job."

Ashnod stepped through the glowing disk. The light surrounded her and saturated her. For a moment she thought she heard, faintly, the voice of an old woman shouting. But then that passed as well, and she was in another world.

The first thing that she was aware of was the heat: not the desert heat, dry and comforting, but a wet, damp heat she had not felt since the swamps of Almaaz. It settled on her like a blanket.

Now she felt the smell, a pungent scent of rot and decay. No, there was more to it than that, she thought. It smelled of oil and chemicals, too. It smelled of goblin powder, of fire, and of steel. For a moment she thought she was back at Korlinda, fleeing as the bombs dropped around them.

There were colors. A riot of jungle plants surrounded her, all in bloom, bright splotches against a sea of dark green leaves and vines. But the colors were wrong. They were too hard, too bright, too alien, and they had a metallic sheen to them. And the vines—they were uniform, more like cables than any natural thing. She touched one of the flowers and pulled her hand away quickly. Whatever juice the bloom was leaking was slightly caustic and stung her skin.

A dragonfly settled on the flower, but on closer inspection Ashnod saw it was not truly an insect but rather a tiny machine made of silver wire and gold plates. She reached out to grab it, but the dragonfly was gone in a wink, darting deeper into the jungle.

She turned around. Mishra was stepping through the radiant disk, emerging like a swimmer from the sea.

"Yes," he said, "it is just as I remembered it."

"You've been here before?" asked Ashnod.

"Only in dreams," replied Mishra. Indeed, there was a distracted, dreamlike quality in the way he spoke. Ashnod gripped her staff more tightly and looked at the sky. It was overcast and glowed with a reddish hue, like hot coals under a blanket of snow.

"Phyrexia," Mishra said at last.

Ashnod looked at him and said, "The dreams again?"

Mishra nodded absentmindedly. "Words carried on the black winds," he said. "This place is called Phyrexia." He stared into the middle distance, trying to get his bearings. "That way," he said at last. "I think the ground slopes down to a pond or something."

Actually it sloped down to a lake, a large, black mirror covered with rainbow patterns of oil. Several large machines, kin to the *mak fawa* back in Koilos, waded through its oily expanse, dredging other pieces of metal from the lake's shallow floor. There were four of them, Ashnod saw.

"You stay here," said Mishra. "Keep your staff ready."

"What are you doing?" asked Ashnod.

Mishra blinked at her. "I'm going to try to control them. As I controlled our dragon engine." He spoke as if the answer to her question was obvious.

"And if they don't *want* to be controlled?" asked Ashnod.

"That's why you have to keep your staff ready," returned Mishra. "Be prepared to run."

Ashnod waited nervously as Mishra crept forward. One of the dragon engines, the smallest, saw him first, and let out a low, bleating cry. The other three looked up at once.

All four converged on Mishra, the smallest reaching him first. Ashnod held her breath as the small metallic dragon leaned forward toward the newcomer, sniffing him as a dog would a stranger.

Mishra stood calmly, as if being sniffed by engines of mass destruction was a common occurrence.

Then the dragon engine dropped on its haunches and laid its head against the ground. The other three did the same. Ashnod could see these were not identical to the *mak fawa* she knew. Their heads were blunter, shaped more like shovels, and their hides were duller than the brass monster they had left behind.

Mishra waved for Ashnod to come ahead, and she stepped into the clearing by the lake, her staff still at the ready.

Mishra nodded grimly. "It's not the stone," he said. "I thought it was my power stone that controlled them, but it's not. It's me. I can think what I want them to do, and they will do it." He seemed more puzzled than pleased by the discovery.

"Good," said Ashnod, wondering for a moment exactly how good it was. "But these seem large to take back through the portal. Can you master something smaller?"

There was a gong in the distance, the deep chiming of an iron bell. The dragon engines looked up and almost bolted back into the oily lake. The bell tolled again, this time close, and the dragon engines started to waver, caught between their obedience to Mishra and their fear of whatever was approaching. The bell tolled a third time, and Ashnod could now hear the twisting, rending noise of metallic vegetation being ripped from its roots. The three larger engines panicked and splashed back into the lake. The smaller one remained but whined like an engine caught between gears.

Part of the forest to their left disappeared, and a true giant lumbered forward. It was shaped like a land-going ship, set on treads, with a great maw set into its prow. Within the maw were spinning sets of teeth, like great scythes. They ripped through the plants and trees of the jungle with ease. When it struck a particularly large tree, the shattered bits of trunk made the booming, bell-like noise.

And standing above the mouth on a platform was a tall, demonic figure. It seemed to be made of metal as well, and shards of dark bone erupted from its leathery skin. It wore armor that seemed almost a part of it. A rictus grin of exposed skin gleamed along its fleshless face. A pair of horns nested among a tangle of swaying, wormlike tendrils that sprang from its head and swept backward like banners made of human skin.

"Run!" shouted Mishra, but Ashnod needed no encouragement. She followed the *raki* back up the hill toward the glowing disk that led to safety.

The vegetation tore at her robes as she ran, as if it were trying to ensnare her, to hold her in thrall for the dark machine that pursued them. Something tore a long gash along one arm, and a flower fluttered in her face, nearly blinding her with its acid.

She looked back only once, to see that the smallest of the dragon engines had not fled back to the lake but was standing, bleating plaintively. The demon machine with its spinning scythes was almost on top of it.

The machine did not slow down as it rammed the smaller creature. The dragon engine disappeared in a flurry of silver wire and metal plates.

Ashnod turned around and ran faster. Behind them, the machine had turned and was pursuing them up the hill.

Mishra was waiting at the portal but would not go through without her. She dived into the portal headfirst. Part of her mind noted that they had not truly established that the disk led back to the caverns. But, she thought wryly, anywhere they landed would have less terror than the Phyrexian beast that followed them.

She sprawled across the cold stone floor of the chamber, her staff skittering ahead of her and slamming against the far wall. She turned in place, and saw Mishra nimbly dash through the disk as well. He turned to the book-shaped embankment, and his hands hesitated over the collection of glyphs. He touched one, and nothing happened.

Ashnod shouted, and Mishra reached out to grab the power crystal from its cradle among the mirrors. He pulled it from its socket and cursed as the warm crystal burned his flesh. The stone that could power the *su-chi* was insufficient to maintain the great Thran machine and was overloaded with power. Mishra dropped the smoking stone, and it smashed against the floor into a hundred shards.

The golden disk winked out of sight.

Ashnod held a hand to her chest and felt her heart thundering against her rib cage. For the first time she considered the idea that the *mak fawa* might have other masters in addition to Mishra, and that those masters might object to trespassers.

To Mishra she said, "The creature on the machine. You knew what it was?"

Mishra nodded, gasping for breath. Ashnod said, "From your dreams?" Mishra nodded again.

"Remind me to pay more attention to dreams," Ashnod muttered quietly, half to herself.

Mishra shook his head and blew on his burned fingers. "We got what we came for. Come along, now."

Without the *su-chi*'s power stone in its cradle, the lights began to flicker again. Mishra headed for the mouth of the cavern at a rapid clip. Confused, Ashnod followed.

She caught up with him at the entranceway. "What do you mean," she said, "we got what we came for? We had to leave everything behind and slam the door behind us to avoid that . . . that machine demon."

Mishra held up a hand. "Shush. Watch."

There was a tremor that ran up the length of the canyon, and Ashnod saw one of the surviving buildings along the valley floor cave in on itself. Then, near the cavern entrance, the ground erupted. A shovel-headed dragon's head launched from the sand like an arrow, trailing its serpentine neck behind it. There was another eruption and another dragon's head. And then a third. The three engines from the lake, transported from there to here. All three clawed their way from the sand and half-slithered, half-rolled toward the cavern entrance.

They knelt before Mishra, recognizing him as their new master.

"Impressive," said Ashnod. "So what do we do now?"

Mishra smiled. It was an unpleasant grimace, but it was the first smile Ashnod had seen from him since they entered the canyon. "Now?" he said thoughtfully, as if turning over possibilities in his mind.

He looked at the dragon engines and said, "Now we call another peace conference."

* * * * *

Back in the cavern, there was a flicker of light, and the golden portal opened again. This time it could only manage to create a disk a few inches in circumference. A leathery hand, its flesh dotted with shards of dark metal bone, reached through the small portal and clawed at the air. Once, twice, a third time, it scrabbled about, looking for something solid to grab hold of. Then the lights of the portal wavered again, and the hand pulled quickly back, withdrawing seconds before the portal closed entirely.

And everything was quiet in the Caverns of Koilos for another few years.

Chapter 13

Peace Talks

The offer of peace talks came after a year of semi-regular fighting along the northern desert borders of the Sword Marches. It caught Tawnos and the rest of Yotia by surprise.

The offer came without warning or preamble. A Fallaji rider appeared at one of the Yotian outposts under a flag of truce, bearing a message for the Queen of Kroog from the Qadir of the Suwwardi. The message was relayed to one of the ornithopter bases deep within Yotian territory and from there borne by air to the privy council at Kroog.

The council consisted of the queen, the seneschal, the Captain of the Guard, and Tawnos. For a brief period a year earlier Urza had attended the meetings faithfully, but soon he began sending his apprentice as his proxy. With the arrival of the qadir's message, though, Urza appeared in the council at the queen's right hand. Tawnos stood behind the Chief Artificer's chair and to one side. The apprentice noticed that Urza's eyes did not leave the ornately scribed scroll now spread before them.

"An offer for peace," said Kayla.

"An offer of truce," corrected the seneschal, with a slight quaver in his voice. "A cessation of hostilities, a pulling back of forces, while peace is being discussed."

"How bad are the hostilities?" Kayla turned to the Captain of the Guard. The Newest Captain, as he was still thought of by many, was a thoughtful man and paused before he responded.

"Sporadic but serious enough," he said, and paused again. The mannerism bothered Tawnos, but the others at the table had grown used to the captain's habit and let him gather his thoughts.

"They fall into two groups," he said finally. "One seems to be a traditional raid of the Fallaji type, a rapid push into our territory, looting a random town or caravan they encounter, then retreating before our forces can arrive. The other type of assault is carried out by a larger, more organized force that seems intent on destroying a specific target such as a bridge, a mill, or a fort. The dragon engine often accompanies these raids. There is less looting but more destruction."

"Those are organized attacks," said Urza softly. "The others are just parties of desert raiders, seeking their own loot and glory. The attacks with the dragon engine are more organized and have a firm objective in mind." His eyes did not leave the parchment bearing the truce offer. "Those organized raids have my brother's approval and show his planning."

"Approved or not," ventured the seneschal, "the effect is to demoralize the people of the Sword Marches and all along the River Mardun. The Fallaji regularly raid the territories on the far side of the river, and rumors swirl that they plan an attack across it sometime in the near future."

"Are they indeed planning such an attack?" asked Kayla, her voice firm and her manner dispassionate. Tawnos noticed that in council she usually let all sides speak, then made her decision.

The seneschal looked at the captain, who paused, then said, "We have no knowledge at this time. We have fortified encampments on the far sides of the river, with bonfire towers to warn of us of any massed movements. The river is wide enough that even if they found or built sufficient boats, we would be prepared for any assault long before they could launch it." Another pause. "However, maintaining garrisons along the Mardun stretches our resources even further."

Kayla thought about what the Newest Captain said, then nodded. "We can use the ornithopters for additional patrols."

"Those resources are stretching thin as well," said Urza. "We have nearly thirty machines in six patrols of five each. If we get the power stones from Argive for which we have asked, then we can double that number, but the Argivian Crown is being"—the lean man bit his lip—"reticent."

Kayla nodded again. From what Urza had told her, the Argivians were practically swimming in power stones, most of them from Tocasia's original encampment. However, it appeared that prying the stones from the ground was simple compared to prying them from the Argivians' hands. Instead she said, "What is the status of the flights?"

Urza answered while the captain was pausing. "Five of the flights are in the field, at bases throughout the northern Sword Marches. The sixth is here at the capital. The Sword Marches flights operate from permanent bases. I was thinking that we could establish a series of such bases along the border and move the flights from one to another as need be."

The captain frowned and said, "That would be taxing on the pilots."

"We have more capable pilots than we have craft for them to fly," Urza replied. "The additional camps would give us sufficient maneuverability and increase our ability to respond. And perhaps they would give us the same element of surprise that the Fallaji are currently enjoying."

The captain shook his head. "The pilots need their rest."

"Should the machines sleep just because the men do?" asked Urza. There was a brittle irony in his voice.

Tawnos had seen this battle before. When it came to the ornithopters, the Master Artificer held more sway than the Captain of the Guard did. The captain paused for a moment, then shrugged his shoulders in defeat.

Kayla watched the interplay coolly, then said, "Urza, provide any plans for multiple bases to the captain. In the meantime, it sounds as if we are stretched thin indeed."

"We have more than just ornithopters," said the captain. "We have foot patrols, civilian riders, and cavalry patrols." He paused for a moment, and looked at Urza. "But yes, the continual raiding has stretched us thin."

"Then we will accept the offer to talk," said Kayla. "Perhaps together we can come up with a solution."

"Unlikely," said Urza. "Their demands, made back at Korlinda, were direct and left little room for negotiation. They want all the land they consider 'traditional Fallaji territories.' That includes the Sword Marches. Are you prepared to give that to them?"

Kayla shook her head firmly. "It is part of my father's legacy, for good or ill. Still, we will talk, if nothing else, to show the Yotia they deal with now is not the one they dealt with at Korlinda."

She rose from her seat, indicating the council was ended. The captain and seneschal rose as well. Urza, however, remained seated.

The Chief Artificer reached out and tapped the parchment. "The question is," he said to Tawnos, "are they the same Fallaji we dealt with at Korlinda?"

* * * * *

The offer was accepted, and word was relayed back to the borders by ornithopter. Negotiators set a date at the end of the next month, at Kroog itself. A route of safe passage was proposed by the Fallaji through the heart of the Sword Marches. The Captain of the Guard protested, and the seneschal counteroffered a route along the Mardun River, just skirting the edges of the contested borderlands. The seneschal expected the Fallaji to reject any deviation from their demands but was pleasantly surprised when they accepted the alternate route without change.

In the capital city of Kroog, preparations were subdued. Anti-Fallaji graffiti was carefully washed from the alleyway bricks, and a great open area was cleared before the city's thick walls for the expected troops. Again, the seneschal was pleased to discover that the Fallaji would be bringing little more than an honor guard. He was less pleased to hear they would also bring the dragon engine.

Urza and the Newest Captain took their own precautions. The palace troops were drilled to within an inch of perfection, and the normal garrison was supplemented by troops from the coastal regiments. They recalled a second flight of ornithopters from the Sword Marches to Kroog to join the five craft already there. Urza wanted ornithopters aloft directly over the Fallaji procession as it moved south, but the Fallaji bridled at this, making their displeasure known through the seneschal. For several days, Tawnos was sure that negotiations would break down over this point, but Urza at last relented. There would, however, be a regular cavalry escort while the Fallaji were in Yotian territory.

Urza also took pains to review all the pilots of the ornithopters at the capital, in some cases interviewing the young men himself. Tawnos accompanied the Chief Artificer on several of these interviews, though he was puzzled by Urza's action—most of the pilots were handpicked and trained by Urza in the first place and were intensely loyal to the Prince Consort.

As Urza talked to them, though, Tawnos saw what the artificer was worried about. Loyalty was not an issue; it was assumed, and indeed, Urza was considered halfway between a legend and a saint by his pilots. His questions focused on how the pilots felt about the Fallaji, about the desert, about the long-running battles they had been fighting. He was, Tawnos realized, looking into their temperaments, trying to discern if any would, accidentally or purposefully, attempt to finish the job the warlord had started. He was examining them as if they were just another component in a larger device, checking them for signs of wear and tear.

Indeed, there were two individuals who confessed a hatred of the Fallaji, and one who promised his loyalty even when he disagreed with diplomacy. Urza relocated these young men to other flights and replaced them with more even-tempered individuals.

In considering Urza's actions, Tawnos realized the Chief Artificer had been caught by surprise once before and did not want to repeat the mistake a second time. With a precision that the apprentice had previously seen the Chief Artificer dedicate to his inventions, Urza investigated every unit stationed at the capital. He knew every merchant who had claimed injury from the Fallaji. And, Tawnos knew, Urza had walked every inch of the walls that flanked three sides of Kroog, and along every inch of the shore of the Mardun, which served as the fourth protective barrier for the city.

Still, the older man had little hope for the negotiations, and said as much to Tawnos. The qadir wanted nothing less than the land that Kayla's late father had conquered, he reiterated, and she would not give it up.

"Then why negotiate at all," Tawnos asked.

Urza sighed deeply and said, "Sometimes even foes should get together to talk. Nothing may come of this talk, but if the sides can discuss without incident, that gives hope for the next meeting."

Tawnos thought there was more than that. The meeting for which the Chief Artificer was planning so carefully was not Fallaji and Yotian, he realized, nor queen and qadir. The meeting was between himself and his younger brother.

* * * * *

The messages started arriving soon after the Fallaji reached the borders of the Sword Marches, arriving at regular intervals, as Urza had ordered. The Fallaji contingent was smaller than that which they had presented at Korlinda, as the qadir had promised. The dragon engine was present, but it was being used to pull a great metal wain, almost as big as itself, with huge, gearlike wheels. While hitched to the wain, the engine moved slowly, keeping pace with the rest of the troops.

The Yotian council argued about the presence of the wain. The seneschal suggested it might be a gift. The Newest Captain thought it might contain additional troops. Urza told Tawnos it was a display of power, a reminder that Mishra had not been merely resting since Korlinda. In the end Kayla chose not to make an issue of the unexpected addition to the Fallaji party. Urza ordered one of the flights, grounded at the border, to return to normal operations, and a second to parallel the Fallaji party, remaining to the east and out of sight.

On the fifth day of the Fallaji journey southward, five days before the arrival of the party in Kroog, there were new rumors of a massing of Fallaji troops on the far northern border of the Sword Marches. The seneschal thought that, if true, it might be one of the more traditional raids, perhaps by individuals who wanted to see the negotiations crumble. The captain argued that, regardless of purpose, any Fallaji incursions would be disastrous at this time and the ornithopters were needed to scout in the desert.

Urza at first refused, only to be overruled by Kayla. Reluctantly, the Chief Artificer allowed three flights (including the one shadowing the dragon engine) to be reassigned to the far north. Urza did not explain to Tawnos the factors that convinced him to change his mind, but several of the household staff heard a serious row in the royal quarters. Tawnos knew that Urza spent the next few nights working late at the orniary. The Chief Artificer claimed to be working on improvements to the avenger-style automatons, but thereafter he attended the council only when specifically summoned by his wife.

On the tenth day the Fallaji arrived before the walls of Kroog. The battlements had been hung with colorful banners, as if festive bunting would conceal the strength and purpose of the stonework beneath. The walls were bedecked with most of the populace of Kroog as well, as were the windows of every building that commanded a view of the visitors. The merchants had made a killing selling telescopes, an Argivian fancy consisting of two polished lenses set along the length of a metal tube. Indeed, Kroog seemed a city of observers as the Fallaji party neared. Her Majesty, the Prince Consort, Tawnos, the seneschal, and the Newest Captain waited with other bureaucrats at the north gatehouse for the Fallaji to present themselves.

There were fewer Fallaji than there had been at Korlinda, and the sunlight sparkled off the polished brass of their wide helmets and heavy shoulder ornaments. But few counted the number of men, for the dragon engine captured everyone's attention.

Tawnos, standing with the others at the gatehouse, was amazed by the beast. It was as if a living thing had been transformed into a machine. It was a dragon whose muscles had been replaced with cables, its hide with plates of metal, its eyes with great gems. It moved like a living thing as well, with little flinches and muscle tics, swinging its head slowly from one side to another, apparently curious about its surroundings.

Urza had told Tawnos of the engine and had said that Mishra found it beneath the desert. But this was no Thran creation, Tawnos thought, and it was as far removed from the Chief Artificer's avengers as a living bird differed from the ornithopters. Tawnos was impressed, and that was with a prior warning from Urza. He could only imagine what the rest of the populace were thinking.

The dragon engine was in harness, like a caravan ox, and pulled the huge wagon almost as large as itself. The wain, though, held no sense of wonder as did the mechanical beast harnessed to it. The wagon looked like a metallic four-story inn that had been suddenly given wheels and turned loose on the world. Its sharp angles and exposed rivets marked it as originally being of Thran design. Numerous portals and battlements bristled along its flanks, set with catapults and small ballista. The weapons were unloaded for the moment and wrapped beneath tarps that no more concealed their purpose than the banners did the walls of Kroog.

Kayla had ordered the ornithopters displayed outside the walls, one flight to either side of the north gate. They were on the ground, their crews standing ready next to them. They were intended both as reassurance and as warning, much as a sheathed sword laid upon a table might remind one's opponent that while there was no intention of treachery, the negotiators were prepared to fight. The pilots, in blue and white tabards, waited patiently by their machines. The Fallaji formed a line opposite them, a respectful distance away.

The dragon engine and its burden drew up before the gates and came at last to rest. As it did so, Tawnos noted something Urza had not mentioned. A dull throbbing came from the beast as fluids gurgled through hidden tubes and hydraulic joints shifted in place. The humming was akin to a heartbeat, and Tawnos could feel it more than he could hear it.

The machines came to rest, and after a short interval, a door opened in the side of the great wain. A staircase was lowered, and down the stairs came two figures. Neither was the qadir. Instead Mishra led the way, followed by his assistant. Tawnos had not met either, yet from the way Mishra carried himself, Tawnos knew he must be Urza's brother.

The younger brother was shorter, heavier, and dark-haired, with a tightly trimmed beard. But there was something in his walk, and in the face beneath that beard, that marked him as kin to the Chief Artificer of Kroog, Prince Consort of Yotia. Mishra was bedecked in the flowing robes of a desert prince, his head bare, and his face beaming with a great smile. He blinked in the afternoon sun and waved to the crowds on the battlement. There were catcalls among the responding cheers, but the younger brother seemed not to notice.

Yet much as the wain was diminished by the dragon engine that served it, so too was Mishra dimmed by his companion. She was a slender woman with hair the color of bloodstained rubies, dressed in dark clothes, a flowing cape billowing behind her. She carried a simple, unadorned staff of black wood and seemingly did not recognize the crowd's shouts, for she kept her gaze forward. From Urza's description, Tawnos knew this must be Ashnod.

No qadir emerged from the metallic wain, and in the gatehouse the Yotian leaders held a quick conference. If the qadir was not present, noted the seneschal, then the queen should not appear either for the initial welcoming. A group similar in protocol should respond to the Fallaji's initial delegation. More might be taken as a sign of weakness, less as an insult.

That meant Urza and Tawnos would greet the new arrivals. The Chief Artificer nodded, his face stiffening slightly as he saw his brother on the field. Tawnos thought the artificer would rather speak with his brother privately, but this was not to be. The queen would remain at the gatehouse as the artificer and his apprentice met the Fallaji representatives.

Urza was stiff and formal as they crossed the open space between the city and the Fallaji. Tawnos kept an appropriate two paces behind and to the right, marshaling his own features to a calm demeanor.

Urza stopped before Mishra and Ashnod and without preamble raised his empty hands slightly, as if he were a priest giving benediction. "Welcome to Kroog, Brother," he said.

Mishra flung both arms outward, and for a moment, Tawnos thought the younger brother was going to rush his elder and hug him. Instead, Mishra bowed deeply. Tawnos noted that Ashnod gave a short bob of the head as well.

"We are honored by your invitation," said Mishra, rising again. The smile on his face could be earnest, thought Tawnos, or it could be the pasted-on smile of a Fallaji trader.

"We are honored by your presence," said Urza, though his words sounded to Tawnos's ears dry and bloodless. "Is your qadir with you?"

"Alas!" said Mishra, bowing again deeply, "I fear that his Most Wise and Earnest Presence could not accompany us on our mission of peace and mercy. Our empire is wide now, and there are other matters that require his attention."

Urza was silent for a moment, and Tawnos could see the muscles tighten along his jawline. "We should have been told if your leader was . . . otherwise occupied," he said at last.

"We understand your disappointment," replied Mishra quickly. "Be assured that it is shared by our most puissant and powerful master. I will not lie to you, Brother. After his last experience with your people, he wishes to be cautious. He has entrusted to me the power to negotiate fully on his behalf. However, if we are unwelcome because of his absence, we apologize and will humbly retreat the way we came." He bowed a third time.

Tawnos realized the younger brother was not making his exaggerated movements for Urza but rather for the large number of Yotians lining the walls. Even if the Chief Artificer had wanted to, he could not now send the Fallaji representatives away.

Tawnos held his face in a mask of solemn indifference, as he had back when as a lad he listened to his uncles speak. He kept his eyes forward, looking past Mishra into the middle distance.

After a few moments, he realized he was looking at Ashnod over her master's left shoulder. She too had the impassive look on her face of a child who is expected to behave herself while the parents talk.

Tawnos blinked, realizing the red-haired woman might think he was staring at her, and moved his gaze a few feet to the left toward one of the wheels of the great metal wain.

As he did so, Ashnod caught his eye and winked. It was a flutter, accompanied by the ghost of a smile. Tawnos started, his eyes darting back to the scarlet-haired woman. But by that time her face was an impassive, diplomatic mask.

All this occurred in the time it took for Urza to respond. "You are welcome as the representative of your people," he said. "Let me present you to the queen. If you will follow me?"

A brief bow here, and Mishra added softly, "And let me say you are looking well, Brother. I would have been heartbroken if you had perished at Korlinda."

"It is . . . " began Urza, and paused. The world seemed to turn around them for a moment; then he continued, "It is good to know you are safe as well. About Korlinda—"

Mishra held up a hand. "We can speak of the matter at length. Let me say that I have given it much thought over the past year. We will talk. But for the moment, we should not keep your queen waiting."

Urza's face tightened for a moment, then relaxed, and he nodded. "Of course." With that he spun on his heel and walked back toward the gate. Mishra followed, accompanied by the woman. Tawnos brought up the rear.

The red-haired woman hesitated as she passed the apprentice. She turned slightly, and said, "You must be Tawnos." She held out her hand.

Automatically, Tawnos took her fingers and bowed slightly over them. "I'm sorry. Yes, I'm Tawnos, apprentice to Urza. You are Mishra's chief apprentice, Ashnod?"

Ashnod withdrew her hand, and again a small smile played over her face. "Chief and only," she said. "It's typical of those two that they wouldn't bother to introduce us. Brilliant, Mishra is, but he sometimes has the social graces of an atog. It must run in the family, eh?"

Tawnos tried to form a response, but by the time he had thought of something relatively innocuous, she had turned back and was following the two brothers toward the gate. Tawnos shook his head slightly and brought up the rear, arriving at the gate as Urza was presenting Kayla, rolling off her various titles like a schoolmaster reading the roll.

" . . . Flower of the Mardun, Warlord's Daughter, Queen of the Yotians, and Warlady of Kroog, my wife, Kayla bin-Kroog," concluded Urza. "Mishra, the chosen representative of the Fallaji. The qadir was unable to attend and begs our forgiveness." Tawnos noted that Urza was looking at the seneschal as he said it, and that the nervous man flinched at the implied accusation. Kayla offered her hand to the younger brother.

"Urza spoke to me of your beauty," said Mishra, bowing deeply over her hand. "But I had forgotten his capacity for understatement. For him a majestic tree is only so many board-feet of lumber, and a desert vista only so many miles to cross. So, too, I see that he has seriously unvalued your charm."

A small smile played across Kayla's face. Tawnos thought the queen was amused, though she had long since become immune to fulsome praise. "Urza had spoken of his brother," she said, "but I must admit that I was unprepared for one so eloquent."

"I have few regrets in life," said Mishra, still grasping the queen's hand lightly, "and one of them is that I never had a sister. With you as my brother's wife, that is now remedied." With that he loosened her hand, and she gently withdrew it.

There were other introductions: Ashnod, Tawnos, the seneschal and the Captain of the Guard, and arrangements were made for the Fallaji to bivouac around their dragon engine. But the part that Tawnos remembered later, after it was all said and done, was the stony stare with which Urza favored his younger brother as Mishra flattered Kayla, and Mishra's toothy white smile as he regarded his brother's wife.

* * * * *

Sounds of the fight carried all the way down the hall. Tawnos had passed a gaggle of chambermaids speeding away from the royal quarters. Then he heard the arguing voices reverberate like steel balls against the surrounding walls. Closer still, the air itself gained weight and potency. He felt as if he were back on the seacoast watching a squall wade ashore, pushing the air in front of it. Undeterred, he pressed forward.

The door to the quarters was shut, but that did little to blunt the noises from within. This close, Tawnos could make out words, and he paused a moment before knocking.

"The answer is no!" shouted Urza.

"Its a good trade!" rejoined Kayla just as loudly. "They will leave the Sword Marches alone!"

"It's not yours to trade away!" thundered Urza. Tawnos had never heard the Chief Artificer that loud before, even when he was bawling out the most incompetent of apprentices.

Tawnos hesitated at the door. Would it be better to interrupt and make them aware that their fight was resounding through the palace, or to wait for a lull in the shouting?

Tawnos knocked. There was a testy growl of, "What?" from the other side, coupled with a more feminine, disciplined, "Enter."

Tawnos entered the room cautiously and said, "The Fallaji delegation is waiting for the tour of the orniary, Chief Artificer."

Urza shot his apprentice a look as frosty as the Ronom Glacier. Yes, thought Tawnos, this was a particularly bad time to interrupt. Across the room, Kayla was standing, hands folded in front of her. In the privy council, that usually meant that a particular subject was closed.

"If you want me to conduct the tour . . ." added Tawnos, but Urza already had his hand up.

"I'll be there," said the Chief Artificer, as Tawnos knew he would. The idea of his brother padding through his research area without

Urza being present was unthinkable.

To his wife, Urza snapped, "This discussion is not over, my wife."

Kayla nodded curtly. "You are correct, my husband."

Urza gave a sharp half-bow, and left the room. Kayla said, "Tawnos, remain a moment."

Tawnos looked at the Chief Artificer. Urza scowled, then gave Tawnos a nod. "Come along when you can," he said, and then he was gone, his formal cape billowing behind him.

Tawnos turned back to the queen. "Your Majesty," he said, then added, "Ma'am."

"You heard our 'discussion' out in the hall?" she said.

Tawnos took a deep breath. "I think they heard your 'discussion' in the domes of Tomakul."

Kayla smiled and slumped into one of her chairs, a heavy, throne-like monster with ornately carved arms.

"I did not hear much of it," continued Tawnos quickly. "The stonework carries the intensity but not the nature of your words."

Kayla laced her hands, templed her fingers, and touched them to her lips. "Would you say the talks have gone well these past few days?"

"Very well," replied Tawnos. And indeed, they had verged on phenomenal, considering the abortive talks in Korlinda. Gifts had been presented. Toasts had been exchanged. Platitudes had been spoken, and effusive compliments had been offered. Private meetings between Kayla and Mishra had led to discussions among the Fallaji and in the privy council. The good feelings between the two sides had culminated in Urza's offer to show his brother his orniary. In return Mishra had offered to let Urza and his assistant look at the dragon engine and great wain. Things were going very well indeed.

"And Ambassador Mishra?" asked Kayla. "Your opinion of him?"

Tawnos hesitated, unsure of what Kayla wanted to know. "He is . . ." The apprentice searched for words. "He is like his brother, only different. More effusive. More willing to talk."

"But no less guarded," said Kayla.

Tawnos thought for a moment. Yes, despite all the talk and praise and compliments, Mishra remained even more closed than his brother. He seemed earnest, but was his earnestness the truth or only a mask?

Tawnos realized he would never think of Urza in that fashion. "I rarely know what Urza is thinking, but that is because he is quiet. I don't know what Mishra is thinking, because he is talking."

Kayla gave a small smile and said, "He is very charming, and I have heard that the desert traders have the ability to talk a snake out of its skin. Do you think he has the ability to enforce any deal made here?"

Tawnos nodded. "He brought the dragon engine with him. The men who follow him apparently think well of him."

Kayla was silent for a moment, then said, "Do you think we can trust him?"

Tawnos held up his hands. "I don't think we have given him much chance to prove our trust so far."

"Indeed," said Kayla, and pressed her fingers to her lips. "What if I were to tell you that Mishra was prepared to sign a treaty recognizing Yotia's claim to the Sword Marches?"

Amazed, Tawnos said, "The qadir is willing to do this?"

Kayla held up a finger. "I said 'what if.' Diplomacy is filled with what ifs, idle ideas that are launched. If they fail to fly, they are quickly denied and more quickly forgotten."

"Like prototypes in the orniary," smiled Tawnos, and he thought about the nature of the offer. "What would be the price for such a boon?"

Kayla nodded. "Their declared price involves protection of Fallaji natives among our populace, guards for their caravans within our land, and a token payment for the land seized, but no formal apology for seizing it. Along with a recognition of the qadir as ruler of the united Fallaji people. In national terms, these are very small things indeed. But there is one last piece, and that is the sticking point."

Kayla was quiet for a moment, and Tawnos did not interrupt the pause. When she spoke again, it was in cool tones.

"What are the abilities of Urza's stone? The one he wears around his neck?"

"His Mightstone!" said Tawnos. Light broke over him. "Mishra wants his brother's talisman!"

"What does it do?" persisted Kayla. "He is rarely without it."

Tawnos thought about what he had seen Urza do with the stone. Slowly he replied, "It seems to make artifacts and creatures more powerful within a limited range. He uses it to heal flawed power crystals, but it seems to work that way only in his hands. And he holds it when he is thinking, though that may be just force of habit."

"Goodsir Mishra has his own stone, mate to his brother's," said Kayla. "Has he told you that?"

Tawnos was silent for a moment, then shook his head.

"I was surprised at that as well, the more so that it was Mishra who told me," said Kayla, a ripple of irritation evident in her voice. "So the stone has some power, and Mishra wants it. Mishra said his stone sang to him. Does Urza's stone sing?"

"Not that I have noticed," said Tawnos.

"Nor I," agreed Kayla. "The ambassador may be using some desert idiom I am not familiar with, so it may just be a flowery allusion. Yet the fact remains that Mishra is willing to guarantee peace, backed by his dragon engine and other devices he has hinted at, all if Urza will give up his stone."

Tawnos shook his head. "Urza would not do this, I think."

"You think correctly," said Kayla gloomily. "Hence the 'discussion' that shook the halls of this palace."

The queen of Yotia placed her palms together, fingers extended, and twisted them a quarter-turn against each other, then back. It struck Tawnos that he had seen Urza use the same mannerism when faced with a problem in design. He wondered if the queen had picked up the habit from her Prince Consort, or the Chief Artificer from his royal wife.

"I do not think it would do the nation harm if Mishra was to get the other half of his stone," she said.

"But it might do Urza harm," replied Tawnos. "In doing so, it could harm the nation."

"Agreed," said Kayla, again twisting her palms against each other, then setting them down in her lap. "But can I let this opportunity pass by? Am I condemning the Sword Marches to continual raids and the rest of the country to a constant military footing because of an item coveted by both brothers?"

Tawnos was silent for a moment, then said, "Urza is right."

Kayla's face fell, but Tawnos added, "You both need to talk more on the subject. You and Urza. You and Mishra. Mishra and Urza themselves. Perhaps there is some common ground that frees the Sword Marches. Perhaps Mishra is merely testing the waters, trying the prototype of an idea to see what your reaction is. Perhaps he asks for the stone and will settle for something else, something you don't know he wants yet."

Kayla sighed. "These are the problems of rulership. There are some situations that resist all easy solutions."

"Which is why I am trying to avoid providing you with any," said Tawnos.

Kayla nodded. "Your talents are wasted as Urza's apprentice, Tawnos. You would make an excellent seneschal."

Tawnos winced comically. "You already have an excellent

seneschal. And were I not Urza's apprentice, who would you talk to about the Prince Consort?"

That sally brought a true smile to Kayla Bin-Kroog's face. "Agreed. Now be off with you. But be sure to tell me later how the brothers are getting along."

Tawnos rejoined the Chief Artificer at the orniary as Urza was explaining the better control of the wing surface with a double-bend structure. Mishra was attentive and seemed to ask all the right questions, leading Urza each time into his next point. Urza, for his part, was scholarly but not pedantic about his work. To Tawnos there seemed to be no friction between the brothers, and he deemed it likely that the subject of the stone had not arisen on either side.

Tawnos looked around. Most of the rest of the Fallaji seemed bored beyond human conception, and the students present had heard most of Urza's explanations before. They were staring at odd bits of the orniary, trying to keep from falling asleep.

Ashnod, however, was watching Tawnos. When he looked her way, she turned her head back to the two brothers. Then, as soon as he turned away, he could feel the pressure of her eyes on him. It made him very uncomfortable.

Tawnos had assumed from what Urza had said that Ashnod was Mishra's lover as well as his student. Yet the two did not behave as intimates. And that earlier wink (if it were truly a wink) and now these stares-that-were-not-stares told a different story entirely.

The talk lasted through most of the early afternoon. Mishra made a number of small suggestions of his own concerning the design, while Urza pointed out what other changes they would necessitate. Finally it became clear they would not have time to tour the dragon engine as well that evening, and indeed there would be much rushing-about if that evening's state dinner was to go off as planned. Mishra was effusive in his apologies.

"I can see that you've achieved much here. Once there is peace, I hope to be able to establish my own small foundry and laboratory," he said.

"When you do," responded Urza, "let me send you the notes on my teaching experiences. I discovered that certain methods work better than others in holding the attention of young men."

"As if we never had that problem when we were young," said Mishra with a laugh, and Urza managed a tight smile.

Yes, thought Tawnos, Urza had not entirely forgotten the argument with Kayla, but he was not going to let it spill out before his brother. It would not be he who created an incident, not he who spoiled his wife's hopes for peace.

The state dinner was held within the great courtyard, an open-air celebration in the Fallaji style to honor the guests. Every cushion and throw rug in the palace was pressed into service, and a fine repast of roast lamb and spiced chicken was laid out for the attendees, who sprawled alongside low tables. The Fallaji, after too many suppers in stiff-backed chairs, were notably at ease, whereas the Yotians continually shifted and moved to find suitable resting places. The seneschal had found a band of Muaharin musicians in the city who had no qualms about playing for members of the Suwwardi clan, and the air was filled with their high-pitched strings and hearty shouts.

Kayla sat with Urza on one side of her, Mishra on the other. She spoke with both, though she was mostly attentive to her husband, at one point offering him a date stuffed with cheese. He did not let her feed him but rather took the fruit from her hand and smiled at her, popping the treat into his mouth. Those city folk who watched the royal couple were no doubt delighted by their display of affection. To Tawnos it was a sign that perhaps the storm in their private quarters had blown over. Mishra, for his part, when talking to Kayla, continually extolled some virtue or another of desert life.

The meal ran eight courses, in the Yotian tradition, but all the courses were of Fallaji dishes. In addition to the lamb and chicken there was a broiled fish done with hot peppers, salads of spinach and goat cheese, and all manner of salted meats. Everything was served with a pungent wine smelling of cinnamon. The wine, called *nabiz*, was as potent as it was pungent, and Tawnos noted that a number of the Yotians used it to offset the discomforts of sprawling across the pillows. Most of his table consisted of Fallaji lieutenants, who laughed among themselves, and once, when a recognizable tune appeared from the band, rose to engage in a long line dance. Mishra joined them, keeping pace with their kicks and flourishes.

A shadow moved along Tawnos's side. "Interesting, no?" asked Ashnod, as she settled down next to Tawnos.

"Traditional warrior's dance," replied Tawnos. Ashnod held out her cup, one of the gold ones from the warlord's tenth anniversary celebration. Tawnos reached for the ewer of *nabiz* and refilled the goblet.

Ashnod made a rude noise at Tawnos's words. "It's one more boys-only tradition," she said with a slight slur in her voice, and Tawnos wondered how much wine she had had already. "The Fallaji are typically chauvinist, and the Suwwardi the worst of the pack. Mishra had to practically club the qadir over the head to agree to negotiate with a woman in the first place. Women should be out raising the children and baking flat bread, not getting involved in politics, war, religion, science, or any of the rest of that 'boys' stuff.' "

Tawnos did not let his surprise at Ashnod's words show. "Times change for all of us," he said. "Perhaps the Fallaji will change as well."

"Not in my lifetime or in yours," returned Ashnod. She pressed a slim hand against her bare breastbone and stifled a burp.

"They are here, negotiating with a woman, and things are going well. And you, a woman, are among their number," Tawnos said.

"I am merely tolerated," replied the red-haired woman. "I am Mishra's apprentice and assistant. The great Mishra is as much the leader of the Fallaji now as the qadir, and the chiefs trust him more than they do the fat young pup currently running things. So they put up with me. And the Fallaji legends say things about dangerous women with red hair." She set down her cup and ran both hands through her long tresses, arching her back as she did so. "So they fear me as well."

"Should they?" asked Tawnos. He knew he was feeling the effects of the *nabiz* work through his system as well, but he could not suppress his interest in this woman.

"Fear me?" said Ashnod, with a devilish smile. "I'd like to think so. But if Mishra left them tomorrow, I would be gone as well before nightfall; of that I have no doubt."

Tawnos made no comment and instead looked at the dancers. Most of the Fallaji had joined the dance, which had transformed from a line into a spiral curling in on itself. Mishra led the procession and had enticed the spindly seneschal to accompany him. The birdlike man tried to mimic Mishra's steps and did an admirable job miming the steps, bows, and shouts. Other members of the palace staff had joined the procession, but both unfamiliarity and spiced wine worked against them, reducing them to mere shufflers in the procession. The Fallaji did not seem to mind and in fact seemed to spur them to increased gyrations and bellows.

"Things are going very well," said Tawnos.

"Better than you could imagine," said Ashnod softly.

"What did you think of the orniary?" asked Tawnos.

"More impressive than I expected," replied Ashnod, shaking her hair back. "Master Mishra is jealous, you know. Not that he'd admit it, but he's been talking about getting a place to set up his own work for years. I think that's why he wants this peace treaty. He's been recruiting artisans from Tomakul and Zegon, but he has no permanent place for them."

Tawnos nodded. Ashnod was sharing more than she should, but he had no problems listening to her. "Still," he said, "it is a pity we ran long at the orniary. I would have liked to have examined . . ." Tawnos stared into her stormy eyes and almost lost his thought. ". . . Mishra's dragon engine," he finished lamely.

"Who's to say you can't?" asked Ashnod.

"Well, there is always tomorrow," said Tawnos.

Ashnod shook her head. "Not tomorrow. Tonight."

Tawnos stared at her. "There's a banquet going on."

"Later," said Ashnod. "Listen. Can you get past the Yotian guards on our wing of the palace?"

Tawnos thought for a moment. "They know me. I don't think there would be a problem."

"And I can get past the brass hats guarding the engine," said the woman, shaking her head again. "They know me and fear me, remember? I can give you a private tour. Interested?"

Tawnos stammered for a moment, and Ashnod added, "Come on. We're supposed to be students. That means we can occasionally play hooky. You've never played hooky?"

"Never," said Tawnos, and realized he was blushing. "Well, hardly ever. You?"

Ashnod's face became suddenly stern, mocking her companion. "Never," she said in a low, masculine tone, then smiled and winked. A definite wink this time. "Well, hardly ever. So, are you interested?"

Tawnos realized that it might be an opportunity to gain additional insights into Mishra for the queen and the Chief Artificer. "Yes," he said at last. "I think I'd like that."

"Dandy," said Ashnod, rising smoothly from her seat without a sign of the effects of the alcohol she had been consuming. "After the midnight bell, then. Come to my quarters. And bring a civilized, decent dry wine, will you? All this desert wine is like liquefied candy."

With that she was gone, disappearing along the edges of the cluster of drunken Fallaji and Yotians, all bellowing and shuffling to the music, forming an ever-growing maelstrom of celebrants.

Chapter 14

Night Moves

Tawnos picked out a white wine from the larder's private stock, which the palace cook assured him was the finest vintage the Korlis vinyards had produced in a hundred years. Still Urza's apprentice felt more like a spy than a scholar with a jug of wine. As an afterthought he picked up his yarrow wood serpent, the one that had impressed Urza years ago. He wound the toy's spring, set the latch, and put the coiled wooden snake in his pocket.

Off across the city, the midnight bell was tolling. Servants would be clearing the banquet by now, and those revellers not capable of making it back to their quarters would be rolled to a convenient corner and covered with a blanket until morning. Urza and Kayla had left arm-in-arm, their heads bent together in conversation. Mishra had completed one last dance with his men, then bade them return to the encampment. He and Ashnod would be staying at the quarters provided in the palace. At the time Tawnos thought that the availability of soft beds and running water had something to do with that decision.

After talking to Ashnod, Tawnos had stopped drinking the *nabiz*. However, the other drink being offered was a thick, syrupy coffee served in small cups. The mixture turned his stomach slightly, and left him feeling nervous.

At least Tawnos hoped that it was only the coffee and the *nabiz* that had unsettled his stomach.

Tawnos paused at the hallway leading to the guest quarters, then changed direction, heading instead for the orniary at the far end of the palace. It was only past midnight. Urza would still be awake and could tell him what to look for in particular when inspecting the metallic beast.

The apprentice arrived to discover Kayla quietly backing out and closing the door of the orniary, watching into the workshop as she did so. She gave a small jump when she saw Tawnos standing there, then raised a finger to her lips.

"He's resting," she whispered.

"It is early for him," said Tawnos quietly.

"Its been a long day," she said, "and a good one, for him."

"Yes," said Tawnos. "He and his brother seemed to be getting along."

Kayla pushed a loose strand of hair back, and a small smile broke across her face. "Yes, that," she said, "among other things. In any event, I don't think you should disturb him for a little while."

Tawnos nodded, suddenly aware that he was carrying a bottle of white wine with him. Fortunately, Kayla did not say anything about it. Regardless, he shifted the jug slightly behind him and asked, "About the, uh, discussion you two had, earlier."

Kayla shrugged, and moved away from the door. "We've talked. We had a good talk."

"And what did he say?" asked Tawnos.

Kayla hesitated for a moment, then said, "He didn't say no."

Tawnos gave a sage nod. "Well, that's a start."

"A good start," agreed Kayla. "Now, I think we both have other places to be at the moment."

Tawnos blushed slightly. Of course the queen had seen the bottle, and made the assumption he had some late-night rendezvous. Tomorrow he would tell her the truth of the matter and the nature of the dragon engine. For the moment, he merely bowed and retreated back toward the guest wing.

The guest quarters consisted of a separate wing of the palace of Kroog, and Ashnod and her master had been placed on separate floors, each in a huge encampment of suites. A handpicked group of servants, known for their open ears and shut mouths, had been assigned to the wing, along with a number of loyal guards. The Fallaji were allowed to keep their own bodyguards, with the understanding that they too would be under guard. After the second night Mishra had dismissed his own guards as a sign of his trust in their hosts.

The arrangements were very Kroogian in nature. Each offer of beneficence concealed some implicit method of control. Tawnos wondered how much of it was Urza's doing, and decided that there was little involving his brother's visit that the Chief Artificer was not aware of.

The guards raised their short pikes to let him pass. Tawnos knocked and the unlatched door opened beneath his knock.

Ashnod was working at the table, fitting wires around an animal skull, which had been affixed to her dark wooden staff. She held up a hand as Tawnos entered, "One moment," she said and looped a small strand through the skull's nostrils. "There. Done." She looked up.

There was a curious fire in her eyes that Tawnos had seen before. He had seen it in Urza's eyes when he was working on a new refinement of an invention, and in the mirror when he himself was helping the Chief Artificer.

Ashnod blinked and the fire banked for the moment, but now that Tawnos had seen it in its full glory, he could still detect it. "Just a little project I've been puttering with," she said, setting the staff aside.

Tawnos looked at the staff and noted that the animal skull fit snugly over the end. "Anything you need help with?" he offered.

Ashnod shook her head. "Just a craft to keep my hands busy." Then her eyes lit up. "Ah, you've brought the wine! I'll get the goblets! We'll do a toast, and then take the jug with us to the engine!"

Tawnos set the wine down on the table and seated himself at a bench. "I hope that this is not too late."

"Not late at all," said Ashnod, saluting the other apprentice with a pair of brass cups, their stems crossed and clenched in her small fist. "I'm used to working on Mishra's time. He's up early and to bed very, very late."

"The Chief Artificer is much the same," said Tawnos, pouring the wine. "I've learned to catnap."

Ashnod took her cup. "I never could do that. But that thick coffee they drink in the desert, *sanduq*, works for me. One cup and I can stay awake for a day and night. Then I fall into a coma from exhaustion."

Tawnos rubbed the back of his neck. He had had no less than four of the small cups at dinner.

Ashnod raised her goblet. "A toast! To the madmen who are our masters!"

Tawnos blinked. "Madmen?"

Ashnod lowered her cup slightly. "To Mishra and Urza?" she suggested.

"To the brother artificers," responded Tawnos and returned the toast. Both took a sip of the wine. Tawnos had never cared for the smell or taste of white wine, but after the heavily spiced meal and pungent drinks it was a gods-send.

Ashnod took the seat opposite the tawny-haired apprentice. "So you don't think our masters are mad?"

"Well, divinely inspired sometimes," said Tawnos. "But mad?"

"There is a fine line between the two," noted Ashnod. "Can we say that the gods or madness control them? How many times has your Urza suggested something completely irrational, only to be proven correct?"

Tawnos shrugged. "I always assumed he had a reason for his actions, even if he did not share it with me."

"Humph!" said Ashnod. "I thought it was a tradition that apprentices always complained about their masters. You were a toy maker, I hear. Didn't you complain about the master toy maker then?"

"Well, the master toy maker of Jorilin was my uncle, so I never—" said Tawnos, then stopped as Ashnod broke out in peals of laughter.

Ashnod must have read the disappointment in Tawnos's face, because she quickly cut her chuckling short. "You sound like a baby duck, always following along behind its mother duck. Such loyalty is so sweet. So your first master was a relative, and your new master is . . .?"

Tawnos shrugged. "He is Urza. He knows more than anyone else I've ever met."

Ashnod looked at Tawnos, and said in a low voice, "Gods below, you're serious, aren't you?"

Tawnos shrugged again. "Sure. Why have a mas . . . a superior who doesn't know more than you do?"

"But, you know things he doesn't, right?" said Ashnod, motioning with her now empty cup.

"Well, yes," said Tawnos, pouring the wine for her, and then, as an afterthought, topping off his own goblet. "But of the important matters, he knows more than I do."

"And that's why we stay with them, then? They know more than we do?" said Ashnod.

"In part," said Tawnos, leaning back. "A small part. I mean Urza is demanding, and precise and hard to follow sometimes when he's hot on an idea."

"Mishra's the same way," said Ashnod. "And you get the idea that when he explains something to you, its as if he's reigning himself in, choosing simple words and small ideas that you can understand. And he expects you to keep up with him."

Tawnos chuckled now. "That's Urza sometimes. You saw the wind chamber in the orniary? Urza had it built so students could prove their modifications of the ornithopters would *not* work, saving him the trouble of explaining it and them the trouble of building a full working model."

"Or nonworking model," said Ashnod, and Tawnos smiled at that. "Like I said earlier, at the feast, Mishra really envies the sense of place that your brother has. Big palace. School of assistants. Regular supplies." She paused for a moment, then added, "Beautiful wife."

Tawnos responded, "There are things in Mishra's life that Urza envies. There's the dragon engine, of course."

"He does?" said Ashnod, looking over her cup. "Urza said that?"

"Once you get away from machinery, Urza doesn't *say* much," replied Tawnos, "but you understand his moods, his looks. What he talks about, and more importantly, what he doesn't talk about."

"Ditto for Master Mishra," said Ashnod. "Or rather, he talks, but he avoids certain subjects. And you can tell what's on his mind by what he doesn't talk about. It appears like a genie in the center of the whirlwind."

"Right," said Tawnos, "and Urza feels that Mishra has a greater sense of freedom, sometimes. Urza feels that he has to be so responsible for everything, and the desert offers freedom. What's so funny?"

"Nothing," said Ashnod, stifling a giggle. "But it's amusing that the Fallaji are currently in the iron grip of a petulant child-man. If you think the desert means freedom, you've never met the qadir."

"I think Urza would much rather be working on artifacts than trying to support a nation," said Tawnos.

"Agreed for Mishra as well," said Ashnod, raising her goblet in another toast. "It's the love of artifacts that binds them together and probably us to them as well. There's something about getting beneath the skin of a new device."

"Understanding a new concept," agreed Tawnos.

"Unlocking its inner secrets."

"Understanding the design philosophy behind it."

"Feeling its power."

"Comprehending its purpose," said Tawnos, "and expanding its abilities."

Ashnod laughed again, and it was a relaxed laugh. "There are so very few of us, you know. I'm one of the few that can talk to Mishra and understand him."

"I feel much the same way with Urza," said Tawnos. As an after-thought, "And with you as well."

"I won't try to use small words," said Ashnod.

"I'll try to keep up," said Tawnos.

"Its all so difficult," said Ashnod. "I mean, I feel doubly walled-away from everything. First, a powerful woman among the Fallaji is an exception, not a rule. And second, being an intelligent being among the desert people is so—"

"Frustrating," suggested Tawnos.

"Exactly," said Ashnod. "Pour me another."

"We should see the engine," said Tawnos.

"There's time," she said. "Time for everything in the world."

Tawnos poured, and said, "I went back to Jorilin a few months ago, and was telling my aunts and uncles what I was doing. And they were very polite and appreciative, but I don't think they understood my work at all."

"At least they were appreciative," said Ashnod. "I get hostile stares from the Suwwardi. But it was the same at Zegon. At first I thought it was because I was a woman, but then people were distant because I was smarter than everyone else. It's frustrating, to be smart. It separates you from the rest of the populace."

"It is difficult being different," Tawnos admitted.

"And I bet the continual work keeps you away from your family. Your friends," said Ashnod. "Your wife."

"I'm, uh, not married," said Tawnos.

"It wasn't you I was talking about," said Ashnod. "But you don't even have a regular young lady, I'll bet."

"Well, I have been busy," said Tawnos defensively.

"I rest my case," said Ashnod, slapping the tabletop with the fleshy part of her palm. "Just like Mother Duck Urza. You're working for the most powerful man in Yotia and you don't have the girls flocking to you?"

Tawnos shrugged. "What about you?"

"Among the Fallaji? Hah!" She slapped the table again. "I really think they have to have a breeding program to produce such oafs!"

"What about Mishra?" asked Tawnos.

Ashnod's chuckle died. "Mishra," she said, and her eyes grew a bit misted. "Early on, yes. But it wasn't as much a relationship as it was a power thing. Sort of who-can-control-who. And it got old fast, and soon he was back to worrying about his precious engines. I don't like playing second to machinery."

Tawnos nodded. So there had been a relationship between Mishra and his pupil, but that was apparently in the past. But there was something else in her words that he almost missed.

"Engines?" asked Tawnos.

"Pardon?" Ashnod blinked.

"You said he worries about his engines," said Tawnos. "Plural."

Ashnod pulled up short. "There's the dragon engine. And the great wain it's pulling. The Fallaji call that engine a war machine, but Mishra told everyone to not refer to it as such during the talks. It might make the Yotians nervous."

"Uh-huh," said Tawnos, filing away that bit of information for later. Perhaps a tour of the war machine was in order as well.

Tawnos decided to push a little further. They obviously weren't going to get to the dragon engine until the wine was gone, and perhaps not even then. "So does Mishra have the power to enforce a peace?"

"If he wants it, yes," said Ashnod. "The qadir will whine and moan, but most of the lesser sheiks already back Mishra. The tribal chieftains want it all one way or another. Either the glories of war or the bliss of peace, without a middle ground. They're like machines that way. Easy to command and control."

"So what does Mishra truly want?" said Tawnos. "I mean, Urza can help with him establishing his own school, if that's his goal."

Ashnod shook her head. "The Fallaji way is not to accept aid, or gifts, or charity. It is to take what they want, through trade, or force of arms, or guile, or whatever else is required. The old warlord figured that out, but I don't think good Queen Kayla has a clue."

Tawnos frowned. "Mishra is not Fallaji. He is Argivian, like Urza."

Ashnod countered, "Mishra has lived among the Fallaji, and come to lead them. He understands their ways better than Urza understands the Yotians. No, Mishra at his heart is jealous of his brother, and wants what belongs to him."

Tawnos thought of his discussion with Kayla earlier in the day. "The stone."

Ashnod nodded. "The stone. Mishra told me the one he carried was once a larger stone, split in two through his brother's actions. Did Urza tell you the same?"

Tawnos worked his mouth, but no sound came out. "We never talked about it, and I never thought to ask."

"Baby Duck!" spat Ashnod, "Mishra envies his brother his soft life and laboratory and beautiful wife. That's true. But what he really wants is the stone."

"Is it worth trading away the Sword Marches for it?" asked Tawnos.

"Its worth *talking* about trading the Suwwardi Marches for it," laughed Ashnod. "The Fallaji get what they want, by war or guile. And if everything's gone well enough, he's already succeeded."

Ashnod realized at once that she had said too much, and put a hand over her mouth. At last she said, "I shouldn't say anything else about that. Diplomatic secrets and all that. We should go see the dragon engine."

Tawnos rose, his mind running through the events of the past day. Meeting Kayla outside the orniary. The fact she was doting on Urza at the banquet, where earlier they were going at it hammer and tongs. The fact that she was insistent Tawnos get along and not bother Urza. They both had places to be, she had said.

He didn't say no, she had said.

"I have to go," Tawnos said.

Ashnod rose across from him. "We have all night."

"I think I need to talk to Urza," he said.

"It's late, even for Urza," said Ashnod. "Perhaps if I accompanied you."

"Hopefully not too late," muttered Tawnos, and paused by the door. He turned and said, "You'll have to stay here, I'm afraid. This has been a very interesting evening, and I hope that I'm wrong about what I'm thinking, because I would like to talk to you again, later."

And with that he was gone, and the short pikes of the guards were visible as the door swung shut. Ashnod shook her head behind him, cradling her brass goblet in one hand. Outside, Tawnos was shouting for the guards to find Ambassador Mishra.

Said too much, she thought. And too soon. She shook her head and drained the goblet of the last of the wine.

Then she went to her jewelry box and removed a pair of earrings. She pried the iridescent stones from them and put the skull-headed staff back on the table. Slowly but with practiced skill, she started to fit the small power stones into the skull's eyes.

* * * * *

Tawnos had to shake Urza awake. The Chief Artificer did not rouse when his apprentice burst into the orniary, nor when he called his name. There was an overturned ewer of the pungent wine on the floor, but only a thin stream issued from its wide mouth. Similarly, a pair of half-empty goblets left sweating circles on the plans on the work desk. Urza was curled up tightly in a blanket, snoring softly, on the day cot he would use when working late or when fighting with Kayla.

Tawnos shook Urza's shoulder, hard, and the artificer was awake in a moment, sitting bolt upright, his eyelids beating rapidly to blink back the sleep. "Tawnos? What? Is there a fire? What's wrong?" Beneath the blanket, Urza was half-dressed, and those clothes he was wearing were bunched together in odd shapes.

Tawnos looked at Urza, and said, "Sir, your stone."

Instinctively Urza's fingers went to his chest, where the stone normally hung. They closed on empty air. Immediately he raised the hand to touch his neck, but the chain that hung there was missing.

"The stone!" he said, the last dregs of sleep banished from his eyes, replaced by a hot fire. "Where is it?" He immediately began tearing up the bedclothes and blankets.

"Sir," said Tawnos, "I ran into your wife as she was leaving here. . . ."

"Kayla?" said Urza, looking up. Then his face turned stern. "Kayla," he said again, a dagger's edge in his voice.

Urza became a flurry of action, gathering his banquet regalia into some semblance of order. He grabbed the cape, looking for the loops, then abandoned it entirely, cursing and flinging it across the room. Then he was at the door, bellowing for Tawnos to follow.

Tawnos was taller than Urza, and should have been able to catch up to the smaller man easily. But Urza moved as if he was an ornithopter incarnate, gliding through the halls at inhuman speed, passing the guards as if they were no more than ghosts. Tawnos was himself stopped by guards from the guest wing, who informed him that Mishra was not in his quarters. A full search of the wing revealed nothing, they added. Would Tawnos want them to seal the palace and send a runner to the Fallaji encampment to determine if Mishra had returned there? Tawnos hastily agreed, but by the time he concluded this brief conversation, Urza had vanished ahead of him.

There were shouts again from the royal quarters as Tawnos approached, but this time both of the voices were male, and booming. In addition, this time the door was open, nearly ripped from its hinges, and Tawnos thought it opened with a sharp kick as opposed to a twist of the latch. From the doorway issued an ever-changing spectrum of light.

Tawnos paused in the doorway and raised a hand to peer past the light. It issued from Urza's Mightstone, and from Mishra's gem as well, forming the poles of a magnet, with the light itself acting like metal filings stretched between them. Urza had regained his stone, and now was snarling at his brother across the room. Mishra was shouting something else incomprehensible back at him, the warm smile of the Fallaji ambassador replaced with a feral snarl. Their words were lost in an angry humming of energy between the two stones. Between them, against the far wall, was Kayla bin-Kroog.

Tawnos noticed that Urza was not the only one who had dressed in a rush. Mishra's clothes were in an equal disarray, and the queen had a sheet wrapped around her torso, clutched at her chest. She saw Tawnos and her face shone with relief. She said something that Tawnos could not hear over the throbbing pulses of the battling stones. She took a step forward, toward him.

Tawnos threw up his hands and shouted for her to stay back. Whatever was happening between the stones, and between the brothers, involved energies he neither recognized nor trusted.

It could have been Tawnos's shout, or his wave of his arms. Or it could have been seeing Kayla, stepping almost into the energies between the two stones. Or it could have been a moment of weakness on Urza's part.

But Urza dropped his stone. Only for an instant, and he still gripped it in his hand. But he dropped his stone, and it was enough.

A violent rainbow of energy spewed forth from Mishra's stone, and slammed into Urza. The lanky Chief Artificer was bodily lifted up by the force of the blow and flung backward, against the armoire, breaking the doors of that cabinet inward from the impact.

Then suddenly the energy from Mishra's stone went out, and it was as if those within the room were suddenly plunged into the dark, so great was the magnitude of difference in the light. Tawnos blinked and started toward where he knew Urza lay. Someone heavy and burly, Mishra, he realized later, slammed into him, brushing past him and out the door.

Kayla was at Urza's side already, crying as she knelt next to his prostrate form. Urza's eyes were open, but showed only the whites, and his breath was shallow and frothy. Still clenched in his hand was his Mightstone, a rainbow of colors leaking between his fingers.

"The temple amulets," said Tawnos to Kayla. "The ones Urza made. Do you have one here? Perhaps we can . . ."

Kayla was nodding but neither had time to finish his or her thoughts. The stone clenched in Urza's hand began to pulse more, to flash through the spectrum, and into ranges that Tawnos felt more than saw. Slowly, Urza's other hand raised, and grasped the stone, and his breathing became more regular. His eyes closed, and when they opened again, they were normal.

No, they were not normal, Tawnos realized. They were filled with emotion. Filled with rage.

Urza got up. Kayla tried to restrain him, to tell him that he should rest until the temple priests arrived, but he brought up an arm to ward her off. He brought it up too hard and too fast, for he knocked Kayla with it. She sprawled backward, and Tawnos rose with his superior, putting a hand out to Urza's shoulder.

Urza batted the offered hand away. "Where is he?" he snarled. His hair was a tangle, and Urza looked more like a madman than an artificer.

Tawnos said nothing, but looked at the door. Urza was striding toward it at once. Kayla shouted after him, but he did not look back.

Kayla was sobbing now, her tears staining the sheet gathered in front of her. "I tried," she said, then took a deep breath, "I tried to do the best thing for my country, Tawnos."

Tawnos could not think of anything to say, but there were more shouts in the hallway. Tawnos helped Kayla to her feet. "Get something on, and bring guards," he said, and was out of the doorway as well.

There was a great clamor toward the guest wing, and Tawnos thought that Urza had found his brother all too quickly. There were shouts and screams and an unearthly flickering of light. He ran for the wing, hoping to prevent any fatalities.

Instead of Urza and Mishra he found Ashnod. She was wielding the staff that she had been working on earlier. Now its eyes glowed with the eldritch nature of power stones, and lightning coursed along the wires that had been spun along the skull. There were several of the guards down along the hallway, most of them clutching their heads and moaning.

Ashnod was swinging the staff back and forth, the gold-lit skull trailing a shadow of color. She was unharmed as yet, but sweat cascaded down her neck and shoulders.

The leader of the guards was preparing a massed attack, but Tawnos put a hand on his shoulder, and indicated that he wanted to try to disarm the woman first.

Tawnos stepped into full view, hands raised and empty. Ashnod paused for a moment, then barked, "I want to leave now. Is there a problem?"

Tawnos tried to smile, conscious that he looked as insincere as he felt. "There has been a bit of an incident," he said. "I'm afraid you're going to have to stay for a while."

"I'm afraid not," said Ashnod, and brought her staff up, the skull-head oozing golden fire.

The blow hit Tawnos square in the stomach, and he could feel the pain rush from that center to the extremities. His stomach heaved and he felt the bilious rise of vomit in his throat. Still he remained on his feet, and grasped at his cloak, trying to find something that would break the effect of the staff's energies.

His hand closed around the coiled wooden snake that he had in his pocket. He pulled it out, thumbing the winding latch open as he did so. Stars danced in front of his eyes, but he had a good enough idea of Ashnod's position to throw the snake at her.

The wooden serpent flew through the air, uncoiling, rattling, and hissing as it did so. Ashnod shouted something and raised the staff higher against this new attack.

Tawnos was moving the moment that Ashnod spared her attention from him. Charging forward, he tackled her, hard, in the midsection. The staff pinwheeled away in one direction while the wooden snake scuttered in the other. Ashnod went down in a heap, and the guards were there immediately, their short pikes pointed at her.

Tawnos kept his footing, and towered over her, gasping for breath. Ashnod raised her now empty hands in surrender.

"Well, it turns out the baby duck has teeth," she said, slowly getting to her feet, the guards surrounding her. "There are new surprises every day."

Chapter 15

Parry and Thrust

Tawnos felt that the entire weight of the Kingdom of Yotia now rested on his shoulders, and he did not like it one bit.

Four months had passed since the fateful argument, and in that time there was no sign of Mishra. He had vanished from the palace, and the Fallaji, the dragon engine, and his war machine had vanished from the gates soon after midnight.

The Fallaji had been prepared for their departure; of that Tawnos had no doubt. Mounted scouts were dispatched that evening up and down the river, but there was no sign of them. Urza had to wait for morning to dispatch the ornithopters, and that was when the scouts had discovered that a ferry barge upriver had been seized and sunk on the far bank.

The assumption was that Mishra and his engines had fled west into the trans-Mardun territories that bordered on Fallaji territory. Then from the east came a report that a collection of brass helmets and Fallaji gear had been found by a farmer, indicating that Mishra's forcers were making instead for the Kher Ridges. Soon after a horseman arrived from the Sword Marches, declaring that a great metallic beast had been spotted, there, moving only at night and heading north.

Military units were shunted first one way, then another in response to each new rumor. To make matters worse, Urza took to the field with one of the ornithopter flights and moved continually from one sighting to the next.

It had been four months, and Urza had still not returned to Kroog nor sent any message to his wife the queen. Tawnos received numerous orders for new developments and changes to the ornithopter design and instructions for coordinating the production of a line of avenger-style automatons. But these messages were always technical in nature, without a hint of curiosity about Tawnos's own well-being, nor that of Urza's wife, nor the situation in the capital.

The last was deteriorating quickly. A rumor had spread that the Chief Artificer's evil brother was hiding among the Fallaji traders still in the city, plotting an insurrection. The resulting riots killed seventeen Fallaji, including, Tawnos had heard, one of the musicians who had played at the banquet. Those with ties to the desert fled the city and other Yotian cities as quickly as possible. This created another rumor that the first rumor had been planted by Mishra so he and his men could escape in the confusion.

The resulting violence overmatched the capabilities of the temples to cope, as resources earmarked for study and supplies were suddenly diverted to the homeless and the wounded. The priests clamored for more of the magical talismans Urza had created early in his career there, but the artificer was not present to create them.

Tawnos heard that people were now beginning to doubt their leaders. If Urza was so wise, ran the common tale, why could he not find his own brother in his wife's own land? Either Urza was not as smart as the people had thought, which was unsettling, or Mishra was much smarter, which was even more troubling. Now rumors of invasion of the Sword Marches or of the trans-Mardun territories were regular fare in the inns and taverns, and many of the merchants spoke of relocating to the coastal provinces for the duration of the hostilities.

Indeed, there was some confusion among the common folk about what exactly had happened at the end of the conference. The general story was that Urza and his brother came to blows, but the nature of the argument was not clear. Some said it was about the Sword Marches. Another story was that Urza had accused Mishra of stealing his ideas and making his dragon engines. No, it was the other way around, others said; Urza had stolen the idea of the ornithopters from his brother. There were a few comments about Kayla herself, but those were only voiced by low individuals in shadowy bars and were given no credence. Or at least Tawnos hoped that was the case.

The confused mood of the city was matched by that in the palace. The Captain of the Guard was frantic, as his orders were regularly countermanded by those of Urza from the field. The seneschal, who had warmly welcomed the Fallaji, was now frantically trying to prove he was as tough as the old warlord himself had been.

The queen kept to her quarters, and would see a select number of people, using the matron as a last line of defense against intruders. She would speak to the seneschal, the Captain of the Guard, and Tawnos, and not to anyone else. Unfortunately for the remnants of the privy council, most of her commands were along the lines of, "Do as you see fit," superseded only by, "What would Urza want?"

And to make matters worse, the matron had informed Tawnos (through numerous allusions and euphemisms) that Her Majesty was "in the family way." Indeed, when Tawnos spoke with the queen, she seemed more haggard and tired than usual. Tawnos sent Urza a gently worded dispatch detailing Kayla's condition but received in return only a list of corrections to the armature of the avengers.

Tawnos could not understand the coldness of Urza's response until he did the math. Given the phases of the Mist Moon and the advancement of Kayla's pregnancy, she would have had to have conceived sometime during the week of the meetings with the Fallaji, probably toward the end of that week, before Urza left the city.

Urza had departed hot on the heels of Mishra. Tawnos did not like to consider what that might mean, but he had no doubt Urza realized it at once.

And last there was the problem of Ashnod, still held as a hostage in the guest wing of the palace. All attempts to contact the Fallaji to negotiate her release had failed. A number of people wanted her executed for crimes that remained as fuzzy as the explanation of what happened between Urza and Mishra. The staff with its sickening energies had been a surprise to Tawnos, and the guards had stripped her room of anything with which she might be able to make a weapon. The staff remained in Tawnos's care. The device itself was a beautiful creation, and he sought permission from the queen to speak with Ashnod about it. At least, that was the excuse that he gave Kayla.

"Where did you get the knowledge that helped you build the staff?" he asked at one point. "Was it an old text? A scholar? A wanderer from another land?"

Ashnod remained perched on the windowsill, the morning sun shining resplendently on her hair. She said nothing.

"It will be easier if you talk," said Tawnos. "Keeping silence isn't going to get you anywhere."

Ashnod's head snapped around to regard Tawnos. Then she smiled and said, "I've got a joke. Care to hear it?"

Tawnos looked puzzled.

"Matron and the queen are talking. Matron says, 'Whatever else you say about that Mishra, at least he dresses well.' And the queen says, 'Yes, and quickly, too.' Whatayathink?"

"That's *not* funny!" sputtered Tawnos. "You know, there are temple inquisitors who have put themselves at our disposal just to wring your secrets out of you."

"But you're keeping them at bay," said Ashnod, sliding off her perch. "And why is that, Baby Duck?"

Tawnos bristled but kept his voice calm. "Because they might . . . damage . . . you. Any knowledge you have might be lost."

"I might choose to die with my secrets rather than betray Master Mishra," sighed Ashnod. "You are *so* naive, and *so* kind. No wonder you're the queen's favorite."

"What do you know—" said Tawnos, defensive again.

Ashnod waved her hand. "There's not a lot to do here, so I listen: to the guards, the chambermaids, the people outside the window. I think you're keeping me around because you need someone to talk to. Mama Duck, Urza is gone, and poor Kayla is wrapped up in blaming herself. That's why you're here."

Tawnos did not reply but kept his head on his chest, regarding the table. A long silence spread out between the two.

Finally Ashnod sat down at the table across from Urza's apprentice. "The way I see it, it's a question of approach," she said at last. Her tone was calm, almost conversational.

"What is?" Tawnos responded.

Ashnod sighed and shook her head. "The staff! Wasn't that what we were talking about?"

"Among other things," said Tawnos, the hurt still in his voice.

"Don't be like that," snapped Ashnod. "Look. Have you worked in a slaughterhouse?"

Tawnos blinked. "I worked as a fisherman once."

"Completely different," said Ashnod. "Fish are low creatures, barely worth the spine they have. If you work at sawing up carcasses, you notice how the joints fit, how the nerves are arrayed, and how the skin peels back."

"I've dissected creatures," said Tawnos, "Birds, for example, to study their wings for the ornithopters."

"But never one that was still alive when you cut into it, correct?" asked Ashnod. Tawnos did not respond, but his face gave away his answer. Ashnod continued, "As I said, there's a difference of approach. You and Mama Duck Urza don't want to get your hands dirty, to deal with the blood and skin and muscle and nerves and fluids.

You'd never have stumbled on the idea of frying an opponent's nerves with something like my staff."

"I don't know if that's a responsible goal," said Tawnos.

"Beside the point," said Ashnod sharply, slapping the tabletop with her palm. Tawnos saw the fire in her eyes again, the inventing fire. "You're looking at the bird wing and thinking about how to duplicate it. I'm looking at the bird wing and thinking about how to incorporate it, how to make it function again. If I were building ornithopters, I would have used roc wings. I'd have kept them alive with their own blood and nutrients and tethered them to the housing."

"That's impossible!" said Tawnos.

"A girl can dream," said Ashnod and smiled again. "But I think that's what they did with the dragon engine. The original builders, I mean. They didn't try to duplicate a dragon with metal and cable, like the old Thran would. Rather they started with a dragon and built outward until the machinery replaced the dragon entirely."

The fire blazed in the scarlet woman's eyes again. "You can't be afraid of living things, or dead things for that matter," she said. "Living tissue is one more set of tools we can use. If we only get past our backward concept that it's somehow inviolate, we can truly make progress."

She looked at Tawnos and shrugged. "That's what I think, at least. Mishra might disagree. I think the answer is within the body, not outside it."

The discussion had taken a disturbing turn for Tawnos. In an effort to divert it into other channels, he said, "Where do you think Mishra is now? Is there a special hiding place he has?"

Ashnod shook her head. "He doesn't need to hide right now. He has his brother right where he wants him, running all over the place looking for him."

"Was that his plan?" asked Tawnos.

Ashnod paused a moment, then shook her head. "I don't particularly know that Mishra had a plan. He is very good at setting things up, but then he throws caution to the winds and spins the wheel of fate."

"Madness," muttered Tawnos.

"Or divine inspiration," countered Ashnod.

"So he didn't let you in on his plans," continued Tawnos.

"If he did, would I be here, living in all this luxury?" Ashnod waved her hands at the bare walls of her quarters. "No. And it's not that he's secretive, though he is. I really don't think he had an exact plan when he came to Kroog, but I do know he'd be happy with the result."

Tawnos sighed. "I wish I could believe you."

Ashnod frowned, then spread her hands. "Look, I'll give you this one free of charge. Mishra is not one to let an opportunity pass, and with Urza 'thoptering all over creation, this is an opportunity for Mish to hurt his brother and hurt him bad. And the qadir is such a hothead that he'll declare a full *jihad* at the drop of a brass hat. So something *is* coming."

"But you don't know what or where," said Tawnos. Ashnod shrugged.

"One more thing, then," she said. "You wondered how I got the staff in here?"

Tawnos said, "I assumed our guards were lax during the festivities."

Ashnod smiled; it was a dazzling smile. "The black thunderwood staff I walked in with. You saw it on the first day; who could deny a woman her walking staff? The skull *was* smuggled in. But the gold wire was sewn into the hem of my bodice, and the power stones were brought in among my jewelry."

Tawnos looked at the tabletop. He had watched her assemble the weapon without realizing it. "There's a point to this?"

"Only this," said Ashnod. "All the components came together at the right moment to produce the staff. That's what's going to happen, regardless of what it is. Everything will come together at once, and . . ." She motioned with her hands. "Boom!"

Tawnos stood up. "You've given me something to think about. Several things, in fact."

Ashnod rose with him. "Yes, and one of the things will probably be, 'Can I trust her?' The answer is, 'No you can't, but you should at least listen.' Okay?"

Tawnos nodded and turned toward the door. Ashnod called out his name, and he turned back toward her.

Ashnod leaned forward and kissed the apprentice. Tawnos started as if prodded by a dagger thrust.

Ashnod ignored the reaction. "That's thanks. Thanks for not turning me over to the temples. And thanks for coming and talking to me. You're a good duck." And she smiled.

Outside, in the hall, Tawnos rubbed his cheek where Ashnod had kissed him. The skin was still warm.

"Urza," muttered his apprentice, "wherever you are, you'd better get back here soon."

* * * * *

Lieutenant Sharaman had the privilege of delivering the report to Chief Artificer Urza. He and another pilot had discovered Mishra's war machine at the center of a large encampment three hours' flight to the west. It was the first sighting of one of Mishra's engines since the troops had begun this wild-goose chase, and Sharaman was delighted to finally see some results from their work.

The Yotian fliers were at their third base camp, each one pressing deeper into the enemy territory of the Great Desert. The Sword Marches were weeks away by foot, and everything at the camp had to be flown in. Sharaman longed for the relative luxuries of the home base: hot meals, attentive women, and most of all, hot water to bathe in. However, mentioning such desires was a quick way to lose one's wings, and Sharaman would rather fly than have the attentions of the most attractive women in Yotia.

Urza was seated beneath his tarp, hunched over a makeshift table. At the table was a hand-drawn map of the desert. In addition to pursuing his brother, the Chief Artificer was conducting the first true survey of this area. Evenings were filled with reports of hills, ridges, dry washes, and a number of curious rock piles that the Prince Consort referred to as Thran sites.

Sharaman stepped beneath the tarp, clicked his heels, and saluted. "Sire, we have a sighting of the great war machine."

Urza did not look up from the map. "Report," he said.

"A large encampment of tents with the war machine at the center."

"Where?" snapped Urza.

"A quarter-day's flight from here, fifteen degrees south of due west."

Urza traced the line Sharaman had defined. "Yes. That would make perfect sense. If we had continued on our present line of attack we might have missed it. My brother did not take into account wide lateral patrols, it seems."

To the lieutenant he said, "Were you spotted?"

"No signs," said Sharaman. "They tend to hide from us, now."

"Indeed," said Urza, raising one eyebrow. "Best to assume they know we've spotted them, and they are likely to be already packing camp. Ready all the ornithopters. Take all the goblin bombs."

"Sire?" asked Sharaman.

"Is there a problem, Lieutenant?" The Chief Artificer looked up for the first time. His face was lined and drawn, more so than would be accounted for by the continual desert wind.

"It is late in the day, Sire," said Sharaman, choosing his words carefully.

"I am aware of the time, Lieutenant," said Urza. His voice was icy. "But if we wait for the morrow, Mishra will be gone."

"It will be dusk before we arrive," protested the ornithopter pilot.

"And it will be midnight if we keep talking about it," snarled Urza, "Now get to it. I want the entire patrol in the air in fifteen minutes!"

Sharaman stiffened, saluted smartly, and retreated. As the pilot left the tent he was already bellowing orders to the other fliers and support staff. There was an immediate eruption of activity as the various artifice students beetled over the machines, making final preparations. Those pilots who had flown with Urza before had begun checking their machines as soon as they saw Sharaman head for the Prince Consort's tent.

Sharaman did not like it. An evening attack was dangerous and meant either setting down in enemy territory for the night or risking treacherous night winds and cool spots on the flight back. Still the Chief Artificer was not to be denied, particularly in the matter of his brother.

They were ready in ten minutes: five ornithopters plus Urza's own craft. All were the double-bend wing design now, of the type in which Urza had flown to Korlinda. Urza's craft remained the best of the lot and was the best maintained. It had a wingspan half-again as long as the others and carried twice as many of the dangerous goblin bombs. The latter had been flown all the way from the Sword Marches and were kept cool and wrapped in damp cloths.

The flight toward the enemy was uneventful, though Sharaman was aware of the lengthening shadows of the hills and the silhouettes of their craft fleeing ahead of them over the rough ground.

When they crested the last rise, the camp was still there, the tents of white cloth shining red in the light of the dying sun. In the center, glowing like an ingot, brooded the hulk of Mishra's war machine.

Something struck Sharaman as wrong, but he could not put his finger on it immediately. He had little time to think of it, for Urza waved his wings in the attack signal.

The six ornithopters broke into two groups of three. Sharaman led one, while Urza commanded the other. Urza's half of the flight activated their wings and beat to gain altitude, while Sharaman's banked and began a low bombing run over the camp.

Sharaman locked his wings in gliding position and reached around for the goblin bombs. Without looking down, he heaved one after another over the edge of the ornithopter's canopy. These attacks were intended to frighten and disorient the camp natives. Real accuracy would be needed at the end of the bombing run, when the target would be the great war hulk.

There was no immediate response from the ground, and Sharaman looked ahead. The great metallic wain, some fifty feet in height, was looming ahead. They were dropping faster than Sharaman had anticipated, and Sharaman considered re-engaging the engine and gaining a bit more altitude before reaching the hulk.

Then the war machine opened fire, and his exact elevation was the least of Sharaman's problems.

The war machine came alive as they neared. Windows slid open and cupolas rotated to reveal ballistae, catapults, and other devices that Sharaman did not recognize. Something rose from the center of the war machine that looked like a great water pump, but instead of water this last device spat fire.

The air was filled with all manner of shot: stones, arrows, and huge ballista bolts. Sharaman slammed open the wing locks and engaged the engine, hoping to rise above the torrent of incoming missiles. He avoided the bulk of them, but one great ballista bolt, an arrow the size of a small tree, drove into his right wing. Worse yet, the bolt had a barbed head and did not pass through the wing entirely. Suddenly the craft was pierced, like a butterfly on a pin, and weighted down. Sharaman was unable to stay aloft.

The lieutenant cursed and hit the emergency disconnect lever to disengage the wing entirely. The lever was jammed by the force of the bolt's blow and would not budge. Sharaman looked around for something with which to pry it loose, aware that he was already losing altitude quickly.

Then he saw the box of goblin bombs and cursed louder. The bombs would explode on contact, and if they were on board when he hit the ground . . .

Sharaman ignored the release mechanism, having determined he was going to crash but equally determined to not leave a huge crater in the process. He picked up the entire crate of bombs from its cradle and shoved it over the side of the craft's housing.

He was horribly low now, for the bombs detonated almost immediately, striking the ground and sending up a wave of billowing black and red force. The force of the blow flipped the ornithopter upside down, and it crashed that way, sliding into one of the sunlit-red tents.

Sharaman guessed he could not have been out for more than a moment; the smell of flames brought him to. Breathing hurt his chest, and there was a numbness along his left leg. Still he knew he had to get out before the flames reached him.

Sharaman pulled himself from the wreckage slowly. His left leg could not take any weight. He pulled a small knife from his vest, ready for any of the Fallaji who might suddenly attack now that his wings were clipped.

But there were no Fallaji. The tent he had slammed into was empty. The only flames were those created by his own goblin bombs.

That was what had bothered Sharaman when he was flying, he now realized. It was evening, but there had been no cooking fires. The camp was abandoned already.

They left the war engine, he thought. He half-stumbled, half-hopped, to a broken pole from the tent and used it as a support.

His initial attack had been a disaster. The only sign of his two fellow pilots were twin plumes of billowing smoke where their racks of goblin bombs had exploded upon crashing. He hoped the pilots had had the presence of mind to jettison before they struck.

Already the second wave, led by Urza's white ornithopter, was pulling into position.

Sharaman looked at the war machine. Why were there no people coming out to fight him? Were they all at their posts?

Then he realized there was no one in the camp at all, including at the war machine. The weapons were firing automatically, responding to some device the Chief Artificer's brother had crafted to detect and assault trespassers.

They were fighting ghosts. And they were dying for it.

Sharaman tried to wave off the attacking wing of three craft, but Urza and the other pilots either ignored him or assumed he was one of the Fallaji. As soon as they neared the war machine, the great wain released another volley of bolts. Both Urza and one other pilot pulled their machines up in time to avoid the onslaught, but the third was not so lucky. It flew into a flurry of small arrowshot. The arrows were not enough to damage the craft, but they pierced the housing and killed its operator. The ornithopter pulled into a spiral to the right, a slow, deadly glide that was punctuated at the end with an explosion.

The other two craft were still making for their target, the smaller craft in the lead. Sharaman tried to understand why the Fallaji would leave behind the mighty war machine unguarded, the engine that Mishra had brought to Kroog as a demonstration of his abilities.

Unless it was a trap, he realized. All this was a stylized **and** ornate trap.

Sharaman shouted, but the lead craft was already dropping its load of goblin powder over the side. The first bomb struck the war machine . . .

. . . And the entire device detonated. The lead ornithopter was enveloped in flame, disintegrating in mid-flight. Sharaman flung himself to the ground as bits of flaming metal rained down around him.

When he looked up, Urza's was the only craft left in the sky. Its white wings were on fire now, and it trailed a banner of smoke. It made a beeline for the oversized rear wheel of the now-ruined war hulk.

The ornithopter struck the wain's wheel and evaporated in a great explosion as its double cargo of goblin bombs exploded. The great wain rocked, then slowly tumbled over on its side, its burning wreckage slamming into the desert sands.

Among the smoking wreckage, framed by the fires of the great wain, a figure moved. Sharaman hobbled toward it, unsure if he should greet or battle the figure.

It was Urza. His flying cloak was singed and burning in several spots, and there were numerous cuts along the right side of his face. He clutched something to his chest, something that glowed as brightly as an ember. Urza coughed into the burning sleeve of his other arm and then started to beat the sleeve against his leg, extinguishing the smoldering blaze.

"Trap," he said as Sharaman reached him.

"Yes, Sire," said Sharaman.

"Should have"— another long, smoke-filled cough—"should have seen it coming." He shook his head. "Any others?"

Sharaman looked at the smoking plumes around the camp. "I don't think so."

"We should go, then," said Urza. "Long walk back to camp. Longer walk back to Yotia."

"Sire?"

"What?"

"I'm afraid my leg's broken," said Sharaman. Despite everything he felt embarrassed to mention it.

Urza's face twitched, as if Sharaman had mentioned some small, niggling problem. Then his eyes cleared, and the Chief Artificer said,

"Of course. So it is. You rest here. I'll get some splints made. We'll check the other craft to see if there are any supplies or perhaps a temple amulet among the wreckage. Then we'll walk back."

"As you wish, Sire."

Urza turned and regarded the smoking hulk of the war machine. He shook his head, and Sharaman heard him say, "Brother, why did you do this? Why the elaborate and costly ruse?"

Sharaman wondered that as well. When they finally reached the Yotian border weeks later, they would both know the answer.

* * * * *

The attack came at dawn and was totally unexpected. Word had come that Urza's flight had failed to report in, and, reluctantly, Tawnos had dispatched the home flight to the north to aid in the search. That left only a single large training machine in the capital itself. Later Tawnos would wonder if dispatching the last organized flight had been the signal for the attack, if Urza's disappearance in the desert had enheartened the qadir's troops for the assault, or if it had been Mishra's plan to attack regardless of what happened to Urza.

Kroog was bounded on three sides by stout walls and on the fourth by the Mardun itself, and it was across that great river that the desert-dwelling Fallaji came. Urza (and Tawnos, and most of the rest of Kroog) had felt that any assault of the trans-Mardun territories would be sufficient warning for the capital. To ensure their own safety, the Yotians had established a set of beacon towers along the far bank to give warning.

It had not been enough. By strength or by trickery, the Fallaji had overpowered the beacon tower guards in the dead of night, and by morning they were ready with their assault.

The morning was a foggy and wet one, the mists pooling over the Mardun itself. The river fishers, among the first ones up in the city, had the first and only warning. Beneath the lightening sky, as they were loading their nets into their boats and making ready to get under way, one of the crew shouted and pointed toward the center of the river.

There were other craft already on the river drifting toward the city docks. There were barges, rowboats, and hastily built rafts and ferries stolen from upriver.

They were loaded with men: armed men with flowing robes beneath their armor, curved blades, and wide brass hats.

The river fishers were alone in their discovery only for a moment, for the next instant the warning beacons across the river came to life, billowing great jets of flame into the sky, heralding the dawn. But the beacons were not set as warnings but rather as declarations of war.

Some of the fishers fled their boats, but other remained long enough to see the great serpentine heads of the dragon engines burst from the gray waters of the Mardun and tower over Kroog's docks. Grasping the shore with their front claws and churning the soft mud of the riverbank beneath the treads, the dragon engines waded into the city. There was the sound of a great machine inhaling, and the leading beast exhaled a torrent of liquefied flame. Behind it, the first wave of Fallaji landed, bellowing war cries as they clambered onto the docks.

The city of Kroog was under assault.

* * * * *

Tawnos had been sleeping at the orniary, as he did often in these later days, when the runner came. The messenger was no more than a young girl and was frightened beyond belief. Tawnos sent her to round up what students she could find from the barracks and to tell them to ready every available avenger and the remaining ornithopter. And if he did not return before the palace was assaulted, the students were to use these devices in their own defense.

Tawnos dressed as he ran toward the royal quarters. The seneschal and the Captain of the Guard were already there, arguing with the queen.

"I am staying," she said. Already she was beginning to show her pregnancy.

"Your Majesty, for your own safety . . ." begged the captain.

"As a temporary relocation . . ." added the seneschal at the same moment.

"I am staying," said Kayla firmly. "This is my home." She looked at Tawnos. "I want to stay."

"That may not be wise," said Tawnos. "Best prepare for flight now and feel foolish about it later." To the captain he asked, "What is the situation?"

"There was no warning," said the captain. "Rafts of Fallaji devils are coming downstream. More are pouring into the river wards all the time. The naval station and the fishermen's docks were hit first. And there are dragon engines; three at least, maybe four. They seem to be leading the assault, spreading destruction ahead of them. We've regrouped all the troops in the capital, but the people are blocking the streets."

"Open the gates," ordered Kayla. "Let the people escape the city."

"But the enemy—" objected the captain.

"Is already within our walls," snapped Kayla. "Do we need to sacrifice the people as well?"

The captain nodded. Tawnos asked, "How long before they reach here?"

The seneschal stuttered and spat, "Th-there is no indication that they are—"

"These are Mishra's engines," snapped Tawnos, a new steel in his voice. "Where *else* would they be heading?"

The captain thought for a moment, then said, "An hour. Two if we're fortunate. Is there anything you have on hand to help?"

"I'm working on it now," said Tawnos. To Kayla he said, "Pack what you can carry. If it comes to this, we will need to flee." Kayla started to complain, and Tawnos added, "Take my advice this time, please. Prepare for the worst, hope for the best. Have the matron help you." He looked around, suddenly noticing that the matron's impressive bulk was missing. "Where is she?"

There was a silence for a moment, then the seneschal stammered, "Sh-she has a sister in the River Wards. Said she was worried about her."

Tawnos's lips made a thin, grim line. "Pack," he said. "I'll be back."

The students were already at the orniary when the chief apprentice returned. Five avengers were in working order, though each required an operator to stand close and give commands. Tawnos assigned five of the oldest boys to take them and report to the captain. He scribbled a hasty note to the captain that the boys should be kept together and used to fight the dragon engines. He added that if the avengers fell, the boys were to flee the city as quickly as they could.

There was only a single ornithopter ready, but it was a huge craft capable of carrying a fully armored avenger easily. Tawnos ordered the remaining boys to pack this craft full of Urza's notes and prototypes.

One lad hesitated; he was one of the young ones, in his first year of studies. "Sir, aren't we going to fight?" he asked.

Tawnos nodded. "Yes, but we need to protect our knowledge. Get it to safety first."

"But," said the youth, sputtering, "we can use the ornithopter to fight, can't we?"

Tawnos looked down on the young man. "Fight? How? We could drop bombs on them. But they are in *our* city, and we would be bombing *our* people. The avengers will buy us time, but probably they can't defeat the dragon engines by themselves. Do you understand?"

The boy looked at his feet. "I suppose. I would rather fight."

Tawnos looked at him grimly. "And I would rather win the fight," he said. "Do you understand the difference?"

Another pause, then, "I suppose so."

"Good," said Tawnos. "Because you're going to fly the ornithopter. If you have to fight, you will. But remember that the important thing is to get the ornithopter, and particularly the books, away to one of the more remote bases farther east. If they have fallen, then head to Korlis, or even Argive. Do you understand?"

The boy nodded, and Tawnos helped the youths load the ornithopter. In the distance there came the sound of explosions and, once or twice, of shouting. Finally the huge ornithopter was loaded, and Tawnos gave the lad the Jalum Tome. As he took it, the boy said, "My brother, he's another student here. Sanwell."

Tawnos hesitated. "Do you want me to send him with you?"

"He's one of the older students," said the boy.

Tawnos nodded slowly. He had sent the older students with the avengers into battle.

The boy said, "If you see him, tell him I left. And tell him not to worry."

"Your name is Rendall, right?"

"Rendall," agreed the boy, setting the great book on his lap.

"I'll tell him when I see him, Rendall, and the gods speed you," said Tawnos. And gods help us all, he added to himself as the boy engaged the power stone and the great craft came to life.

The great ornithopter strained at its pulleys and leaped into the sky in a single bounce. It did not make the low, climbing circle common in training flights. Instead it flew arrow-straight to the east. Behind it, there was the screeching of the dragon engine that witnessed its departure. That made Tawnos feel slightly better. If Mishra was going to take Urza's city, he was not going to take Urza's knowledge.

He dismissed the rest of the students, telling them to take what they could carry and head east as quickly as possible, regrouping at the caravan town of Hench. And if that had fallen, he said, make for the coast or Korlis. He looked at their faces and knew that a few would go for weapons and join the melee, but enough would have the common sense to let the school survive.

Tawnos took Ashnod's staff from its holder and left the orniary for the last time, making for the guest wing. The guards were still at their positions outside Ashnod's door. Tawnos dismissed them, ordering them to help protect the palace.

"Helluva of a party," said Ashnod as he entered. "Pity we're missing it." Her words were light, but her face was drawn and concerned.

"I need your help," said Tawnos. "We need to get out of the city."

"We?" asked Ashnod. "Does that include me? I mean, these are my people coming to call."

"These are the Fallaji!" shouted Tawnos. "Do you think they can tell the difference between you and any other non-Fallaji woman in the middle of the battle?"

"If I have my staff, they will," replied Ashnod calmly. "Give it to me."

"Promise to help," said Tawnos. "Promise to help me get the queen to safety. Or, if we're captured, guarantee her safety."

"Why should I help your precious queen?" snapped Ashnod harshly.

"She's pregnant, " said Tawnos.

"I hope you don't think you're appealing to my motherly instincts—" began Ashnod.

"Mishra may be the father," interrupted Tawnos. "Do you want to tell him his child died in the taking of the city?"

Ashnod sat down. "Whoo," she said. Outside the window there was an explosion. Too close for Tawnos's mind. "Never even heard that rumor. Are you sure?"

Tawnos looked at his hands. "No."

Ashnod shook her head and chuckled. "Well, that's good enough for me. I promise to help get your precious queen away from here, or if you're captured to guarantee fair treatment. Can I have my staff now?"

Tawnos hesitated for a moment and then gave her the staff. She ran her fingers over it and said, "I expected you to dismantle it."

"I did," said Tawnos, heading for the door. "And I rebuilt it. Let's go."

The hallways were empty now, and through the windows of the promenade Tawnos and Ashnod could see the rising plumes of smoke. Through it, far off in the city, Tawnos saw a dragon engine.

"There was more than one," he said bitterly.

"Yep," said Ashnod. "I told you, but you weren't paying enough attention."

"Maybe I should have given you to the priests," snarled Tawnos.

"Then who would help you now?"

They ran into the queen and the seneschal at the entrance to the royal quarters. The seneshal was carrying a large carpetbag filled with the queen's personal effects.

Ashnod looked at the queen's swelling belly. "You *have* let yourself go!" she said.

Tawnos asked, "Status?"

The seneschal stammered and said, "B-bad. The avengers slowed the lead dragon engine, b-but it just pulled back and let tribesmen overwhelm the avengers and their operators. Some people think the queen has already left the city in an ornithopter."

Tawnos mentally kicked himself. It had not occurred him to use the ornithopter to rescue the queen and not Urza's notes. Or himself, for that matter.

"We need to make haste," said the seneschal. "The engines will be here any moment."

The earth shook, and a deep, fiery roar proved the seneschal wrong. The dragon engines had already arrived at the palace of Kroog and were slamming their great shovel-like muzzles as battering rams against the walls.

The hallway rocked, and half of it slid away, breaking apart under the assault of the engine. Stonework and furnishings suddenly collapsed as if a great blade had cut through the palace itself. In the wake of the cave-in, more of the hallway slid into a churning dust cloud.

Tawnos grabbed Kayla and pulled her close to him onto more solid ground. The seneschal was not so fortunate. The ground beneath him broke like brittle ice in the spring, and with a scream he toppled forward into the abyss. Kayla shouted as the seneschal vanished in the churning debris, still clutching Kayla's carpetbag.

Ashnod lashed out an arm and grabbed Tawnos's shoulder. "Let's go. Her Majesty can get new luggage later."

Tawnos's brows furrowed in anger, but there was no time for argument. The entire royal wing was slowly coming apart beneath the treads of the dragon engine. The beast screeched again, and the three, Ashnod, Tawnos, and Kayla, fled down the hallway, away from the assault.

They made it to the main entranceway before they ran into Fallaji troops. An honor guard, noted Tawnos briefly, from the look of their hats and carved gold epaulets. The three refugees were descending the main staircase when the desert tribesmen spilled into the hall beneath them.

For a moment both parties froze. Then Ashnod took a step forward down the stairs and shouted, "These people are under my protection!"

A large figure separated from the rest of the Fallaji. This one was dressed in resplendent armor of tooled leather and was fat to the point of obesity.

"You are a woman. You cannot offer such protection."

Ashnod stiffened, and Tawnos realized that the two knew each other. "I am the apprentice of your *raki*, O powerful one," she said, venom in her voice. "I can do as I please."

"A pity," said the fat Fallaji, "since in all the confusion of the battle, my men killed you before we knew who you were. I am afraid Mishra will have to understand, later."

Ashnod looked shocked. "Why are you doing this?"

The fat one smiled. "Mishra depends you, as a man leans on a crutch. My father once said that it is a bad thing for a man to have a crutch. I do this to make Mishra stronger." To his men he said, "Kill them all."

Tawnos shouted and pulled his blade, pushing Kayla behind him. Ashnod screamed an obscenity and brought up her staff. The golden-wired skull hummed and spat sparks.

The Fallaji soldiers did not make it farther than the bottom two steps. They went down, clutching their necks and bellies from the painful force of Ashnod's attack. Even behind her, Tawnos could feel the intensity of the assault. Kayla huddled against him. The queen was muttering to herself, and Tawnos realized that the words were prayers to one god after another.

The soldiers collapsed in gasping piles, but Ashnod did not let up her attack. Instead she turned her staff on the fat one who had threatened her. The staff's tip glowed a brighter shade, and the wires incandesced, glowing from their own heat. The fat one clutched at his throat and spun around in place like a puppet, but Ashnod did not relent. Tawnos could see blood spurting from the man's ears, nose, and eyes. When Ashnod finally lowered her staff, the fat one collapsed in a heap, dead among his unconscious soldiers, a puppet with his strings cut.

Ashnod slumped as well, and Tawnos reached out to steady her. She was bathed in cold sweat, and a thin trickle of blood streamed from her nose.

"I really," she said, rubbing the blood off on her sleeve, "I really *have* to fix the glitch in this staff's design."

Tawnos helped both women down the stairs, past the dead and unconscious men. He paused only slightly at the fat one, lying with his ruined face oozing blood. "You knew this one?"

Ashnod looked at the face of the dead qadir of the Fallaji. "Some desert nobody," she said bitterly. "Mishra is better off with him gone."

Kayla wanted to head east, joining the refugees fleeing the city, but Ashnod took them westward instead, toward the docks. They were stopped by two Fallaji patrols, but each time these soldiers recognized Ashnod's claim that the two Yotians were under her protection. That was fortunate, thought Tawnos, for Ashnod was nearly dead on her feet from the first battle and could not sustain another.

They had passed through the front of the fighting now, and all that was left behind the advancing army was blackened devastation. What houses were not crushed by the engines had been set alight, and flames guttered at every window. There was no one in the streets but the dead. Tawnos found one of the avengers, its legs removed by the Fallaji, still flailing around in circles in the middle of one of the plazas. Taking a moment, Tawnos deactivated it and removed the power stone. There was no sign of the device's operator.

At last they reached the docks. The quays were abandoned, like the rest of the city. Ashnod chose one of the smaller of the attacking boats, still moored at a wharf. "Here," she said. "Get in."

"We should go east," said Kayla weakly.

Ashnod shook her head. "Mishra's troops are going to be chasing refugees east for the next two weeks looking for you," she said to Kayla, and turned to Tawnos. "And you. And anyone else connected with Urza. Head south to the coast, then go east from there."

Tawnos helped Kayla over the gunwales of the rowboat. The Queen of Kroog fled to the far end of the vessel and pulled her cape tightly around her. Tawnos turned to Ashnod.

"You knew this attack was coming?" he asked. "I mean, now?"

Ashnod shook her head. "If I did know, and if I had told you, would you have believed me? I've given you what you want. I'm going now." She clutched her staff as if Tawnos might try to take it from her.

"They might still kill you," the apprentice said.

"Less of a danger now. Trust me on that one," she said. "If I find Mishra, everything will be fine. You take care of Her Majesty. You *really* think she's carrying Mishra's whelp?"

"I don't know," said Tawnos softly. "I'm not sure she knows either."

Ashnod shook her head. "Still playing the baby duck, even when the mommy ducks are heading for the abattoir. Your loyalty will put you in a spot someday where even I can't help you. Best of luck, Duck!"

She kissed him quickly, but long enough for Kayla to observe. Then, with a wink and a wave, the scarlet-haired woman disappeared back into the burning city.

Tawnos watched until Ashnod vanished among the smoke and burning ash. Then he took the long pole and pushed the boat away from the docks, into the main current of the river.

The apprentice and the queen watched the city burn as they floated away from it and watched the smoke that marked its pyre long after the flanking hills hid the devastation from direct view. The rest of the journey for that day, and for the next few days, was in silence, as they moved sluggishly down the river. The sense of loss, and their responsibility for it, weighed heavily on the occupants of the tiny craft.

Chapter 16

Aftermaths

It had taken Urza nearly a month to return to the wreckage of Kroog, first walking out of the desert with the wounded Lieutenant Sharaman, then regrouping the embattled Yotian forces in the Sword Marches and organizing an orderly retreat south. The Sword Marches fell behind them, and most of northern Yotia as well. But there was nothing left there to fight for and nothing to sustain an army.

The Fallaji harried their flanks but left them alone. Urza's forces got within two days' flight of Kroog, which was still in enemy territory. The Prince Consort (and *de facto* ruler, in the continued absence of the queen) took a trio of ornithopters to the wreckage.

Mishra, now known to Yotians as the Butcher of Kroog, had abandoned the city, and his dragon engines left little standing. The massive walls themselves had been left untouched, though their mighty gates had been worked from their hinges and splintered. Everything within the walls had been burned, and that which resisted burning had been crushed beneath the dragon engines' treads. A gray rain of ashes and dust fell on the city for three days after the razing. There was little looting afterward because there was little to loot. All that was left were the walls and a slope of gray rubble leading down to the Mardun River, and beyond the walls a scattering of lean-tos belonging to refugees too stubborn or stupid to move elsewhere.

Three ornithopters alighted on the low hillock where the palace would have been. Urza and Sharaman climbed from their machines, but the third pilot remained with his craft, ready to take off at the first sign of trouble.

There was nothing to do except watch and nothing to see except the ash-covered rubble. Urza stood in one spot, then moved a few feet over, then moved to a third location. Occasionally he picked up a bit of rock or let a handful of soot sift between his fingers. It seemed to Sharaman that the ruler was trying to imagine what building stood there and where he would be within that building.

There was a great pile of rubble that had been burned, blasted, and then cleared. At first Sharaman thought it had been a great court, but he soon realized that it was the site of Urza's orniary and that it had been scraped down to bedrock. Urza stood in the dead center of the cleared circle and knelt down, putting his hands over his eyes. There was not even any rubble left for him to touch.

People began to drift in from the gates. Sharaman tensed for a moment, but he realized these were little more than Yotian refugees from the camps outside. Leaving Urza to his revelry, Sharaman went to meet them.

Sharaman had been in Kroog a handful of times, the first when he received his flight training. It had been an amazing city to a boy from the eastern provinces, a boy who had been given a ride in an ornithopter when Urza flew to Korlinda. Now that was a lifetime ago, and mighty Kroog was a dead ruin.

Sharaman went and talked to the refugees, then returned to where Urza stood, a young boy in tow.

"Sire," he said gently.

"And I always accused my brother of not finishing anything," said Urza softly. Then his eyes focused and he turned to Sharaman, once more the Chief Artificer. "What?"

"There are people here," said Sharaman. "They want to know what to do."

"Do?" said Urza, his voice sounding strangled. "What can they do? Tell them to head south, or east, or west, or wherever they think they can find safety. Tell them that there is nothing for them here."

"Perhaps it would be better if they heard it from you," said Sharaman.

Urza looked at Sharaman. "And say what? That I'm sorry I failed them? That I'm sorry that I wasn't here for them? That I'm sorry that my brother fooled me? That I'm sorry that my wife and my apprentice and my work are all gone?"

Urza's voice rose as he spoke, and Sharaman wondered if the Chief Artificer would weep. Instead the older man shook his head and said, "No, I have failed them. They should go find someone who has not failed and follow him." For the first time he noticed the youth. "And this is?"

"He says he's one of your students," said Sharaman.

Urza peered at the youth. "Perhaps. Your name is . . Rendall?"

"Sanwell, Sire," said the youth. "Rendall is my younger brother. He's the one Master Tawnos chose to fly the ornithopter away."

Urza looked at Sharaman, and there was a new light in his eyes. "Ornithopter? Then someone escaped this with an ornithopter?"

Slowly, Sanwell told the story, which he had heard from another student after the battle. His younger brother had taken most of the important papers and designs and flew them east. No, no one else went with him. Yes, with orders to go to Argive if need be to escape the Fallaji. No, he didn't know what had happened to Master Tawnos and the queen. Sanwell's avenger had been overwhelmed by a number of desert fighters. It had taken out a number of them, but there were too many of them.

When he was done, Urza rose, and there was a new fire in his eyes. "So, my brother," he said, "you didn't finish this, either. Sharaman!"

"Yes, Sire!"

"I want you to take our remaining forces south. Regroup what you can and fortify the ports."

"Yes, Sire. And what of you?"

"I am going to find the knowledge that Tawnos saved for me. Rendall!"

"Sanwell, Sire."

"Are there any other from the school here?"

Sanwell looked around at the desolation. "No, Sire."

"Then you'll come with me," said Urza sharply. "We have to find out where your brother went with my work and begin again."

"And this time," said the Chief Artificer among the wreckage of Kroog, "this time, I will not stay my hand or feel mercy for you, Brother. This time there will be a reckoning. I swear it!"

And as if in response to his words, a cold wind blew up from the river, scattering ashes around his feet.

* * * * *

The Caverns of Koilos had visitors. Non-Argivian visitors.

They were from a monastery along the northern shores of the continent, a theocracy that celebrated the power and the majesty of the Thran, and more importantly, their devices. They claimed a large territory, but they had been relatively reclusive. They found that other cultures did not share their respect for the machine's workings, that others sought to barter them, like the Fallaji, or to make pale shadows of the Thran creations, like the Argivians. So they remained a quiet people, venturing out only rarely beyond their borders.

Until the dreams came. They began over a year ago, first one brother, then another, then a third, all consumed by the same vision: a world of machines far beyond the abilities of the Thran; living engines of steel and cable, of indestructible hearts pumping vital oils through the body; steel leaves and saw-toothed grasses; a world that rained oil and bloomed with mechanism.

In short, paradise.

And the dreams enraptured the dreamers with its siren call, urging them to leave their lands, to come to the center of the dream, and to work miracles there at the center.

Under the urgings of the dream, the Brotherhood of Gix responded. Two dozen of the most trusted brothers, those who had served the cause of the machine most devotedly, left their homes and headed south.

They avoided the Malpiri tribesmen who regularly raided their lands, but a few fell to the dangers of the desert itself—exposure, heat, and bandits. Only a dozen arrived at Koilos a year later, and they were an emaciated lot, dressed in windblown rags and possessing a wide-eyed, fanatical expression.

As they traveled, the dreams grew stronger in them. The dreams showed them the canyon that would lead them to their goal, and the cavern that they would find there. They pulled out ancient stones that glowed of their own light and journeyed within the cave, stepping around the wreckage of ancient machines that had been tested and found insufficient in the eyes of their great machine god.

At last they stood before the great machine. They took their gathered light stones and placed them within the machine as they had been instructed by their dreams and passed their hands over the mysterious book of glyphs. The fact that they could not read the glyphs bothered them not. The only thing that mattered was the dream, and the dream told them what to do.

The monks of the Brotherhood of Gix were not surprised when the lights of the cavern flickered to life around them, nor when the machines themselves began to sing, communing with each other and singing praises to their god. Delight flickered on the faces of the Gixians, knowing that their dreams were about to become reality.

A great disk formed in the middle of the air, like an oil puddle that had been turned on its side. It shimmered with a rainbow of colors not found on this earth, for these were rather the colors of dreams. The pool widened to the height and width of a tall man, and something stepped through it.

It was tall and humanoid. It seemed to be wearing an armor of black metallic snakes, but to the monks' delight, they recognized that it was the skin of the being, a skin of metal and coils. Its face was skeleton-white and it sprouted more tendrils from its head, great blood-colored serpents.

As one, the monks fell to their knees in worship.

The godly being, servant of the machine god, stood before its glowing portal. It sniffed the air, as if experiencing it for the first time. It stretched its sinewy cable-muscles and turned its head from side to side, testing the extent of its body.

One of the monks, the leader among the survivors, slowly rose and spoke. "Welcome, most holy creation. What may we call you, that we may better serve you?"

The machine being looked at each of them, and there was a soft mental caress as its mind touched theirs. It had been the one to send the dreams, they realized. It had been the one to call them to this place.

The machine being's lips whirred as they formed themselves into a smile. "Gix," it said at last, in a voice only Mishra and Ashnod had heard before. "You may call me . . . Gix."

PART 3

Converging Trajectories

(29 AR  57 AR)

Chapter 17

Mishra's Workshop

The imperial court had changed while Ashnod had been away, which was no surprise to the apprentice. In the year since the fall of Kroog, she had left and returned a half-dozen times, and upon each return she discovered some new wing or pit or chamber had been added to the court of the new qadir of the Fallaji.

Mishra had selected a site on the northwest tip of the Kher Ridges, with a dominating view of the arid lands to the west. Through a trick of the weather patterns, this area was well watered and was swathed in trees so large that they might have been planted by the Thran themselves. They were some type of oak, with thick, heavy trunks and long, horizontal branches. Already some of the quarters and laboratories were being nestled among those branches. When Mishra became qadir, Ashnod reflected, he wished to set down roots. Perhaps, among the great trees, this was what he meant, literally. The first time she had seen the site, she had trouble believing that such huge growths had blossomed in a land that was elsewhere bone-dry and arid.

Surrounding the grove of great trees, most of the smaller timbers (still great, towering oaks and younger maples) downslope had been cleared. Part of the clearing was for cultivation, but more of it was for smaller foundries and forges. Already the residue of those forges spilled slag, the unusable remains of their industry, down the slopes and into the streams at the foot of the hills.

The latest addition was a great barn that dominated an area at one end of the encampment. It was constructed of half-hoops of metal with fabric stretched between them. Already slave laborers were laying stonework for permanent walls along the base.

247

Ashnod let a slave-stablehand take her horse and entered the workshop proper. One of the great trees had died eons ago, leaving a massive stump over sixty feet high and twice that in diameter. Mishra had the stump hollowed out and converted into his own private workshop to rival the crushed orniary in now-dead Kroog. Now that workshop towered above her, the windows carved through its outer bark lit by fires within. The windows were oddly shaped, formed more by the twists of the once-living bark than by Mishra's own needs. To Ashnod, the windows looked like malignant, winking eyes.

The rooms within were similar—odd, strange shapes that resembled teardrops or spirals or multi-planed solids. Rooms rose slightly from one end to the other or were constructed of numerous terraces, each with different machinery. Ashnod had no doubt that there were additional rooms within the structure that had not been there when she had last been present. Such was the sprawling nature of the new qadir's domains.

One thing that had not changed was the treasure piled in the hallways, the remains of the initial looting of Kroog. There was gold platterware and cracked crystal, gems spilling out of wooden boxes split by rough handling, and rare vases of blue and white glazing with longitudinal cracks running from rim to base. All of it was gathered to celebrate the power of the *Raqi* of the Suwwardi, their new Qadir-by-Acclamation of the Fallaji Empire, the mighty Mishra.

One wall had been cleared to allow diplomats, supplicants, courtiers, and other parasites to wait at Mishra's whim. Ashnod did not have to wait, of course, and breezed past these poor wretches. She felt the pressure of their eyes as she passed and smiled. That was one of the good things about returning to Mishra's workshop.

The workshop proper was two parts library, two parts workshop, and two parts throne room. A great dark oak throne had been pushed against one wall, piled high with pillows and resting on a carpet of pure, regal purple, pulled from the wreckage of the palace of Kroog.

The throne was flanked on both sides by piles of books. There were books looted from Yotia and shipped from Zegon and Tomakul, huge folios and small personal diaries, scrolls and tablets and all manner of journals, bound in leather of beasts both common and forgotten. Ashnod noted, not for the first time, that many of the volumes had gathered a thin patina of dust and had not been disturbed since their initial placement.

Ashnod thought of Urza's workshop. Even cleaned and organized for their visit, it had a cluttered look. But it was a busy clutter, an organized chaos, one that was continually in motion, continually evolving. The books in Mishra's workshop might as well be blank for the amount of use they saw.

Mishra was not on his throne. While the others cooled their heels outside, he was at a great slate board, another prize of the war, that had been hung along one curved wall. Mishra had been working in multi-colored chalk, and out of the rainbow smears of his writings and frequent erasures, there arose the portrait of a dragon engine's head, bedecked with arcane letters and illegible scribbles.

Hajar, ever-faithful Hajar, stood by the throne and announced Ashnod's presence, which was fortunate, for Ashnod felt that Mishra would not bother to look up otherwise.

Mishra regarded Ashnod, and the apprentice could sense a tenseness, a coiled-spring nervousness, in the master. He tapped the chalk against the slate a few more times, then tossed the chalk into its box, and padded toward his throne.

"Report," he grunted as he retook his place among the pillows.

With each of her visits Mishra had become more brusque, more abrupt with her. Elevated to the supreme position and with the added responsibilities of running the far-flung empire, he had no longer any time to be polite, even if he had the inclination.

"Plunder from the Yotian provinces," said Ashnod, proffering an inventory list that Hajar took. She folded her hands before her for a dry recitation. "Four thousand pounds of gold, six thousand of silver, including two thousand buillon, seventeen vases in good condition filled with gemstones worth . . . "

Mishra waved away Ashnod's words, and said, "Books?"

Ashnod sighed. Master Mishra had become more impatient of late. "Five new volumes on alchemy not in your collection. Three volumes on optics. Two on hydraulics that may be of vital interest, and one volume on metallurgy in the Yotian style, which may prove invaluable. One on clocks which sings the praises of its author. Records of gem-cutting, tinsmithing, and architecture. The standard collection of journals and diaries that will have to be read to determine if they contain anything useful. A large number of maps, most of Korlisian trading routes."

Mishra nodded, folded hands before him, and patted his fingers together. "Usable resources."

"Three new mines have been seized, bringing the total to seventeen," said Ashnod. "There were eighteen, but Yotian rebels pulled the main support frames out from one, choosing to seal themselves inside rather than surrender. Four foundries have been dismantled and are being relocated here, and they should be operational within two months. Smaller forges are being set up in the Suwwardi Marches. Lumbering continues in northern Yotia, but under armed protection."

Mishra nodded again, and said, "News."

"More of the same," said Ashnod. "The surviving Yotian towns along the coast are willing to pay tribute and swear fealty, at least on the surface. However, raids and rebellions are common from the Suwwardi Marches south. As a result, any timetable involving Yotian resources is questionable at best. There is no shortage of slaves from among the captured revolutionaries and fallen towns."

Ashnod was gilding the truth at best. For the first time the Fallaji were controlling a population not of Fallaji blood and with it the traditional ties to the qadir. A more heavily armed presence was needed in Yotia to control the people and guard the plunder. That tied down manpower, and the Fallaji hated to be tied down.

Mishra did not pursue the nature of the unrest in his new conquests. Instead he simply said, "And my brother?"

"Still beyond the Kher Ridges," said Ashnod. The report always devolved down to this simple question and Ashnod's simple response. The plunder, the resources, the knowledge were all secondary to the activities of Mishra's brother.

"As far as you know," said Mishra.

Ashnod sighed, trying to hide her impatience. Since taking the mantle of command, Mishra had changed, and not for the better. "As far as we currently know. Ornithopters have been sighted along all the major passes eastward. But there has been no organized Yotian resistance. Urza is said to have established an encampment in Argive, near the Korlis border, but Korlis swears neutrality in the matter in exchange for access to Fallaji markets."

Hajar made a huffing noise. Most of the Fallaji considered the Korlisians as bad as the Yotians, spreading honeyed lies of friendship while driving the hardest of bargains. Were the Korlis merchants truly interested in pleasing the Fallaji, they would have captured Urza and turned him over when Mishra's brother had crossed into their territory.

"What is he waiting for?" said Mishra, patting his fingers together. "It's been a year."

"The loss of Kroog and most of northern Yotia has struck him hard," said Ashnod. "He may simply be in hiding."

"He never hides," said Mishra hotly. "He plots. He plans. He is still in communication with the Yotian towns, I am sure of it, and the rebels act on his command. He is waiting for the right moment. For the moment of weakness. Of inattentiveness. And then . . . ," Mishra raised both hands to indicate the magnitude of his brother's imagined revenge.

Ashnod bit her lip, then said, "If that is the case, perhaps we should lay siege to the remaining Yotian towns and plunder them as well, denying him any further resources. Our dragon engines have been quiet for surprisingly long."

Mishra made a grunting noise and slid off his throne. He motioned for Ashnod to follow as he headed for a side door to his throne room. Ashnod followed, and the rear of the procession was brought up by Hajar.

The side door led to a spiral stairway that corkscrewed through the once-living wood of the workshop. That in turn led to a postern gate alongside the massive stump. Mishra walked through the new barn, a curious Ashnod and an impassive Hajar in tow. A few of the slaves building the walls paused to watch them pass and earned a beating from the slavemasters for their effrontery.

The interior of the new building was a single room dominated by two great machines. Small figures, scholars sent by Zegon and Tomakul, and students from among the brightest of the Fallaji, climbed over the machines like ants over a carcass.

The first of the machines looked very much like a carcass. It was one of the dragon engines, lying on its side. Its lower treads had been removed, and the plates along its belly had been pried loose to reveal the network of cables beneath. These had been uncoiled, like entrails, to reveal pumps and servos within the heart of the beast. Several small gems glittered weakly within the great wounds of the creation, but for the most part it was an inert thing, a dead creature.

Alongside it was a second dragon engine, which resembled the first as a child's drawing of a horse resembles the real creature. It was all hammered angles and sharp edges, and lacked the graceful, fluid styling of the partially dismantled creature beside it. Its face was similar, but frozen in a parody of the original dragon engine. Its muscles were not fluid cables, but roughly hewn slabs of metal held together by rivets and welds.

The second dragon engine was under construction, and as Ashnod watched, the scholars and students managed to get it to raise a foreleg. It was functional, but it looked less a living thing than the damaged beast next to it.

"It was injured in Kroog," said Mishra, regarding the fallen dragon engine, his face almost pained by the sight, "against one of my brother's accursed avengers. It survived the battle, but one by one its systems began to fail. It faltered, it was paralyzed along one side, and then it went blind. There was nothing for it but to slowly monitor its decay. None beyond this encampment know this."

Ashnod shrugged. "You have the other dragon engines."

"And the same may happen to them," said Mishra hotly. "I don't know what tricks my brother has planned, and with each day, he may have more of them. Can you imagine what would happen if one of these engines collapsed on the battlefield? What if the enemy saw that my creations were defeatable?"

Ashnod thought about it, then nodded slowly.

"And my brother is capable of defeating them. This I know," said Mishra. "If only I had remained alongside it, but no, instead I chose to take an engine in a fruitless pursuit of one of Urza's ornithopters, thinking it held possible hostages. A small error on my part, but a fatal one for this engine. If I had remained in Kroog, this one would still be functional."

If you had remained in Kroog, thought Ashnod, you would likely not be qadir now. But Mishra knew nothing of that, nor of her involvement with Tawnos and the queen. She only nodded.

Mishra waved at the other construct. "And *this* is but a shadow. A puppet crafted to resemble the original. It has most of the power, and none of the grace of the original. None of the sentience. None of the life. There are secrets locked within the dying body, terrible secrets that are beyond our power to duplicate. Perhaps Urza . . ." Mishra's voice trailed off, then returned with iron behind the tone. "Urza could, which is why we must ready these new engines, new devices, to keep him at bay."

Ashnod said, "Master Mishra, I think I can help."

Mishra turned to her. "You can rebuild the dying engine?"

Ashnod looked at the carcass of the original dragon engine. It looked like carrion, picked apart by beetles. She shook her head. "Your own plans proceed apace. Allow me to return to my own studies, and I can give you weapons to defeat your brother."

"I need you to oversee the plundering of Yotia," said Mishra. "Only you know what is valuable and what is dross."

Ashnod shook her head. "Much of what is valuable from Yotia has already been taken, or can be demanded as tribute, or has been pirated away to Korlis. You don't need me to scavenge, milord. You need me to think. To help you build."

Mishra thought a moment, and Ashnod continued, "I have had time to think of matters, both in my forced rest as a guest of Kroog and later, seeking books and information for you. I believe that I can wrap a machine around a spark of life. I believe I can merge the living and unliving together. I can give you the army to defeat Urza."

Mishra rocked slightly back and forth, then shook his head. "I need you to be my eyes, my ears beyond these walls. There is much I need to have done, and so few, like you and Hajar here, who I trust to do it."

Ashnod tilted her head to one side and said, "A pity. Urza would trust Tawnos with such a matter. Indeed, it was Tawnos the Student who distracted you with that fleeing ornithopter, for Urza the Master had trained him well. Are you saying that Urza is a better master than you are?"

A red storm of rage formed on Mishra's face, and for a moment Ashnod wondered if she had pressed too far. But Mishra took a deep breath, and the anger subsided slightly. Sharply, he said, "What do you need to produce such an army?"

Ashnod kept her gaze level, as if she had anticipated this request. "My own lab, away from prying eyes." She nodded in mock reverence to Hajar. "Most of the books on biology and anatomy from the plundered libraries. A portion of the resources sent as tribute. Surgical tools from Zegon. And slaves. Both skilled ones—smiths and glassblowers—and ones that no one will care if they are lost."

Mishra was silent for a moment. "Will criminals do?" he said.

Ashnod nodded sternly. "Criminals, traitors, revolutionaries, deserters, those whose disappearance will not be mourned. What I am thinking would be distasteful to some" —she nodded at Hajar again— "but necessary for us to build an army to defeat your brother. That is one reason I would want to keep the encampment a secret."

Mishra paused for a moment, then said, "Do it."

"I cannot promise results today," said Ashnod quickly, "or tomorrow or the next. But with my research and your rebuilt dragon engines, we can hunt down your brother and destroy him, wherever he hides."

"My brother does not—" Mishra stopped himself, then nodded. "Take what you need. Send me reports. I want to know what you're doing. And make it quick. My brother will not lie waiting for his chance forever."

Ashnod added, "You should know what I propose to do. It is not a gentle process."

Mishra said, "These are not gentle times. And we are not a gentle people. Do what you must, but give me the weapons that I need. Do what you must."

Ashnod bowed low, and Mishra spun on his heels, retreating back up the hillside to his warped workshop. Hajar, his silent ghost, followed in his wake. After they returned to closed doors, Ashnod thought, the Fallaji assistant would counsel his qadir against trusting the scarlet-haired woman. Or he would commend the qadir on his wisdom and be relieved that the woman would no longer be a regular participant in Mishra's court.

It mattered not to Ashnod. She waited until both figures were out of sight, then she allowed a slow smile to spread across her face. She had gotten what she wanted—her own shop and the freedom to pursue her own studies.

And she had learned something else. Whatever else Mishra was, he was afraid. Afraid of his brother. Afraid of being punished for stealing his brother's woman, for destroying his brother's house, for breaking his brother's toys. It was a useful tool to use in dealing with the new qadir, but one she had to be careful not to blunt with overuse.

"Speak the magic word and the gates to the treasure swing open," she said to herself, thinking of an old Fallaji legend. "And the secret word is *Urza*."

She watched the ants scuttle over the two dragon engine carcasses, stripping one to provide life for the other. Then she returned to her own quarters to finalize her plans for the future.

Chapter 18

Urza's Tower

It was three years after the fall of Kroog that Tawnos finally rejoined Urza in the most southwesterly of the Argivian provinces. They were hard years, and their toll showed on the apprentice's face: years of running and hiding, of flight and patience, of work and abandoned work.

Kayla was with him, and Harbin, her son, born in the midst of a monsoon outside Jorilin and now two and a half. They were also accompanied by two animated statues Tawnos had created during that horrible, second winter, when Fallaji slave-taking patrols had forced them to flee into the Kher Ridges.

They had finally made their way into Korlis itself, but even then they did not believe they were safe. The Korlisians were still trading with the Fallaji, and though they were negotiating with the Argivians on a pact of mutual protection from the desert raiders, Kayla wondered if the fugitives would be turned over to Mishra's representatives as a sign of the merchants' good will.

They traveled in secret, and mostly at night. They did not give their real names, though there were enough who recognized Kayla's profile, particularly in the Yotian coastal towns, to provide needed aid. It was that very recognition, and the threat of exposure it brought, that convinced the former queen to head north and east, toward Argive and sanctuary. When word finally reached them that, yes, Urza was in Argive near the Korlisian border, the three—accompanied by their two artificial protectors—made their way to Urza's Tower.

This was more easily proposed than accomplished. Urza had selected a site far from towns or villages, hard on the flanks of the Kher

Ridges themselves. The vale of his tower was cloaked in a continual fog, fed by mountain streams cascading to the valley floor around it. To a casual observer, it was a shadowed mountain glen, similar to hundreds of others along the western borders of Korlis and Argive. But this vale curved and extended slightly to the north, and in that northern pocket, hidden by the mists, Urza built his sanctuary.

Out of those mists came five murky figures, a man on horseback, a woman and a boy on a sturdy pony, and two silent statues tirelessly keeping pace.

The tower itself was made of white stone and topped by a golden cupola. It looked slender and lonely, flanked by the valley walls themselves. Kayla noted that there was no sign of activity about the place. She commented that it looked as if it had been abandoned.

Tawnos agreed. In the old days, in Yotia, there would have been ornithopter patrols continually in the air over such an important site. Indeed, were it not for a loyal Yotian expatriate found in a nearby town two days previous, they would have missed the tower entirely.

The child, Harbin, squealed and twisted in his place in front of his mother. The misty air was a delight for the child, and he kept trying to reach out and grab a handful of it. Tawnos tried explaining that air could not be caught, at least not with one's hands. The boy listened, stern-faced, nodded in agreement, and attempted to grapple with the air the moment Tawnos's back was turned.

Tawnos pulled up his mount a hundred paces from the tower. The place was silent as a tombstone. Where were the protections? Had Urza truly abandoned this tower, or had they already been spotted? But if the latter, why was there no welcome?

There was a movement to Tawnos's right, and he suddenly wheeled the horse in place. Out of the mountain shadows came the reflection of light on metal and a curious low chirping sound.

A figure stepped into view, followed by a second, and a third. They were a cross between men and metallic insects, their long, antlike heads perched on spindly necks. They looked as if they were wearing metallic armor pitted by flecks of rust. Then Tawnos realized this armor housed their bodies. Beneath the plates the apprentice could see the mechanisms and levers clatter, forcing the creatures to move forward. Their knees bent backward, like the avengers, though these constructs were barely as tall as a man's shoulder.

They were armed with heavy cleavers mounted on poles, which they brandished at the travelers. The machines were silent; the chirping was nothing more than the wear of metal on metal, of pulleys hissing from cables running through their loops, and of brass trip switches setting and re-setting.

Tawnos heard a strangled cry and looked toward Kayla. There were another three on her side of the road, similarly armed and armored. The two groups were converging on the travelers.

Tawnos barked a command at the statues, one of the five they understood, and spurred his mount forward, shouting for Kayla to follow. The horse, a weathered old beast, whickered a complaint and moved forward slowly.

Equally slowly the two clay statues turned toward their assailants. Each had been taught to recognize weapons and to attack those bearing them. The number of targets confused the statues for a moment. Then each statue chose a wing of the assailants.

What followed was a silent battle, one without shouts or cries. The clay statues were armed only with their fists, but they were huge, hamhanded fists, with a great deal of power behind them. The metal automatons were quick, and with their weapons had a reach the statues lacked. A deadly ballet ensued, punctuated by the ring of hard blows landed on armor and the soft chopping noise of blades digging into earthen flesh.

The two lead automatons of each wing got too close to the statues and were rewarded with hammer blows to the face. One dodged, but the other caught the blow head-on. Its spindly neck snapped, and the head fell across the creature's back, still held by a tangle of loose wires. The rest of the body did not recognize the loss but still flailed at the clay opponent with its chopping blade.

The blades dug deep, but the clay closed up as soon as the blades cut through it, like soft dough incised by a bread knife. One of the chopping blades got hopelessly mired in the clay creature, and the statue reached out and grasped the automaton's head. It squeezed, and bits of automaton became permanently lodged in the statue's huge hand as it shattered the creature's skull.

Two of the automatons fell back, then counterattacked as one. The clay statue raised an arm to ward off the blow, and both attempted to chop at the same arm. The first blade cut deep, and the second deeper still. There was the dull ring of metal on metal and a snapping noise as the second automaton cut through a metal bone at the heart of the clay statue's arm. The statue raised that arm, but most of the clay was sloughing off of it now, revealing a thin metal framework beneath.

While the automatons and statues battled, Tawnos and Kayla rode for the tower. If Urza was there, then these would be his creations, and he could call them off. If he was absent, the tower might provide some sanctuary until the clay statues had defeated their foes.

Tawnos shouted at the tower and saw movement along the upper battlement. A tall, familiar figure raised a whistle to his lips.

There was the short piping of three notes, and Tawnos turned in his saddle to see the automatons had ceased their attacks. Unfortunately, the clay statues still saw them as threats, and one snapped off another neck before Tawnos shouted the word for them to stand down. The clay statues halted as well, one in mid-punch.

Tawnos looked up, but the figure was gone from the battlements. The front door opened and a second figure emerged.

This was not Urza, but he had the leanness of the Chief Artificer, and Tawnos wondered if he had been mistaken about the figure seen above. This man was dressed in the uniform of a Yotian officer—a flier, by the looks of the shadows where patches and insignia once hung. He was a lieutenant, or had been, back when the Yotians had an armed force.

The figure dropped to one knee before the mounted figures. "Your majesty," he said to the queen. "Goodsir Tawnos. The artificer bids you welcome to his tower. If he had known you were coming, he would have deactivated the guards. I am Sharaman. Please enter and make yourself welcome."

He went to Kayla's horse to help her dismount and instead received a handful of young Harbin. The former lieutenant looked as if he had been handed a bag of live snakes and quickly (but gently) put the sandy-haired child down while Kayla dismounted.

The lad ignored his brusque treatment but instead craned his head up toward the battlements. Tawnos looked up and saw the flicker of the familiar figure of the Chief Artificer as Urza moved back into the shadows of the balcony doorway. Then the slender figure was gone entirely.

Tawnos dismounted as Sharaman said, "If you will follow me. I am to make you welcome and to escort you to the artificer."

Kayla said, "That will be fine."

Sharaman paused and then said, "Your Majesty, I apologize. I was instructed to make both of you welcome but to bring Goodsir Tawnos to Master Urza. I hope this is not a problem."

Kayla and Tawnos looked at each other. Tawnos had been sure Urza would wish to see his wife first, after all these years. Now there was a tightness to the queen's lips, and she nodded her agreement.

Sharaman put the queen and Harbin in an austere waiting room on the lower floor, informing them he would return with drinks and sugar wafers. This endeared him immediately to Harbin, who squealed as Kayla gave her assent. The former lieutenant took Tawnos up several sets of stairs.

"How is he?" asked Tawnos at one landing.

"He is," said Sharaman briefly. "He's been through a lot."

As have we all, thought Tawnos, but he said nothing as Sharaman pushed open the final door and stood aside for Tawnos to enter.

The apprentice stepped into Urza's study, and Sharaman closed the door softly behind him. The room was tasteful and tidy, verging on severe. A thin rug partially covered the wooden floor, and several tilted drawing boards stood near the windows, all covered with plans in various stages of development. A ball-and-socket joint, carved of yarrow wood, lay on a small worktable, next to an open book.

Urza himself was at the balcony, his back to Tawnos, looking out over the foggy vale and the remains of the earlier battle. His hands were clasped behind him. Tawnos waited. At last Urza let out a great sigh and turned toward Tawnos.

"I had expected a message, first," the older man said.

Tawnos saw the lines on Urza's face, a small collection at the corner of each eye. His eyes seemed deeper as well, more sunken in their sockets, and his hair was turning fully to the shade of spun white gold. He wore his work smock, but it was clean and well pressed.

Tawnos said, "Messages can be intercepted, sir. And we were not sure of your location until we passed the Argivian border."

Urza nodded offhandedly and took another deep breath. Then he forced a smile. "It is good to see that you are alive. I worried when there was no news."

"We spent longer than we should have in Yotia," said Tawnos.

"Yes," said Urza, pressing his palms together and twisting them slowly. "I suppose you had to. Look on my desk, would you? On the book holder there."

Tawnos walked over to the desk. "The Jalum Tome," he said at last.

"The Jalum Tome," repeated Urza. "You succeeded, Tawnos. All the knowledge you loaded into that ornithopter. Young Rendall made it to Argive, and everything was waiting for me when I finally got to Penregon. Most of my work, and our papers. There was some loss, but nothing that could not be recouped. One student packed a list of laundry to be picked up, thinking it was an important paper, but under the circumstances it was a brilliant move." Urza looked at Tawnos. "Thank you."

"It was my responsibility," said Tawnos bowing slightly.

"And more than adequately discharged," said Urza. "Those statues you brought with you. Very impressive."

"Clay over a framework of wicker and metal," replied Tawnos.

"That is more than just clay," said Urza. "It seemed to shrug off the blows of my own soldiers."

"Yes, sir," said Tawnos, wondering why they were speaking of such matters while Kayla was still waiting. "It was from a deposit we found when we—when Her Majesty and I—were hiding in the mountains. It had the property of flowing and rejoining when cut. At first I thought it might contain something similar to the Thran Stones, but now I am not sure. If I could locate the primal nature of this earth, we could make wonderful creations."

"Yes," said Urza, and suddenly pointed toward a corner of his workshop. "That chest. Look inside."

Tawnos looked quizzically at the older artificer, but did as he asked. When Tawnos opened the coffer, he was nearly blinded by the light of the stones within.

"Power stones," he said.

"Aye," said Urza, pride in his voice.

"I've never seen this many in one place," remarked the apprentice.

"Aye," repeated Urza. "While we were doing the best we could with what we had in Kroog, the Argivian nobles have been collecting them for over forty years. There's much more than that, more than enough to power any number of devices. That's what the Yotian soldiers operate off of."

"Yotian?" said Tawnos, a small stab of pain in his voice.

Urza held up his hands. "A small conceit. My guards. They're smaller than the avengers and easier to produce. I call them Yotian soldiers because they will, I hope, prevent Yotia's fate from visiting Argive and Korlis. An old friend once told me there was power in names. And perhaps . . ." Urza let his voice trail off.

"Perhaps that will take back Yotia for the queen," said Tawnos.

"For the Yotian people," said Urza quickly. "For the people who trusted me and whom I delivered into my brother's hands."

"Your brother has his hands full of them at the moment," said Tawnos. Urza did not reply. "I understand he leads the Fallaji, now."

Urza nodded. "The universe changes. Yotia falls. My brother leads the Fallaji. In Argive the crown has lost almost all of its power, for it let Yotia worry about the desert tribes, and now Yotia is gone. The nobles hold most of the power in Penregon, and they are very, very concerned about the Fallaji crossing the ridges and attacking."

"Are you?" asked Tawnos. "Worried, that is."

Urza opened his arms to include the room. "This is the result of that worry, Tawnos!" he said. "I can duplicate this tower in five days, given sufficient materials. I am working on a way to have the Yotian soldiers themselves build it. Imagine a line of these forts, manned by unsleeping soldiers, protecting Argive and Korlis from the Fallaji. Protecting them from my brother."

Tawnos nodded. "I was surprised not to see any ornithopters."

Urza shook his head. "They're needed to the north, patrolling the passes. Besides, sending an ornithopter aloft is sending a flare for the enemy, showing him where you are. That's another lesson learned at great price." Urza stood there for a moment, grinding his palms. "Did I tell you we have another school, in Penregon this time? Rendall is there, and his brother Sanwell. He survived, along with a handful of others. The school is being overseen by an old friend, Richlau. Did I ever mention Richlau before?"

"Urza," said Tawnos softly.

"I don't think I did," continued Urza. "Anyway, there is a whole raft of young nobles—well, not young anymore, but individuals who once worked with Tocasia and who know about artifacts, who value them and are willing to help me in my research."

"Urza," said Tawnos again.

"More than just power stones. I mean manpower, training, and re-sources. Argive is a rich country."

"Urza!" said Tawnos a third time, sharply.

"What is it?" asked Urza testily.

"Kayla is here," said Tawnos.

"I know," the artificer said, and there was a long pause. Then he said, "I know" again, and there was a longer pause.

"You should go down to meet her," said Tawnos. "And your son."

"Is he really . . . ?" started Urza, hotly, but letting the question die.

"He has your hair," said Tawnos.

"He has my father's hair," said Urza, and turned to look out the window again. "I wish you hadn't brought them," he said after a time.

"By all the gods of Yotia!" shouted Tawnos, and Urza jumped at the sound of the younger man's voice. "We have been running and hiding for three years now. I delivered your son, yes, *your* son, in the middle of a thunderstorm. I bring them all the way here, and *you* don't want to see them? Do you still hate her so much?"

Urza turned pale, and Tawnos was afraid the older man was going to flinch, to flee, to pull back further within himself. "No," he said at last. "It's not that. Not entirely. It's just that I failed. I failed to see what was coming. I failed to anticipate my brother's plans. I failed her, and I failed her nation."

"And I failed," said Tawnos grimly. "And she failed. We've had to live with that failure every step of the way from Kroog. Is that what it is, Urza? Are you ashamed that you're just as fallible as the rest of us?"

A long silence between them for a moment. Then Urza sighed and said, "I'm a storm crow, Tawnos. A bird of ill omen. Disaster follows in my wake, and I don't want to hurt her anymore. I don't want to hurt anyone anymore. Only a fool would be at my side."

"Then call me a fool, for one," said Tawnos. "I would like to go back to being your apprentice. Kayla would like to go back to being your wife."

Urza turned away again, and Tawnos saw him raise his hand to his face, perhaps to wipe away a tear. Yet when Urza turned back, his face was patient and calm, and his eyes were clear. The artificer smiled. "I have no need of an apprentice. And your skills with those statues prove that you are a master artificer in your own right."

"Well, if you don't need an apprentice, you need someone who will get behind you and give a good thwack from time to time," said Tawnos. "That's a job I can do as well."

"And do well," said Urza. "I need a friend, and you've been one to me. And to the queen. You have not failed either of us."

"You're wrong," said Tawnos, "but we can talk about that some other time."

"Indeed, we can," said Urza, then nodded his head. "Let's go down and see my wife. And my son."

Slowly they descended the stairs from the tower. Tawnos wondered if sound carried as well in the tower as it did in the old palace of Kroog. Urza stopped once to point out some feature of the tower to Tawnos, then shook his head and pressed on. He realized, Tawnos thought, that he was delaying the inevitable.

They reached the waiting room. Tawnos waited at the door. Sharaman set down the tray of sugar wafers and retreated to the hallway as well. Neither man left, but neither remained in the room.

Kayla rose, and Urza walked over to her. They embraced, but it was a polite embrace, each resting hands on the other's elbows. Still, they did not part, and Tawnos could see tears welling in Kayla's eyes.

"It is good—" rasped Urza, his throat tight. He cleared his throat and said, "It is good to see you again."

Kayla's mouth moved, but Tawnos did not hear the words.

"Hey!" said Harbin, at their feet. He pulled on Urza's smock and the artificer looked down at the lad.

Harbin looked at Urza, and with all the power that a two and a half year old can muster, said, "Unca Tawnos says you're my daddy. Are you?"

Urza looked at Kayla, then down at the small child. He knelt and took the lad's small hand in his own.

"I suppose I am," he said. "And I'm very pleased to meet you after all these years."

Chapter 19

Exchange of Information

Gix the demon received the report from one of his monks, but no words were spoken. Instead the monk knelt beside the demon's makeshift throne, and the demon's elongated finger clasped the top of the monk's skull. The monk let out a low moan as the talons dug slightly into the skin and demon's claws connected with the nerves beneath the flesh.

It was a heady moment for Gix, slightly intoxicating. These fleshy creatures were filled with sensation. Even the monks, whom Gix had learned possessed an existence that was removed from the experiences of others of their race, were a cornucopia of emotions, a pit of conflicting desires, a rich, breeding tidal pool of feelings. The electric thrill of touching those feelings, even vicariously, rushed through him like a shot.

The demon would be loath to admit it, but he found the experience unlike any at home in Phyrexia. Delicious. That was the word for it. The touch of the monk's nerves was delicious.

The emotions subsided—fear, anger, passion, concern, bliss—and Gix began to scan the monk's mind. The monks prided themselves on their machinelike organization, but Gix found their minds a tangle of clutter, a jungle of conflicting thoughts more impenetrable than his homeland's jungles. Slowly Gix extended his own consciousness, taming the wilderness and pulling the answers he needed from the living skull of his worshiper.

There had been those who had protested against his tender probings; they were buried in the sands outside, buried next to the weak, who collapsed in on themselves at the first gentle mental touch. Only the strong and the willing remained in the demon's service, which was as he thought it should be.

He had learned much of the world through the monks, much about a world so different from his own, as organized as a goblin parade and as structured as an overturned anthill. Even those words were looted from the monks' minds, for the pure chaos of the world did not connect in any way with his old life beneath the oily skies of Phyrexia.

This was a world filled with rogue units without coherent masters of any type. Perhaps this world had had masters once, but they died or went away, leaving brawling children in their place. There was an old, dead race called the Thran. Perhaps they had been the masters. But they were gone and left their toys behind—simple, uneducated machines without a glint of true sentience, and now some of these squalling children had unearthed those toys and were playing dangerous games.

One of the children had found the way into Phyrexia and stolen toys from his betters. He'd stolen from those who would come looking for his devices. He'd stolen from Gix.

The child was called Mishra, the monk's mind said. He was the master of the Fallaji, a crude and brutal people who lived in the dry regions. But to say he was their master was giving him too much credit, for all he was doing was riding a wave of their bestial organic nature. The tribesmen he led would slam against other bands of creatures like a random marble in a maze. This Mishra provided no more true guidance than an ornamental spur on a diabolic machine.

There was another, Mishra's subordinate, but the red-haired one did not shine in Gix's mind as did Mishra. He was the thief. Mishra was the one whose mind had brushed his all those years ago. Mishra came to him in dreams. (Had he dreamed before he encountered Mishra? Gix wondered. He had no memory of doing so.) Mishra invaded Phyrexia and took the dragon engines, the *mak fawa*, the creatures of the first sphere.

Mishra must be punished.

But Mishra was not alone, for there had been another in that initial mind touch, years ago, a shadowy figure alongside Mishra. At first he thought it was another subordinate, similar to the Ashnod-subordinate. But Gix soon realized that this other was instead a similar unit, issuing from the same basic components and manufacture. A brother, the monk's mind said, though the word carried different flavors and sensations than when referring to other priests.

The brother, Urza: another master of another crude, brutal people. There seemed no end to such barbarians, the children of unknown, abandoned masters. Once Gix sensed Urza's existence he could see him clearly—cut from the same cloth as his brother, no more and no less than Mishra was. Their minds seemed ordered, or at least more ordered than most he had encountered.

Each brother carried a legacy of the old ones, of the Thran. It was a stone split in two, each half containing the summation of the earlier stone yet altered to fit the organic unit they had bonded with. Gix could feel the crystalline longing of these halves, of the attraction they held for each other, and of their repulsion.

The stones stood like beacons to Gix, and even without the monk's surrogate senses the demon could feel their power. The beacons had moved little in the past few years. One lay to the west, across a patch of uneven mountains. The other was in the south, among another barrier of titanically broken ground. They called to him. They pleaded with him to take them back to Phyrexia, back to where they would be truly used.

When he had first come into this fleshy world, Gix thought he would merely slay the thief and return with the recovered dragon engines. He could feel their calls as well, though one became weak and flickered out of existence a few years previously. He mourned for that one and almost sought vengeance.

But now there was more to his mission. He could touch the dreams of the thief when he was in Phyrexia, but in this world he could touch neither Mishra's dreams nor Urza's. Now they seemed proof against his blandishments. Was this part of the power of their stones or of the world itself? The stones seemed important. Should he recover them as well? And were these two organic children a danger to Phyrexia? If they had broken through the barriers, would not others?

Faced with questions, Gix was logical and precise. He sent his monks out to gather information. Once the information was garnered, he sucked it deliciously from their minds and formulated a plan.

Gix willed his orders into the mind of the monk. There was another low moan as old information was pushed out of the monk's mind and organic circuitry rewired to comprehend the new orders. Gix had learned, through fatal trial and error, which parts of his worshipers' minds they needed for basic functions, and he left those untouched.

Gix lifted his hand, and his talons slid loose from the flesh and nerves of his servant. The monk pitched forward, into the waiting arms of his brothers (brothers to a lesser extent than Mishra and Urza). The monk would be tended and cared for, and when his mind healed he would pass on the message of the god.

They were to gather their brethren and go to this Urza and to this Mishra. They would become part of their brutal and crude organizational units, part of their tribal courts. They were to watch, and they were to report. And when the time was right, they were to call Gix from his throne in the caverns of Koilos, and he would punish the brothers for their crimes against the machines. For their crimes against Phyrexia.

And he would take the stones from them, thought Gix, flexing his fingers before him. Droplets of the monk's blood spattered against the demon's chest, hissing and bubbling as they struck.

Yes, thought the demon. The stones were his by right of conquest. He would take them back to Phyrexia.

Chapter 20

Transmogrants

Ashnod's reports to Mishra over the following months were regular, if not fully detailed. A few words on progress to date. A revised schedule of deadlines. A list of new supplies needed: sand for a particular type for glass; metal from a particular forge; fabric of a particular weave. And slaves—always more slaves.

The last were plentiful, but the remaining resources were beginning to wear thin. Most of Yotia had been plundered, and entire villages were now being impressed to work the mines that had not yet been stripped clean. The caravans from Tomakul and Zegon were less frequent than they should have been, and the quality of their tribute had fallen off. A number of representatives of those cities were dispatched to Ashnod as an example to the others. The Korlisians, still hiding behind a gauzy mask of neutrality, were increasingly troublesome. Mishra was convinced their caravans were havens for Argivian spies who reported everything back to his hated brother.

Mishra found that Ashnod's experiments served to increase loyalty and discipline among his own troops. It was soon reported that thieves and deserters were sent to Ashnod's camp and never returned.

Finally, after many months, Ashnod appeared before Mishra with a working prototype. It listed heavily to the left. It drooled. It shuffled on two feet. It had oversized pins through its wrists, ankles, elbows, and knees, and metal plates strengthening its neck. It was hairless. It lacked teeth and had dark smudges where there once had been eyes. Its skin resembled bluish, cracked plaster, and it looked as if it had been cooked in wax. It could not speak, but made soft, mewling noises. It stank.

When Ashnod gave it the command, it disarmed and almost killed three of Mishra's elite guard and ignored the pain as a fourth guard finally pinned it to the floor with his spear. It tried to fight its way up the impaling pole to claw at its attacker before its organs failed and it died at last.

Mishra was pleased and gave Ashnod permission and resources to build an army of her "transmogrants," of these things that were once living beings but now were little more than organic automatons, controlled by Ashnod's word.

If Ashnod noticed the fearful and disgusted faces of the Fallaji as her prototype was hauled from the room feetfirst, she said nothing. Nor did she notice the dark-robed northern priests among the assemblage, who whispered to each other in excited tones.

* * * * *

Despite the relative success of the first prototype, it took nearly a year for Ashnod to refine the process and guarantee a success rate of more than fifty percent. She spent another year organizing the transmogrified beings into something more than a shambling horde.

The red-haired woman's methods were simple and ruthless. She bleached out the minds and wills of her captives as she pickled their skins, making them tough, resilient, and mostly mindless. The rudiments of intelligence remained—enough to follow simple orders. But any trace of personality was gone. It was good that the process warped the body as well as the soul, Ashnod reflected. It would do little good for a Fallaji warrior to recognize a criminal cousin among her ranks.

Finally the unit was ready for Mishra's use. The timing was excellent. The Korlisians were traitors, the new qadir had decided, and needed to be made into an example before they grew more powerful. Argive was protecting the northern passes, but if the qadir's armies broke through in the south, near Korlinda itself, the Fallaji would have a foothold on the far side of the mountain chain.

Mishra sent Ashnod a message to ready her warriors for battle. The artificer replied that she wished to lead the attack herself. In his workshop, the other captains complained to the qadir. How could a woman lead? they asked. What real man would follow a woman? Particularly a woman with ill-omened hair?

Mishra thought about their complaints and sent another query to Ashnod, detailing his desire for her to contribute to the attack, though he made no mention of leading it. Ashnod took note of the exclusion and returned a second letter, the heart of which was that unless she controlled the entire army, she could not guarantee the performance of her forces.

There was a lull in communications, until Mishra issued a formal declaration making Ashnod a brevet general for the duration of the campaign into Korlis and commanding the other war captains to defer to her.

Mishra himself decamped from his workshop for the Suwwardi Marches, where the army was gathering, to review the troops and confer with the war captains one last time. Several, including old Jarin of the Ghestos clan, expressed one last time their concern about Ashnod's leadership.

"She is a woman," Jarin repeated at his final meeting with the qadir. Ashnod was not present, for she was readying her transmogrants for the long march. "An uncaring woman at that," the old man added.

"She is my assistant," said Mishra. "I trust her in all things."

"Do you trust your war captains less, Most Wise of the Wise?" asked Jarin.

"I trust all to do their duty toward the Fallaji people," replied Mishra.

"She is not Fallaji!" shouted Jarin, and several of the other war captains whispered to each other heatedly. "She traffics in the unspeakable! Her abominations frighten the horses and disturb the men. She uses outlander wizardry!"

Mishra's face clouded and he snapped, "I am not Fallaji, either, humble servant! Do you want to do without my outlander wizardry as well?"

Jarin's voice stuttered, then finally fell silent. A long, tense moment passed, but no other voice came to Jarin's defense. Even Hajar was a stone-faced enigma at his master's side.

At last the war captain of the Ghestos clan knelt before his qadir and said, "I appreciate the opportunity to voice my concerns, Most Mighty One, and understand the wisdom of your puissant decisions."

The talk moved to other matters, but Jarin did not raise his voice again. The other war captains, though they agreed with the old man, did not broach the subject.

In the morning there was a grand review. Mishra and his aides, including Hajar, gathered beneath their pavilion as the troops passed in review. There were Fallaji in the crowds, and Yotians as well, nervous and uncertain among the desert dwellers.

The troops were dressed in their best finery, armor and robes that would be packed away in the baggage train and only removed again when and if they reached Korlis's capital. Three units of cavalry trotted past, bedecked in flowing red robes that flickered like flames. Despite his earlier outburst, Jarin was allowed to retain control of the Ghestos cavalry, and he rode, expressionless, at the head of his unit.

The sun shone off the wide brass helmets of the foot soldiers, moving in precision review past their qadir. Then came the skirmishers, younger and a bit less organized, most of them younger sons just entering the military. Then the scouts rode past on their nimble horses, cantering in ornate patterns back and forth before the pavilion. And with each the Fallaji cheered, and even the Yotians present remarked on the grandeur of the warriors and their relief that the troops were heading somewhere other than Yotia.

Ashnod arrived with her horde of transmogrants. There were nearly three hundred of the creatures lined up in orderly rows. They moved not with the precision of trained troops but rather with an eerie lockstep, for they were controlled by the same mind. Not a trace of individuality showed itself among them, as if they had been cast from the same mold. They looked as if they would topple over as they shambled forward, but they marched as a single unit. The beasts were clad only in rough tabards of brownish Yotian cloth, and those garments looked like an afterthought.

Ashnod rode at their head, astride a great black charger. Her cape matched her scarlet hair, and she wore an ornate set of black and red armor—custom-made, it was said, in Zegon. The armor bristled with spikes and was polished to snare the sun and blind the onlookers.

The cheers died as she passed before the stand, and the applause was sporadic at best. Mishra's aides sat immobile as rocks next to the qadir and did not respond. The qadir raised his hand in benediction to Ashnod, and she returned the salute. Neither paid attention to the lack of enthusiasm among the others.

Last came the dragon engines, four new ones, operated by crews working within their bellies pumping the bellows and keeping the steam pressure high to drive them forward. There were renewed shouts of encouragement as they towered over the populace. Only two of the engines would be sent east with Ashnod. The other two would be sent south along the Kher Ridges, to be "spotted" by the Korlisians, drawing troops away from the Fallaji main attack.

The crowd's spirits rose with the passing of the dragon engines, and after the review the qadir treated the populace to a feast. At the banquet Ashnod sat at Mishra's right hand, and there was no doubt about the trust he placed in his general. Jarin was seated at the far end of the platform, but many of the other Fallaji, including Hajar, stopped to offer words of encouragement to the old Ghestos.

With the coming of the morning the army was gone, east into the mountains, into Korlis beyond.

The path they trod was similar to that Ashnod and Mishra had used to reach Korlinda many years ago. The journey was less smooth than hoped. In the first place, the new dragon engines were not as nimble as the originals; they moved slowly and required a great deal of space in which to turn. In addition, they were noisy, venting steam and clattering like sacks of old nails. This bothered the cavalry troops and made Ashnod realize that any element of surprise would be lost.

Then there were the transmogrants themselves: slower than the other troops, slower than the dragon engines themselves. Yet they were tireless. Each day the regular foot soldiers and cavalry outdistanced the shambling, demiliving creatures. And each day, around the midnight bell, the living automatons lurched into camp. Ashnod remained with them and spoke little to the other war chiefs during the journey.

At the end of the tenth slow day in the mountains, the advance scouts spotted an ornithopter. It sighted them as well and retreated back down the pass, flapping its oversized wings in panic.

That evening, after midnight, the generals held council. It would take two days to free themselves from the mountains entirely and to reach the relatively open land of the upper Kor valley. The Korlisians, probably with Argivian support, would be waiting for Mishra's forces before they could extricate themselves fully from the highlands. A tight battle would be disastrous for the normally mobile Fallaji cavalry.

"Alas and alack!" said Jarin, turning his palms upward, "we seem to be undone. For the merchant nation's mercenaries will be rushing for the pass, seeking to hold it against us! And we cannot turn back in good faith without so much as a single drop of blood being spilt. To press on is folly, and to turn back smacks of dishonor!"

"There must be another way," muttered Ashnod, almost to herself.

"If there is," said Jarin, "I have no doubt you will find it. It was for exactly this reason that our qadir, mighty may he be in his wisdom, chose you to lead us."

Ashnod looked into Jarin's face for the slightest hint of insincerity, but there seemed to be none. She thought for a moment, then said, "We must get out of the passes before the Korlisian troops arrive."

"Aye, but we are too slow," complained Jarin. "Would that our engines had wings, so that we might arrive there sooner, but they do not."

Ashnod pressed her fingertips together, and said, "Then we leave the dragon engines behind."

Faces fell around the table, and the arguments began. The engines themselves were useful tools, said one war captain, invaluable in battle. They were mobile forts, said another, a solid center about which men could cluster for defense. A third officer noted they provided protection for the army from the ornithopters, whose pilots had learned the dangers of straying too close.

A smile flitted across Jarin's face, but he said nothing.

"The engines are too slow," said Ashnod finally. "We have the transmogrants to provide a solid center to the line."

"Your abominations are slow as well," noted Jarin.

"Then they will leave now," stated Ashnod. "They will be waiting for you at the entrance of the pass." She turned to Jarin. "Unless you have a better plan?" she asked silkily.

No one did. The meeting was over, and Ashnod was gone again, leading her shambling creations ahead of the army and leaving the *mak fawa* to catch up as best they could.

The army reached the vale of the upper Kor before the Korlisians could respond fully. Still, word reached Ashnod of a large force of Korlisian troops coming up the valley. Scouts had spotted ornithopters in the skies above the Korlisian troop column, proof—if there still were any doubt—of that nation's complicity with Urza's Argivians. The Korlisians would be within striking range the next morning.

That was more than enough time for Ashnod to lay a trap.

The plan was simple. The foot troops were drawn up in the center of the plain, flanked on one side by all three units of cavalry. The transmogrants stood in the center of the line, serving as an anchor, hidden behind a thin line of foot soldiers. The skirmishers would engage the enemy van, drawing it to attack the line. The transmogrants would be revealed, and on Ashnod's signal the cavalry would sweep in along the flank, destroying the Korlisians utterly between the swift-moving horses and the unyielding transmogrants.

Jarin was politely unimpressed. Fallaji cavalry was made for quick strikes, he observed, not for running down entire units of the enemy.

"New uses for old tools," said Ashnod, who was thoroughly tired of the older Ghestos war chief.

"And if the Korlisians do not take your offered bait?" asked Jarin. "If they encamp and wait for reinforcements?"

"Then the dragon engines catch up, and we fight a more traditional battle," snapped Ashnod. "Tell me, Captain, would you question Mishra's orders so often and so heartily?"

The older war captain stiffened, then replied through clenched teeth, "I have my orders, which are to follow you. We will deploy along the flank and await your signal."

In the morning the Korlisians arrived, a force equal in number to the Fallaji forces. Two ornithopters were present, though one darted east at the first sight of the Fallaji troops. Reporting back to Urza and Tawnos, thought Ashnod. Surely neither artificer would be present here. There was no sign of war machines among the troops, nor did she see additional ornithopters.

The skirmishers engaged the leading edge of the Korlisian troops, firing slings and light bows. Several units of the Korlisians charged forward but were mastered by their captains and brought back, and the enemy formed into regular units. The Korlisians made extensive use of mercenaries, Ashnod recalled, so they would be better disciplined than most of the Yotian rabble. Then again, there were likely Yotian sellswords among the Korlisians, and that might cause them to charge prematurely.

The enemy force as a body heaved forward slowly. Its center held through tight discipline, but the units along its flanks were already ahead of the main van. They were in a perfect position to be cut off and defeated.

Ashnod smiled as the enemy neared. The transmogrants were in place behind a thin line of swordsmen. To her right, the cavalry rode into view, waiting only for her signal to charge.

The two armies collided like prehistoric beasts, and men began to die. Brass hats with spears kept a number of mercenaries at bay, while swordsmen engaged in a deadly close combat.

Ashnod shouted an order, and the swordsmen at the center of the line parted. She gave another cry, and her transmogrants raised their weapons and began to lumber forward.

Something happened on the opposing side. The center of the main van, where the commander normally would have his own elite guard, parted to reveal a new set of creatures. There were two types among the Korlisians: humans in beetlelike armor, and hulking brutes looking like soft, misshapen ogres.

Ashnod suddenly realized that the beetlelike armor was the outer coverings of humanoid devices, and the soft flesh of the ogres was some type of mud. Automatons, she thought, like Urza's avengers. The Korlisians had prepared their own surprise at the center of their line.

Ashnod cursed as the two centers collided. The transmogrants would have broken a line of normal humans, but these were no ordinary warriors. The beetle men worked with clockwork precision, raising and lowering their razor-tipped blades like farmers threshing wheat. Alongside them, the huge earthen statues waded into the transmogrants, crushing soft skulls with their great hands.

The transmogrants would neither retreat nor regroup. Ashnod had not given them the capacity to understand such orders. However, it was clear to the red-haired general that they were overmatched, a fact equally clear to the other Fallaji footmen and skirmishers. Already they were losing ground, only a few steps away from a full retreat. Ashnod's position was a bubble extending into the Korlisian lines, surrounded on three sides by mercenaries and automatons.

Ashnod gave the order, and heralds gave the signal for the cavalry. A sudden assault on the flank would still break the Korlisian army and allow her own human troops to recover, she told herself. The signalman unfurled a great crimson banner and waved it to the cavalry.

The cavalry did not move. Ashnod stared in disbelief, but her eyes had not deceived her: the cavalry had not abandoned its position. A unit of mercenary archers from Korlis had taken up position opposite it, but the three units of cavalry did not charge.

Ashnod cursed again, and shouted at the signalman. He waved his banner again frantically.

Still the cavalry did not move.

Ashnod looked around. The left flank, farthest from the cavalry, was already crumbling, the Fallaji footmen abandoning their spears, and in some cases their helmets, and falling back. Ahead of her the blades of the beetle men were ripping the transmogrants to shreds. As she watched, an earthen statue picked up a transmogrant, lifted the creature over its head, and pulled it apart by the legs and arms. The rotted remains cascaded down on the statue, but the clay automaton suffered no damage. Indeed, the cuts inflicted on the statues seemed to heal as Ashnod watched. The transmogrants had better success against the beetle warriors, and along the ground lay scattered remains of both dead human flesh and dismantled mechanisms.

Ashnod looked to her right to the cavalry. Now it was finally moving.

Then she cursed. It was moving backward. An orderly retreat in the face of mere archers. It was pulling away.

The sight of the cavalry's retreat destroyed the remaining right flank. The troops wavered and then broke into a run. Both flanks were in full rout, and the only thing holding the center was the remains of Ashnod's unit of transmogrants.

Ashnod wheeled her own horse, a pained look on her face. To abandon her creations felt to her as if the very heart was ripped from her flesh. Nonetheless, they would be destroyed. There was no one else to save them.

She spurred her black charger and left the devastation behind her, hoping that the transmogrants would do enough damage to at least slow their pursuers until the Fallaji were once more under the safe protection of the dragon engines.

* * * * *

The transmogrants had done that part of the job well, for after repelling the Fallaji invasion force the Korlisian advance halted entirely. The enemy might have been more hurt than Ashnod had thought, or they were waiting for resupply. Possibly the mercenaries had clauses in their contracts excusing them from pursuing enemies into the mountains. Perhaps their own commanders were afraid of ambush, thought Ashnod.

Regardless, there was no pursuit, save for the lone ornithopter that trailed them west for a day until they reached the dragon engines. Their surprise shattered, their forces demolished, their transmogrants slain or lost to the last being, the troops gathered around the engines, reversed their course, and began the slow crawl back to Fallaji territory.

* * * * *

Half a month later, Ashnod stood in Mishra's workshop before his dark oak throne. She was sputtering in rage.

"Treason!" she shouted. "I gave a direct order, and Jarin here ignored it! Because of that we were routed!"

"Most Revered One," said Jarin calmly, "we did not see the signal flag for the assault. We had been told by our most revered war general not to attack until we saw the flag. When we saw the battle was going against our forces, we pulled back to provide a screen to protect our retreating troops. More would have perished if we had not done so."

"We were defeated because he ignored the signal flag!" shouted Ashnod.

"I did not see the signal flag," said Jarin, his face impassive. "Nor did the other war captains."

Mishra patted the tips of his fingers together. "Do you say that my trusted assistant is lying?"

"No, Most Wise Among Us," said Jarin, quickly, "only that we did not see it. Such are the fortunes of war. A daring plan often comes to naught because of a simple thing." He looked at Ashnod and added, "Or because of a simple mistake in judgment."

Ashnod looked daggers at the Ghestos chief but said nothing. Jarin added, "We did retreat in good order. Most of the cavalry was unharmed, and the dragon engines were undamaged. There were, however, heavy losses among the footmen, and the brevet general's own . . . special forces . . . were lost."

"What a surprise," muttered Ashnod. Mishra ignored the comment and dismissed the war captain.

"Can you believe his lies?" the red-haired woman shouted as the door was still closing behind Jarin.

Mishra's face was tense and concerned. "I had hoped your endeavor would prove successful. Success ennobles many an experiment. If you had pressed into Korlis, if your creations had secured us a beachhead, then the war chiefs would be lining up to tell me how they knew you could do it all along. Needless to say, they are not doing so."

"It's all lies," replied Ashnod. "They're afraid of me. Of us. Of what we can do. Of our creations. The battlefield does not belong to human warriors. The dragon engines proved that. The transmogrants proved that."

"The battlefield is still theirs," said Mishra. His voice held no expression. "Their swords succeeded where your mindless creations did not. But you leave me with another problem. Some of the chieftains think that I listened to you too much in this matter, that I showed weakness by depending on you."

"Weakness!" shouted Ashnod. "Let them try to run an army in the field."

"I will," said Mishra. "Because I am sending you to Sarinth."

There was a long pause.

"Sarinth is on the other side of the empire," said Ashnod at last.

"Hard on the shores of Lake Ronom," agreed Mishra. "A nation rich in metals and wood, material that we need here. I want you to secure the fealty of their leaders."

"You want me out of the way," accused Ashnod.

Mishra held his hands open. "You are the most trusted of my lieutenants. I fear for your safety among the other chiefs."

"You should fear for their safety instead," spat Ashnod.

"I do," said Mishra. "Which is another reason to send you to Sarinth. Take a small force of men you trust with you. Gain their fealty."

"And if Sarinth doesn't want to swear fealty to us?" inquired Ashnod bitterly.

"Then I will send a larger force," said Mishra, "under a real commander."

Ashnod bristled but said nothing.

Mishra's eyebrows arched, and a kindly look passed over his face. It was an expression Ashnod had not seen in a long time.

"My student," he said, "you do many things better than any man, better than any individual, in my empire. But you are part of that empire, and you must go as your qadir commands."

Ashnod bowed formally. "I respect your wishes, Most Wise Among Us," she said woodenly. "Let me make my preparations for departure."

Mishra smiled and said, "One more thing."

Ashnod turned at the door.

"Leave Jarin alive," said the qadir. "It would be . . . difficult . . . to explain it if he something horrible happened to him so soon after this conversation."

Ashnod's brow furrowed, but she nodded.

The door closed behind her, and Mishra let out a deep sigh. Then he rose from the throne, padded over to his great slate board, and began to reconfigure the legs of his new dragon engines.

Chapter 21

Ivory Towers

Loran, Scholar of Argive, arrived at Terisia City in the early summer of the fifth year after Yotia's fall. It had been a long journey, from Penregon down to Korlis, then west by a coast-hugging boat across the storm-tossed Shielded Sea, north to Tomakul, and finally west over the wastes of the desert by camel to the borders of the city-state itself.

Loran wondered if, had she known the true distance of Terisia City from Argive, she would have left her home at all. Indeed, many of her fellow nobles had tried to dissuade her from the journey. But she could not remain in Penregon. War fever had seized the nobility, a disease that apparently clouded the mind and convinced those infected by it that Urza, who had failed to save Yotia, was nonetheless their salvation from his brother's hordes.

Loran was less than convinced. Yet in the drawing rooms and councils of Penregon her doubts were met by indifference at best and scorn at worst. She had opened correspondence with the archimandrite years before, and when the Terisian scholar extended an invitation to her she knew she would take it. Now, after long months, she stood at the gates of the great ivory metropolis.

Terisia City rose above the neatly cultivated fields that surrounded it and was visible from miles away. The city was a gem set in a great ring of white stone. Its roofs were glass and crystal, and they scattered the sunlight like prisms, surrounding the streets below with rainbows. When the hard winter rains struck, Loran was assured by her guide, the entire metropolis would rattle and resound like a shaken tambourine.

The city walls were of white stone, hauled from the distant Colekgan Mountains to the north by dwarves and their giantish slaves. Great towers of similar white stone ringed the city. They reminded Loran of chess pieces left behind by some idle god. Even these towers were works of art, for they were lovingly decorated with bas-reliefs of mythological beasts, winged lions, and elephants.

It was within one of these ivory towers that Loran was to meet the supposed "Mistress of the Order of the Ivory Towers," the archimandrite of Terisia City, first among equals of the tower scholars. Loran had no idea which tower belonged to the archimandrite, but she inquired at the city's main gate. She hoped to send word of her arrival, then to settle in some inn within the city.

Standing by the main gate was a broad-shouldered, bearded man with a wide-brimmed hat and a walking stick. As she spoke to the guards, the man removed the hat and mopped his brow with a rough handkerchief. He turned at the sound of her voice.

"You seek the Mistress of the Towers?" he asked. "Come. I'm heading there myself."

He turned away and walked a few paces, and Loran noticed he was lame in one leg. He hobbled along, resting heavily on a short metal stave. The man stopped and turned and looked back at the woman. "Argivian, by your accent," he noted.

Loran nodded, puzzled.

"You would not be Loran, the scholar from Penregon?"

"I would be," replied Loran. "But you have the advantage of me."

The man turned and limped back toward her. Loran met him halfway. "Feldon," he said, bowing over her offered hand. "Another scholar like yourself. You understand how I realized it was you?"

Loran paused for a moment. "I don't suppose there are many Argivians this far west."

Feldon nodded, and Loran noticed he wore his long hair swept back over his ears, without a braid. In the warmth of the region, it was no surprise that the man was sweating profusely.

Feldon said, "Your arrival has been expected. Come, let's see the archimandrite together."

Loran motioned toward her guide, still standing by his camel. "I have still to find lodging."

"Ah. Allow me," said Feldon. He hobbled forward two paces and ejaculated a rapid string of Fallaji words, accented in a dialect that Loran did not know. The guide responded in kind, and Feldon fished a coin from his heavy coat. He tossed the coin to the guide, who caught it with a deft motion, smiled, and bowed.

"You're staying at the same inn I am," said Feldon, turning back to the Argivian scholar. "Don't worry. If your guide had been less than an honorable man, you would not have gotten this far. Come along." And with that he limped forward again.

He reminded Loran of a bear. Of a great bear, she thought, that had accidentally wandered out of the mountains and been mistaken for a human. She smiled at the thought and quickly caught up with him. The last was easy, since he paused every few steps to mop his brow and to complain of the heat.

"You are not from Terisia City either," said Loran.

"Northern uplands, near the glacier," answered Feldon. "Came down here to check the libraries. Useless things, the libraries. Couldn't find any runes that matched."

"Matched?" asked Loran.

"This," said Feldon, holding up his metal walking stick. The head had been twisted into an ornate curve.

"It's a staff," Loran said.

"More of a cane," returned Feldon. "But look along the shaft."

Loran reached out and steadied the proffered object. Along the length of it were markings—little more than scratches, but definitely organized in a recognizable pattern.

"They aren't Thran," she said at last.

"Nor are they dwarven or goblin. Or anything else that anyone around here recognizes," said Feldon. "Found it in the glacier. I've been studying it."

"The cane?" asked Loran.

"The glacier!" said Feldon with a broad smile. "The big one that pours into Ronom Lake. Glaciers are frozen rivers, you know, and they move, glaciers do. Not that you'd notice, but they slowly come down the mountain, scraping clean the land in their path. Found this one at the base of the glacier, and I've seen others buried within its heart."

Feldon continued his lecture as they continued around the perimeter of the walled city. They passed the first tower and came to a stop at the second. Feldon bellowed another string of words at the female guard before the door, this time in a language Loran did not even recognize. The guard bowed and stood aside for Loran and Feldon to enter.

"Sumifan," he said by way of explanation. "They have a tonal quality to their language that makes discussion quite maddening sometimes. The same word has several different meanings if you vary the pitch."

"You study languages?" asked Loran.

"When I am not studying glaciers," replied Feldon, with a private smile. "Actually I ended up knowing so much about language because I needed to know more information about glaciers and could not read the old scrolls or hear the old tales in their original tongues. So I learned language as a matter of course. Your specialty is artifacts, correct?"

"Old Thran devices," Loran specified.

"Like the two brothers," grunted Feldon. "Mishra and Whatsisname."

"Urza," said Loran.

"Dangerous things, artifacts," said Feldon, and there was something in his voice that made Loran wary. By this time they were past the reception hall and in the main room.

The chamber was larger than Loran had expected and was dominated by a heavy table of lacquered oak. The walls were lined with glass-fronted bookshelves, within which were locked all manner of folios, scrolls, librams, and curios. Already the keeper of the tower, the archimandrite herself, was moving toward them.

Gliding would have been a better term, for the archimandrite, a sliver of a woman with a pale and narrow face, did not seem to walk as much as she hovered above the stonework floor. Her long black hair spilled down her back in a single fall. Loran thought of the way she had worn her hair as a girl, back in Tocasia's camp. That seemed a lifetime ago.

"Good Feldon," said the archimandrite. Her voice was soft but firm. Loran could sense at once that she was used to others quieting in order to hear her.

The sweating scholar managed another low bow, then turned his entire upper body toward Loran. "Gracious Archimandrite, may I present Loran the Argivian, scholar of Thran Artifacts. Also a woman kind enough not to interrupt while I go on about my glaciers."

The archimandrite curtseyed gracefully, and Loran returned the courtesy. "It is good you have arrived," the woman said. "Let me introduce you to the others."

"The others" consisted of a bald couple, man and woman, seated at the far end of the table. The man, a rotund little fellow, rose as they approached. Loran extended a hand, but the man instead slapped both hands across his chest, his fingers touching his breastbone. Loran took this as a greeting and lowered her hand accordingly. Feldon smiled at the exchange, and the archimandrite made no mention of it.

"Drafna, founder of the College of Lat-Nam," said the bald man.

The seated woman made a small coughing noise. It was little more than a clearing of the throat, but Loran and Drafna noticed it.

Drafna cleared his throat and said, "Co-founder of the College of Lat-Nam." That brought another small cough, and Drafna began a third time, "Co-founder of the *present* incarnation of the College of Lat-Nam." He turned and looked at the woman, who said nothing but merely smiled. "My wife and co-founder, Hurkyl."

Loran curtseyed, and Hurkyl made the same breastbone-touching greeting as her husband. Hers was both more graceful and more tentative. Loran stared at the bald woman. She had almond-shaped eyes, and ornate designs had been tattooed into the bare flesh of her shoulders.

The archimandrite motioned for Loran to take a seat, while Feldon pulled out a great, dark oak chair for himself, hung his hat on one of the posts jutting from the headpiece, and lowered himself down, gripping his cane as he did so.

"I thank you for the invitation, Mistress of the Towers," said Loran, "and I should tell you at the outset that I come with the knowledge of the Chief Artificer of Argive, though not as his representative."

"That would be Whatsisname," said Feldon.

"Urza," said the archimandrite levelly and raised her hand to signal the servants. The archimandrite seemed young to Loran at first blush, but now she realized the woman was older than she. The grace of her movements had been honed by years of practice.

A servant, another Sumifan, arrived with coffee. It smelled of honey and was not as thick and syrupy as the Fallaji mixtures with which Loran was familiar.

"Despite this lack of official authorization," continued Loran, "I have brought along the notes on Thran artifacts that the Argivians have collected over the years, culminating in Tocasia's notes from her digs." She turned to Feldon. "Tocasia taught me what I know about artifacts, and she also taught Urza and Mishra." To the archimandrite she said, "Unfortunately, Urza would not allow me to bring any information about his own work. I had to travel through innumerable miles of land held by his brother, and he feared any data sent might fall into the wrong hands."

"Understood," said the archimandrite, and in that word made sure that Loran knew there would be no questions concerning Urza's work—at least not at this meeting. "But you do carry other knowledge that is valuable to us," the archimandrite continued. "You knew the

Brother Artificers as children."

"Yes," said Loran, "though I was very young at the time myself."

"Did they hate each other even then?" asked the Mistress of the Ivory Towers.

Loran paused and thought for a moment. "No. They were rivals, I suppose. All brothers are. Urza was smarter, or rather was more studious. Mishra was nicer. He got along better with others."

"This would be the same Mishra that leveled Kroog?" inquired Feldon, his voice dripping with irony.

The archimandrite ignored him, instead saying, "But they did not hate each other when you knew them."

"No." Loran turned to Feldon. "But they have changed. I have not seen Mishra since Tocasia, our mentor, died, but he is said to be a cruel desert warlord, a demon to Argivians and Korlisians alike."

"Is he?" said Drafna.

Loran shook her head. "I cannot say what he is now, or why. But it is difficult for me to equate the young man I remember telling stories by the fire with the Butcher of Kroog."

"Time changes us all," said the archimandrite. "But what of his brother? What of Urza?"

Loran shook her head again. "Urza has been hurt very, very badly. He seems to have pulled back into himself. I talked to him just once, to tell him I was making this journey. He was . . . not cold, but detached, as if everything was a cryptic message that could be solved only if one had the right cipher."

The archimandrite leaned forward in her chair. "So you do not think there will be a resolution between the two without further conflict?"

"No," said Loran flatly. "I don't think there will be. In Argive, when I left, they were building a string of towers along the borders, filled with clockwork soldiers of Urza's design. There are new mines across the hinterlands, and most of the streams have been dammed to provide additional power. When I passed through Tomakul and Zegon, portraits of Mishra hung everywhere, and people felt he would lead them to a great and powerful future. No, there will be no resolution without war."

"Told you," said Feldon. The archimandrite frowned.

"What does it matter what two screaming brats do on the far side of the continent?" said Drafna sharply. "It does not involve us at all. Let them brawl and leave us to our own work. If they would rather fight than study, is it our responsibility?"

"It's more than that," said Feldon. "Things like this have a tendency to spread. First it's the Fallaji against the Yotians. Now it's against the Argivians and the Korlisians. How long before we get dragged into things on one side or another?"

"This qadir of the Fallaji is facing eastward with his forces. We are to the west. We are not his worry," said Drafna.

"Really?" snapped Feldon at the bald man. "I was talking to a Sarinthian merchant this morning. Apparently Mishra's devil-girl apprentice, Ashnod the Uncaring, was in Sarinth, 'negotiating' for the timberland and mineral resources of the state. Apparently the negotiations consist of Mishra giving Sarinth the choice of either handing over the goods or having the Fallaji come and take them."

"I'd like to see them try," offered Drafna.

"That's what the Zegoni said," muttered Feldon. "And they're being bled dry as a vassal state of the Fallaji domains. The Yotians, too, for that matter."

"The qadir's representatives have approached Terisia City's council as well," said the archimandrite softly. "They have been politely refused. What will happen when they arrive with their dragon engines at our gates?"

"Or at yours, Drafna?" asked Feldon.

The co-founder of the College of Lat-Nam made a harrumphing noise but said nothing.

"Terisia City is an ancient place," said the archimandrite, speaking to Loran but for Drafna's benefit. "It has many defenses. The great white towers that ring the central city are but one of them. But these defenses are old and might not be sufficient to withstand an assault from without. Our people have been at peace for longer than any remember, and they have no love for war."

"It doesn't matter if you love war or not," said Drafna, "if one is coming your way."

"Exactly!" thundered Feldon. "That's what we need to prepare for! Otherwise the various western nations and their knowledge and scholars will be picked off one at a time."

"You could ally with Urza," said Loran. "Since Mishra is your closest fear."

The archimandrite and Feldon looked at each other, then at Loran.

"Whatsisname may be as bad as Mishra," said Feldon. "The example of his defense of Yotia is not encouraging."

"We do not want to avoid one master merely to accept another," said the archimandrite, softly but clearly.

Loran thought about the Mistress's words. "That's true," she said. "I'm afraid Korlis has become little more than a province of Argive. More and more of its decisions come from Penregon in the name of coordinating the war effort."

"Exactly," said Feldon again. "We have to find a third path."

The archimandrite leaned forward, and Loran felt herself drawn forward as well. "We have many scholars within our walls and know of more scattered through the western part of the continent. I propose we gather them here to form a union, a conclave, a gathering of knowledge that is able to stand up to either of the brothers' machines."

"I know several Sarinthian scholars who started packing the moment Ashnod arrived in their capital," said Feldon. "And there are some shamans and witch women from up near the glacier who could aid as well."

"The reputed song mages of Sumifa might cooperate, as well as astrologers and diviners who have fled Zegon," added the archimandrite.

"No," said Drafna. The others looked at the bald man. "No," he repeated firmly. "This is not for us. Lat-Nam is far enough away that we do not have to worry about desert tribes. We are not interested."

There was the shadow of a cough, so quiet none would normally hear it. Drafna looked at his wife, who cleared her throat again. Feldon raised an eyebrow, and the archimandrite kept her face a passionless mask. Drafna scowled.

"I meant to say, we shall see," said Drafna, shooting a glare at the other scholar of Lat-Nam. "I have reservations, but we will make all our resources and knowledge available." He took a deep breath and laced his pudgy fingers together. "After all, we might learn something as well."

The archimandrite turned to Loran. "And you, Loran of Penregon. Will you join our union?"

Loran sat silent for a moment. She had come seeking knowledge, but was it knowledge that might be used against either of the brothers? Didn't she owe Urza and Mishra more than that? Could she turn over copies of Tocasia's notes to people who, even with the intention of defending themselves, would search them for a way to defeat the brothers?

She thought of the ever-growing mines and factories that filled her homeland, and of the other noble families that seemed determined to declare Urza their patron saint. Of the Fallaji who seemed to have deified Mishra. Would Tocasia want either man to use the knowledge she had taught him in that fashion?

Loran took a deep breath, like a diver about to plunge off the pier. "Yes," she said at last. "I will join you."

Chapter 22

Urza's Miter

"How can you stand these collars?" asked Tawnos, tugging at the starched fabric around his neck.

"I can't," replied Urza. "When I was a child, I hated any ceremony that forced me to dress up. I think it's one reason religion fell out of favor among the nobility: it was too uncomfortable to dress for."

Both men wore stiff cotton shirts with even stiffer woolen jackets accompanied by heavy woolen pants. Each garment was ironed with knife-edge folds. Leather boots, new and shined to an incandescent glow, were equally unwieldy. To Tawnos they felt more like lead weights than footwear. The ceremonial gear was mandated by the most august of ceremonies in which they were about to take part. Tawnos wondered if they could just send the outfits and stay home themselves.

Reflecting, Tawnos thought the pair had gotten off lucky. There were costumes and ceremonial uniforms among the gentry that reminded him of a ship under full sail, so festooned were they with ribbons, banners, and medals. But Argive had never had a Lord High Artificer and Protector of the Realms before, nor a Master Scholar. As a result both men were shielded from the worst of past pageantry.

Tawnos had always heard the Argivians were a dour, serious people. Even the way they treated such a celebration was further proof, he thought. Never had he seen so many people dead set on enjoying themselves. They were single-minded—even grim—in their pursuit of pleasure. The past month had shown that beyond a doubt.

There had been celebrations beyond measure in Penregon. First a royal wedding between the young crown prince of Argive and the granddaughter of the redoubtable lord of Korlis. Then the official notice of abdication of the venerable (if weak) Argivian king in favor of the crown prince and his new bride. Then there was the official recognition of the combined kingdoms of Argive and Korlis (though Korlis was effectively subsumed politically into Argive). And now came the final act: recognition of Urza as Lord High Artificer and Protector of the Realm of the combined kingdoms.

The nobles of Argive were behind it all. They had been feuding with their crown for years. The king (now referred to as the Old King) advocated a policy of containment and appeasement of the desert tribes. That policy had been destroyed with Kroog, along with whatever power the king still held. The nobles were behind the royal marriage, along with the merchants of Korlis. They were no doubt instrumental as well in convincing the Argivian king to relinquish his crown. Tawnos knew for a fact that the nobles had pressed Urza to accept the scepter and miter of the Lord Protector of the Realms.

What Tawnos did not understand is why Urza had accepted the position. When Tawnos put the question to him, the artificer offered a weak excuse; at least it seemed weak to Tawnos.

"In Yotia," said Urza, "the warlord let me build my devices, but I had little control over their use and never sufficient resources to develop them properly, even as Chief Artificer. Now, as Lord Protector, I can control the use of my devices and will have full access to sufficient resources."

"I'm not sure about the nature of that control," returned Tawnos. "From what I've seen, even leaders are driven by events and situations beyond their control. That includes the will of the masses. Already there are those who call to retake Yotia."

"That may well yet happen," said Urza, "but it will occur with a mechanized force, one filled with avengers, mechanical soldiers, and the new sentinels we're designing."

"It may happen before we have a chance to finish the work," said Tawnos. "In fact this new position may bring you under new pressure to launch an attack."

Urza ground his palms together slowly. At last he shrugged. "You may be right, my former student."

"Then why accept the miter and scepter?" demanded Tawnos.

"I have another reason," said Urza, and closed his mouth firmly.

Tawnos wanted to press Urza about what such a reason could be, when the door to the room flew open. A small metal bird fluttered into the room, chased by young Harbin. The seven year old laughed and lunged at the small bird, which dodged his blows effortlessly and circled the room.

Tawnos whistled a short tune, and the bird came to rest on the mantelpiece. The boy also quieted immediately, suddenly aware of the others in the room. "Uncle Tawnos," he said with a smile. Then his face turned stern. "Father, I'm sorry for interrupting."

Urza smiled gently and said, "No interruption." He looked at the bird. "One of yours?" he asked Tawnos.

Tawnos shrugged. "A small distraction, using some of the ideas we've been working with. It avoids the boy's blows because it detects the air moving in front of his hands, much as an insect would. He can catch it if he moves slowly, but I have never seen a young boy who had that much patience."

Urza nodded. "Yotians may have many souls, but at your core you are still a toy maker."

Lady Kayla, Queen-in-Exile of Yotia, had entered behind the boy, while a servant carrying her cloak remained outside. "Harbin! You know better than to disturb your father and Tawnos!"

Urza allowed himself another gentle smile and said again, "No interruption. On a day like this, it would be hard to get any real work done anyway. Come in, and let us toast our good fortune."

Tawnos turned to pick up an oversized "elephant" bottle of red wine, a gift of the nobles. The Argivians liked their wines bloodred and furniture-polish bitter. Urza fetched two goblets, one for each of the other adults, and his own chalice. The last had been Urza's own handiwork. He had converted the central pump that had worked the last of Tocasia's onulets, a beast now as mythological in Argive as minotaurs and rocs.

Tawnos poured a small amount for himself and for Kayla and a more generous helping for Urza.

Urza raised his chalice in a toast. "We have passed through fire over the past few years, and that has tempered us. Now the fires grow hotter still, but we are stronger, and we are proof against the flame. To Argive and Korlis!"

"To the memory of Yotia!" said Kayla.

"To the new Lord High Artificer and Lord Protector of the Realms!" said Tawnos.

"To the new Chief Scholar!" replied Urza, and metal clanked between them. Urza drained his cup and said, "We had best be moving along. If we are late, the Argivians will make being late part of every ceremony from here until doomsday!"

Urza started for the door, then paused. He whistled a small tune, identical to the one Tawnos had used minutes before. The mechanical bird unfurled its wings and sailed off the mantelpiece. Harbin swatted at it but missed, and the bird fluttered around the room, dodging the young boy's best-aimed shots.

* * * * *

The ceremony itself was typical of all Argivian ceremonies: long-winded and stifling. Tawnos had thought he would not survive the wedding earlier in the month, but this was infinitely worse, for he and Urza were at the center of the activity. There was no chance to sneak out when you were on the podium with all eyes on you.

The Great Hall had once been a cathedral to a god now forgotten and out of fashion. It was packed with all manner of Argivian nobles, clad in finery that swelled their forms to twice their size. In addition the incense used in the hall was overwhelmed by the clashing odors of perfume worn by the Argivian women (and some of the men). Tawnos wondered if he could afford to sneeze in his tight outfit, and his eyes watered.

The Argivians bothered Tawnos, and the nobles worst of all. Owing to the former apprentice's Yotian origin, most tended to treat him like some rustic relative. He always felt he was out of place in Kroog, a boy from the coastal provinces in the big city. At least, though, in Kroog he was among Yotians. Many of the Argivians seemed to assume that all Yotians had trouble with the language. They spoke slowly and loudly to him.

Worse still were those Argivians who acted as if he were still no more than Urza's apprentice. Occasionally they did not address him at all in the Lord High Artificer's presence, as if he were no more than a hanger-on, a dogsbody, a servant to Urza. Even when the artificer made sure to mention Tawnos's inventions, such as the triskelion, a mobile fortification, the eyes of the nobles glazed over and Tawnos could almost hear their ears clicking off.

No, thought Tawnos, worst of all were the stiff collars. He reached for his but halted his fingers in time. It would be just like a rural bumpkin to pull at his neckline in the middle of a ceremony.

The ritual was interminable. There was a presentation of honors; a recognition of foreign delegations; a recognition of important nobles that was effectively a roll call for the entire cathedral; a platitude by the Chamberlain of Argive that was longer than most sermons. This was followed by a listing of good things that had happened of late, which were (truly or otherwise) ascribed to the efforts of Urza and his faithful assistant, Tawnos.

The tawny-haired man's position on the podium gave him a chance to sweep the crowd with his eyes and pick out faces. Kayla and Harbin in the front row. She seemed nearly wilted in her gown but was still game, while the boy had surrendered to boredom a half-hour back and was now kicking the sides of the pew in a desultory fashion. The apprentices were led by Richlau the schoolmaster, the senior students Rendall and Sanwell at his side. Sharaman was in full military harness and looking almost comfortable in his dress uniform.

There were others: Argivian noblewomen in full regalia, and young courtiers vying with them for flashiness. Korlisian merchant lords, more restrained, but still bedecked in the most sumptuous of fashions. There were dwarven diplomats from the Sardian Mountains, a dour group of diminutive people who made the Argivians look positively festive and the Korlisians evenhanded. Their mountains held much of the resources that Urza needed, but they were willing to trade their metals and stones for gold, which Urza considered a minor metal of little real value in the battlefield.

There were Yotians present, dressed colorfully but simply. They were refugees who had fled to Argive after the fall and represented some of the most powerful families in the region, yet next to the Argivians they seemed like poor relations.

There were also others of whose identity Tawnos was unsure. There were a band of fur-wearing barbarians from Malpiri, and a group of priests, black-robed savants with mechanical devices hung around their necks. Gixians, Tawnos reminded himself, from a monastery far to the northwest. Urza had received an offer from them to aid in his studies, but Tawnos found them too fanatical in their devotion to the machines themselves. They treated even the ornithopters as if they were living creatures. It made Tawnos nervous, and he avoided them, as did most of the rest of the populace, who had no time for gods of any stripe.

The chamberlain's invocation ground to a close, and he was replaced by the lord of Korlis, whose voice was slightly more pleasant but who seemed intent on showing everyone that her nation could be just as long-winded as the Argivians. She spoke of the recent events, of the erecting of the defensive towers along the borders of both Korlis and Argive, and of the continual ornithopter patrols that kept them safe from the Fallaji devils.

It was more than just Urza's devices that kept them safe for the moment, Tawnos thought. Word had reached Penregon that Mishra had plundered most of Yotia and drained Zegon as well, and was looking for new supply sources. Apparently the attempts to fold Sarinth, far to the west, into the Fallaji empire had not gone well, and a huge force had settled there to besiege the principal cities. Instead of gaining needed resources, Mishra had succeeded in opening another front. Should he continue in this fashion, Urza's brother would soon surround himself with enemies.

Of course the situation was not lost on the Argivian nobles, nor on the Korlisian merchants who wanted to reopen their precious trade routes. Now was the time, they said, to press the advantage. Now was the time to retake Yotia. Now was the time to put Mishra in his place.

Urza had surprised Tawnos with his response to the noble demands. In Yotia he retreated to his orniary and let others do the talking and planning. Now he met with the nobles and the merchant lords whenever possible and never shirked from showing them some new device or implementation. They, in turn, had opened their vaults to him, allowing him access to power stones, land, and other resources needed to build.

Tawnos thought he knew Urza's plan. The artificer would continue to build his avengers, ornithopters, sentinels, and soldiers until he had more than any dragon engine could best. Only then would he move against his brother.

Tawnos hoped Urza would have time to carry out his plan. Given the enthusiasm of the Argivians and the greed of the Korlisians, he was not sure.

The lord of Korlis finally surrendered the podium, and his young majesty presented the titles. Urza knelt (a feat in itself, considering the stiffness of his costume), and the young king placed the Lord High Artificer's mitre on Urza's head. Then he laid the scepter of the Protector of the Realms in Urza's hands. The crowd burst into applause as Urza rose and recognized their cheers.

They were quieter for Tawnos, but only slightly. He received the heavy velvet robes (lengthened to cover his large frame) of the Chief Scholar. He knelt as well, and the king placed a golden circlet on his head. Even kneeling, Tawnos was almost as tall as the king and had to bow forward to prevent the Argivian from having to reach up.

Then the benediction, and Tawnos swore he saw the entire audience shudder to a man as the chamberlain remounted the podium and launched into a rousing screed against the Fallaji devils. That was what was missing, Tawnos thought. There were no Fallaji present, at least none who would announce their heritage. The chamberlain declared Urza to be Lord Protector of all the lands not held by the Fallaji and their allies.

In other words, all lands not under the rulership of Mishra.

Finally the ceremony was over, and the people filed out for a ceremonial banquet, which would be dominated by even more lengthy speeches. Every merchant and noble with at least some claim to the title would rise and deliver his own thoughts on the matter.

Tawnos couldn't wait.

Back in his chambers Urza smiled and pulled the miter from his head. It was a heavy thing, and Tawnos had wondered if the older man would fall over from the weight.

Urza hefted the miter, clearly delighted. Finally Tawnos said, "I've never seen you this cheerful when the people praised you in Kroog. Is it the fact that they are your own countrymen that makes you smile?"

Urza looked up, puzzled for moment. Then he smiled broadly. "You think that is it? That I have become a vain old popinjay, thriving on the adulation of the crowds? Look into my new hat, my former student, and see the truth of the matter."

Tawnos moved over and looked over the brim of the upturned miter. Gemstones were sewn into the lining of the tall hat. That was why it was so heavy.

No, not gemstones, Tawnos realized. Power stones, pure and unflawed. There were more than had been in the chest Urza had shown him five years ago.

Tawnos looked at Urza, and the Lord Protector beamed a warm smile. That was why he had put up with all the pomp and trappings of the ceremony, the Chief Scholar realized. That was why he had endured the speeches and courted the nobles and why, while claiming modesty, had accepted the post of Lord High Artificer.

All to gain more power. All to gain more resources.

Urza left the miter in Tawnos's hands and went to fetch his chalice before the pair left for the interminable banquet. Tawnos shook his head. His former master had not changed at all. His devices were still at the center of his universe.

Tawnos did not know if that knowledge made him feel better or worse.

Chapter 23

Circles of Protection

The Brotherhood of Gix summoned their master to Mishra's workshop.

The priests did so only because Mishra, the Artifice Qadir of the Fallaji, was going to decamp soon, moving westward to the caravan city of Tomakul. The Sarinthian front had expanded into a full-fledged war, and Mishra needed to be closer to action. Already manpower had been stripped from occupied Yotia, and troops were making the long trek north and west to the wooded shores of Ronom Lake

The Gixians knew of these decisions, for they had infiltrated most of the daily workings of the workshop and the surrounding factories. Over the past few years they had become a regular part of Mishra's court and were for the most part tolerated. They had spun that tolerance into a web of information. Little came to Mishra's factory that did not reach the Gixians' ears and, through them, their master's.

The mines were mostly tapped out now, said the reports from Yotia, and entire mountains were being stripped away for any resources they could provide. Similarly, the tribute of men and supplies from Zegon was drying up. Far-off Almaaz had bought its own protection by sharing its mystic song mages, but Mishra was now depending on that nation for iron and lumber as well.

Then there was Sarinth. There were the official commander's reports of great dragonlike wyrms that haunted the forests, and light troops who struck from ambush. The city of Sarinth itself, immured to years of assaults from the Yumok nation to the north, was as hard to crack as an iron-shod chestnut.

There were other Sarinthian reports, these from Ashnod and

harder for the Gixians to get their hands on, though not impossible. These reports were friendly and conversational, but they never failed to mention the problems of the current Fallaji commander and the inevitable tragedy that would ensue if the red-haired woman were not immediately given free reign in military matters. Mishra held firm to his decision: he did not give her a command, nor did he call her back to his side, and the Gixians approved of both decisions.

And last there were the reports from the east, from the passes through the Kher Ridges to Argive and Korlis. The war there was a slow, grinding process, as two titans hurled themselves against each other. Urza was busy, of that there was no doubt, ripping huge chunks from the Argivian landscape to feed his own war machines. The land was ringed with towers that appeared almost overnight, each tower containing mechanical protections. The camp was awash in rumors that the Argivians were about to cross the mountains and the desert and press on into occupied Yotia. Mishra was forced to relocate his court to Tomakul, closer to the heart of his empire, closer to the siege of Sarinth, and farther from the thinly defended Yotian border.

This last item was a bad thing for the Brotherhood of Gix. Such a move would disrupt their organization, which they had shaped into a perfect machine. So they gathered in their quarters (situated beside the spillage from one of the great iron foundries) and called their master.

Their chant was logical and precise, their motions practiced and machinelike. They had been taught how to call upon Gix before they left Koilos, and the demon had left precise instructions when to call upon him. Now, in the windowless room of their small quarters, the twenty-four brothers chanted the proper dirges and motioned their hands in the proper manner, carving symbols in the air.

In return, the air winked at them, coalescing into a great pillar of blackish smoke, smelling of burning oil. There was the sound of crashing gears, and from the smoke stepped their master, Gix, resplendent in his living armor, his snakelike tendrils flexing and coiling from the back of his head.

"You have summoned me," said Gix. "I trust it is for a good reason."

* * * * *

Gix moved unseen through the darkness of the desert night, a landscape hidden from the heavens by clouds of smoke and illuminated from beneath by the light of the foundries that ran around the clock.

The great trees that had originally cradled the factories were dead now, their lumber sawn up and used to make catapults, rams, dragon engines, and other war machines. The surviving stumps had been hollowed out and converted to barracks and foundries and plated with sheets of thin copper. There were still humans about, both warriors and slaves, but much of the work was now done by automatons—great clanking beasts that shuffled mindlessly from one task to the next.

It was no Phyrexia, thought the demon, but it was a good start.

His followers had been correct. Once Mishra relocated his command center, he would be tougher to strike at. Further, it might take years for the human artificer to raise Tomakul to the same wonderful level of civilization that he had achieved in this region.

Now was the time to strike, the demon thought, before the advantage was lost.

Gix moved like a spirit through the empty hallways and mechanized forges. He left his children, the priests, behind, after rewarding them with a touch of the dreams of Phyrexia. They lay in a stupor now, dreaming of their mechanical paradise. Gix moved best alone.

Were he discovered, Gix knew that with but a thought he could easily return to Koilos. He had gained an affinity with the desert caverns over the years, and simply by willing it so he could travel there. He needed help from his priests to be summoned elsewhere, but he could go home at will.

Gix allowed a narrow smile to cross his lipless face. He thought of Koilos as home now. Not Phyrexia, to which he could not return, not at least without first punishing the interloper. Not without taking from the trespasser his valued stone of power.

There was only one incident *en route* to the workshop. An automaton from one of Mishra's factories crossed before him. Sensing something unfamiliar, it stopped in place, whirring menacingly. Gix was uncertain if the machine had the rude sentience to recognize him as a stranger or if it was merely sounding an alarm as an automatic reaction.

In the passing years he had developed an understanding of these simple machines made by clumsy mortal children. Gix reached out mentally to the artifact, caressing it with soft words as a human would comfort a wounded animal. It did not matter if the animal understood the words, only that it understood the intent behind them. The priesthood back in Koilos had been rebuilding the old *su-chi* automatons, and this one was little different from them.

The machine shivered for a moment as Gix's mind touched the small shard of power stone that served both as its heart and brain. The demon changed only a few small matrixes within the crystal itself, but those were enough to convince the lead-minded device there was nothing out of the ordinary and no alarm need be sounded. The automaton stopped whirring and soon scooted out of sight.

Gix entered the workshop, gliding past bleary-eyed guards who no more noticed his passing than they did the smoke that now rose from the surrounding landscape. The demon's feet did not touch the ground as he floated effortlessly to the thief's chambers, where his minions had assured him his prey awaited.

Indeed he was present: slumped backward in a work chair before a great board made of slate, a piece of chalk still clenched in his hand. Gix's mechanical eyes swept the room. It was filled with books, most of which were covered in a thick coating of dust. At the far side, near a heavy wooden throne, another man, a Fallaji guard, was asleep.

Gix nodded. One less being he would have to kill immediately. He moved toward the inert form of the sleeping Mishra.

The human looked almost cherubic in slumber. His beard was now flecked with bits of gray, and his hair was cropped at the neckline behind him. Mishra was wider now than he had been when he had entered Phyrexia, the excess weight spilling over his beltline. There were small wrinkles beside his eyes, and lines stretched across his forehead. The crown of rulership had rested heavily on that head.

But Gix could sense an alertness about the man, even in slumber. His mind was working, dreaming of new devices and new plans. Even in rest there was the sense of motion about him. The demon would have to move quietly.

Originally Gix had thought to merely excise the top of the man's head and scoop the brains out slowly, to make Mishra aware of what was happening to him before he perished. Now, seeing the man think even when asleep, Gix decided to merely slash his throat and take the power stone for himself.

The power stone. It lay within a small pouch hanging from around Mishra's neck. Gix could feel the crystal's presence, just as he could feel Mishra's, or feel the automaton's heart. The ordinary human across the room was a statue, a lump of earth by comparison. Both Mishra and his stone exuded a sense of power that Gix could almost taste.

The demon held up a finger, and a single needle-sharp talon extruded from his fingertip. He leaned forward. One swift cut, he thought, along the base of the jawline, from ear to ear.

There was a noise, a humming so soft that only Gix could hear it. Beneath the folds of the human's vest, within its pouch the gem began to glow in rainbow colors. It flickered to life of its own volition, the colors spilling from the gathered opening of the bag and bathing Mishra in its light.

Gix froze for a moment and not of his own will. The stone was aware of him as he was aware of it. Somehow, it could prevent him from carrying out his plan. He pressed a hand forward, and with every inch progress became more difficult, until at last it was like pressing through forged iron: solid and unrelenting.

Gix shook his head in puzzlement. There was no indication earlier that the stone offered any personal protection to its holder. Yet he could not lean forward and end this one's life.

The demon changed his goal. He would take the gem itself and then kill the human for his insult.

The gem seemed to sense Gix's intent and flashed brightly as the demon reached for its pouch. Gix pulled his hand back and let out a hissing curse. The stone's proximity had burned him like acid, and wisps of smoke rose from his scalded hands.

Across the room, the other human stirred in his sleep. Gix tucked the burned hand under his arm, muttering in a clicking tongue of the pain.

Gix looked at the slumbering Mishra and let out a low, catlike hiss. The stone offered some protection to itself and its user, at least from creatures such as the Phyrexian. It burned him as he approached.

No, not burned, thought the demon. It was attempting to recognize him and to dominate him, to command him, as it had commanded the dragon engines years earlier. The stone, though itself unthinking, recognized his sentience, and it rejected him as dangerous. That rejection was the burning.

Gix perched on the edge of the worktable. The stone protected the man. The stone protected the stone while in the man's possession. Gix thought about it for a few moments, then smiled.

The answer was to change the nature of the stone, or to change the nature of the man.

The stone was half of its original, and perhaps its protective nature stemmed from that cleaving. It was seeking its mate, thought Gix. Perhaps it had somehow determined that Mishra was its opposing half. That would explain the wards that kept a Phyrexian creature such as himself at bay.

Unify the halves, and the entire crystal would be restored. Gix could take it back to his homeland.

And the man? Gix looked at the sleeping Mishra. Perhaps he could be changed as well, altered to something that would serve Gix's masters better as a live slave than as a dead example.

Yes. It would take time, but Gix had little but time. Mishra was separated from his fellow humans by his intelligence, by his position, and by his power. Could Gix recruit him, and his brother for that matter, into his world?

Would that not be a more fitting punishment than just killing them?

Gix let a lipless smile spread across his face. Yes, there were more ways to kill a creature than just by ending its life. Sometimes all you had to do was give it what it wanted.

Gix tilted his head back and barked a short string of clicking syllables. Within his body, small alterations were made, and he called out to the machines in the caverns of Koilos. They answered his call and pulled him back to their warmth and comfort. In an instant he was gone.

In Mishra's workshop, Hajar stirred and inwardly cursed for allowing himself to drift off. The preparations for relocating to Tomakul had drained the life from him as well as from Master Mishra.

Hajar padded over to where Mishra was sleeping, still seated in one of his chairs. His vest had come open, and the pouch containing his talisman, his multicolored stone, lay on his shirt. Hajar smiled and tucked the pouch back within Mishra's shirt, covering the qadir of the Fallaji with a blanket.

The guard blinked and sniffed the air. There was an odor present, a mixture of burning coal and machine oil; probably the result of a wind shifting its bearings and blowing over some sulfur pit or workroom.

Hajar shook his head. He for one would be glad when they were quit of this place and back under the desert sky. He checked the doors to make sure they were locked, then retreated back to his own position and drifted back to sleep, dreaming of that desert.

In their quarters, the Brotherhood of Gix dreamed as well, dreams sent by their masters. There were new orders, said the dreams, and it would require that they serve in Mishra's court longer than had been planned. But the rewards would be great once they succeeded.

All the dreams in Mishra's encampment that night were pleasant.

Chapter 24

The Third Path

Loran moved down the curved hallway of the tower with practiced grace. For the first year of her tenancy among the ivory towers, she had regularly gotten lost, for the corridors and walls were not straight but rather curved to fill their outer shape. Slowly she had stopped thinking in terms of north and south, and instead estimated in terms of distance from the tower's center and the angle from the entrance. Now the towers were no longer an enigma to her.

The archimandrite had noticed her growing assuredness, of course—she seemed to notice everything—and congratulated her on the matter. "Drafna still rises from meetings and heads for the wrong door," she said.

Drafna was confused by many things but proved to be brilliant with artifacts. He could postulate an entire artifact from the merest scraps and was rarely incorrect in his assessment. As he pored over Tocasia's notes he occasionally reminded Loran of the young Urza and Mishra, so intent was his desire for understanding.

On a daily level, Drafna proved to be a trial. He regularly disagreed with whatever the majority seemed to prefer. Were it not for Hurkyl, he would have left the Union long ago.

Hurkyl held the leash, and Loran soon realized many of Drafna's discoveries were in fact made by her and only relayed through the balding scholar. She was a timid woman, almost to the point of being invisible. In the three years Loran had been at Terisia City, she had heard the woman complete a full sentence only three times. In many ways, Hurkyl reminded Loran of herself as a young woman.

City life seemed to agree with Hurkyl. She, her husband, and all their students back in Lat-Nam, apparently, had shaved their heads because the school was mostly underground and shaving of all body hair kept the lice at bay. Since staying at the ivory towers of Terisia City, Hurkyl had allowed her hair to grow out and proved to have thick, luxurious tresses that caught the light like strands of obsidian cord. Drafna had returned to Lat-Nam several times, but Hurkyl always remained. The archimandrite was the center of the Union, but Hurkyl was one of the keystones of that group, as well as Feldon and, despite himself, Drafna.

And, Loran had come to recognize, herself as well.

The halls were full of lesser scribes and scholars as she wended her way to Feldon's private sanctuary. The city was quickly becoming a refuge for those individuals who saw their work threatened elsewhere. Most were from the lands bordering the Fallaji empire, but there were numerous expatriates from Zegon, Tomakul, and other Mishra-held cities. To Loran's surprise, there were some from Korlis and Yotia as well, and some dwarves from the Sardian Mountains who did not trust Urza and the Argivians.

There had also been an infusion of charlatans, tricksters, hoaxers, and outright frauds. Yet for every three such con men (and con women) there was an individual who carried a useful device, an old scroll, or something that added to the growing body of knowledge kept in the tower. Loran would have evicted the lot of them, but the archimandrite had taken them in, and the Union was stronger for it.

Then there was the Brotherhood of Gix. Their order of black-robed monks venerated some sort of machine god, which should have made them invaluable in working with ancient artifacts. But their love of the artifacts approached fetishism, and they were continually judging both the artifacts and those who used them. To those careless enough to ask, they explained at length that they held Urza and Mishra both unworthy of the great devices they had built and believed the two would be punished for their effrontery. The brotherhood left little doubt that it had the same opinion of Drafna and herself. As a group, they seemed to be holding something back as well, listening to everyone but saying little in response save to offer praises to the machine.

Feldon had brought back with him some seers from Sarinth and shamans and witch priests from the Yumok nations of the mountainous northern coast. These last were heavy men with sallow skins, sweating profusely beneath their furs and seal-hide capes. Loran could see why Feldon got along with them, for both he and the Yumok priests were uncomfortable in the warmth of Terisia City.

The archimandrite brought the scholars and librarians of her city. They ranged in quality and temperament from enthusiastic bibliophiles to hidebound book-straighteners. The latter would rather die than let anyone open their cherished tomes and risk the information within escaping. Still with kind words and a steely will the archimandrite pried their holy texts from their hands.

There was one bitter disappointment. The song mages of Sumifa refused the offer of the Union. Instead, they had thrown in with Mishra and were using their skills in his service.

"I don't see why that's a problem," Drafna said upon getting the news. "The Sumifans—all Almaazians, for that matter—are an irritating people at best. Their language is filled with trills and warbles, and it's hard to understand them."

"They have a version of old knowledge," said the archimandrite calmly. "Their songs carry some sort of power, which allows them to calm, and to some degree control, savage beasts."

"Hokum," snorted Drafna.

"Perhaps," responded Loran, "but there might be truth behind their claims, some natural effect we are missing. There might be something we can learn from."

"If there is anything at the core of their teachings," said Drafna, "it is wrapped under so much folderol and mummery that it's generally useless to us. Like that machine god of the Gixians. Now there's a bad lot: creepy fanatics with delusions of mechanical utopia. They're just not all here." The scholar tapped his bald pate repeatedly for emphasis.

Feldon usually started frowning the moment Drafna opened his mouth. Now he slapped the table with an open hand. "Don't dismiss the song mages out of hand. Just because we don't understand a phenomenon doesn't mean it doesn't exist."

Drafna turned frosty. "I find it hard to believe that music truly calms the savage breast, that's all."

"I find it hard to believe in men flying in Thran artifacts," snapped Feldon. "Or in mechanical dragons, for that matter. But we live in a world where they exist, and I, for one, want to be prepared for them."

Now, at Feldon's door, that conversation came back to Loran. Feldon and Drafna had become opposite poles in their discussions. Was that why Feldon had asked her to come to his personal study, as opposed to bringing something before the entire group?

She knocked, and a heavy voice bade her enter.

Feldon's study was spartan—a low table piled with books in an orderly fashion; a few chairs around a low table; and a small slate board along the wall. The room was lit by a single window. The heavy bear of a man was seated before the table, which was clear but for one item.

"Did you hear the news?" Loran asked as she entered.

Feldon glanced up with a haggard look. "About Yotia? Drafna told me about it at breakfast. It's ancient history already."

Loran nodded. Even rumors took their time traversing the length of the Fallaji empire. But some refugees from Zegon had arrived in the city the previous evening with important news: Urza had made his move across the Korlis-Yotian border and was liberating cities from the overmatched Fallaji.

"Ancient history," said Feldon. "By the time the news reaches us, Whatsisname could be in Tomakul."

"Or have been stopped by a counteroffensive," noted Loran. "But you did not ask me up here to discuss the news from the battlefronts. What's wrong?"

"What do you make of this?" the lame man asked, motioning Loran forward. "Yumok fishermen brought it up with their nets; the same group that delivered that coral helmet a year ago."

It was a cross between a bowl mounted on a thick pedestal and a squat, wide-rimmed goblet. The bowl was about a foot across, with a pair of heavy handles mounted on each side. The bowl appeared copperish, but it was unlike any copper Loran had seen before. The device reminded Loran of a sacrificial bowl used by the old religions of Argive.

"It's called a sylex," said Feldon, his eyes not leaving the bowl. "At least that's what it calls itself. And it's from Golgoth, which I've never heard of either."

"You know what it is?" asked Loran.

Feldon tipped the bowl toward Loran. The interior of the bowl, which would normally be smooth, was covered with small incised figures that seemed to spiral before her eyes from the rim into the base.

"Its purpose is written on it," said Feldon.

Loran narrowed her eyes. "These are Thran glyphs," she said at last.

Feldon nodded. "I can't read those characters," he said, then pointed to another curving line of characters. "But these are Fallaji characters, written in an arcane style that I can read. These resemble the song markings of the Sumifans, and these match the incisions on my cane. These"—he pointed to a few other lines—"are unlike anything I've ever seen. Do you know what they mean?"

"A way of reading Thran," said Loran. "A master cipher to a host of old languages."

Feldon smiled. "Indeed. If only the message it bore was not so grim."

Loran raised an eyebrow. "And it is?"

Feldon leaned forward over the bowl. "I don't have all of it, but I think I have most of it. It's called a sylex, and it's from Golgoth, as I said. Whether Golgoth is a land, a king, or its maker, I have no idea. It is supposed to herald the end of the world."

Loran looked at Feldon and said nothing.

Feldon shook his head. "I know what you're thinking. Mummery and claptrap. That's one reason I didn't bring it forward to the others. Drafna thinks I'm going to start hanging strands of burning incense and spinning prayer wheels any day now. But listen to the translation of the archaic Fallaji: 'Wipe the land clear. Bring the ending. Topple the empires to bring a fresh start.' And this: 'Call the end, fill with memories of the land.' Sounds pretty dense."

"Fill with memories," said Loran. "Sounds like something out of a charlatan's patter. Old magics that require the whisper of a dying sun and the smile of a cat. And wasn't there an old Fallaji legend of a city in a bottle, which survived when the rest of the world was to be destroyed?"

Feldon looked up. "You don't believe it then?"

Loran shook her head. "I think this is a wondrous find, which will unlock many other mysteries for us. Perhaps it carries some warning of an ancient time. But no, I don't believe it."

"Touch it," said Feldon, leaning away from the bowl. "Go ahead, touch it."

Loran reached out and grasped the side of the bowl. There was an instant feeling of disquiet, as if the sun had suddenly passed behind a cloud, leaving her in shadow. She looked up, and the entire room seemed to have dimmed. Out of that dimness, she thought she heard a cry, the plaintive lament of a young child, though so faint that it was almost below her ability to discern.

She released the bowl's edge, and the world returned to normal. The sun passed from behind the cloud, and the child's cry was gone entirely.

"You felt it too," said Feldon.

Loran nodded and sat down opposite Feldon, the sylex between them. "There is something here."

"Something we don't understand yet," said Feldon. "Is it a warning? Or a weapon?"

Jeff Grubb

"But what does it mean?" asked Loran. "Fill with memories?"

"Has Hurkyl taught you any of her meditative techniques?" inquired Feldon.

"She's taught the archimandrite, who's passed a bit on to me," said Loran. "But there are a number of meditative techniques used by scholars to focus attention and concentration, ranging from the songsmiths of Sumifa to—"

Feldon interrupted her with a hasty wave of the hand. "But Hurkyl, our silent compatriot, what of her meditations?"

"The archimandrite said 'she sits in the morning and thinks of her home in Lat-Nam, of the azure-colored waves, white with froth, suspended over the shore before crashing down.' I think it calms her to think of home," said Loran. "While it is fresh in her mind, it keeps her from needing to return to her island."

"Anything else?" asked Feldon.

Loran shrugged. "There have been some interesting incidents," she said. "The archimandrite mentions that after her meditating sessions, Hurkyl's quarters become neater. The books are shelved in their proper order, and her styli are back in their case. No one remembers putting them away, of course."

"You believe that?" said the bear of a man gruffly.

"I think we need to research the matter further," returned Loran. "If it were anyone else but Hurkyl, Drafna would be shouting from the parapets that it was all bunk and hokum."

"Yes," agreed Feldon. "But have you tried the techniques? Have you thought about your homeland?"

Loran shrugged again. "I don't really want to think about Argive at the moment or what is happening there."

"Yes, I suppose so," said the bearish scholar. "I'm going to have to learn that technique, I suppose. Sounds like it might be akin to filling something with memories of the land."

Loran did not answer but looked at the bowl. She reached out for a moment but did not touch it again.

Feldon said, "If it is a weapon, is it one the brothers could use?"

Loran shook her head. "I don't think so. There is no mechanism here, no set of weights and cables, no obvious source of its power. All there is is a warning and the bad feeling that surrounds it."

Feldon nodded. "I agree. And yet why do I feel so loath to tell the others about it?"

Loran concurred with the feeling. "Tell the archimandrite at least," she said. "And make a parchment rubbing of the interior. The translations within will prove invaluable to our work. Then put it in a safe place, secure from any would-be thieves. Just in case it is what it says it is."

Feldon nodded again, but his eyes were on the sylex. "It's a little tempting, though, isn't it? Wiping everything clear and starting again?"

Loran rose and paused at the door. "Yes," she said, "but your glaciers would probably melt. And then what would you study?"

Feldon allowed himself a weak smile. "You speak the voice of reason. No matter how bad things are now between Mishra and Whatsisname, it hasn't gotten all that bad yet."

Loran smiled as well and left Feldon to his studies. Outside the room, in the curved hallway, she touched the hand that had held the bowl. It was numb, and feeling was only now starting to return to it. She flexed her fingers and tried to will the nerves to respond.

Loran shook her head. It hadn't gotten all that bad.

Yet.

Chapter 25

Rack

Tawnos was in chains. A set of manacles bound his wrists no more than a foot apart, and a second set similarly constrained his ankles. The chains of the manacles were gathered together at his midsection where another, longer chain secured the entire collection to a large iron ring in the floor. He could not stand up fully, much less move comfortably.

Not that there was much room to move in or places to go if he could. The room was without furniture save for a single stool. A grate above allowed in some diffuse light on an irregular schedule, and another grate in the floor carried away waste. A single iron door with a shutter was set along one wall. A human skull leered in the corner, the remains of a previous occupant. Other than that, nothing. Nothing but him and his chains

A pity, really, thought Tawnos, because the war had been going so well up to that point.

Mishra had spread himself too thin, and the combined kingdoms of Argive and Korlis took advantage of the weakness. Mishra managed to hold the northern passes well enough, but the defenses into Yotia were threadbare at best. Raiding from the combined kingdoms intensified, until finally a group of Korlisian volunteers were trapped in Yotia and massacred.

The Martyrs of Korlis were noteworthy for both their youth and the fact that they were not in the pay of anyone else. Instead they were true patriots of their nation, the sons and daughters of merchant lords. Their slaughter electrified the southern of the two united countries, and demands rang out to the combined king to take action immediately.

It had happened as Tawnos had predicted, before Urza was ready, but later than Tawnos himself had anticipated. The Lord Protector had sufficient manpower to throw his machinery south without seriously depleting the northern passes. With most of Mishra's forces heading west to Sarinth, no one expected a strike against Argive.

There *were* strikes, of course, but they were badly planned and hastily launched and dealt with by the forces at hand. Instead, a full army of Argivians and newly patriotic Korlisians headed south and west, backed by ornithopters, Yotian soldiers, a variety of avengers, including the new sentinel model, triskelions, and a four-part flying creature called a tetravus. The legions spilled over the borders and into occupied Yotia.

The Fallaji garrisons were not enough to hold the borders but sufficient to offer more than token resistance and prevent a quick campaign. The Fallaji began a regular retreat over the next year, withdrawing from one province to strike in another. They burned the territories to which they never intended to return.

By the fall of the first year the areas south of the wreckage of Kroog were freed from Fallaji rulership, if not their raids. This included Jorilin and the other coastal cities. By the end of next year, the Fallaji had been driven from most of Yotia with the exception of the trans-Mardun provinces and the Sword Marches. Seven enemy dragon engines had been destroyed in the process in pitched battles that tested Urza's machines to the utmost.

The land was wrecked by the despoiling Fallaji and the wars of liberation, but it was retaken at last. Tawnos rode to cheers at the head of the army through the streets of recovered towns. To hard eyes as well, from those who had suffered under the Fallaji and wondered what their former queen was doing, safe and secure in Penregon.

They got their answer soon enough. Yotia was incorporated into the combined kingdoms of Korlis and Argive, without so much as asking the newly freed people. The queen would not return, and Yotia would be a vassal state for the unified kingdoms. After more than ten years of war, Yotia had traded one master for another.

Tawnos understood this at the time. He knew it was the only way to convince the Argivian nobles and Korlisian merchant lords to help mend the shattered landscape and feed a population whose fields had been burned by the retreating Fallaji. But the part of him that was Yotian did not like it, and it was clear others felt the same way.

There was a similar reaction to the Lord Protector's next decision. The people assumed that Urza would clear out the rest of the provinces, restoring a complete Yotia. Instead he eschewed retaking the Sword Marches of his father-in-law. The army massed for an assault across the Mardun, making for Tomakul itself.

The Yotians muttered and talked about the Korlis merchants, and how the Korlisians lusted to regain their protected trade routes to beyond Tomakul. Tawnos knew better—Mishra had apparently made Tomakul his base of operations, and Urza was coming for his brother.

The procedure was slow, methodical, and utterly relentless. The advance was held to thirty miles a day, though some of the automatons could travel farther than that. At every night's stop one of Urza's towers was erected, fitted with great mirrors and signal fires to communicate with its neighbors. A permanent garrison of men and machines was stationed, and the remainder pressed on.

As they pressed westward the resistance stiffened, and more manpower was called for. From his headquarters in Penregon, Urza was finally forced to weaken the passes in order to supply the main assault. In addition the Lord Protector hired mercenary units, promising plunder when Tomakul fell. The Korlisians were nervous about the decision to offer Tomakul to the sword, but since most of the mercenaries were theirs, they abided by it.

By this time Tawnos was leading the army westward, though officially in a capacity advisory to General Sharaman. Tawnos knew the strengths and weakness of his machines, and the general trusted Tawnos's judgment sufficiently to translate the Master Scholar's advice into orders. They were within sight of the great golden domes of Tomakul when everything fell apart.

Fallaji cavalry had struck along the length of the supply line throughout the march and on several occasions had taken a tower, forcing part of the army to double back to re-establish their lines of communications. At first the attacks had been sporadic, but now they were almost continual. Indeed Tawnos blamed their defeat in part on the regular nature of those attacks. The Argivians had been immured to the continual raiding, and as a result they didn't realize the nature of the assaults had changed.

Tawnos also blamed the defeat on lack of adequate information. Sarinth's capital had fallen as they pressed west, after years of siege, and no one told the Argivian force. Most of the Sarinthian countryside was still in revolt, but the nation's great walled city had finally fallen and troops previously tied down in siege were now flooding south, bearing down on Tawnos's column.

Urza had taken too long to arrive at Tomakul, and Mishra now had the opportunity to respond in force.

First were the dragon engines. Mishra had lashed together at least a dozen, most of those clanking imitations, plus two of the ones that had leveled Kroog. These moved like panthers and struck without mercy. There was also a new type, one that could fly, and it scattered the ornithopters like sparrows before a hawk.

Then there were the transmogrants: zombielike beings that had once been men but now were shambling engines of destruction. These bunched up against their assailants, and Tawnos's clay statues were slaughtered in droves. The transmogrants had been taught to pull the clay from the statues' forms, like ants cleaning a carcass. The amorphous clay had not the chance to regather itself.

Neither did the Argivian army. From its position farthest forward, it was driven back to post after post: retreating, fighting, then retreating again. Word arrived that new Korlisian mercenaries were coming up the line, bringing with them the mechanical garrisons from the previous towers.

The reinforcements never materialized. Instead the retreating Argivian forces found one of the towers in the hands of Mishra's cavalry, who had flanked the line of march and now bore down on the remains of Sharaman's force with Urza's own automatons.

The field was covered in blood and resounded with the screams of the valiant and the dying. Tawnos held his own for a short while, surrounded by a pair of his clay statues. He formed one island of an archipelago of Argivian defenders, ringed by Fallaji swordsmen and unliving opponents. The sky belonged to flying engines of destruction.

Then there was an explosion and darkness.

He woke in the dark of the pit. He had been bruised badly, particularly around the face, but was otherwise unharmed. He had now been conscious several days, by his own count, and except for an unspeaking guard who slapped a bowl of gruel-thin porridge before him, there had been no visitors.

There was a soft clicking noise as the shutter to the iron door slid open. A flash of dark eyes sparkled on the other side, and it slid back.

Then the door was open, Tawnos winced at the brightness. Several figures stood in the doorway, silhouettes against the light beyond them.

The foremost strode into the cell and removed her gloves. She wore spiked armor.

"Hello, Duck," said Ashnod. "I hope you've enjoyed your quarters. It's not much, but it's better than you deserve."

* * * * *

"It's called an oubliette," she said as two guards brought in furniture. "It's apparently an old Fallaji tradition from back when they took prisoners on a regular basis. A dimly lit cell, perfect for making personal enemies disappear. Tomakul is tunneled with them. We had to clear some of the bones out of this one so we could put you here. The skull was left as a reminder. Its owner starved here, ignored by the guards and abandoned by her captors."

The guards brought in a heavy chair with thick pillows for padding. Ashnod set herself gently down on the pillows. The guards placed a small table before her. The table had clawlike legs that gripped the rough stone floor. Ashnod tried to shake the table, and when it did not move she nodded her approval.

The table was fitted with a single manacle. One of Tawnos's hands, the right one, was freed of his wrist cuff and forced at dagger point through the table-mounted manacle, palm upward. The guards fastened the cuff shut with iron pins, and two of them left. One remained.

"There are those among the Fallaji who want you dead," said Ashnod. "They are, fortunately, outnumbered by the ones who want you to suffer a long time first."

She pulled from her bag a circular device looking like a flat plate, to which an odd set of struts and wires had been attached. She slid the plate forward beneath Tawnos's right hand. The remaining guard placed the dagger's edge against Tawnos's throat as Ashnod attached small clamps to each of his fingertips. The clamps drew blood as they pricked his flesh.

Tawnos waited until the dagger had been withdrawn from his neck, then said, "And which group do you represent?" His lips felt like lumps from the earlier, unknown, beating.

"As always, I represent myself," the red-haired woman said, throwing a knife-edge switch before her.

Tawnos convulsed as a charge of energy passed up his hand and into his body. He nearly fell from his stool, but his hand was firmly manacled to the table, and the table was firmly set on the floor. He twisted and turned as the current ran through his body.

Ashnod tripped open the switch. "It works," she said.

Tawnos gasped, "What . . . is . . . ?"

Ashnod replied, "The Fallaji have a number of traditional tortures: rack, thumbscrew, and garrote. Mishra had worked his own version of the rack, years ago, designed to cause maximum discomfort for minimum effort. This"—she patted the device that had ensnared his hand—"is a smaller version of my own rack. Like it?"

"Love it," gasped Tawnos. "Fits you perfectly. Why don't you just kill me?"

"That's one option," said Ashnod. "One I don't want to be forced into."

"Ashnod," said Tawnos, "when you were our prisoner, we treated you well."

"Here's a hint, Duck," said Ashnod. "By Fallaji standards this *is* being treated well. Most of your compatriots have been killed. Mishra doesn't even trust Yotian slaves anymore. He thinks Urza can read their minds at a distance. Mishra wanted to deliver your head, pickled, to Momma Duck Urza. I talked him out of it; said you had knowledge we could use."

"I won't tell you anything," spat Tawnos.

"I know," said Ashnod calmly. "But it was either this or the pickling jar."

"Why tell me this?" growled Tawnos. "In the hopes I'll tell you something useful?"

"In part," said Ashnod.

"And with your friend listening?" asked Tawnos.

Ashnod shook her head. "Understanding Argivian is considered to be a black mark in the Fallaji armed forces these days. Watch." She turned to the guard and said clearly, "I turned your father into a transmogrant. And your grandfather and your brother too. Because they were insufficient bedmates." The guard said nothing.

Ashnod turned back. "See? If I said the same thing in Fallaji, he'd be after my blood." She turned to the guard and barked out a command in the desert language. The guard started to protest in the same tongue, and Ashnod shouted at him again. The guard hesitated, glowered at Tawnos, then left the cell. The door swung shut behind him. The shutter opened briefly, then closed.

"Now you have to do me a favor," said Ashnod.

"I'm at your disposal," said Tawnos bitterly.

"My back is to the door," she said. "And I figure our guards will be checking regularly on my progress with you. So when the shutter opens, give me the high sign and I'll give you a little dose."

"Why would I do that?" said Tawnos.

"Because if you don't, I'll have to zap you randomly just to keep up appearances," she said, and threw the knife-switch again. Tawnos's body stiffened as the charge roared up his arm. "The secret word is 'traitor,' okay?"

"Easy to remember," said Tawnos. "Just stop doing that."

"Oh come on," said Ashnod with a smile. "This is nothing close to a lethal dose for a man your size and age. Trust me, I know."

"I believe you," said Tawnos. "Those transmogrants, the zombie men. They are yours, aren't they?"

"What do you think?" she said, smiling.

"They're horrible," said Tawnos.

Ashnod's smile flickered for just a moment, and when it returned there was a forced feeling about it. "I thought you, if anyone, would understand."

"They were once living men," hissed Tawnos.

"Emphasis on once," returned Ashnod. "They were criminals, slaves, prisoners; people they were going to kill and leave out for the vultures anyway! I found a use for them!"

"Traitor!" snapped Tawnos quickly.

Ashnod threw the switch, and another bolt of energy blasted through Tawnos's arm and shoulder. It seemed to him that she left the switch closed for slightly longer than she needed to. When Tawnos recovered, she continued.

"The desert has only two resources. The Thran relics are one, and Mishra has gone as far as he can with them. The other is people. They're a resource too."

Tawnos said nothing.

"I'm not afraid to get my hands dirty," said Ashnod.

"Or bloody," added Tawnos angrily.

Her hand hovered over the switch, then pulled back. "We don't have all the wealth of the eastern nations," she said defensively. "We have to make do with what we have."

"You don't take care of what you have," said Tawnos. When Ashnod looked at him, confused, he said, "You've stripped Yotia to the ground."

Ashnod's eyes lowered. "Yes. That. I argued against that, too, but Mishra overruled me there. That ever happen with Urza?"

Tawnos hesitated for a moment, then nodded. "More often than I want to think about. Why was it a bad idea?"

"Didn't I just agree with you?" asked Ashnod.

"Yes," said Tawnos, "but I probably won't like your reason why."

"Because it's a waste of resources," said Ashnod. "Of material and manpower we might have held and used later."

"Thought as much," said Tawnos. "Traitor."

Another flip of the switch, though this one was not as long as previously. Nevertheless, Tawnos was sure that his heart had stammered in its beating in the middle of the jolt.

"But you were overruled," continued Tawnos, when he could breathe again.

"Uh-huh," said Ashnod. "Mishra's been putting distance between the two of us for years now. He wants my transmogrants, my battle armor, and my other creations, but he doesn't want to be seen as depending on me. It's a sign of weakness among the Fallaji, and even after all these years he depends on their support."

"The other chieftains," said Tawnos, guessing whom she meant.

"And others," returned Ashnod. "He has an aide from way back who's like his second shadow. And then there's the Gixians. They would just love to go pawing through my notes."

"Gixians?" inquired Tawnos. "The Brotherhood of Gix? Machine worshipers?"

"Yeah," grunted Ashnod. "Nasty little creatures."

"They're in the Argivian court as well," said Tawnos. "Your spies?"

Ashnod shrugged. "Don't know. They may be playing both sides against the center. I don't trust them."

"Nor I," agreed Tawnos. "Less now that I know they're working with Urza's brother as well. Traitors."

Another throw of the knife-switch, and Tawnos yelped. Finally he said, "I don't know if I can take much more of this."

"Agreed," said Ashnod. "And we've spent long enough for me to claim you'll be a very hard nut to crack. Loyal unto death to Momma Duck Urza and all that."

"So they will kill me, now," spat Tawnos. "Was that what all this was? One last chance to taunt me?"

"One last chance to see if you're as smart as I am," said Ashnod, sharply, "and one more chance to embarrass the others on whom Mishra depends so heavily. If everything goes well, a chance to have you owe me a favor. A girl can never be owed too many favors."

"I don't understand you," said Tawnos.

"You will," said Ashnod, "if you're as smart as I think you are. For now, this discussion is over." She flicked the switch shut again, and the pain radiated through Tawnos's body until finally the darkness swallowed him.

Tawnos did not know how long she kept the charge going, but by the time he recovered the guards were back in the room and he had been freed from the table and its device. His right hand was a tight ball of pain as they refastened his original chains.

"But you didn't ask anything," he gasped. "About the artifacts."

Ashnod knelt beside him and hissed, "I don't *need* to ask anything. We have the remains of your precious artifacts. They will tell me more about Urza and you than a year and a day of torture would."

Then she was gone, and the room was in darkness again.

For a long time he sat in the shadows, slowing his racing heart and his labored breathing. Once the shutter in the door opened, then shut again after an unseen watcher determined Ashnod had not killed him.

Tawnos slowly opened his hand. Clenched tightly in his palm were two of Ashnod's earrings and a spool of golden wire. The gemstones in the earrings glowed with their own internal light.

She wanted him to prove he was as smart as she was, he thought.

Tawnos allowed himself a smile, and crawled over to the skull that had been left in his cell.

* * * * *

Ashnod was summoned to Mishra's court in the palace of the old Pasha of Tomakul. It was a month after her discussion with Tawnos, and three days after she had filed a final report on Tawnos's artifacts. There were definitely design components she could incorporate into her own work.

She did not find Mishra at his workbench. Instead he was seated on the former pasha's throne, patting his fingertips together. Slowly.

Ashnod had been surprised by Mishra's appearance when she first returned from Sarinth. The man had let his waistline grow, and there were jowls beneath the silver-flecked beard. He was decked in his desert robes, billowing things that made him seem all the fatter. He had tucked into his belt the symbol of Sarinth itself, a razor-sharp ankh.

The strain of the war was telling on him, thought Ashnod. He had been afraid of his brother's response for years, and when it finally came, he beat it back. Now he was afraid of the next assault.

Beside the throne and slightly behind it was Hajar, trusty and silent as ever. On the other side was one of the Gixians, a repulsive priest with a hunchback and mismatched eyes.

Ashnod knelt, then rose to hear Mishra's words.

"Tawnos escaped his dungeon cell five nights ago," he said quietly.

Ashnod frowned. "Why was I not informed?" she said hotly. "Has he been found?"

"Not yet," said Mishra.

"And no one told me?" snapped Ashnod. "I might have aided the pursuit."

"Or hindered it," said the Gixian.

Ashnod gave the priest a look that clearly showed she was sizing him up for the transmogrant tank. "What do you mean?"

Mishra answered instead. "An accusation has been made about your involvement in this matter."

"My . . ." said Ashnod, letting her voice trail off in astonishment. "Who makes such wild accusations?"

Mishra said nothing, but the Gixian priest laughed. It was a nervous, clicking chuckle.

"You did meet with the escaped prisoner," said Mishra finally.

"Once!" said Ashnod hotly. "Almost a month ago! On your orders! To ascertain whether he would break under the rack. I quickly determined that he would not and left him there to rot. It was there in my report."

"Of course," said Mishra smoothly, waving aside her comment and the report. "The fact of the matter is, Tawnos made his escape by means of a device similar to your own staff."

"Pardon?" Ashnod wondered if she was acting sufficiently surprised by the news.

"A device that weakened his guard," continued Mishra. "A device that allowed him to immobilize a patrol that had almost snared him. A device similar to that which you used against me once before, at the walls of Zegon."

"That proves nothing," said Ashnod, then took a deep breath. "I was relieved of my own staff when I was captured in Kroog. Tawnos could have examined it then and prepared himself for the eventuality of capture. It is not my fault if your guards did not search him sufficiently."

"And your conversation," said Mishra, ignoring her words. "Very unusual interrogation technique."

"My methods have been suited to your needs before," said Ashnod, but she felt a cold chill run down her back. Had one of the guards been able to understand them?

As if reading her mind Mishra said, "While the guards spoke only Fallaji, to prevent them from communicating with the prisoner, they did have fairly good memories. Their recitation of the words proved interesting. They did not understand any of the words, so the translation was garbled, but they paid special attention whenever you mentioned my name."

The cold chill became a winter blast. Ashnod said, "If you do not trust me, Master, next time send along a guard who speaks the prisoner's language. I am sure there were mistakes in what they heard and reported to you."

"I would be inclined to believe you," said Mishra, "were it not for one last piece of evidence. Priest, if you please?"

The Gixian chuckled and held out his hand. In his palm were the setting to a pair of earrings. The gemstones had been removed.

"Found them in the sewers beneath the cell," said the priest, with a giggle.

"Amazing what people lose," said Ashnod coldly.

"Indeed," said Mishra, looking over Ashnod's shoulder now. "They look similar to a set I've seen you wear. Except those are now missing. And these are missing the power stones that would have been at their centers."

Ashnod opened her mouth and shut it. Mishra's mind had been made up before Ashnod arrived at the door, and he'd paid not the slightest heed to anything she had said. Even were she innocent of the accusations, the circumstances damned her.

And she was not innocent.

"Milord," she said, switching tactics, "were you aware there are members of the Brotherhood of Gix in Urza's court?"

Mishra's face was calm, but there was the barest twitch of his lips at the mention of his brother's name. Instead he said, "You know that from your interrogation of my brother's student?"

"Yes," said Ashnod.

"Was that in your original report of the interrogation?" asked Mishra, his eyes narrowing.

Ashnod realized her mistake. While claiming her honesty and innocence, she had revealed there were things she had not reported. She kept her face emotionless and said, "I did not want to make *wild* accusations"—she nodded at the priest—"without proof."

"And do you have proof?" said Mishra.

"I was waiting for confirmation from other sources," said Ashnod, "but thought you had best know of it now."

"I know of it," said Mishra, "because the good priest here has informed me of the situation. Which you had not. You've made their case for them."

Ashnod grasped at straws. "Surely I am not to be singled out because a prisoner escapes."

"You are not," said Mishra shortly.

"There are the guards," said Ashnod.

"They are already dead," said Mishra, "at my command."

Ashnod paused for a moment. "I see. And my fate?"

She looked at Mishra and thought she saw his face soften, but only for an instant. "You are banished."

"Most Revered One, I—" started Ashnod.

"Banished," said Mishra, slightly louder. The priest giggled and rubbed his hands together. Yes, Ashnod thought bitterly, the Gixians had their paws in this from start to finish.

"Urza would not treat his apprentice so shabbily," said Ashnod hotly.

As soon as the words left her lips she knew they were a mistake. Mishra's face burst into an emotional storm. "*What* my brother *would* or *would not* do is no concern of yours!" he thundered. Ashnod felt the force of the words like hammer blows.

Mishra leaned back in his chair. The momentary storm had abated, but the fire was still in his eyes. "You are banished from this court and from the Fallaji empire. Leave now. If you are found anywhere within my lands after sunup, you will be put to death. Slowly. Am I clear?"

Ashnod looked into Mishra's face, then nodded. "As glass," she said. She bowed low and retreated from the throne room.

She stormed through the halls, making for her quarters. No, she realized, the rest of the brotherhood was already there, going through her notes and books, stripping her lab of her personal discoveries, looting her possessions. They would like nothing better than to delay her, then to claim Mishra's order as a chance to get rid of her once and for all.

Instead she went to the stables and took her favorite horse, the black charger that had carried her from the battlefield in Korlis. She took only the clothes on her back and the knowledge in her mind.

That would have to be enough.

She rode out of the pasha's royal complex and reined the horse in. The street led east and west. East to Argive, a road most likely watched, or west to the unknown.

She pulled the horse's reins and began the long trek to the west, to Terisia City and the lands outside either of the brothers' control.

The guard at the gate noted her decision and informed the priest of Gix who had asked him to keep an eye out. The priest reported to his superior, who whispered it to Mishra. Mishra merely nodded and began to plan the next campaign of his glorious empire.

Chapter 26

Clockworks

Tawnos almost made it to the border before the *mak fawa* caught up with him.

He had almost expected it. He had been extremely lucky so far, and he knew that luck would run out sometime.

After his escape he had cut north and east across the desert, making for the passes of Argive instead of following the route of ruined towers back to Yotia. That had shaken the immediate pursuers. He spent some time among the Sarinthian refugees on the shores of the Mardun but traveled mostly alone and at night. He rode by the soft light of the Mist Moon when he could and by the erratic sputtering of the Glimmer Moon if its larger sibling was not in the sky. Neither moon had been aloft the previous evening, and, close to his goal, Tawnos decided to risk traveling by day.

He had almost lost his horse and his life to one of Mishra's inventions earlier in the day. The creation was some sort of reactive device, similar to Urza's sentinels. In this case, the device lay beneath the sands, waiting for a trespasser.

As Tawnos rode through the device's domain, the sand around him began to churn, like water coming to a boil. Tawnos tried to reign in the beast, but the horse bolted, taking the scholar with it.

He was lucky again. Had he stayed Tawnos would have been trapped. Metallic coils and saw-toothed arms erupted from the sands, flailing blindly in all directions. A rasping shriek rent the sky from the ground-shattering creature. Far off in the distance behind Tawnos came an answering scream.

Tawnos clung to the horse's mane, looking behind him as they fled.

The coils and arms twitched briefly, then slowly pulled themselves back into their sandy pit, covering themselves as they retracted. In another moment the ground was as it had been before.

Tawnos felt a cold trickle of sweat run down his back. If the device had merely attacked, he would only have had to avoid it or outrun it. But it had signaled that it had been tripped, and something farther back had answered the scream.

Tawnos dug his heels into the horse's flanks and rode hard for the passes, hoping not to meet any other hidden traps *en route*.

He looked back once to see a cloud of dust on the horizon. Pursuit. Tawnos pushed the horse harder, but when he looked back again there was already a dark dot at the base of the cloud, ripping up the desert as it passed.

A dragon engine. The land was rising now, and small, stringy shrubs dotted the rock outcroppings. Tawnos thought about hiding, but instead he chose to make for the pass. Most of the dragon engines were large, clumsy beasts and would have trouble negotiating the rocks easily.

He looked back a third time and could make out the details of the dragon engine's form. It was one of the recent ones, and though it was a smoother, sleeker creation than the earlier Mishra-manufactured models, it still did not compare to the monstrosities that had leveled Kroog. Even at a great distance, Tawnos could see the beast's head lurch back and forth like that of a spastic insect.

Tawnos smiled, but the smile died as great wings sprouted from the creature's back. They unfurled in the afternoon sun and began to beat as the engine charged forward. The cloud of dust disappeared as the mechanical creature sailed aloft.

Tawnos cursed and jabbed the flanks of his mount hard, spurring it to a full gallop.

He would not make it, he thought. Flying dragon engines had destroyed most of his air support at Tomakul. There was nothing in the Argivian arsenal that could stand up to them.

For a moment Tawnos considered abandoning his horse and hiding, but instead he pressed on. If he could reach the narrow passage at the beginning of the pass, he might be able to find an Argivian outpost before the dragon found him.

He almost made it.

Tawnos did not see it, but he could feel the pressure of the air as the beast dived above him. There was a roaring, and heat scorched his back.

The horse screamed and stumbled, jolting him from his saddle. Tawnos dived forward, arms swung before his face to protect himself. He managed to twist and land on a shoulder, but the force of the blow rolled him to one side of the rocky outcropping.

The Chief Scholar gagged on the smoke rising from his burning horse. It was still alive and thrashed in agony as its flesh burned away.

Tawnos felt pity for the horse, but the objective part of his mind also noted that the dragon engine had breathed some sort of flaming jelly, a substance that was not extinguished even as the horse convulsed in the dirt. Something new to worry about, he thought.

Tawnos looked up and saw that the dragon engine was above him, pulling up for another swooping dive. There was little cover that the flaming liquid could not breach, and the scholar had no doubt that the engine had sensed his movement and was coming back to finish the job.

That was when the metal-winged birds appeared. They were like a cloud of insects that rose from the east and swarmed the great engine. At first Tawnos thought they were real birds that had somehow been driven into battle. Now he saw they were small constructs, each no larger than a man. They swooped and dived around the larger engine as sparrows harrow a hawk.

The dragon engine craned its neck back and struck against one of the smaller winged machines. The avian nimbly darted away, warned of the assault by the change in air pressure caused by the dragon's movements.

Though wracked with pain, Tawnos smiled. He knew what the bird artifacts were and who had built them. And from whom the builder had gotten the original idea.

The bird machines dived and darted around the dragon engine. The engine managed to remain aloft, but the avians were faster than its snapping jaws. It breathed its ignited fluid, but that only brought down a single opponent. The remainder flocked around it, and, beating its wings frantically, the dragon engine lost altitude.

The bird machines had razor-sharp beaks and tore the outer housing of the dragon engine away. There were several holes already in the *mak fawa's* back, bored in concentrated attacks from the smaller machines.

Tawnos watched as a small bird machine flew into one such tear in the engine's fuselage, near the joint where the dragon engine's wing strut met the body. There was a skittering, crunching noise, and then a small explosion. The wing folded in on itself, trying to retract back into the body. The dragon shrieked in almost living pain and pitched to the left.

It plummeted to the ground, its one good wing still trying to scoop the air beneath it.

Tawnos crouched as the dragon engine struck the ground two hundred yards west of him. Even at this distance he could feel the heat of the explosion as its liquefied tanks of fire ruptured and the entire creature went up in an incandescent ball of flame. Tawnos shielded his eyes from the flame, and when he could look again, nothing remained but a burned-out shell of metal ribs. If the engine had been operated by crewmen, they were dead.

The metal birds swooped and regathered in a flock, a chaotic combining and recombining of individuals in different flight patterns. Then they organized themselves into a V-shaped formation and winged eastward toward the pass.

Tawnos limped along behind them, making for Argivian territories.

* * * * *

"Clockwork avians," said Urza, setting down his favorite chalice. "And yes, they were based on your toy for young Harbin."

"I had assumed as much," replied Tawnos, settling down in one of the overstuffed chairs that now dominated Urza's reception hall. His wounded arm was in a sling, but the Master Scholar was otherwise unharmed.

Urza lowered himself into the opposite chair. The Lord High Artificer's hair was pure white now, and the lines around his face were deeper. Tawnos was sure Urza had lost weight since he last saw him, and he knew the older man now used spectacles with which to read. Despite himself, Tawnos reached up and ran his fingers through his own hair. It was starting to thin in the back.

"After you were . . . captured," said Urza, "I sat down with Harbin and went over all your old toys. He knew in what order you had built them and kept them in good working condition. There were some bits of brilliance among them, you know."

"Mostly ideas and fancies that did not seem to have immediate use," said Tawnos.

"Indeed," said Urza, with a wry smile. "Well, the avians had an immediate use. Those flying dragon engines were bad enough, and when they started breathing this liquid fire . . ." He held up his hands. "We were hard-pressed by your absence. We thought you dead."

"I wasn't," said Tawnos. "Not quite." He flexed his right hand.

"I'm glad you weren't," said Urza, and Tawnos saw the older man meant it. He could imagine Urza at the drawing table, turning over and over in his hands one of Harbin's toys that his son had outgrown, shoving aside the memories of their work together in order to unlock the design secrets of Tawnos's creations.

The moment passed, and Urza cleared his throat. "The avians were a gods-send. They were simple, cheap to produce, and easy to target against Mishra's larger machines. One of the enemies of this war is distance. By the time any weapon moves from the front to somewhere it can actually do damage, a counterweapon has been created and deployed. The clockwork avians have given us a chance against the flying dragon engines, but by the time we had regrouped to make another assault, Mishra had a new guardian on his borders."

"The ground-breakers," said Tawnos. "I met one the same day I was attacked by the dragon engine."

"Nasty," agreed Urza. "They slow the army down, which gives my brother still more time to prepare a counterattack."

"What was the liquid fire?" asked Tawnos. "The substance the dragon engine breathed."

"Another new development," said Urza, "apparently out of Sarinth. There are deposits of oil and thicker, more viscous fluids that bubble out of the ground there. My brother has found a way to break down that liquid to its component parts, and one of those parts is highly flammable, like goblin powder. It almost destroyed the army before we got the avians in the air." He paused for a moment. "We still hold Yotia."

"And the passes in Argive and Korlis," said Tawnos.

"But we haven't been able to press forward since then," concluded Urza. "We're still waiting for him to make his move. To attack somewhere so we can react. Neither side seems to have the power to make a major push nor the time to adequately secure the borders. And in the meantime, we're draining our resources at a faster rate."

"I noted more foundries on the way back to the capital," said Tawnos.

"More foundries, factories, and mines," returned Urza. "We have felled most of the forests from Korlis and are buying metal from the Sardian dwarves. The merchants are starting to complain about the amount of gold heading north, and they are agitating for a campaign against the dwarves themselves. They want us to fold the dwarven territories into ours and their resources with them."

"And your opinion?" asked Tawnos, thinking he should have asked, "And your decision?" instead.

"I don't want to attack without good reason," said the older man, "but I'd prefer to keep the dwarves at an arm's length. You can't trust anyone just because they claim to distrust the Fallaji empire and want to be your friends. The Gixians did that."

Tawnos nodded. One of the first results of his return had been the rounding up and imprisonment of the priests of Gix. The fact that they were advisors in Mishra's court made many people in Argive very nervous and others very embarrassed.

"The priests of Gix had wheedled their way into the school while you were gone; did you know that?" said Urza. "And right under Richlau's nose, too. He was redder than a setting sun when it all came out."

"Nice to know there was some good from all this," said Tawnos.

A silence fell between the two men. Urza frowned slightly, and ground his palms together. "I've been working on your clay statues as well," he said at last. "I have an idea about using that primal clay material without the framework. It would be more malleable that way."

Tawnos looked at his mentor. "Urza, what's troubling you?" He knew the older man well enough to recognize when Urza was talking around a subject.

The Lord Protector raised a hand to argue, then shook his head and was silent for a time. "Harbin," he said at last. "He wants to be an ornithopter pilot."

Tawnos nodded slightly. "We've talked. He rode out to meet me."

"Like a flash of lightning, as soon as word reached Penregon of your return," said Urza. "When we first heard about the Battle of Tomakul, and feared you dead, he wanted to run out and join an army unit. To avenge you, you know."

"I know," said Tawnos somberly.

"His mother was shattered when she thought you dead," said Urza, shaking his head, and looked off into the middle distance. "When I came back from a campaign, Harbin never rode out to meet me."

Tawnos shrugged. "I know he respects you."

"Respects, yes," Urza said irritably. "He's always so polite and respectful. His mother has taught him well, there. But we don't really talk. He knew all about the toys you made for him, but he has no interest in artifice beyond how it can be used. He's bright, but that basic sense of curiosity is missing. And he thinks the world of you."

"He respects you," repeated Tawnos. "He just grew up around me."

"Yes," Urza let his voice trail off, as if his thoughts took him some-

where else. Then he said, "So he told you he wants to fly an ornithopter?"

"About the second set of words out of his mouth," said Tawnos,
"after he made sure I was still alive."

"And you think?" Urza raised his brows.

Tawnos sighed. "He's fourteen. That's a good age to start training.
He's quick, and he's bright, as you said yourself. He'd make a good
pilot."

"His mother will have me slain if I do," said Urza. "She doesn't
want her son exposed to the war. She wants him safe and secure. He
should go into government, she says. She's already arranged a marriage for him when he's of age, you know?"

"He's told me," said Tawnos.

"She mentioned it in one of her correspondences," said Urza, nodding at a pile of unanswered mail. "Nice family. Argivian nobility."
He ground his palms together. "But the problem is, everyone is
needed in the war. Everyone. My own factories are operating under
skeleton staffs as more men and women are needed for duty. I've tried
using goblin slaves in the workshops, but they create as many problems as they solve. How can I demand everyone suffer for this accursed war, then protect the boy? But if I don't, his mother will be
heartbroken. I don't really want to do that either."

Tawnos looked at the older man. Urza could reason out the smallest detail of a device, but real life always confounded him.

"I think you should let the boy take the training," said Tawnos at
last, phrasing his thoughts carefully.

"Well, he's made his case to you," said Urza.

"And made it well," said the former apprentice. "He's smart and
has good reactions. If he's expected to eventually lead, he'd best start
now."

"But his mother—" began Urza.

"Will have to accept it," finished Tawnos. "I'll speak with her and
remind her that I came back in one piece."

Urza shook his head. "If he's lost in battle—"

"I didn't say you should send him into battle," said Tawnos. Urza
raised an eyebrow, and Tawnos continued, "Just let him train to
become a pilot. Then make sure that his assignments are in more
peaceful parts of the kingdom. Don't send him to Yotia if an assault is
brewing, but have him run messages to Korlis. Scouting missions.
Aerial surveys. There are more than enough jobs for an ornithopter
pilot that do not involve direct contact with the enemy."

Urza looked at his hands. "He won't like it."

"Then he'll complain about it," said Tawnos, "and if he comes to you, you can point out how bad it would look if the Lord High Artificer and Protector of the Realm used privilege to put his own son in a combat unit over other deserving young men."

Urza rubbed his chin. "He'd hate that."

"Yes he would," said Tawnos. "You see, I have no desire to see Harbin endangered. But I think shielding him from everything will not help him either."

Urza chuckled and hoisted his heavy chalice. "It is good to have you back, Tawnos. I have been lessened in your absence."

"And I in yours, Urza," said Tawnos, raising his own goblet. But as he spoke he heard swift footfalls in the hallway outside. Both men turned toward the door as the messenger arrived, grasping the door frame to bring herself to a halt.

"Chief Scholar," said the messenger. "Lord High Artificer." She gulped for air. "A message has come from the spies. Mishra's army is on the move."

Both men looked at each other. Then Urza said, "Where? Yotia? The Passes?"

The messenger shook her head and inhaled deeply. "Terisia City. He's headed west. For Terisia City."

Chapter 27

Sylex

The ivory towers were burning.

The invaders had first swarmed from the desert more than a year ago and almost overpowered the defenders in the first wave before the gates were closed and the great metal bolts of the portcullises secured. There were thousands of them: grim-faced desert warriors and mindless machines, spilling from the east like hungry insects. They looted the surrounding land, and what they could not carry they burned. They were at the gates of Terisia City within days.

They failed to take the city. The gates were shut in their face, and Mishra's army was turned back. The next spring they returned with a contingent of siege equipment, battering rams, and dragon engines.

Then began the siege, a slow and torturous process that wracked the city and its people. The towers proved their worth, for the enemy could not get close to the walls without suffering withering fire from the spires. Each tower was in turn protected by the city walls behind it and by the adjacent towers. The entire city was wrapped in a cocoon of stone and protected by a bristling array of ballistas, archers, and grapeshot catapults.

A flying dragon engine made an attempt to burn the city to the ground, but as it flew overhead it disintegrated from the firepower and shot brought to bear against it. There was no second attempt by Mishra's forces to fly over Terisia City.

Through it all there had been no clue as to the reason for the attack. The city had attempted to parley with the invaders, but any attempt to reason with them was met with arrowshot and swords.

The intervening winter bought the city time, and the leaders used that time to fill the city granaries, remove its innocents, and strengthen its defenses. The Union used the interval to press forward with its studies.

It had been enough, for the siege stretched into months without a sign of either side breaking. The scholars in their ivory towers had kept one of the two most powerful armies on the continent at bay while they continued their own work, as they attempted to discover all the secrets of the third path, the path that was neither Mishra nor Urza.

That path was charted by Hurkyl's meditative techniques, as Feldon had predicted. The key lay in concentrating on the memories of one's homeland and pulling forth the unknown energies from those memories and that land. Hurkyl discovered the energy, but the archimandrite named it, calling it mana. Loran thought at the time the name was misleading, smacking as it did of old Fallaji tales of wizards and not of science. But despite the name, the archimandrite had succeeding in researching and refining this mana, had distilled it down to its base elements. And she turned those base elements into a weapon against the desert warriors.

But now Hurkyl was dead, the archimandrite was missing, and the city of the towers had been betrayed and occupied by the Fallaji. The ivory towers were isolated, surrounded within and without, and one by one they began to fall under Mishra's concentrated assault.

The Archimandrite's Tower, one of the few that survived intact, was in disarray. In the center of the Archimandrite's Hall, Drafna bellowed at the Sumifan guards, shouting final orders for a sortie. His balding pate was barely visible over the shoulders of the gathered guards, but Loran knew the scholar's shout anywhere.

Drafna stood up on a chair to be better heard, and Loran saw the wildness in his eyes, the manic intensity that seemed to grip the scholar like a fever since Hurkyl had perished. The passage of time had not weakened that fire. He had been there when his wife had died at the gates of the city, when the Gixians had betrayed them.

They had all seen the dangers without but had ignored the rot within. The other scholars had paid scant heed to the machine-worshiping priests as they moved among them, saying little but listening a great deal. The Gixians had learned much in Terisia City, and the scholars often treated them as a harmless, if backward people. When the priests of the brotherhood felt they finally knew enough, they betrayed the scholars and opened the city gates to the enemy.

Hurkyl, ever attentive, figured out what was happening and convinced Drafna to rally those guardsmen who remained loyal. Drafna's forces tried to press back the Fallaji assault and close the gates before the enemy could enter the city proper. But Mishra's troops were ready for the assault and had a trio of dragon engines ready to capitalize on the treachery.

Drafna's forces were scattered at the gates, and the dragon engines began to roll forward. That was when Hurkyl revealed to the enemy the greater power the Union had gained through her studies.

Loran had watched from the closest of the towers during the assault, trying to bring the catapults to bear against the advancing dragon engines without harming the loyal garrisons. Hurkyl stood at the city gate, and for a brief moment she was alone before the three dragon engines. She looked like a frail doll, dressed in azure, her thick black hair flying like a pennant behind her. She closed her eyes and silently raised her arms, and around her the world began to change.

A glow enveloped her, a sapphire hue as blue as the seas around the island of Lat-Nam. It radiated outward, casting a new set of shadows against the ground. The human troops wavered under the light, and the dragon engines . . .

. . . disappeared. They were not destroyed, nor did they simply fail or retreat. Instead they slowly faded from view. The surroundings became clearer and clearer until the engines seemed to be no more than colored fog.

Then they were gone, gone through the actions of one woman.

Hurkyl staggered from the force of her mystic work, and Mishra's human forces took advantage of her weakness to press forward. Her sapphire-blue glow was dimmed, then extinguished entirely beneath a wave of spearmen. Hurkyl had defeated the artifacts but not the warriors who accompanied them.

Loran saw Drafna trying to lead a charge to where his wife had disappeared beneath the spearmen, trying to hack his way through the enemy to reach her, but it was too late. The bald-headed scholar was driven back to another tower, and the city itself fell to Mishra's forces.

The city was sacked and burned, its surviving populace butchered, and its glass roofs smashed so that not a single pane remained whole. The scholars in the towers collapsed their tunnels back into the city itself, sealed their windows against the smoke and the cries of the martyred, and prepared for the worst. First one, then a second, then a third of the ivory towers fell to the invaders, who moved in a circle around the city itself like an apocalyptic clock.

There would be no salvation from the Fallaji, no last-minute rescue. Loran had received correspondence from a friend still in Argive, months out of date but speaking of a rebellion among the dwarves of the Sardia Mountains. Urza would have his own hands full, Loran realized, and there was no one else to oppose Mishra in the west.

Nature brought a brief respite. A sandstorm blew up out of the desert to the east, carrying a heavy, thick load of dust that reduced visibility and halted Mishra's army entirely. Many of the scholars used the storm as cover to escape from the city itself, taking with them what they had learned about the new teachings. Some said the archimandrite had fled, though others said she had been captured by Mishra, and still others said the sandstorm was her doing, as the banishing of the dragon engines had been Hurkyl's.

Yet the storm would not last forever, and with its passing the ivory towers would again begin to fall, one after another. Those scholars who had survived were preparing to abandon the city entirely now. The land beneath the towers was honeycombed with tunnels, and enough survived to allow a safe escape to the hinterlands.

Drafna bellowed another set of orders at the Sumifan guards and servants, who moved with the calm, relaxed demeanor with which Sumifans did all things. Loran looked around but did not see Feldon. She had been sure he would make it to this tower, if he could.

She found him in his study, staring at the Golgothian Sylex. He looked up briefly from the copperish bowl and sighed as she entered. "Fill it full of memories, and start over again," he said. "Scrape it all clean, like a glacier."

"If what it says is true," said Loran. "However, I think it would be as dangerous to the user as to its target."

Feldon grunted and rose. "I agree. Drafna ordered me to fetch every bit of artifice in the tower. He intends to lead a sortie with the surviving guards, to fight his way all the way back to Lat-Nam if he has to. He's in a fey mood, that one. I think he'd be more happy if he died than if he made it out. Anyway I sent everything else down but this. . . ." His voice died as he stroked the side of the sylex.

"Do you think it will work?" asked Loran. "That it will end everything, as it claims?"

Feldon looked at her. "Do you want to find out?" he asked.

Loran looked at the bowl for a long moment, her thoughts racing.

Then she shook her head. "There's too much we don't know about this."

Feldon nodded. "Agreed. But if we do not use something like this, what should we do with it?"

"We should destroy it," said Loran.

"I don't know if we can," said Feldon. "It's been beneath the sea for who knows how long, and it has resisted every attempt to take a sliver of metal from its side. Perhaps Hurkyl could have done something to it with her mana. . . ." Again he let his voice die. He looked at the bowl for a long time. "I don't want to give it to Drafna," he said.

"Are you afraid he'd lose it?" asked Loran.

"I'm afraid he'll use it," corrected Feldon. "Since Hurkyl died, he's been, well, strange. I don't think he really cares if the rest of the world survives or not."

"His world died with his wife," Loran said, and Feldon nodded in agreement. "So take it with you yourself. We have to leave soon."

"With my game leg I won't get far," said Feldon. He tapped his cane against his twisted limb for effect. "I'm going to try to get out, but I think I'd better be traveling light."

There was a pause, and Loran said, "You want me to take it. That's where this is going."

Feldon gave a bearlike shrug. "You're leaving as well, either by the tunnels or with Drafna's charge."

"By the tunnels," said Loran. "And you're coming with me."

"Too old, too lame," he said. "You'd make better time without me. And there's better chance of the knowledge surviving if we split up. There's a small town at the foot of the Ronom Glacier, called Ketha. I'll meet you there within the year if I survive. But, yes, you should take it."

Loran pursed her lips. "Why me?"

"Have you been able to use the meditative techniques?" asked Feldon. "Have you been able to pull the mana from the land?"

Loran held up her hands. "I don't believe that this is magic of any type. It's merely science that we have yet to understand."

Feldon leaned against his chair. "The answer would then be, no you have not."

Loran looked at Feldon, then at the bowl. He was right. She had not been able to master the techniques, either because her own memories of home were too faded or her home was too remote. Or the land was no longer as she remembered it. She considered that option as well and wondered if that was part of the "science" of this new and untried field. At last she shook her head.

"That's why you should take it," said Feldon. "I've had small success myself, though I think of the mountains and ice when I do it. Everyone seems to be different and can manifest slightly different effects. Yet you have not, and that is why you should take it."

"Because if something bad happens, I will not be able to use it in a moment of weakness," said Loran flatly.

Feldon looked at the woman and let out a deep, heavy sigh.

Loran took the bowl. The feeling of shadow descended upon her as she grasped it, and she almost let it go. Instead she hefted it, looked at Feldon, and said, "Do you have a bag for this?"

Feldon produced a battered backpack, one of his own from his glacier-exploring days, and Loran slid the bowl into it. It was heavy, but its weight was minor compared to the aura of dread that surrounded it.

Loran and Feldon made their good-byes, and she hugged him. When they parted there were tears in her eyes. "Come with me," she urged.

"We'll scatter like geese," said Feldon. "They can shoot only so many of us."

"Small comfort if you're one of the geese that's shot," said Loran. "Look after yourself."

"You as well," said Feldon. Then she was gone.

Feldon packed the last of his own belongings in a second backpack, pausing as he heard Drafna bellowing orders, readying the surviving troops for their assault. By now Loran would be in the tunnels, hopefully still free of Mishra's forces and the hated Gixians.

Feldon hoisted his pack and shook it, trying to move the heavier items to the bottom. Below he heard the great doors of the tower swing open and the cries of the men and women who were going to fight their way past Mishra's army. At least, he thought wryly, that's what they hoped.

Feldon counted to a hundred just to assure himself they would be gone, then counted to a hundred a second time. Then, gripping his walking cane securely in one hand, he began to hobble his way down to the tunnels. As he limped along, he mumbled prayers: for himself, for the rest of the surviving scholars, for Drafna, for the archimandrite, and for Loran. Particularly for Loran.

* * * * *

A month later, Loran lay dying, her right side smashed and twisted by the rockfall. A few feet away from her, the sylex had spilled out of its backpack and lay glimmering among the rubble.

She had made it to the foothills of the Colekgan Mountains before disaster struck. The surviving populace had flowed through Mishra's lines like water through a steel sieve, spilling in all directions, seeking escape to every cardinal point save east. Loran had joined a group of Yumok nationals who wanted no more than to quit these supposedly civilized lands and return to their upland homes.

They were moving through the first passes when the avalanche hit. It struck without warning. One moment a caravan of refugees wound its way among the cliffs, the next there was thunder from a clear blue sky and a rain of stone and soil as the path disappeared. Loran heard screams and shouts around her, but they were soon lost in a torrent of rock.

Not after all this, she remembered thinking. She made a silent, impassioned plea to gods long ignored. She remembered thinking as well this was no accident.

She had been right. Now that the dust had settled, figures moved among the debris.

At first she thought they were other refugees who had survived the rockslide and were searching for survivors. She tried to raise an arm to call them and realized she could not move her right arm. Her entire side was a thick smear of blood along her travel cape, and it hurt to move her head to look at it.

Suddenly she realized the figures were not Yumoks. They were dressed entirely in spiked armor with heavy, flowing capes. They moved among the debris, poking at bodies nonchalantly with their swords.

They were looters. They had set the avalanche, she realized. They had brought the mountain down on the caravan to scavenge the bodies.

She must had shuddered or spasmed in pain at the thought, for a voice over her right shoulder called, "We've got a survivor!" The voice was muffled behind steel but fairly close.

"Good," responded another voice, this one female and unmuffled. "I was afraid that you did your job too effectively, Captain."

Loran tried to turn herself about to see who was talking, but she could only twitch. Heavy, gauntleted hands lay on her shoulder, and she felt pain radiate from her wounds. A face hove into view, hidden behind a thick metal visor. It looked like one of Urza's automatons, save for the fact that there were human eyes behind the eyeholes. They were not particularly warm or comforting, but they were human.

"Alive or dead?" asked the female voice.

"Alive, but not by much," said the man behind the visor. His breathing was as sharp as her own, and Loran realized what was in those eyes. Pain. There was pain in the soldier's eyes.

"We don't need by much," said the woman. The armored figure stepped aside for a moment, and Loran saw the woman. She was dressed in similar, spiked armor, but lacked a helmet. Loran could see thick red curls spilling onto her shoulder plates. "We just need a little information," the woman continued coldly, "and then she can die like the others." There was no pain in this red-haired woman's eyes. Only power.

"Milady, look at this," said the soldier, coming back into view. He was carrying the bowl-shaped sylex.

Loran must have tried to move, twisted in place, tried to say something. All she knew was that a moment later she was in intense pain, pain that seared through her like a blade. When her senses cleared again, she saw the red-haired leader turning the sylex over in her hands.

Ashnod, she realized, and wondered if her lips formed the words as she said them. But word was that Ashnod had been cast out from Mishra's camp. What was she doing here, with her own soldiers, then?

"Interesting," said Ashnod, running her slender fingers along the inside of the bowl, tracing the script within as it spiraled to the base. "Most interesting. And I think our little friend knows about it. You're no Yumok, nor a Fallaji. Some scholar from the east, perhaps?"

Loran said nothing and wondered if she would be able to die before anything else horrible happened to her. The stories of Ashnod's cruelty were legendary.

The red-haired woman seemed to read her mind, for she said, "We're going to have to nurse this one back to health, Captain. And then she has *much* that she's going to tell us. I'm *sure* of that."

Loran willed herself to die, but her only reward was Ashnod's laughter.

Chapter 28

Argoth

Gwenna watched her invader from her perch on the interwoven upper branches of the trees. She spotted this one first, and therefore it was her claim, her invader. The others were going back to the hamlet to send messages farther south to Citanul and Titania's Court, to ask for judgment on this development. Until then it was her duty to watch him and judge the invader.

She had never seen an invader before, though there were enough stories about invaders over the years for her to know they came in all shapes and sizes. They were similar in that they were not from Argoth, usually driven to shore by the storms that protected the island. All invaders were similar because they had no contact with the land at all and did not understand it.

This invader was mannish, like the druids of Citanul, Argoth's only true city. The invader was taller than these druids and had sandy blond hair gathered in a horse's tail behind its head. It was dressed in blue pants and white shirt, with a blue jacket that now hung from the side of its craft. The invader said something in a language Gwenna did not know and kicked the machine. Gwenna assumed it was a mannish curse, invoking mannish gods who never listened anyway.

Gwenna herself was elvish, as were most of the natives of Argoth. There were pixies, treefolk, and all manner of other forest dwellers on Argoth, but the elves were the smartest and most refined of all the races—at least in Gwenna's opinion. There were only a few of the mannish breed, and they tended to keep to their holy orders and stone retreats. Gwenna wondered why, since there were so many elves in the world, most of the invaders from the old tales were mannish in nature.

337

Invaders almost always came by sea, their boats smashed on the surrounding reefs or pulled into small maelstroms around the island's coast. They were usually waterlogged, battered, and weak by the time they arrived, and as such put up little or no fight when it was time to kill them. This one, however, came from the air and seemed to be in much better shape for it.

The invader's craft looked like a wounded bird curled up on the white sand of the beach. If Gwenna had not seen it land, she would not have thought it could fly at all. Indeed it was hardly much of a flier. More of plummeter, for it dived like a cormorant for the beach, pulling up only at the last moment. Even then, it had smashed into the sands with a bone-thumping crunch. One wing was twisted at an odd angle now as a result of that crash.

Titania's Law was fair but firm on the matter of invaders. They should be watched, and word sent back to Citanul, to Titania's Court. If it damaged the island (as most invaders did, sooner or later), it would have to be destroyed.

Gwenna could not imagine why this particular invader needed to be destroyed, but such was Titania's Law, serving the great goddess Gaea. This invader looked mostly harmless, unlike a waterlogged savage. But those were the rulings of the land: observe the invader to see what crimes it committed against the land, and then, when the order came from the court, dispatch it before it could cause any further damage.

So Gwenna watched.

* * * * *

Harbin circled the crashed ornithopter, then kicked it again. The blow did not do anything to repair the smashed device, and it made him feel only slightly better about his situation.

When his father agreed to allow him to train to be an ornithopter pilot, he dreamed of flying such a craft into battle. Instead, he had spent a dozen years on routine matters. Running messages and orders throughout the combined kingdoms of Argive, Korlis, and Yotia. Conducting surveys along the northern coast of Malpiri. Carrying diplomats and bureaucrats from Kroog to Penregon. They were vital assignments, but safe ones.

He tried to be reassigned to a combat unit, or at least to a garrison unit, but received no aid from his elders. Mother had been adamant against his flying in the first place. Father had been cool and distant, as always, and spoke about the importance of not showing favoritism. That was very much like Father: the perfect answer to every question. Even Uncle Tawnos was sympathetic but did not attempt to change matters.

There had been excitement in his work. He was once assaulted by Malpiri tribesmen when on the ground and discovered Fallaji raiding parties four separate times. On one such occasion, he was pursued by a flying dragon engine and outflew it, bringing it within range of one of his father's clockwork avian flocks. Yet still, while most other pilots had been moved to the front, he had been left behind in relative safety.

Harbin smelled a plot, and the plot stank of his elders' collusion. He tried once more for a combat posting and was told that after his present tour of duty he should settle down to a training position. He was twenty-six now, they said, practically as antique as the first primitive ornithopters. Melana, his wife, would like him to take the training position, but then his wife spent all her time in Mother's court and would like nothing more than for Harbin to abandon flying altogether.

There was a rustling among the forest leaves, and Harbin tensed, his hand going automatically to his sword hilt. The rustle continued, and soon a pair of eyes on multicolored stalks raised from the impenetrable green. The eyes blinked at Harbin in the sunlight, then pulled back and retreated deeper into the forest. Harbin caught a flash of yellow and black striping and realized he had been looking at a forest slug, though one almost as large as himself. The slug was more afraid of him than he was of it.

Harbin shook his head and realized that he was still gripping his sword hilt. The blade was one of Tawnos's "new metals"—lighter, stronger, and more versatile than the blades previously in use. The blades had proved useful in combat and had turned the tide in a number of critical battles against Mishra's forces.

Harbin carried one of the first of the new metal blades, and his craft had been one of the latest longer-winged, lighter creations from Urza's workshops. Had it been a lesser craft, it would not have survived the storms that drove him to this strange beach.

More collusion of the elders in controlling his life, thought Harbin. More unwanted protection that probably saved his life.

The storm had come out of nowhere as he skirted the Korlisian coast. He tried running from it but was driven farther and farther out to sea. He tried to climb above it, but the rising anvil of the thunderstorm kept towering over him like a great wave. It was as if the storm held its own intelligence and was intent on keeping Harbin from escaping its grip.

At last he flew into the storm itself and was battered for three days and three nights by its fury. Howling winds threatened to snap the wings and peel back the protective housing, while bolts of lightning chained around him. Odd electrical fires danced along the wings and the guide pulleys. For one horrible moment the entire craft had been inverted, and Harbin saw the sea rise before him like a wall of water before he regained control of the craft.

Then the storm was gone, and he was in clear air. Behind him the storm still boiled like soup, but ahead there was land, a huge rolling expanse of greenery. Where the land met the sea there shone a bright strip of white sand, gleaming like a beacon. Exhausted from three days of continual battle against the sky, Harbin brought the wounded craft down hard on the beach and felt something give as the craft landed. He tumbled from the ornithopter and collapsed on the sand in exhaustion beneath one of its half-folded wings.

It was afternoon when he awoke, and Harbin could not be sure if he had slept a few hours or a few days. He had been undisturbed, and fortunately he had set the craft down above the high tide mark. Brushing the sand from his uniform, he surveyed his surroundings and the damage to his craft.

His world was a straight line of beach of such a white brilliance that it hurt his eyes. The sky above was a crystalline blue, unmarked by clouds overhead, but turning first white, then gray, and finally black along the horizon out to sea. The storm was still offshore, waiting patiently like a cat at a mousehole.

Inland was a verdant jungle, seemingly untouched by man. It began at the beach's edge with a thick tangle of low-lying vegetation, but soon mounted in towering, white-barked trees of a type that Harbin had never seen before. The forest was so ancient that the upper branches were interlocked, forming huge canopies.

Harbin wondered if perhaps this was the way Argive had looked, long before Father and Mishra began their continual war. Before the lands were strip-mined and the skies turned dark from the factory smoke. Perhaps this was the way paradise was supposed to look.

Harbin took a sighting on the sun. He was south of civilized lands, farther south than the southern Korlisian coast. He had no idea of his longitude. Home could be due north, or northwest, or northeast. If he guessed northwest, Harbin figured, if he flew that direction, he would probably hit land. Eventually.

Harbin looked back at his craft. It was mostly in good shape. Some of the wires had snapped, and the pulleys along one of the control surfaces were stripped, the result of his landing. The worst effect of the storm had been to splinter the right wing strut. It held up to the brunt of the storm, but cracked halfway through. It would have to be replaced before he took another chance with the winds aloft.

Harbin kicked the craft a third time but not as hard. Then he opened the housing and pulled out the repair kit every ornithopter carried.

Within the steel box was a collection of tools: a hammer, and an axe with two spare heads; a flexible piece of saw-toothed metal; spools of wire and spare pulleys; spools of thinner catgut and steel needles to repair holes in the wings; a balled coil of rope. He thumbed through the box. Fishing hooks. Tape measure. Emergency rations. Flint and tinder. An oversized hat to protect him from the sun. Harbin looked at the collection and felt Father's heavy hand again. It was as if his elder thought of every contingency for such a crash. And Urza probably had.

Harbin gnawed on a chunk of smoked meat and walked around his craft a few more times. With the exception of the main strut, he could take the ornithopter aloft immediately. But he would have to find the right tree for the replacement strut.

That meant going into the jungle, the one with the huge black and yellow slugs in it.

Harbin hoped the slugs were the worst of the dangers in the primeval forest. He hefted his axe and headed into the thick vegetation.

* * * * *

Titania's rules on invaders were straightforward and strict, and Gwenna knew what the response to her report would probably be. Still she followed the letter of the law in dealing with the latest invader. She watched.

Of course word would come from the court that if the invader had not damaged the land it should be captured. If it had damaged the land, it should be killed. And of course, given time to communicate, even mystically, back to the court and to gain a response, it was inevitable that the invader would do something to damage the land and would have to be destroyed.

Gwenna felt a slight touch of sympathy for the invader. It did not know it was signing its own death sentence by stealing Gaea's bounty without permission.

Perhaps that was Titania's intention after all. Titania spoke for the goddess Gaea, and the elves, pixies, and treefolk listened.

The invader moved gingerly though the border vegetation, trying to find a path through the undergrowth. The scrub and vine maples tugged at its pants, and the water dripping from the canopy above left dark stains on its white shirt. Gwenna started after it, moving quietly from tree to tree by the interlocking branches, remaining out of sight. Once she brushed a dead branch, and sent it clattering to the forest floor. She remained perfectly still as the invader scanned the area, looking for her. Then it set out again, and she followed, an arboreal shadow.

Once he was past the scrub vegetation on the beach, the territory opened up beneath the great trees. The soil was thick here with rotted vegetation, and the canopy was broken only by blown-down and toppled trees. The fallen giants served as nurse logs for new growths, straining for what little light penetrated the leaves above.

The invader stopped at one of these glades and chose a particularly straight sapling of yarrow wood. It circled the tree three times, then nodded and pulled a strip from its shirt and tied it around the trunk at about eye level. Then it headed back for the beach in a clear line. Though it did not use it, the invader carried an axe in its hand.

Gwenna knew in an instant what the invader's intent was. By cutting down the live tree it would sign its death warrant. The messengers would return and they would say, "Has the invader damaged the land?"

Gwenna would be forced to respond, "Yes, it cut down a sapling."

The messenger would say, "Then the invader must be similarly cut down."

And to Gwenna that seemed a waste. She wanted to know more about the broken bird thing that the invader rode. How could it fly and carry a mannish invader? There had never been a winged invader before. Perhaps they needed to learn more of it and leave it alive.

Gwenna quickly scouted the area and found a nearby deadfall, where a huge paleroot had recently blown over in a storm, taking other yarrows and tangleoaks with it. She found an uprooted yarrow about the same size as the one the invader marked. This tree had been recently killed by the fall. She offered the proper prayers to Gaea and removed the dying branches of the yarrow with her own blade, then pulled the entire sapling to where the invader would return, and laid it across the path.

The invader returned with a large coil of rope and found its way blocked by the fallen sapling. It was confused, then looked at the tree it was about to fell, then at the deadfall. It shrugged (a curious, mannish shrug), and tied the rope to the fallen sapling, taking Gwenna's offering and sparing the living tree. It pulled and struggled and cursed (in its strange language) and finally dragged the dead tree back to its campsite.

Gwenna felt relieved she did not have to kill the invader immediately.

The invader came back within the forest one other time, to find fresh water. It didn't kill anything then, either, instead surviving on food it brought with it and fishing in the gentle surf. Fishing was permitted by Titania; she only protected the land.

The invader spent most of its time hacking at the yarrow, then removing one of the bird thing's wings and replacing it with the spar it had carved. Gwenna watched but found its actions boring and confusing. It would measure something, cut it, measure again, cut again, and eventually trim the new spar to resemble the old. These actions seemed a waste of time to Gwenna.

The nights were warm, and the invader did not light a fire, though it obviously laid one. As a signal to others, perhaps? she thought. Were there more of these flying men in the world?

On the fourth night the invader retired early, and Gwenna crept down from her arboreal perch, leaving the forest and crossing onto the beach itself. She felt odd without the protection of the trees above, but her curiosity had gotten the best of her.

The invader was sleeping in the belly of its wounded bird, now sporting a new wing of roughly hewn yarrow. She was close enough to see the invader clearly now and thought about how much like a child it looked. Soft cheeks and a smooth forehead. She was close enough to touch it, to draw her dagger across its throat as it slept.

She could do it, too, and claim that the invader had despoiled the land in some way and as such had to be destroyed. But in her heart she knew she could not lie to her fellows, and besides, Gaea would know the truth. If Gaea knew, Titania would find out.

And she was still curious how the bird thing worked.

The invader struggled in its sleep, reacting to some threat in its dreams. Gwenna darted out of view, and the young mannish invader mumbled something and twisted in its sleep again. Gwenna circled the craft once more and knew that it was a made thing that smelled of dead wood and oily resins. Then she retreated back to her hiding place to continue the watch, as Titania would have wanted it.

In the morning Gwenna was startled awake by a new sound, a sound that convinced her in a moment she had made a mistake in sparing the young invader.

She could see the beach from where she perched, and the bird thing was moving now. The invader was within it, and the bird thing was flapping its great wings. There was a high, whining noise that hurt her ears, and the sand billowed out in great dusty clouds beneath the moving wings. The invader's craft took a single, low hop on the beach, then a second, and then shot into the air like an arrow.

Gwenna watched the mechanical creation gain altitude, the wires that ran through its wings singing as it caught the wind like a kite. The bird thing began to circle and spiral upward over the warming sand of the beach. Gwenna wondered if it was going to fly deeper into the island's heart and how she was supposed to follow it if it did.

Instead the bird thing increased its altitude until it was a small dot, then flew northwest, toward the continual line of storms that marked the borders of Titania's influence.

Gwenna came out of the beach again, watching the small craft as it became smaller still and finally disappeared entirely from her sight. She had not expected the bird thing to fly again. She had not expected the invader to be foolish enough to escape. She had no doubt it would fail in the attempt and be driven back to shore elsewhere along the island coast.

But if it was driven back or destroyed by the storm, she did not see it.

An elder came to her two days later and found her still at her post, waiting for the bird thing to return. She told him that she had watched the invader as he repaired his craft and then departed.

The elder asked, "And did it damage the land while it was here?"

Gwenna replied, "No, it did not."

The elder thought for a moment, surprised by the answer. Then he said, "Then you did the right thing not to slay it if it violated no law."

And that was that. The invader did not return that month, nor in the month that followed, nor in the month after that. No one found the remains of the invader or its bird thing along the rest of the coastline, and it was assumed it had been destroyed by the storms that surrounded and protected Argoth.

Gwenna was unsure. There was a nagging in her stomach about the invader; about the fact that she kept it from despoiling the land and thereby preserved it from death. She wondered if she had done something wrong in letting it live.

To Argoth's pain and her own shame, she would live to see how wrong she had been.

Chapter 29

Mana and Artifice

The assistant announced Harbin's arrival to the Lord High Artificer and Protector of the Combined Kingdoms of Argive, Korlis, and Yotia. Harbin did not wait for Urza to respond but was in the room already, hot on the assistant's heels, not giving his father a chance to send him away.

"Father, you must see me," said the younger man.

"And see you I do," returned Urza, pushing his glasses back up on the bridge of his nose. He nodded to the assistant, and the young girl retreated to her own studies.

Harbin looked at his father. Urza was leaner now and his frame had taken on an almost birdlike quality. His hair was snow-white and had receded to expose most of his careworn brow. He wore his spectacles all the time now, not just when working. He looked old and tired.

"You have read my preliminary report, sir," said Harbin, politely but without preamble.

"Yes," said Urza, patting a small stack of papers. "And I must say you were fortunate. The storms of the southeast have shattered boats and sent good men to the bottom. Both your mother and your wife were beside themselves with worry. I trust you have seen them and reassured them."

"I sent word to them, Father, but came here first," said Harbin.

Urza looked at the young man, surprised, then nodded. "You found something beyond the storms," he said.

"An island," said Harbin. "More than an island, a huge landmass to the south and east of Korlis. Heavily forested, but I noted from aloft there were huge mountains as well, as big as the Kher Ridges. I kept multiple sightings on my return, and even given the storms I think we can find it again."

Urza said nothing but merely ground his palms together slowly.

"There's enough lumber there to launch an armada of ornithopters against the enemy and enough ore within those mountains to make new legions of avengers," continued Harbin. The young man's face was alight with possibilities. "This is the chance to tip the battle in our favor for once."

Urza held his silence, and his eyebrows furrowed. Harbin said, "Sir, have I said something wrong?"

Urza's eyebrows rose, and he shook his head. Harbin wondered where his father's thoughts were while he talked. Instead Urza said, "Harbin, what was it like flying back to Penregon?"

Harbin thought for a moment. "It was unremarkable, sir."

"What did you see of the land while you were aloft?" asked the older man.

Harbin shrugged. "Mines, factories, farms, towers, outposts. Nothing out of the ordinary."

"Hmmm," said Urza. "Nothing out of the ordinary. Argive was once a land of rolling hills and manor-house estates. Did you know that?"

"I know the histories, sir," said Harbin.

"Histories that I was alive for. Korlis was covered with forests, though now not a tree stands between its capital and the coast. Yotia was an open territory of fertile fields. Now its fields are barren, and the Sword Marches is a plain of blackened glass."

"That is because of Mishra's inventions," said Harbin quickly. "His ground-breakers and armageddon clocks. He would rather destroy the land than to give it up to you."

"Yes, those are the qadir's inventions," said Urza, not even speaking his brother's name. "But have I been any better with my creations? The land has been ripped asunder in our pursuit of resources to fight this war. There are reports from among the surviving Sardian dwarves that burning rain falls from the sky into their land, searing the flesh and corroding any exposed mechanism. The qadir has plundered nation after nation. Have I been any less effective in my own work?"

Harbin was silent for a moment, then said, "This is unlike you, sir. Is there other news I should know of?"

Urza let loose a small smile. "Why is it everyone knows when I am troubled except me?" he said and turned back toward his desk. "I've been going through Richlau's old papers. You knew him?"

Harbin said, "He was the Master of Apprentices at the Artificer's School." Then he paused and added, "I didn't know he was dead. I am sorry."

"Happened while you were away," said Urza. "I knew him when we were very young. He died of natural causes in his library. But still, his death has troubled me."

Harbin said nothing. They had both become immured to the continual losses of the war, both of manpower and machines, but the passing from simple old age was something that Harbin had a hard time considering. If Richlau had been older than his father, then he must have been very old indeed.

"In any event, I've been going through his personal papers, and found correspondence with another old friend, named Loran." Urza tapped a thick pile of letters. "She was another scholar and went to Terisia City to study when you were very young."

Harbin thought he understood. Terisia City had fallen to enemy forces and been sacked. Since then it had been taken and retaken several times. If Loran was there, she was probably dead as well.

"Loran writes of some meditative techniques they were developing in the city," continued his father. "They allowed the user to manipulate matter and living things. To fly. To jump great distances. To shatter objects. What do you think of that?"

"I would find such a claim . . . dubious," said Harbin. It was the kindest phrase he could think of.

"Dubious?" said Urza, catching the halt in Harbin's voice. "How so?"

"I find the existence of such things unlikely," said Harbin. "Flying without an ornithopter. Have you ever encountered something like this?"

Urza was quiet for a moment, and Harbin wondered, not for the first time, what he was thinking. The older man's hand reached for the amulet that always hung around his neck. "No. Not exactly. Sometimes when I am starting on a new device, there is a spark, a feeling that I get, when everything falls into place. But no, nothing that would allow me to fly without an ornithopter."

"Well, then," said Harbin, "if you did not think of it, it probably does not exist. Sir."

Urza smiled broadly. Harbin relaxed, and for the first time since he was a child he felt comfortable with the older man. "You think too highly of me," the artificer said.

"As any good son should," said Harbin. Urza's face clouded for a moment, and the younger man felt at once he had gone too far. Quickly he added, "If this meditative technique *was* valid, it didn't work against the enemy, did it? Terisia City was sacked and burned, and all the meditation in the world did not prevent that."

Urza said, "Well reasoned."

Harbin replied with a small nod, and Urza picked up the pile of letters, then set them back down. "Before your return," he said, "I was wondering how to continue protecting ourselves from the qadir and his machines. We have almost emptied the land and have little to show for it. We stand, more than ever, on the edge of a blade, poised between salvation and defeat. Perhaps, I thought, if our devices could be developed to work off this meditative energy, this mana . . ."

Harbin was silent, unsure if his father was truly speaking to him or not.

Urza sighed deeply. "No, you're right. There is too much unknown, even if there is some grain of truth at the heart of this. It would take years to discover what the ivory-towered scholars had come up with, and all their work is now among the qadir's plunder."

Urza looked up at Harbin, and his face was stern and self-assured, as it normally was. "But this new discovery, this new land, is an opportunity to finally gain the advantage over my . . . over the qadir. You've done very well, Harbin."

"Thank you, Father," said Harbin. "I've already started plans for securing the island."

"You?" said Urza, and blinked. "Just because you were fortunate to get past the storms once—"

"I should lead any expedition that returns there," rejoined Harbin. "It is a well-reasoned argument." The younger man folded his arms.

"Your mother will not hear of this," said Urza.

"Which is why I came to you first," said Harbin, "instead of talking to her, or to Uncle Tawnos. If you say yes, they will not argue with you."

Urza pulled the glasses from his face and pinched the brow of his nose. "Then you leave me no choice," he said at last. "You will lead the expedition to this new land."

Harbin had expected more of an argument, or at least more fire in the Lord Protector's voice. Instead there was just exhaustion.

Urza rubbed his chin. "Harbin?" he said.

"Yes, sir?"

"Do you dream?" asked Urza.

The question caught the younger man by surprise. "Dream? I suppose everyone dreams."

Urza held up his glasses, and the muddied sunlight caught them. "I dreamed I had made a set of lenses that let me look into the human heart. To see to the core of its being. I used them to look at my brother, and there was only darkness. Only darkness in my brother's heart."

"Sir?"

"Only darkness," repeated Urza, and sighed. "That is why we are going to bring this new island of yours into the war. Because we need to beat back that darkness."

* * * * *

"Bunk! Bunk and camel droppings!" bellowed Mishra, throwing the book against the far wall of his workshop. The offending tome fluttered end over end before its covers spread like a bird's wings and it smashed, spine first, against the far wall. Hajar quietly walked over to the jettisoned book, straightened its pages back into a semblance of order, closed it, and placed it on a growing pile.

"Most Revered One," said Hajar simply, "even among the dross there may be accidental gems."

"Gems? Gems?" snapped Mishra. "There are no more gems among those convoluted daydreams than there is grass in the Suwwardi Marches, these days!"

Hajar started to say, "The Scholars of the Ivory Towers held our forces at bay for—" but Mishra waved a hand at him.

"They had stout walls and good weapons," the qadir rapped out. "This mystic effluence had nothing to do with their success."

"The generals who oversaw the siege and later sacking would disagree," said Hajar.

"Those generals were looking for an excuse for their own incompetence," snarled Mishra. "They found it in the nonsense of those scholars. A dragon engine goes missing, and they blame witches and pixies!"

He might have said more, but his words were already being garbled by the phlegm in his throat. The Artifice Qadir of the Fallaji Empire bent almost double in a long, wheezing fit of coughing.

Hajar waited for the attack to abate. Mishra had grown heavy over the years, and sometimes it hurt his lungs to breathe. The thick yellowing smoke that hung night and day over Tomakul did little to abate his illness. Hajar had recommended Mishra retreat to the clearer desert air, but as in most matters these days, the bodyguard's advice was ignored.

The fit was a short one, and Mishra pulled a silk scarf from his pocket to wipe the sprayed spittle from his lips. "Scholars," he snarled, picking up where he left off. "Mystic energy within the land itself. Tapping into that energy through memorization and meditation. Hokum! We drove the charlatans out of Zegon, and they all fled to Terisia. And I thought there was knowledge there!"

Hajar said, "Even among the dross there—"

"Is more dross!" shouted Mishra. "There is no more truth in those books than in the 'true sight' of some old Fallaji wise woman sitting in the square, trading rose-colored visions for brass coins."

Hajar stiffened at the slur against the Fallaji, but Mishra ignored it. "I hoped there would be some great weapon, some master artifice that could finally defeat my brother," he wheezed. "But all that is here are campfire tales and petty mystics!" Another coughing fit rose to his lungs, and Hajar walked over and stoked the coals, then poured a ladle of water over the red-hot embers. Heat and steam seemed to help His Most Revered One's breathing.

Mishra needed something to help him, and Hajar had hoped it would be among the books looted from Terisia City's ivory towers. Hajar believed the generals when they said the scholars had some sort of *raki* powers that allowed them to defeat the dragon engines and transmograms and to keep the Fallaji at bay for so long.

As Mishra searched, the empire crumbled. They were reduced in the east to skirmishing and petty raids across the Kher Ridges. In the south Yotia was a lawless frontier, at least those parts that had not been turned to glass by Mishra's inventions. The descendants of the ground-breakers, the armegeddon clocks, had fused huge sections of the land to black glass, denying the enemy any use of it. Elsewhere huge plows churned through the dying land in desperate attempts to pull something useful from the earth's bosom. To the west was untamed and barren wilderness, already plundered to keep the war machines going.

The pieces were beginning to fall apart now. There was civil war in conquered Almaaz and revolution in Sarinth. Many of the tribes of the Fallaji were now raiding fellow tribesmen, and discipline was breaking down.

Ashnod, gone these many years, was to blame, Hajar felt. Without her to argue and plot, without her for the generals and war captains to fear and conspire against, the various factions within the empire were turning against each other. Urza was the continual enemy, but he was far away. It was Ashnod everyone hated and feared.

She had been spotted in Sumifa, said one report. No, in the Colekgan Mountains, said another. No, she was seen in Yotia and was going to sell her secrets to Urza, said a third. Nay, said a fourth, she was dead from her own diabolic devices. Whatever the truth, Hajar knew the empire suffered without her.

Mishra's coughing fit subsided, and the qadir again dabbed at the corners of his mouth with his kerchief, an automatic gesture these days. "It is hard for you to understand, Hajar, but know that all of my devices are rooted in some basic principles."

"If you insist, Most Puissant One," said Hajar.

"And this"—Mishra motioned at the ever-growing pile of books— "this school of fools acts as if those basic principles do not exist! You don't need wings to fly or a transmogrant to build an army! All you need is thought and land, and you can wish things into being!" He slapped another book, and a fountain of dust shot out from between its covers. "Pah!"

Mishra raised his kerchief to his mouth and retreated to his throne. He lowered his large bulk into the chair and said, "Call for the Gixians."

Hajar bowed but did not move. "The Gixians?"

"They've been playing with Ashnod's works for years," snapped Mishra. "Perhaps they have some trick I can use against my brother."

"With respect, most honorable one," said Hajar, "there are those who say you rely on the Gixians far too much."

Mishra's forehead creased and he growled, "There are those who also say I rely too much on *you*, Hajar. Now fetch me those accursed priests."

Within the hour three of the priests were brought before Mishra. Hajar had not liked the priests when they first arrived, and he liked them less with every passing year. They had slowly infiltrated the bureaucracy and made themselves invaluable to the empire. Since Ashnod's desertion (no mind that she had been banished; if she had been loyal, she would have remained), they had taken over that woman's laboratories and slaughterhouses. And they had taken over Mishra's own mild attempts at training young Fallaji in artifice, turning the schools into mere extensions of their priesthood.

A pair of young Fallaji men accompanied the head priest as they approached the throne. Perhaps the Gixians saw this as tribute to

Mishra, but Hajar thought of it as an abomination. These young men should have been warriors. Instead they were chanters for a foreign religion.

Worse yet, within the last ten years the Brotherhood of Gix had taken to modifying their own bodies in their worship of the machine. Flesh was woven with links of chain and metal scales, and even limbs were replaced with clunky mechanical devices. They mutilated themselves and declared themselves more holy for their efforts.

The lead priest was such an abomination. He had no eyes; rather a plate of curved metal covered his eye sockets, polished to a mirror's brightness. The plate had been bolted to the priest's face at the temples, and occasionally a trickle of blood would drip down alongside one of the bolts. The priest was dressed in heavy robes, and Hajar wondered what other parts of his body he had modified in the name of his machine god. Hajar suppressed a shudder and decided he did not want to know.

The lead priest bowed, the two Fallaji acolytes following his motions like puppets on a string. "Most Wise, Most Thoughtful, Most Powerful Qadir," said the lead Gixian, "we offer whatever help we may give in your illustrious name."

Mishra rested both hands on his belly, templing his fingers and tapping them softly. "You said Terisia City held great knowledge."

The priest bowed again. "That is so. My fellow brothers walked among their scholars and learned much."

Mishra continued, "I have reviewed much of the material that we have recovered and determined it to be without merit."

Again the priest bowed. "If that is what you determine, that must be correct," he said smoothly. Hajar wondered that the man's spine did not snap from changing opinions so quickly.

"Yet you said they had great power," said Mishra.

Yet another bow. "They may have hidden their true strengths from us or cloaked them in mysticism, assuming that we would respect their beliefs," said the priest. He cocked his steel-shod head and added, "We are industrious but not all-seeing."

"But we have nothing useful from Terisia City, save the traditional plunder," said Mishra, his voice sounding thick again as the fluids began to settle in his lungs. Hajar automatically moved to the hot coals and scooped another ladle of water onto them. Mishra began another long cough, and the priests and Hajar waited for him to finish.

"Most Illustrious One," said the lead priest, "there are some things we have learned."

"Such as?" prompted Mishra.

"Mysteries of the human body," said the mirror-plated Gixian. "We have studied much of Ashnod's work, and we believe that we have . . . " He paused for a moment and then continued, ". . . improved it."

Mishra leaned forward now, his bulk shifting beneath him. "Improved it? How?"

"Ashnod thought of the body as a resource," said the Gixian. "We believe the body is a machine and should be able to be improved like a machine, thereby made more holy. And more powerful."

"More powerful?" rasped Mishra. "How? Can it be used as a weapon?"

The lead priest turned toward Hajar, though how the monk could see without eyes confounded the older Fallaji. "We can talk to you of this," said the Gixian, "away from prying ears."

Mishra nodded. "Hajar, leave us."

Hajar set down the ladle. "Most Revered One, I—"

"I said, leave us," said Mishra again. "I want to hear what the good monks have to say of the matter. Away from prying ears."

Hajar started to argue, then stopped. He nodded, bowed deeply, and left the room, pulling the ornate doors shut behind him.

"Now," said Mishra, smiling and leaning forward toward the three monks, "tell me more."

PART 4

Critical Mass

(57–63 AR)

Chapter 30

War Drums

The demon Gix sat in the cavern of Koilos and feasted on the minds of two of his followers. One was a spy who had come west from Argive and was still obviously human. The other came from the court of Mishra, and she was festooned with rings and other metal ornaments. Her left arm was entirely artificial. Her face was a rictus grin that indicated further work in the jaw and throat.

One priest knelt on either side of the demon, and he gripped their skulls and pierced their flesh with his talons, sucking their memories from them. He savored their experiences, their messy lives and flamboyant emotions, as he took in their knowledge.

The more human priest, the one from Argive, was obviously jealous of his companion. He could not modify his form in the same fashion as she did, for he had to operate among the other humans in Argive's capital, Penregon. But this plain, unornamented one held wonderful information, of the new discovery of the island off Terisiare's southeast coastline. The new land was wrapped in storms, but once past the bad weather there was a land rich for the taking, similar to Phyrexia's first sphere in its wildness, but more organic and disorganized.

He scanned through the mind of the priest from Mishra's court, and there was nothing similar there. Yes, they had raided Ashnod's notes and were already successfully using her work on the human body to modify themselves. And yes, Mishra relied more and more on the priests with every passing month and was now susceptible to the brotherhood's suggestions and recommendations. But Mishra was hurting badly for resources now and had sucked most of the lands dry.

357

But no word of the new island's discovery within the priest from the Artifice Qadir's court.

Gix let the information click through the registers of his own mind. He wanted to reunite the split power stone, but he was not sure now which brother should do it for him. Mishra had been the initial invader of his domain but now was depending on Gix's puppets, the priests, more and more. Urza, wrapped within his own hierarchy of supporters and students, remained an enigma to Gix, but with the resources of this new island he would be able to overpower his brother, given time.

Gix wanted one of the brothers dead and the other sufficiently weakened so that he would not stand in Gix's way. But both humans had been working through their proxies, through their own minions, and had not met face-to-face in decades.

Perhaps, Gix thought, he could change that.

To the metal-studded priestess from Mishra's court he presented information that Urza had found a new source of material to keep his war machine functioning. The woman shuddered as the new data flooded into her brain, and a single, oily tear pooled at the corner of her eye.

Gix ordered the male spy to return to Argive and allow himself to be captured. He must then reveal, only under torture, that Mishra himself planned to take the prize of the island kingdom personally, giving himself a boon of materials and opening the entire southern coast of Urza's kingdoms to attack.

Almost as an afterthought, the demon burned out that part of the man's brain that contained the feelings of jealousy of his fellow monk. The man let out a small gasp.

Machines did not feel jealousy, noted Gix. Neither should their worshipers.

He released the pair, and the woman moaned as the mental connection was broken. The man collapsed, and Gix had to summon a pair of *su-chi*, partially restored by the priests, to drag him off to recover elsewhere. Given the damage done to his mind, there would be little difficulty in his being caught by the Argivians.

Gix leaned back on his throne and clicked his taloned fingers together. Now, finally, all the pieces were falling into place.

* * * * *

Gwenna had been there when the first invader came and was there when the invasion proper began. Titania was no fool, and an invader that escaped the land was expected to return. Gwenna and others of her clan had been recruited to serve as shore watchers for the next year or ten years to guard against the recurrence of men from the sky.

And they did return, from the sky and from the sea.

Gwenna was at the tree line overlooking the pristine white beach where the invader had first landed. It was morning, and the storms that formed the outer barricade of the island were a dark line against the horizon.

Then darker flecks appeared along the gray horizon, slowly becoming clearer and more solid as they sailed out of the rain. The dark blots quickly resolved into large boats. It was a flotilla of ships sailing out of the storm.

There were other flecks aloft, no more noticeable than gnats swarming around the greater shadows. They were the bird things, Gwenna realized. Their small size alongside the greater silhouettes spoke of the boats' huge size. Each of the great ships had to be the size of an entire elven hamlet.

As Gwenna watched, more ships sailed out of the gray storm, and then more still. Some were streaming black smoke, and others white steam; still others billowed out with great sails, torn by their passage through the heavy weather, looking like specters as they neared the shore.

It was an armada unlike any that Gwenna could recall, not even out of the old lore. The invaders were coming to Argoth.

The force was making for a peninsula westward along the coast, and Gwenna began moving in that direction. She thought of moving along the beach, but already the small bird things were overhead, swooping and scouting the area. Instead she kept to the upper levels of the trees, running along the great branches and leaping the occasional chasms within the interwoven branches.

She found young Doril at her watch position, staring at the armada as it bore down on them. The younger elf's eyes were wide with fear.

Gwenna shook her and told the youngling to take word of the invasion back to Titania's Court. But even as she spoke, Gwenna knew that with a force so large, Gaea herself had to know. If Gaea knew, then Titania, their queen, must be aware as well. Still Doril was petrified, and even flight was a sufficient action for her at this point.

The invaders had landed by the time she arrived. Their boats did not moor but drove up onto the beach itself. The bows of the great craft split open, and out of them spilled a torrent of creatures like ants from a ruptured anthill. There were men among them, but there were other things of a type that Gwenna had never seen. Some looked like beetle-headed humanoids, and these took the perimeter of the beachhead. Others were mechanical giants with knees that bent oddly, and they were already unloading supplies. Huge castlelike creations rumbled from the bellies of the ships, bristling with armament and blades. A great machine with a saw-toothed mouth lumbered forward on spider legs.

If Gwenna had any doubts as to her own responsibility in this invasion, they were banished when she saw the figure leading the assault. There, among the mechanical beings and human warriors, was her Invader, the one that she had refrained from killing over a year ago. He was bellowing orders to the men and machines, and they responded to his words. He turned to listen to another man, a taller, older man with broad shoulders. They spoke, and then the younger Invader snapped another set of orders, and the machines bent to his will.

The spider-legged creation lumbered toward the tree line, even as the mechanical giants began to dig the foundation of a fortress above the high tide line. The sawteeth of the great spider behemoth bit into the trees, and sawdust and bark flew in all directions as it chewed its way into the jungle.

Other ships were landing now along the beach, their bellies rupturing and giving birth to other monstrosities. Some of the ships had hung on the reefs, but enough passed through that gauntlet to repeat the scene Gwenna witnessed all along the coastline. Overhead, the sky buzzed with bird things, both large and small.

There was no time to wait for a response from Titania's Court. These were not solitary invaders cast up from some shipwreck. This was a force, armed and dangerous, which within moments of its landing began to assault the land.

Gwenna knew she should wait for official response, but she also knew what the response had to be. If she waited the forest would be lost. Her perch shuddered as one of the great bleachwoods toppled, taking with it two more trees with which it had interlinked branches.

Gwenna retreated, pulling back to the deeper heart of the forest. She needed to gather the rest of her clan and form a war party.

The invaders would not wait for such niceties as permission.

* * * * *

Ashnod stared at the sylex and smiled. It had taken many years, but its secrets were at last hers.

She ran a finger along the bowl's lip. The world seemed to darken around her, and she welcomed that darkness. It spoke of an entirely new type of power, a new resource that she could harness.

She had learned well, though her teacher had needed some encouragement to share the secrets of the ivory towers. The scholar was gone now, though not dead. Ashnod would have found a way to preserve her if she had merely died, but the woman had instead escaped, made off into the night either by herself or with aid.

It mattered little. She left most of her knowledge behind.

It required a different way of thinking, a way Ashnod had trouble understanding at first. Hers had been a world of the physical, like the other artificers. But once the concept existed that the land itself held power, that it only needed to be released, the rest of the theory fell easily into place.

Once you believed in magic, it could happen.

Ashnod lifted her fingertip from the bowl, and the world returned to normal. This device was too dangerous for direct use, but the secrets it revealed were powerful enough to demonstrate her abilities to Mishra and to regain her place by his side.

He needed her aid desperately. The tribes of the Fallaji were finally falling apart, and the non-Fallaji nations they had conquered were wracked by revolution and civil war. Through it all, an ever-increasing wave of devices spilled across the eastern passes from the foundries and workshops of his accursed brother.

She had made her own home in Almaaz, far from its now-ruined capital of Sumifa, and played one faction off against another as that country spiraled into dissolution. At one point she thought she could unite the nation and return to Mishra as Almaaz's queen, but now . . .

He would be much more impressed with the power and knowledge she held than with any mere nation.

There was a shadow at the door—one of her own acolytes, veteran of several sides in the civil war. She had shared some of her secrets with her students but not enough to make any of them dangerous. She told them nothing of the true power of the sylex.

"Mistress?" said the acolyte.

"Speak, Thaxus," Ashnod replied grandly.

"News from Tomakul," he said.

Ashnod looked up, her eyes narrowing. "Out with it."

"Word has reached Mishra that his brother has found a great

island, filled with trees and metals to let him fuel the war effort."

Ashnod nodded. Yes, such news would make Mishra all the more desperate. "Is it true?"

"The Artifice Qadir has reopened the boatyards at Zegon, and has dispatched slaves to build a fleet of his own," said Thaxus. "He intends to take the island for himself."

Ashnod nodded again. Yes, that was very much like Mishra. He needed a new goal to keep his empire together, and the promise of fresh plunder was enough to keep the child-men who were the Fallaji war chiefs in line. And he would need help if he was to succeed. Her help.

The news was at least three months old. Mishra would have finished his ships by now.

Thaxus shifted from one foot to another, and when Ashnod looked up, there was fire in her eyes.

"Saddle my mount," she said, "with supplies for a long trip."

"Where are we going?" asked Thaxus.

"You are not going anywhere," said Ashnod with a wicked smile, one that the apprentices had learned to fear. "I, on the other hand, am going home."

* * * * *

Junior Artificer Sanwell, who a lifetime ago stood with Urza among the ruins of Kroog, found the Lord Protector in his workshop. A great area had been cleared in the center of the room, and a glowing sphere hovered in the center.

The sphere shone with a color unknown to Sanwell, a combination of swirling yellows and greens that seemed to etch their intensity into his eyes so they were still visible even when he screwed his eyes shut against the brilliance. Lightning danced off the surface of the sphere as it spun, unsupported, in the center of the room.

Sanwell wanted to shout, but Urza noticed him and cut the power to the machine himself. The sphere spat one last arc of greenish lightning, then floated gently to the floor. Sanwell noted that the Lord Protector's white hair had been standing on end and surmised that his had been as well, within the field of the great device.

"Rakalite," said Urza briefly, grinning, as if the name explained everything. "Works on the same principle as the old amulets of Kroog, wrapping the body in a protective field that nurtures its healing. What do you have?"

"The spy, Milord."

Urza's smile disappeared, and Sanwell could see the old man make the mental transition from thinking about his devices to thinking about the war. "The Gixian? What of him?"

"We finally got him to talk," said Sanwell gruffly. "I'm afraid we had to break him to do it."

"Of course," said Urza softly. "What did he know?"

"He was Gixian, a priest in the order," said Sanwell. "And yes, he was funneling information to Mishra. He gave us some other names, but they've already fled the kingdom."

"The qadir knows," said Urza sharply. "He know about the island."

Sanwell nodded. "Your brother, the qadir, is said to be building his own invasion fleet and will be leading it to the island himself."

"Tawnos is there," said Urza. "Harbin is leading the expedition." The old man ground his palms together. The motion raised his shoulders, and to Sanwell it made him look like an albino vulture. He was silent for a long moment, looking at where the oddly colored sphere now rested on the floor. He muttered something Sanwell could not hear.

"Milord?" asked Sanwell.

"I'm going, I said," Urza grunted, looking up at Sanwell. His face was exhausted, and all the spirit that had been there moments before had been drained from it. "I'm going to that island. To meet my brother one last time."

Chapter 31

Magic and Machine

Harbin arrived in the Court of Queen Titania of the elves of Argoth.

He had been surprised to discover that the island had its own queen. Indeed he had been surprised to discover that the island was inhabited by more than trees and multicolored slugs. Nothing from his earlier scouting showed clearings, wood fires, or any of the normal trappings of civilization.

But these elves were not normal. They lived in the trees themselves, and had somehow bent them to their own wills. Great cathedrals of open space had been nurtured in the center of the woods, and the elves made their homes among the branches. The Court of Titania was the greatest of those cathedrals, and banners of green, gold, and white dripped from the branches overhead.

Harbin had set down his flight of ornithopters in a clearing about a half-mile away. He was greeted by a small army of elves, dressed in armor made of varnished reeds and armed with razor-tipped bone spears. Darting among the warrior elves were pixies, small humanoids with dragonfly wings, and behind the lines of elves were centaurs and treefolk—giantlike creatures who looked very much like the forest that surrounded them.

Among the armed guard was a single tall elf, almost as tall as Harbin himself. He was dressed in green and white robes that seemed to swirl around him like a cloud. He held his hands out palms upward. Harbin returned the gesture. In Argivian, the elf said, "You are to come with us. No harm will fall upon you while within Titania's power. I am her Speaker."

364

The voice was clipped and precise, another surprise for Harbin. The elves they had fought to date had their own language and showed neither the ability to nor the interest in communicating; only in fighting, tooth and nail, for every piece of land on the island.

The raids had begun almost immediately after Harbin's landing and grew in intensity with each passing month. The shore towers were under assault almost immediately, and the work crews were victims to snipers as soon as they entered the forest proper. It had become necessary to clear the land within a mile of each tower, and even that was a difficult operation. Often the forest itself would begin to grow back unless the brush was regularly cleared and burned.

Then came the major assaults, of elves, centaurs, and treefolk. There were massed battles against crudely armed beings who fought with the passion of raging animals. There were animals among them as well: cougars, wolves, and other wild creatures. At first Harbin thought the armies drove the animals before them, but soon he realized the elves exerted some measure of control over the mindless creatures, much as the Argivians did over their machines. They would make lightning strikes from the tree line, then fade into the forest once Argivian forces arrived. Those who pursued the elves beneath the canopy of green were ambushed.

Battlements surrounded the towers, and stockades of newly hewn lumber were set up a reasonable distance from the ever-advancing frontier. Heavy, modified ornithopters, now called ornibombers, strafed the jungles to clear it of wildlife and elven raiding parties before the lumbering machines even rolled forward. Slowly, the resources were pulled from the land and poured into making more stockades, battlements, and machines.

The losses were horrible, both of men and machines. The Argivians rarely saw their opposition, and then suddenly they appeared, a huge horde of elves, or a flight of pixies, or an army of treefolk. A group of the last had reached one of the shore towers and was shredding supply boats before the Argivians realized the treefolk burned the same as any other tree.

One morning the attacks stopped as quickly as they had begun. Seven days later an elf appeared at the doors of the stockade, unarmed and carrying a scroll.

Harbin himself was at that fort and ordered the guards to open the gates and allow him to parley with the elf but to be ready to shut them should it prove a trap.

It was not. The elf extended the scroll, and Harbin took it from her. It was a map to a location a few hundred miles inland. A note attached, in fluid script, stated that if he wished to parley, he should appear at that location at a certain location and time.

Harbin nodded to the messenger. The elf took a step back and turned to go. She hesitated for a moment, and Harbin almost swore she was going to say something herself. But she only shook her head, and walked back to the tree line. The moment she passed beneath the shadows of those trees she was gone.

The time given was not sufficient to relay word back to Penregon, and, after some concerns, Tawnos allowed the young man to go to the meeting but insisted he take a flight of ornithopters with him.

Now the Speaker led Harbin beneath the trees and into the Court of Titania. He had left two men behind to guard the ornithopters and took two with him. But if the queen violated her word of safe passage, it would matter little whether they were together or apart.

They were preceded and followed by pale elven warriors, their faces painted with chalk. The procession was flanked by other races that watched as they marched by. Once Harbin swore he saw a human face among the crowds, but it was gone and he could not pause to find out.

At last they were let into the great cathedral itself, bathed in green light from the leafy canopy overhead. The ground was firm and even (much of the land beneath the trees was boggy and uneven, slowing their work even further). A long processional was cleared, flanked by still more elves and pixies, straining to look at the invaders. Near the front were humans dressed in brown robes and hoods. They looked daggers at Harbin as he passed.

At the end of the processional was a great dais, its steps rising to a white marble platform that ended in a throne as green as the heart of the forest. Seated on the throne was the queen herself.

Her beauty was unearthly. No, Harbin realized; her very being was unearthly. Her face seemed like a jade mask, narrow and pointed at the chin. Her form was lithe and lean and, if she were to stand, she would be taller than Harbin. She was decked in tendrils and vines, the brilliant yellow-green of new shoots, but her eyes were deep, old, and unfathomable.

The Speaker motioned for Harbin to remain at the base of the dais and took a position two steps up and to one side of the queen. Titania's face tightened as she regarded Harbin, and the man had the feeling she was mentally peeling away his flesh to get a look at the soul beneath. It was not a pleasant sensation.

There was a silence for a moment. Then the queen spoke, and her words were music. Harbin realized her tongue was related to the elven languages he had heard before as chamber music was related to barbarian chants. Her voice transfixed him and held a fire all its own.

The Speaker said in his clipped tones, "I speak for Queen Titania. Titania speaks for the goddess Gaea, most bountiful and all-powerful. Argoth is under the protection of Gaea and home to her children. You are not welcome here, and you should leave."

For all the soft trills, it was a blunt message. Harbin responded. "I bring the welcome of the combined kingdoms of Argive, Korlis, and Yotia, its king and people. I bring the welcome of the Lord Protector of the Realm, Urza the Master of Artifice. I am Urza's son, Harbin. Speak to me as you would to him."

The Speaker relayed the message to Titania, and Harbin wondered why the vine-clad woman smiled for a brief instant. Then she spoke again, and the Speaker translated.

"She knows who you are and what you are," he said. "She wants to know if you understand what she just said."

Harbin took a deep breath. "Tell her I have heard her words. But also tell her that our people will not leave this island."

Again, the words were relayed, and Titania's response was short, like a dagger thrust.

"Then your people will die here," said the Speaker. "You have despoiled the land and must be punished. That is Gaea's Law."

"If I may," said Harbin, raising an empty hand. "Titania should know that my people need the lumber on your shores and the minerals beneath your hills. We are at war against a greater, darker power and need every resource we can muster."

The Speaker did not even wait to translate this, but merely repeated, "She knows who you are and what you are. You are not welcome here, and you must leave."

Harbin raised his other hand. "My father's brother threatens all our land with great machines of mass destruction. Without the lumber and ore to protect ourselves, we will be destroyed. With our destruction, Mishra will find your land and destroy it as well."

The Speaker translated, and Queen Titania remained silent on her throne, her face impassive. Harbin had expected a more immediate reaction.

Then it occurred to him. Queen Titania was not truly present in this great hall. The beautiful creature before him was a mannequin, a puppet operated from afar. It looked truly alive, but it was nothing but vines and wood. Was the unseen Titania considering his words, or was she busy elsewhere, conferring with advisors?

Finally Titania spoke, and the Speaker's face tightened as he listened. To Harbin he said, "Your enemy has already found our land. He has landed on the western shores with a force as great as your own. Like you, he is already despoiling the land that he touches."

"It is as I told you," said Harbin. "He has great and powerful engines of destruction."

"And how are they different from *your* engines of destruction, human?" said the Speaker, without relaying the message to his queen.

Harbin fumed for a moment, then said, "Tell your queen that if she will ally with us, we can defend her against Mishra."

The Speaker paused for a moment, then relayed the message. The response was short and guttural, and Harbin did not really need the translation.

"She says, 'No thank you,' " said the Speaker diplomatically.

Harbin was exasperated. "You don't understand. Unless you ally with us, unless you allow us to harvest some of your resources, Mishra will sweep across your land. Only as an ally can you hope to surv—"

Harbin was cut off by a long, tremorous outburst from the queen. Her face was filled with anger, and Harbin marveled for a moment at how lifelike the mannequin seemed.

"The dwarves of the Sardian Mountains were your allies," said the Speaker. "Where are they now?"

Harbin was stunned. "How do you know of the Sardian Dwarves?" he blurted.

"The goddess Gaea knows all. She speaks to Titania," said the Speaker. "Titania speaks to me. Where are your former allies?"

"I never heard them called allies," said Harbin, recovering. "They were another race that bordered Argive, in the mountains. We traded with them for metal and then discovered they were trading with Mishra as well."

"You killed them," said Titania, in a language clear and understandable to Harbin's ears. "Your people killed the Sardian Dwarves. Few survive, as slaves or exiles, but their mines have been plundered and their halls are now warrens for goblins. Is this the fate of your allies?"

Even in rage, even speaking his own language, her voice was beautiful. Harbin stammered, and said, "I was only a youth at the time, but—"

"And Yotia?" said Titania. "Your mother is Yotian, human. How has that nation fared as an ally? Is not its northern border a sheet of fused sand and black glass?"

"That is not my father's fault!" said Harbin hotly. "It was Mishra who did that!"

Titania did not listen. Instead, she tilted her head, as if listening to music that no one else could hear.

Then the queen of the elves stiffened in her chair and screamed.

Harbin took a step back, along with most of the court. The queen's face was contorted, and Harbin could see parts of her wooden mask splinter as she screamed. Leaves fell from her vine-covered dress and grassy tendrils spun out of control. She twisted once in her chair and was still.

Harbin was suddenly very much aware of where he was: deep in the heart of unknown territory. Surrounded by beings who had fought his work since its inception. Protected from them only by the word of their monarch, who had just screamed in pain as he yelled at her.

Harbin did not turn around, but he imagined every elf, centaur, and pixie in the forested vault was drawing his weapon.

But as quick as Titania's attack came on, it passed. The queen stirred and collected herself, and Harbin saw that her green garments were regrowing themselves.

Yet when she looked at him, Harbin saw that her eyes were deep, tired pools, and she suddenly seemed worn and haggard.

"You and the other invaders stink," she said simply and quietly. "You smell of metal and machine oil. Both sides despoil our land, and both sides will be driven out. Argoth is not yours, Child of the Artificer. It belongs to neither your father nor to his brother. Go now. Tell the other humans this message: Leave now or be driven from our shores."

Titania lowered her head. The Speaker said, "This audience is over."

Harbin wanted to press his point, to warn Titania further of the danger of Mishra, but her mannequin was already unraveling, the vines and grasses pulling away from the form, rotting as they separated. Finally all that lay on the throne was a jade mask.

"You will be protected as long as you remain within our lands," said the Speaker. "Now you must go."

Harbin and the two other pilots were escorted from the halls, Harbin walking alongside the Speaker. There were so many questions here, so much said and not said. He had failed in that the Argivians needed the wood and ore and he could not get permission. But he knew that permission would never come from this strange queen. What device did she use to animate her puppet? And was she present, even now, watching them?

There was another human face in the crowd, his face grim and angry. Harbin thought of the brown-robed men and asked the Speaker, "There are men here?"

The Speaker nodded but did not lose a stride. "There are. But they are no friends of yours, Artifice Child. They hate artifacts and all devices and fled to our isle to escape them years ago."

Harbin thought for a moment and said, "That is how you know about Urza and Mishra, then? They are refugees from the mainland."

The Speaker smiled. "The Druids of Citanul came here centuries ago, Child of the Machine Maker."

"But you said they hated artifacts."

"Do you think," said the Speaker, "that yours is the first empire to rely on the tyranny of the machine? Or the last?" When Harbin did not answer, the Speaker asked, "Why did you bring your flying devices here?"

"The ornithopters?" Harbin said. "It was the quickest way. And it would not harm your precious woods."

"It was a show of power," said the Speaker.

Harbin felt embarrassed. The Speaker was correct. But after seeing what the queen could do, he did not feel particularly powerful.

"Yes, it was," said the Speaker smoothly. "A small show of power. Now allow us a small show of power in response."

They emerged in the glen where the ornithopters had landed. All five machines were there, as were the two Argivians left behind as guards. There were the elvish warriors and more of the brown-cloaked humans. The Druids of Citanul.

"Observe," said the Speaker, and signaled the brown-robed humans.

At once the druids began a chant. It was a low chant, almost felt in the bones more than heard through the ears, and it used the language the Speaker had employed when he spoke to Titania. Their voices rose, then fell, then split into separate choruses, weaving and interweaving among themselves.

The pilots reached for their weapons, but Harbin held up a hand to stop them. None of the elves moved.

Then the ornithopters began to move of their own volition. At first Harbin thought it to be a simple breeze that caught the wings, but their wings began to unfurl to their full limits. Beyond those limits. As Harbin watched, the pulleys along the wings ripped from their grommets and the wires snapped, their sharp twangings punctuating the monks' chants.

One of the pilots shouted and ran for his craft, but it was too late. The ornithopters rose like bucking horses, flapping their dying wings against the ground. For a moment, they looked like wounded, living birds. Then they crumbled in on themselves, their struts and fabric unable to withstand their own sudden animation.

Where the ornithopters had been, there were now five piles of broken wood and hide. Already, the elves and druids were beginning to back away, disappearing into the trees.

"Your show of power. Our show of power," said the Speaker. "Know that we could have done it once you were in the air, but you are under Titania's protection until you leave our lands. You have nothing to fear until you reach the lands you have despoiled."

The Speaker smiled, and it was a mean, self-satisfied smile. "Have a pleasant walk back, human." And he was gone as well.

* * * * *

Mishra had moved faster than Ashnod had assumed. He was gone by the time she arrived in Zegon, gone with the invasion fleet bent on wresting the new land from Urza. Only through personal favors and equally personal threats did Ashnod gain passage on one of the supply ships following in the wake of the initial attack.

She could see the new land before it appeared on the horizon. It was marked by a thick column of smoke that grew as her ship passed through the storms, a dark beacon calling her forward.

The shore was a blackened wreckage of burned stumps, jutting from the ground like rotted teeth. Already the tree line had been pushed nearly to the horizon, and Mishra's factories were already assembled and working full tilt to convert those resources that survived into useful weapons.

Ashnod moved among the wreckage and discovered signs that the occupation had not gone unopposed. There was a shattered hulk that had been a dragon engine not far from the docks at which she had landed, and she passed an open grave filled with the bodies of transmogrants and what looked like elves.

She wanted to seek out Mishra first but upon landing thought better of it. Mishra had banished her and might not be overjoyed to see her. Better to check with the hierarchy first.

She went looking for Hajar instead. She found him, two miles upshore, trying to unmire a war machine that had sunk, axles-deep, in a swamp.

Hajar looked at Ashnod stonily, then nodded. It was a warmer welcome than she had expected. Perhaps the older man was mellowing.

"You are back," he said shortly.

"New horizons, new opportunities," she replied. "Any chance of getting to see his nibs?" She laid her backpack on the ground and hefted a heavy box. "I brought presents."

Hajar said nothing to her but turned the bother of extricating the titanic machine over to an underling. He started walking farther up the shore, and Ashnod followed, carrying both box and backpack. Hajar offered to carry neither, and Ashnod noted there was a slight stoop in the old Fallaji's shoulders as he moved. The years of watching Mishra's back were finally telling on the lean-faced bodyguard.

They arrived at last at a blockhouse, a huge fortress of rough-hewn lumber and unmortared stone. It looked as if this had seen some fighting as well, for the outer walls were scorched by flame.

"I take it that there have been problems," Ashnod said.

Hajar nodded. "The land is occupied and must be taken, inch by inch."

Ashnod nodded in turn. "Any chance of talking with the original owners?"

"A leader of their people appeared here soon after we arrived," said Hajar. "A green woman, wrapped in leaves and coiled vines."

"How did it go?" asked Ashnod, already knowing the answer.

Hajar sighed. A small sigh, but a sigh nonetheless. "Mishra ordered the dragon engines to set her on fire. She screamed and went up like kindling. Then the attacks began again."

"How is he?" she asked as they passed within the heavy gates of the blockhouse. "Mishra, I mean."

"He is," said Hajar, then looked at Ashnod. She saw there was a softening in his lean visage. "And he is not. You will understand when you see him again."

The throne room of the blockhouse was a rough, frontier affair, a rude dais made of slabs of stone with a captain's chair from one of the ships serving as a throne. It was flanked by two Gixians, one with an artificial arm, the other with a steel plate bolted to his face across the eyes.

Hajar remained by the door, and Ashnod noted the pecking order had changed in her absence.

There was Mishra himself. He was thinner and more muscular than he had been when last she had seen him. What mass he retained was now muscles rippling beneath his robes. His hair and beard seemed darker too. Ashnod assumed that the older man had at last surrendered to vanity and used some Zegoni ointment to hide his age.

But his eyes were as alive as they had ever been, as curious and as seeking. Ashnod had forgotten that look over the years.

He still had the razor-sharp ankh of Sarinth tucked in his belt, even though that land was in full rebellion. Ashnod made a mental note not to mention it, as it might still be a sore point. She set the box down and the pack next to it and prostrated herself before the Artifice Qadir.

"I bring you greetings, O Master of the Desert and now Master of the Sea," she said, rising without waiting for him to command it.

"I thought I had banished you," said Mishra grimly. "I said I would have you slain if you were found within my territories again."

"So you did, Most Sage and Just One," said Ashnod, hewing to the formal modes of address until she could discern Mishra's temperament. "And if you truly held this land, I would never choose to risk your wrath by appearing before your court. But it seems there is some doubt about that control at the moment, and I offer my aid to make this land yours."

She looked at Mishra's face, seeking some smile, some recognition that he was glad to see her back. All she saw was a grim fire burning behind his eyes.

"What offer of aid is this?" he said.

"I have wandered far during my . . . extended leave," said Ashnod, opening the top of the chest. "I've learned many things and found many items that may be of use to you."

She pulled a copperish bowl from the chest. "I believe I can use this simple sylex to determine our future," she told him with a smile, holding it aloft.

Mishra did not shift position as he regarded Ashnod and her gift. "You bring me metal dishes?" he said. "Have you become a coppersmith in your absence?"

Ashnod lowered the bowl, disappointed. "More than just a serving dish, Most Powerful One. There are forces in the world beyond those of our mere machines. I have endeavored to master those forces."

"Magic," interrupted Mishra.

"Pardon?" asked Ashnod, startled.

"Magic," repeated the qadir, "like the fools of the Union of Terisia City believed in."

"For want of a better word—" began Ashnod, but Mishra cut her off.

"Magic," he said a third time, "does not exist. It is all tricks, done with smoke, mirrors, and other devices. I have done such tricks. So have you, to fool the credulous. Magic is not real. Do not bother me with such trivialities."

"Most Comprehending One," said Ashnod, "I do not think that the power of the scholars of the ivory towers is trivial—"

Mishra laughed. It was a sharp, barking laugh that Ashnod did not like at all. "I never thought I would live to see the day the great and powerful Ashnod, Ashnod the Uncaring, would become a simple trading-camp charlatan, seeking to con her way back into my good graces."

Ashnod felt her face redden at the rebuke. This was not going the way she had expected at all. She said, "I can offer some small demonstration—"

Again Mishra interrupted. "Save your demonstrations for the gullible, Ashnod. I know your patter well. And I have missed it. But I have changed in your absence, even if you have not." He looked at her, long and hard, and Ashnod, for the first time in many, many years, wondered what he was thinking.

Finally Mishra said, "You are welcome to remain with my forces, Ashnod, or go as you see fit. I lift your banishment. But know that your actions will be watched." There was a slight bob of his head toward one of the priests. "If there is any sign of betrayal, I will personally turn you into a transmogrant. Am I clear?"

"As glass," said Ashnod, frowning. "But may we at least speak in less formal surroundings?"

"You will come when I call," said Mishra, "or you will not come at all. You are brilliant in your own way, Ashnod, and I am sure that, returned to true work, to building artifacts, your talent will blossom again. You may go."

Ashnod hesitated a moment, and Mishra said again, "You may go." There was granite in his voice.

Ashnod bowed again, and retreated from the room. Hajar followed her.

"Well, that went badly enough," she said, then turned to Hajar. "Things have gone downhill around here while I was gone."

"It has been so noted," said Hajar simply.

Ashnod wanted to ask more, to find out how influential the Gixians were, who really ran things behind Mishra's throne, when the door behind them opened. The priest with the steel-plated eyes emerged and bowed, slight and perfunctory, before Ashnod.

"We are interested in your bowl," said the priest.

"That trivial piece of magic?" said Ashnod, raising an eyebrow, "Magic your lord does not believe in?"

The priest bowed again, and Ashnod swore she heard something click and whine as he did so. "The brotherhood is always open to new avenues, and, if they prove true, can present them properly to His Most August and Serene Personage. The bowl, please."

"I think not," said Ashnod.

The priest stared at her, if an eyeless thing could be said to stare at anyone. "We have been charged with keeping an eye on you, former apprentice. We have Mishra's ear, and we can be your best allies in his court." He smiled, and every other tooth was missing. "Or your worst enemies. The bowl, please."

Ashnod looked at Hajar, and said, "Is this the way of the court, now, where petty muggings are common in its halls?"

Hajar did not say anything. Or rather, he looked at the floor beneath them, and his look spoke volumes.

"I see," Ashnod said, and handed the chest over to the priest. "Please accept this gift as a token of my appreciation," she said through clenched teeth. "May there be someone present to administer aid when you choke on it."

The priest took the chest and gave her another toothy smile. "We knew you would show wisdom," he said, "once the situation was made clear to you." And he was gone, back into Mishra's throne room.

Hajar did not say anything after that, but he did not have to. He escorted Ashnod to a tent city where most of the court was camped. She would have a private tent, and, as the qadir had directed, the permission to come and go as she pleased. If she needed anything, she should ask him. And then he was gone as well.

Ashnod lowered herself on her bunk and shook her head. She had returned, but it was not the return of the prodigal that she had hoped for. And Hajar was right. Mishra was both very much as she remembered him and very different.

She wondered if she should stay and decided that she should check out where else she could run before bolting.

She pulled her backpack onto the bunk and opened it, pulling the

Golgothian Sylex from its depths, still wrapped in her clothing. Mishra had been right about one thing, of course. She had become a coppersmith in the years that she was gone. She had become many other things as well. But she had remained a suspicious enough person to bring the duplicate of her own crafting to present to Mishra. It was Ashnod's sylex that the priests of Gix now held, while she retained the original.

Ashnod ran her finger along the edge of the ancient, rune-etched bowl, and the light dimmed slightly around her.

Chapter 32

The Road to Apocalypse

Harbin and his men arrived, footsore but otherwise unharmed, at the edge of Titania's territory. The elven queen had been honorable in her declaration of protection. Harbin felt they had been watched every step of the way, but there were no incidents with the natives. Even the animals seemed to stay clear of them as they trudged the long miles back to the base through the oppressive humidity found beneath the forest canopy.

It was clear when they arrived at the border of her majesty's territory. The forest ended as suddenly as a cliff. One side of the border was the lush, green, and humid world of Titania. On the other was the land of Harbin's father and of the Argivians.

It had been clear-cut, with every tree sawed down and hauled away. Smooth stumps marked the former forest like gravestones, and every bit of detritus and foliage had been stripped. Off in the distance, a huge mound of leaves and vines was smoking lazily, and beyond that, Harbin could see large machines ripping up the earth itself, searching for mineral wealth beneath.

It looked more like the Argive he had grown up in than the Argoth that the elves claimed as their own, Harbin realized. His people had taken the land and made it their own, for good or ill.

Harbin stepped out into the open; the ground immediately became hard-packed, and the sun beat down on him like a hammer. He blinked in the brightness, as each of his men in turn stepped into the sunlight.

Behind them, from the forest, there was the war cry of elvish voices.

As one, the five men bolted across the wreckage of stumps, hoping to make the cover of the burning mounds before the elves caught up with them.

* * * * *

In his lair in Koilos, Gix watched his entertainment through the eyes of a minion.

She was one of the unfortunates among his brotherhood, one of those who had failed the test of the machine. Her limbs had been replaced by servos and mechanisms, but the work was shoddy, quickly failed, and could not be replaced. She lay like a broken puppet at the foot of his throne, her useless prosthetics cast in all directions. She had cried about her fate for a long time until Gix tired of that and sewed her lips shut.

Still she had her uses. Gix gripped her skull and tapped into her mind, watching the contest before them through the filter of her emotion and pain.

Two of the *su-chis* were battling. Gix controlled them as he controlled the woman before him, but did so at a distance. With practice over the long years in this strange land and with the aid of few devices of his own creation, he had become very good at commanding the hearts and souls of these machines.

The *su-chis* stood two paces apart and flailed at each other. One bore a length of chain, the other a club made of the leg of another *su-chi* it had previously beaten in battle. Gix commanded the two automatons to beat each other to pieces, and, loyal to their god, they did so without complaint or comment.

There was no poetry to this battle, for both machines stood their ground, neither retreating nor dodging. Instead they relentlessly hammered away at each other, and the cavern walls echoed with the clang of metal on metal.

As they thundered at each other, Gix's observer watched, flinching with each rasping clash of metal. Occasionally a part of one of the *su-chis* would fly off, and she would start suddenly, her skull firmly in the grip of the demon.

Gix savored the feeling, the sudden rush of adrenaline through the priest's body. Without her senses, her reactions, the battle was merely a study of forces and impacts, of metal and resistance. But through human eyes, the two inhuman machines took on different appearances, and Gix relished the difference.

The combatants were tireless, but in the end the metal itself succumbed before the mindless will of the participants. The chain-wielding automaton wrapped the length of chain around its opponent's neck and snapped its head from its pivots. The head of blue-metal wires bounced off its support toward the throne, and Gix's observer flinched at that as well.

Meanwhile, the now-blind automaton attempted to hammer its opponent with its club. Its opponent let go of the chain and blocked the attack with an upraised arm, which bent under the force of the blow. Sparks began to issue from the joints of the former chain-wielder from the impact, yet it moved smoothly under the blow and reached up with both hands, driving its fingers into the clubber's chest.

The former chain-wielder pulled its hands apart and ripped its opponent's chest open. There was a shower of sparks as the leg-wielder collapsed in on itself, lacking anything at its center to hold it together. Again the observer flinched and tried to turn away, but Gix held her head tightly and commanded her to keep her eyes open, to drink in the eye-searing sparks of the device's destruction.

In an instant it was over. The chain-wielder towered over the broken pile of scrap metal that had been its opponent. Gix felt the fear and revulsion in his observer and drank it like a fine wine.

He let go of her, withdrawing the talons back into himself as she collapsed into a twitching pile at the foot of the throne. Gix rose and strode to the victorious automaton. Sparks rained from its joints, and the battering it had received had caved in part of its skull.

Gix held out a finger and pushed against the victor's chest. The *suchi*, unbalanced, tilted backward, and smashed against the hard stone floor of the cavern. Its arms and legs separated under the blow, and its chest heaved in one last shower of sparks; then it was quiet.

"Unworthy," he said as an epitaph.

Gix looked at the two fallen devices. So very much like the brothers they were: mindless, easily manipulated, and relentless in their assault. And in the end the victor would be vulnerable to Gix.

"Soon," said the demon through lipless teeth. "Very soon."

* * * * *

Queen Titania was dying, thought Gwenna. The queen was dying, and the land was dying with her.

A continual haze pervaded the surviving forest now as more and more of the land fell to assaults of the brothers. From one side Urza advanced, from the other Mishra, and they left nothing in their wake. With each glade that fell, with each knot of trees that was lumbered and consumed by their machines, with each mountain that was strip-mined, the land grew weaker. With the land, the queen grew weaker, and with the queen, the people.

Gwenna could feel it, and so could the others. Their tie to the land, the soft and reassuring touch that they felt in the core of their being, was gone. There was only emptiness. Emptiness, and the smoke of the burning pyres.

Titania had retreated to the most hidden part of her kingdom to plan the last assault, Gwenna had been told. But she had seen the queen before her retreat and knew that Titania would not emerge from her sanctuary again. Her majesty was harridan-haggard and exhausted, for each blow against the land was a blow against her. Gwenna knew that Titania was lost to them and with her the wisdom of Gaea herself and the goddess's protection.

Gwenna would not stand aside and wait for news to come of Titania's surrender, nor for a final battle after their forces were so weakened they would be ineffective. They could stand against one of the invaders, but not both at once. She spoke with others among the elves and decided they must make their own assault.

Then the red-haired human woman appeared to her group of plotters and gave them the opportunity to strike back.

Now she and a legion of comrades had gathered on the denuded shores of Argoth, an area where the despoiling armies had passed but not remained. They waited on the shores for one set of enemies, in order to strike out against the others.

The others rounded the headlands in their strange ships of metal and wood, their internal engines shooting sparks into the night sky. Some of the elves muttered among themselves, and Gwenna heard the word, "abominations." But she would ride in the belly of these abominations if it meant she could fight the invaders on their home ground.

The larger ships remained in the deep waters of the bay while smaller craft came and beached on the shores. The red-haired woman with the ornate staff led the way, followed by a group of warriors swathed in cloth. These later warriors were led by an old human with a narrow face.

The red-haired woman bowed curtly and said in Gwenna's tongue, "Are you prepared for the voyage?"

Gwenna looked at her people. There was nervousness among them, but also anger. Anger at having their homes destroyed and their lands ripped asunder by the invaders. She nodded.

"Then you'd best board and board quickly. As long as you are on shore, you are vulnerable," said the red-haired woman. "Fortunately, the storms offshore have abated, so it should be safe sailing."

The storms were abating because Titania was dying, thought Gwenna, but she said nothing. Instead she merely nodded and gave the signal to her forces. They hefted their weapons and began climbing into the boats. Gwenna paused for a moment and listened as the red-haired woman and the old man made their good-byes. Gwenna did not understand what they were saying and wondered for a moment if the two had been lovers and were now parting, possibly forever.

The thought appealed to Gwenna as she climbed over the gunwales of the boat and took her first steps away from Argoth and into the heart of the enemy land.

"This is risky," said Hajar, as the elves in their armor of shellacked wood clambered into the boats.

"Everything is risky," said Ashnod. "But we need to strike at Urza's boatyards before he can resupply further. We do not have the manpower, but these forest children are mad enough at him to do the job for us."

"You should come along," said Hajar.

Ashnod shook her head. "Mishra will accept your departure, I think, but if I leave, he will come after me."

"He will be angry," said the old Fallaji.

"He will be delighted," said Ashnod, "when you succeed."

"I'll bring the boats back," said Hajar.

Ashnod shook her head again. "Why? So they may be used to bring supplies from Zegon? There is nothing left there. It's all been melted down and chopped down and converted and sent here. We're at the end of things, Hajar. It is now or never."

Hajar was silent for a moment, then said stiffly, "I have missed your way of thinking. The Brotherhood of Gix is not nearly as comforting."

Ashnod said, "I will tell Mishra when he finds out that this was my idea but that you insisted on leading the raid so things would work out."

Hajar chewed over the idea, then managed a small smile. "It has been an honor working with you. You think like a man," he said.

Ashnod's fingers tightened around her staff, but she said, "Thank you, Hajar. I accept that as the compliment you mean it to be."

The boats were loaded, and Hajar was gone, rowing out to the larger craft. Ashnod watched the sparkling lights of the craft until they sailed again around the headland and were lost. Then she began a long walk back to camp, wondering if Mishra would even notice that Hajar and the ships were gone.

* * * * *

"He's sending me home," snarled Harbin, settling down in the camp chair across the tent from Tawnos.

Tawnos looked up from his work but said nothing.

"He says I am needed more back in Penregon," continued the younger man.

Tawnos tightened a nut on the large construct he was working on and said, "He's right."

"Of course he's right," snapped Harbin. "He's always right. That's what being Lord Protector is all about, isn't it? Being right."

Tawnos stood up and regarded his handiwork. "This looks about ready. What do you think?"

Harbin looked at the object. It looked like a large crate, seven feet in length and three in height and depth. It was unremarkable, save that it was made of metal and had a great, heavy lid.

"Looks like a coffin," said the younger man.

Tawnos took a step back, looked at the construct, and smiled. "Yes, I suppose it does. All the better, I guess."

"What does this one do?" said Harbin, putting his irritation with his father aside.

"When I was Mishra's . . . guest, they kept me in a cell forgotten by the rest of the world," said Tawnos. As he spoke, he flexed his right hand, as if to shake out an ancient pain. "I'd been thinking about it and came up with this. It functions with some of the same mechanisms that power the old amulets of Kroog, along with Ashnod's staff from Zegon."

"Uh-huh," said Harbin. "And what does it do?"

"It will keep a body within in stasis—effectively asleep for as long as the power stones operate within it or until the box is opened." Tawnos looked at Harbin. "You see, I've been thinking about what your father will do with his brother once he defeats him. I don't think he could bring himself to kill him, but neither could he suffer him to live. This"—Tawnos patted the top of the lid—"is the third option."

Harbin smiled and it was a warm smile. "Uncle Tawnos, you are now inventing answers to questions no one has even posed yet. You assume we're going to defeat Mishra or take him alive if we do."

"Of course we're going to win," said Tawnos. "We did not come this far to give up."

"I wonder," said Harbin.

Tawnos blinked at the younger man. "You have doubts?"

Harbin shook his head. "Not I, but in talking with Father . . . " He shook his head again. "He seems, well, not despondent, but weary, tired."

"Resigned," said Tawnos. "His has been a long road, and it will finally end soon. I think he knows it. It will end, one way or the other."

"And when it does end," said Harbin, "I want to be here. One way or the other."

Tawnos shook his head. "The elves have gotten their hands on boats and are marauding their way up the coast. We need a good leader to rally the garrison units against them. You are that leader."

Harbin said nothing.

"You wanted the opportunity to lead," said Tawnos, "and the price of leadership is that you have to keep leading, even if you would rather be somewhere else."

Harbin slowly nodded. "You and Father have already talked about this, correct?"

Tawnos shrugged. "He has sought my advice regarding your well-being."

Harbin looked up at the older, taller man, and said, "Will you look after him? Father, I mean. After his well-being?"

"I always do," the Master Scholar replied.

"No," said the younger man, "I mean this. When we parted, he said something that's bothered me. He said 'Tell your mother to remember me as I tried to be, not as I was.' He doesn't think he's going to live through this."

Harbin looked at the ground, and Tawnos said, "I'll look after him. I've been doing it for years, in one way or the other."

Harbin sighed. "I told him I was wrong, too."

"Wrong about wanting to stay at his side?" asked Tawnos.

Harbin shook his head. "A long time ago, he asked me what I thought about the Union's work. About magic. I told him I doubted that it even existed. But now, after seeing the elves and their queen and what they can do without any devices at all, I'm unsure. I feel responsible for convincing him that magic did not exist."

"I don't think anyone ever convinced Urza of anything he did not believe in himself," said Tawnos. "Just remember that there is always something that you don't know, that you can afford to learn."

"Is that why you're still with Father after all these years?" asked Harbin.

"Probably," said Tawnos. "But I have learned much from a lot of people. I guess I assumed that I never knew it all to start with and was more willing to listen to others."

Harbin smiled at Tawnos's words. The older man went to the far side of the tent and rummaged around, finally pulling out a short wand. The device was about the length of Harbin's forearm and had a thick, bulbous tip like an orange. "Here," he said. "A going-away present."

Harbin looked at the device. "What is it?"

"Another machine I developed some time back. It masks the user from the sensory devices of the artifact-creatures. This was a prototype. It doesn't seem to work on the larger beings, but it will help if there are any transmogrants around."

Harbin smiled. "Still trying to protect me, Uncle Tawnos? No, you keep the wand. You'll probably need it more than I do, where I'm going."

"So you will be going?" said Tawnos.

Harbin held out his hands in mock surrender. "Of course!" The younger man gave a smile. "But once these elven marauders are taken care of, I will be back. Count on that."

"Of that I have no doubt," said Tawnos. "After all, you are your father's son."

"Of course I am," said Harbin, a tired smile spreading across his face. "Who else would I be?"

* * * * *

Mishra did not question Hajar's absence nor ask about the missing ships, nor even Ashnod herself. Instead he pushed deeper and deeper into the heartland of the island. Anything that could not be fed immediately into the foundries was killed and burned, and charnel pits dotted the countryside. The air hung heavy with the smoke of what once had been Argoth's forests. Mishra's forces moved with the smooth and relentless efficiency of a machine, mowing down everything in their path.

Finally Ashnod was summoned once more into Mishra's presence. The priests of Gix hung over his shoulder as she entered, like vultures waiting for the lion to make a fresh kill.

"You have been talking to natives of this island," said Mishra without waiting for her to bow and scrape.

Ashnod looked at the leering priests, then said, "Of course. I have been endeavoring to get them to attack Urza's forces as opposed to our own. They have a company of druidical priests that—"

Mishra interrupted as if she had said nothing after "of course." "Do you believe that they could defeat my brother's forces?"

Ashnod looked at Mishra, but his brows were in shadow, and she could not see his eyes. "No," she said simply, "I don't think they could."

"But they could weaken him," said Mishra.

"Yes," said Ashnod. "What is this about?"

Mishra's head snapped up, and Ashnod saw the fire in the man's eyes. "Urza's main position is seven days away. There is a force of elves heading toward it, which is two days away from arriving. If the elves reach my brother first, they may weaken him sufficiently, allowing me to crush him completely. Your thoughts?"

"Urza has many machines on his side," began Ashnod, but stopped as Mishra's scowl grew deeper. "Yes. If the elves attack Urza first, then he will be weakened. But he would win any direct battle with the natives."

"Thank you," said Mishra, turning away. "You may go."

"Milord," said Ashnod, "if there is to be a battle, we need to draw up the plan of assault."

"One has already been drawn up," said Mishra, and the priest gave another leering smile. Ashnod knew who had done the advising in this matter. "We will gather our forces and move in behind the elves, ready to attack after they do. You may go."

Ashnod looked at the priest, then bowed low to Mishra and left his headquarters, muttering as she did so.

That evening there was a celebration among the Brotherhood of Gix. There was a bonfire in their camp and much chanting and singing. Ashnod considered trying to reach Mishra then but decided against it. The Gixians had probably left at least one of their number behind to watch over the Artifice Qadir.

The red-haired woman sat on her bunk, holding the old pack that still contained the Golgothian Sylex. She was to have no role in the battle, it seemed. And no role in whatever would follow it. She thought for a moment and looked into the darkness, the only sound the cheers of the priests of Gix.

Ashnod would have a role, whether Mishra wanted it or not. She pulled some parchment from her pack and a stylus and began composing a letter to an old friend.

* * * * *

The elves never stood a chance, thought Tawnos, sadly. All the valor and bravery and devotion in the world did not matter when you were armed with wooden armor and bone weapons facing remorseless metal and unthinking stone.

They came in waves—elves, sprites, centaurs, and treefolk. Some were riding great wildcats, and others were commanding herds of slugs that wrapped around the legs of an artifact and sucked its energy dry. The sky above rumbled and lanced down bolts of electrical fury, and the ground replied in the thunder of feet moving across the hard-backed surface of the ravaged earth.

And towering above it all was a titanic figure, a living embodiment of the torn forests of Argoth. It was huge and roughly humanoid, but the mane of its hair was trees, and its body was made of the living wood, entwined upon itself to form massive muscles. It born a stone sword that seemed to be forged from the heart of the mountain itself.

Tawnos remembered what Harbin had said about the elven magics, and knew that the elves had somehow animated the power of the forest and bent it to their will.

Urza's forces were quickly arrayed in defense: avengers, sentinels, tetravi, and triskelions, insect-headed mechanical soldiers armed with weapons of new steel and statues crafted out of primal clay. Word was sent down the line for reinforcements as the first wave struck the Argivian lines.

The elves were slaughtered. For every mechanical device that fell, thirty elves perished; for every ornithopter that was brought down, there were fifty pixies. The treefolk screamed as they went up in flames, one after another, and still the elves came on. Tawnos was at the center of the line and felt it begin to waver, then to give under the relentless assault. Tawnos called for more support, but the auxiliary units were already committed to the flanks.

If the center did not hold, then the army would collapse in on itself.

The sky rumbled again, and the ground responded with a deeper cry. And Tawnos knew the reinforcements had arrived.

Urza had his own titan, crafted in the mountains of Sardia before the dwarves betrayed them. It was a hulking giant of stone and metal that towered over everything in its path. A single stride was a hundred feet, and crows and carrion birds had nested in its head. Urza had brought it to Argoth on a great barge, and it had acted as a lighthouse to guide the ships to safe harbor past the storms.

Now it met the only other being on the island that was its equal.

The tree monster bellowed a challenge, and while the colossus was silent, it turned and bore down on its opponent. The two locked in combat that dwarfed the lesser beings around them. The center of both lines broke to give the titans room to brawl, and those elves and devices that were too slow to get out of the way were smashed into the earth.

The stone sword arced through the air and bit deeply into the colossus's side. The great animate statue shuddered, and plates of metal cascaded from its joints like scales shed from a snake. The forest titan reared back for another assault, but the colossus was too fast for it. It grabbed the attacker's arm as it descended and smoothly and effortlessly twisted it from its socket. There was the sound of an entire jungle screaming as the forest beast's arm was ripped loose and sent spinning across the shallow valley.

The forest titan was not to be denied, for as it lost one arm, it swung heavily with the other, a massive hand made of wood and rock. This smashed against the side of the colossus's head, and most of the giant's face became a cloud of dust.

The colossus did not need its head to think or react. It grappled the front of the forest titan with one hand. With the other, it reared back and slammed a fist into the creature's chest like a battering ram assaulting an enemy gate.

The forest thing's body exploded in a rain of splinters that cut down troops within a hundred yards of the brawl. Its legs thundered to the ground in two separate directions, and its head rolled backward and plummeted, screaming as it fell.

That broke the elves' morale completely. Their assault fell apart with their gigantic leader, and they fled from the battle, dropping their weapons as they ran. Those machines that could pursue did so, cutting down the forest-dwellers with neither remorse nor pity.

Yet the forest titan had succeeded, for the colossus could not recover from its attack. The force of the blow ripped the stone statue's own arm from its moorings, and it cascaded to the ground with the sound of an avalanche. Bolts of lightning shot from its metal-plated joints as the great statue slowly dropped to its knees, then sprawled forward, facedown, across the small stream that now ran red with blood and black with oil. The valley shook as it struck the earth.

Tawnos watched the rout and felt sadness. It was not the elves' fault that they were forced to fight for a land they could not hold. They were merely in the wrong place at the wrong time. Had their land remained secret, they would have been spared all this. But once revealed, they were cast in the maelstrom of war with the rest of them. He shook his head as a last group of elves and centaurs tried to rally on a mound of fallen triskelions, only be to overrun by soldiers.

All that was left after that was the cleanup. The bodies were collected and burned, and the artifacts were checked and repaired. The colossus was beyond help, but plates from its hide could be stripped and used for other creatures.

Urza arrived in the evening with additional reinforcements, along with more artificers and mechanics to held with the repairs. Though the elven force was almost entirely wiped out, it had taken a heavy toll on the Argivians.

Then the scout arrived with the bad news. Mishra's force had been spotted five days' march to the west and was making for their position.

Tawnos argued they should pull back, at least to the safety of the coastal forts, but Urza would hear nothing of it.

"Strip the forts within four days' march of here," he said. "We will fight here."

"We are battered and tired," noted Tawnos.

"Our machines are battered, but they cannot be tired," said Urza. "What noncombatant living beings we have we can evacuate in time. Let this battle be at a time and place of our choosing."

Tawnos looked at Urza and saw that Harbin had been right. Urza seemed resigned to battling his brother, regardless of the outcome. It would all end here, one way or another.

The scout also brought a message for Tawnos. He did not say where he had got it, but Tawnos knew who it was from the moment he saw the handwriting.

"Something important?" asked Urza. "Has Harbin had success against the raiders?"

"Message from an old friend," Tawnos said, scowling. Urza was already poring over the maps of the surrounding terrain, and only nodded. Tawnos pocketed the message, and Urza said nothing more on the matter.

Tawnos thought of the date, and said, "If they take five days to get here and attack by the sixth, it will be the last day of the year. Perhaps we can begin the new year with a world at peace, when we win."

"The last day," said Urza softly. "And on the last day, we're equal."

"Pardon?" said Tawnos.

Urza shook his head. "Just an old thought. You get to an advanced age and that's all you have anymore. Old thoughts, and regrets."

* * * * *

In Koilos, the demon Gix heard the chants of his priests in Argoth and knew that it was time to go to them.

All the pieces were in place. The one brother was wounded, and his sibling was bearing down on him. The survivor would be battered beyond belief and in no shape to defend himself. Neither was prepared for the surprise the demon had prepared for them.

Gix smiled as a small point of light appeared near his throne. It grew until it had formed into a disk, like a reflecting pool that had been turned on its side. There was the smell of smoke and the distant sound of crashing gears.

He looked around at his domain within the cavern, at the scattered parts of the demolished *su-chi*. He would soon return in triumph.

He looked at his observer, the poor priestess whose mechanical limbs had rejected her. She implored him with her eyes, for she no longer could speak.

The disk was almost fully formed, and Gix did not have much time. He walked over to her and cradled her head in his hands. His talons pierced the flesh of her scalp and drove through the bone into the brain itself.

Gix opened every synapse in the woman's mind and let the holy fire fill her as every part of her brain fired at once. She jerked and spasmed in his hands, and then was still. He let go of her, and she slumped to the floor, a puppet with its strings cut.

Gix noticed that there was a smile on her sewn-together lips, and he smiled in return as he stepped through the gate and into the final battle between the brothers.

Chapter 33

Tawnos and Ashnod

The Last Battle began before dawn, as the overcast sky was just beginning to lighten. The remaining mechanics on both sides began activating their destructive artifacts, and the thrumming of their engines was a bugle call to both sides. The vibrations grew on both sides as more wings were limbered, treads were checked, and leg armatures were put through their final preparations.

With the first light of dawn, the dragon engines surged forward, forming a wedge and bearing down on the Argivian position. Behind them lumbered two huge flanks of transmogrants, and the remaining Fallaji soldiers decked in Ashnod's spiked armor. Bringing up the rear were Mishra's great ground-shattering engines and war machines, protecting the flanks of the wedge. Behind these lines rose a dozen winged dragon engines, bugling battle cries and breathing flames into the morning air.

Urza had guessed his brother would try a direct assault, counting on the weakened state of the Argivian forces after their battle with the Argothians. For that reason he positioned all Tawnos's mobile fortifications, the triskelions, in the center, supported by war engines of the Lord Protector's own design. The rest of his units were broken into smaller groups of clay statues, avengers, and sentinels. Shapeshifting automatons, made of primal clay worked over adjustable frames, held the flanks. The sky was alive with ornithopters and ornibombers, protected by tetravi and clockwork avians that swarmed upward toward the great flying dragon engines of the enemy.

The armies crashed together with a scream of shattering metal. The dragon engines on the ground moved among the triskelions, hammering them with flame and savage blows, but the great fortresses refused to fall. Urza's war machines were smashed beneath the treads of the dragon engines, slowing them while hordes of avengers and clay statues clung to their flanks seeking to break through their armor to the driving motors within and destroy them.

The dragon engines screamed, and the transmogrants fell upon Urza's flanks. The remade troops were picking at the clay statues like carnivorous apes, but Urza's newer shapeshifting automatons were too much for the reanimated forms of men and elves. Old blood and new oil splattered on the combatants as they slammed into each other.

In the air the clockwork avians swooped and dived at the dragon engines, seeking the weakness in their armor that would allow them to penetrate and spread packets of explosives within. Occasionally there was a metallic scream as an ornibomber or dragon engine lost structural integrity and could no longer remain aloft. The huge engines sprawled into the seething madness below, crushing both ally and enemy beneath their sprawling hulks.

On the far right flank, Tawnos led a squad of Yotian soldiers, heavily armored and looking more like beetles than humanoid automatons, looking for a way into the rear echelon of Mishra's forces. He held aloft the sensory-dampening wand that he had days earlier offered Harbin, and none of the other combatants seemed to notice him or his patrol.

There was motion ahead of him, and Tawnos barked a command. The soldiers formed a wedge behind the old scholar, raising blades made of tempered glass that could cut through steel. Tawnos snapped the attack command, and they lumbered forward, their servos and governing mechanisms clicking as they sought out their targets.

It was a group of priests, Gixians by their robes, and the automated soldiers fell upon them like wolves among sheep. The blades of unshatterable glass rose and fell like scythes, and the Gixians screamed as they fell beneath their razor-sharp edges.

There was the clatter of glass upon metal, and Tawnos at first assumed that the priests were wearing armor. But when he caught up with his weapons, he saw that the Gixians had replaced parts of their own bodies with machinery—large lumbering, clanking prosthetics that denied them the speed with which to escape.

Tawnos looked down at the fallen bodies and wondered if the alterations were voluntary. It smelled of Ashnod's work, but she had never modified the living, only tormented them. Was this something new in Mishra's arsenal?

That was when things started to go wrong.

There was a whirring noise behind him, the familiar whine of one of his own Yotian soldiers approaching. Tawnos half-turned, and in turning realized that the automaton had its blade poised to strike. The Master Scholar stepped back and stumbled over one of the Gixian's bodies.

The fall saved his life, for the soldier's blade cut through the air where Tawnos had been moments before. Another of the soldiers stepped up in front of Tawnos to defend him, and the two Yotian automatons began cutting each other to ribbons.

Tawnos rose slowly, the joints in his knees complaining. He looked around. All the Yotian soldiers were fighting among themselves. Their blades of tempered glass cut into each other, peeling away their heavy armor like orange skins. Already some were falling from the assault, but whether they were attackers or defenders Tawnos could not say.

Tawnos shouted a command for the unit to form up, and the machines ignored him. He shouted the command for them to cease fighting, and they ignored that as well. Finally he bellowed the order that would deactivate the units. They paid no attention to this order. The battered survivors of the contests only lurched forward to seek new targets.

Tawnos took a step back, then a second; then he was running for the center of the line. Two soldiers attempted to follow him but soon fell to fighting each other.

As Tawnos moved along the line, the story was the same. The machines on both sides had forgotten their basic orders and were lashing out at random, striking at any target in their path. He found a unit of clay statues in combat with a band of usually allied avengers, the great automatons pulling chunks of primal clay from the statues' frames. On the horizon, a pair of dragon engines had their necks entwined like mating geese, and each had its jaws wide open, attempting to bite the other's head off. The triskelions had opened fire on Urza's battle engines and on each other, and already smoke was billowing from their frames. Overhead the clockwork avians were attacking the ornithopters, and their needle-sharp beaks ripped apart the crafts' reinforced wings.

Tawnos stumbled across human bodies as well—mechanics, guards, other scholars, and Fallaji warriors. The humans had been the first to be destroyed in the rebellion of the machines.

Tawnos heard someone call his name, and there was a flash of scarlet against a black cloak. Ashnod shouted his name again, and

Tawnos waited as the woman scrabbled over the fallen body of a clay statue. She was bearing her ubiquitous staff and still carried the battered backpack she had possessed the previous evening.

"Is this your doing?" shouted Tawnos over the clashing din. A hundred yards away, a headless dragon engine was using its neck as a metallic whip to breach one of the triskelion towers.

Ashnod shook her head emphatically and shouted back, "It's affecting Mishra's devices as well. Maybe something in the way the machines are getting their commands?"

Now it was Tawnos's turn to disagree. "Nothing like this happened before. Maybe the two brothers' stones—the Mightstone and Weakstone. Could their proximity do this?"

Ashnod shouted, "You tell me. It seems as if everything with a power crystal has a mind of its own."

There was an explosion nearby. Too close. Both man and woman crouched as a fireball bloomed skyward, shaking the ground with its eruption.

"One of Mishra's war machines," yelled Ashnod.

"I'm going to get back to Urza's camp," shouted Tawnos. "Come along?"

"Thought you'd never ask," replied Ashnod.

The two headed away from the line as a great dragon engine, perhaps one of the originals Mishra had brought to Korlinda, rose over the hillock. It regarded the two beings before it as if they were insects.

"You have a command word to control that thing?" asked Tawnos.

"You think it would listen?" replied Ashnod.

The dragon engine hesitated, then turned away, moving back into the heart of the battle.

"Something you did?" said Tawnos, but Ashnod only shook her head. Then a third voice spoke up.

"No, that was me."

He stepped into view, and Tawnos saw a creature of nightmares. He was as tall as Tawnos, with long coils that sprang from the back of his skull-like head and twitched of their own volition. His body was constructed entirely of struts and cables held together by sinews of flesh, which twisted like muscles as it moved. He was the ultimate automaton.

"Demon!" shouted Ashnod.

The creature laughed, and it was a harsh, clicking sound. "Is that what you call one who just saved you from your master's devices? Yes, I can control it, even if you masters can't. I can control most of these

393

creatures now, and when they are done slaying each other, I will take the strongest ones back with me to Phyrexia."

Ashnod dropped the pack and hoisted her staff with both hands. "Get back!" she said.

The demon laughed again. "Now is the time to pack up the toys and go home. Urza and Mishra will die today, and with them fail their hopes and their legacy." He paused for a moment, then added, "And their students."

The demon crouched to leap, but Ashnod was faster. She brought up the end of her skull-tipped wand, and multicolored energies surged forth from the tip.

The creature staggered under the force of the blow but did not fall. "You've grown more powerful," he snarled, but his words were forced.

"I've been practicing," said Ashnod. Tawnos noticed that her teeth were gritted as well. "Tawnos," she shouted, "take the backpack."

Tawnos did not move immediately, instead drawing his own weapon.

"No!" shouted Ashnod, "This one is mine. Take the backpack. In it there's a bowl. Tell Urza to fill it with memories of the land. Got it? Memories of the land."

Tawnos did not move, and Ashnod cursed. "Urza's going to need it, if this *thing* is here!"

Already the demon had risen to his feet and was staggering forward, struggling against the beam of Ashnod's staff. As Tawnos watched, his arms grew longer and his fingers sharpened into talons. Sweat was streaming down Ashnod's face.

"Go, Baby Duck!" she shouted, and redoubled her effort. The demon staggered back a few paces but then resumed his slow progress forward.

Tawnos grabbed the pack and turned, running for the base camp. Behind him the demon screamed and Ashnod cursed. Then their voices were lost in the clanging din of the mechanized battlefield.

Chapter 34

Urza and Mishra

Urza was alone at his camp. The aides and apprentices had fled or had rushed elsewhere as reinforcements or had been killed in combat. Below him, across the haze-filled valley, was a sea of mechanized ruin. Most of the smaller automatons had been smashed now, and only the great behemoths were thundering against each other. An oily smoke covered most of the land, and he could not see the opposite side of the valley any longer.

Urza removed his glasses and pinched the bridge of his nose. So much effort, he thought, for so little result.

Tawnos was out there, he knew, but Tawnos had fought before and always returned home. Harbin was at least safe from this battle, *en route* back to Penregon. Urza realized he should leave now, should pull back.

But pull back to what? The forts had been emptied to bring troops to this battle. There was nothing left in the combined kingdoms to send, even if the boatyards were still functional. There was nothing left of the land with which to build anew.

Urza looked out over the vale and shook his head. He thought of Loran's notes, and he thought of Harbin. The boy had seen what the natives of this land could do and had come to believe there were more powerful forces than just artifice and machinery. Perhaps he was right. But it was too late for that.

Perhaps it was always too late, thought Urza.

There was movement to Urza's right, and he turned, expecting to see Tawnos stepping out of the gathering smoke. Instead it was another figure, this one muscular and young, and dressed in the robes of the desert.

"Hello, Brother," said Mishra.

Urza blinked. Mishra looked unchanged from when they had last met face-to-face, at Kroog. Indeed, if anything, he looked younger, stronger, and more confident. Instinctively Urza's hand went to the Mightstone hanging from around his neck.

"You're looking unwell," said Mishra, a cold smile on his face. "Your machines have sucked the life out of you. That is your error. One of many."

Mishra took a step forward, and Urza's stone began to glow. The pouch around Mishra's neck began to shine in response. Mishra opened it with his left hand and pulled the fist-sized rock from it.

"Two of a kind," said the younger brother. "How long have we fought? And for what, Brother? For trinkets such as these?" He pulled out the ankh with his other hand. "For rulership of nations and people?"

"I just wanted to learn," said Urza, softly. "I just wanted to build my devices."

Mishra took another step forward, and Urza tried to push the younger brother back, forcing his will through the stone as he had at Kroog. As he had back in Tocasia's camp at the beginning of his life.

He was less effective this time. Mishra took another step forward, slower this time, and his smile was fixed and brittle. "You've let yourself grow old, and your light is dimming," he said. "Shall we talk one last time, or must I slay you now?"

"You still want my stone," said Urza, but it was exhausting to speak. He felt age resting on his shoulders, and the stone was a great weight around his neck.

Mishra took another step, and both brothers were bathed in the light now, the multicolored light from their own stones. The two men were only a foot apart. "You think this is only about a mere fractured gem? You think that is where the power is?" Mishra said, and there was effort in his smile. "You still covet my stone, Brother? Here, take it!"

Mishra lashed out with the stone gripped tightly in his hand. Urza dodged to one side but knew as he dodged that Mishra's attack was merely a feint. The ankh in Mishra's other hand came up suddenly, and Urza twisted and stumbled backward, trying to get out of the way of the blade. The light of his stone died as the razor-sharp edge of the ankh streaked across his forehead. Urza's face exploded in pain as he fell back.

Mishra laughed, and Urza reached up to his face. The ankh had carved a deep furrow across his forehead, which already welled with blood. The thick, sticky fluid ran down the sides of Urza's face and stained his glasses a sanguine hue.

"You never realized true power, Brother," taunted Mishra. "You never had to fight for your life. You were always safe in your world of devices and calculations. Now you see you went down the wrong path. You'll die old and alone, and I will take your lands and peoples and inventions and bend them to my will." Mishra leaned forward to deliver a killing blow with his ankh.

Urza felt anger, hot and fresh; and with that anger came action. Were he thinking rationally, he might have tried to retreat, to talk, to plan another assault at a later day. But he was in pain, and anger welled from that pain. He moved instinctively and impulsively.

He dropped the defenses he had erected around him, defenses that had blossomed when the two fought. Instead, he used the energy of the stone to launch a direct assault against his brother.

He used the Mightstone as a focus for his assault, but poured into it his anger at Mishra. He poured all his rage, and all his other emotions as well: how he loved his brother and how he hated him, how their war had wrecked their lives and their world. All this he poured through the stone in one blast of energy.

And as he did so, he felt something give within him. It was as when a muscle suddenly pulled from strain, or a gear changed within a device. Suddenly the mental walls around him fell away, and he realized his brother had been right.

He had never realized true power.

Until now.

Urza knew the power came from within him, not from any device or crystal. He fed that power through the stone and into a single bolt against his brother.

Mishra's chest exploded in a ball of crimson fire, and the younger man screamed and fell. The fire spread through his robes and he flailed his arms as the flames engulfed him. His body blazed brightly for a moment; then he was gone, fleeing back into the smoke that filled the valley.

Urza watched him flee and now realized what had made Mishra so powerful. For Mishra's robes had burned in Urza's assault, and with the robes the flesh beneath them had peeled away from the heat.

Beneath the flesh had been metal. Urza had seen it for only a moment but that was enough. There were plates where Mishra's ribs should have been, and pulleys and coiled knots of steel rope where his muscles should have operated.

His brother had been consumed by his own machines. He had become one himself.

Urza felt the effects of his own assault. Something had changed within him, and once the door was open it could not be closed. He could sense the world around him by more than sight and feeling. He could feel the power within himself and the power within the land that surrounded him.

The land was in pain. No, not just in Argoth, but in all of Terisiare. He and his brother had plundered the earth for its riches, and damaged it almost beyond repair. Now it cried out to him, in a maddening chorus, crying for respite. Crying for release.

There was another flicker of motion to his left, and he raised the Mightstone against a new assault. But this time it was Tawnos staggering out of the smoky fog, coughing and clutching a backpack. The student looked ancient as he staggered forward.

"Urza," said the former apprentice. "The machines no longer obey."

Urza looked over the battlefield and saw it with new eyes. Where before there was the confusion, he now saw another puppeteer pulling the strings. Pulling the strings of the artifact creatures. The strings of his brother. His own strings.

"There was a demon, a creature from Phyrexia," continued Tawnos. "He ambushed me and Ashnod. Ashnod said I should bring you this." He pulled a bowl-shaped sylex from the pack. "Urza, are you listening?"

Urza looked at the bowl and heard the cries of the land around them. "I hear," he said. "More than you realize, now, I hear."

"We should retreat," said Tawnos, "get away from here. If your brother finds us . . ."

"My brother has been here once," said Urza, "and he will be coming back." He took the bowl from Tawnos's hands, and as he touched the sylex, the cries of the land became more intense in his ears. They rose in a deafening cacophony of pain that only he could hear.

"Ashnod says you are supposed to fill it with memories of the land," said Tawnos. The scholar's mouth worked a moment, then he added, "I don't know what that means."

"I know," said Urza, and he *did* know. The moment he took the bowl from Tawnos he knew what its purpose was and how he was to use it. The understanding flowed through him like an electric jolt.

"We should go," said Tawnos.

"No," said Urza, softly.

"Urza, you're hurt—" began Tawnos, but Urza cut him off.

"No," he repeated. "It ends here, for me and for him." For a moment, his eyes focused on Tawnos, and Urza said, "You must go and find a safe refuge. Find some place to take cover."

"Urza, I'm not . . ."

"*Do Not Argue!*" thundered Urza, and his eyes flashed with rage. "Find the deepest cave, the farthest tree, the strongest fortification. Find anything to protect yourself and *Do It Now!*"

Tawnos was gone, and Urza was alone on the hillside. Only for a moment, for there was a clanking and clattering to his right, down toward the valley. The noise grew louder by the moment.

Mishra was returning, and he had brought a dragon engine with him.

The mists parted as the great machine rumbled up the hill toward the wounded scholar, and Urza mentally corrected himself. Mishra had brought the dragon engine as a part of himself..

Most of the flesh had burned away from his brother's form, leaving only a maze of coiled wire and black cables beneath, oozing fluid. The cables had reached out from within his body and merged with those of the dragon engine. This one had been the one at Korlinda, and similar cables had extruded from it to join with Mishra. Machine and man had become one entity.

Mishra's face was largely intact, save for a long, burned scar along one side. The tatters of flesh flapped against the metal beneath as his mechanical jaw opened and closed, bellowing threats. There was a dripping redness along that side that might have been blood.

Urza saw the abomination that was his brother and knew what must be done. He spoke a word and pulled the energies of the land to him.

In an instant, the hillside at his feet slid away, crashing toward the Mishra engine. The man machine was caught by the cascading earth and dragged backward, down toward the valley floor.

It would not stop his hate-filled brother, Urza realized, but it would slow him down. And that was enough.

Urza sat cross-legged with the bowl in his lap. The runes within the bowl spiraled toward the center, but he did not need to read them. Whatever force now coursed through his veins allowed him comprehension, allowed him to commune with the artifact as he now heard the cries of the land. Blood from the gushing wound on his forehead dribbled into the bowl and filled the carved runes with crimson.

Urza summoned his memories, the memories of his life and his studies, and willed them into the bowl. He thought of Argive and of Korlis. He thought of his towers and workshops and of the orniary in Kroog. He thought of lands he had flown over and fought over. He thought of the Kher Ridges and the Caverns of Koilos.

And he thought of a small encampment, now forgotten by most living men and buried by sand, where students of an old woman dug for artifacts of an ancient and forgotten people. Where two brothers learned about the Thran.

The Mishra machine had recovered from the avalanche and was now charging up the hill, its dragon head screaming. Urza looked up and saw his brother's face, half-torn from the metallic skull beneath, and wept for him. The artificer's tears joined the blood and memories in the bowl, and he felt the power well up around him.

The power filled him now, flowing to him from all the lands and all the memories of the things that he had done. His regrets and pride and anger and solitude all poured into the bowl, filling it to the brim, filling it to the bursting point. And beyond.

The Mishra machine had attained the hilltop now, and its serpent head loomed high above him. Mishra was grinning, the smile half-flesh and half-steel. It was the grin of a man triumphant.

Mishra was screaming something, but Urza no longer heard his voice. All he heard was the land, crying for release.

And Urza released the power.

A flash at the base of the bowl spread outward and upward, a new sun brought to the earth and igniting everything it touched. Urza felt the flash for a moment and smiled as it washed over him. His last sight was of his brother, melded to the machine, as both were caught in the blast. The smile on his brother's face turned into a twisted parody as the systems of his body failed. Then the Mishra dragon reduced to its smallest particles, and those particles were caught by the force of the explosion Urza had called into being. They were blown far, far away.

And Urza was gone as well.

* * * * *

Argoth died at last. Those survivors in the land only had a moment to react to the great flash of light on the horizon, when suddenly it was on top of them.

The surviving trees ignited where they stood, blown down by the wind, their stumps uprooted by the undulating earth as ground slid beneath the sea, and new earth shot up from the force of the explosion.

Gaea screamed as the circle of destruction widened.

* * * * *

The men on Harbin's ship who had been looking south were blinded by the light, their eyes reduced to pools of blood from the intensity. The masts and sails of the ship were set afire by the heat.

The ship was suddenly rising, as the sea itself became a mountain and carried the boat with it. The ship rose upward, and Harbin clung to the tattered remains of the rigging, screaming his father's name.

All at once the boat and the man were atop the great swell of the ocean, and Harbin could see, far to the south, the reddish glow of the sky as Argoth burned. He could see other swells, each larger than the one that had just overtaken them, advancing like relentless armies.

His ship was cast down again into the ocean.

* * * * *

Gwenna felt the ground tremble beneath her and heard the cry of Gaea as her land died. They were fighting Korlisians along the coast, and many of the warriors on both sides now cast down their weapons and began to weep. The war was over, and there were to be no victors.

Gwenna noticed the sea was gone, leaving only broad patches of mud and rock. She realized what that meant. She shouted for her warriors to flee to the hills inland and broke into a loping run; she did not see which ones obeyed her.

She was halfway up the nearest hill when the first great waves, each the size of a small mountain, broke against the coastline, smashing everything in their path.

* * * * *

In Penregon, Kayla set down her pen at the sound of distant thunder. But the thunder did not diminish but instead became louder and was soon accompanied by the rushing of winds. The ground shook beneath her, and in another room there was the sound of dishes clattering to the floor.

The room was rocked, and the furniture slid against the far wall and was smashed. To the south there was a great reddish glow, as if all of southern Argive had caught fire.

The door flew open, and Jarsyl, Harbin's eldest, came in, crying and clutching one of his father's old toys, a mechanical bird that Tawnos had made for him. Kayla hugged the child and whispered soft words to him, as outside the house men screamed and buildings toppled.

And a single tear ran down the side of her face as she comforted her grandchild.

* * * * *

In the caverns of Koilos the air wrinkled and pursed, and there was the smell of burning oil as Gix returned to his lair.

He had been damaged, and his movements left greasy footprints and spatters of oil. There was human blood on him as well, on his chest, his talons, and his face, but he had no time to consider his appearance.

He worked quickly, one part of his mind calculating how long it would take for the blast wave to reach him, another wondering if the mountain itself would be sufficient protection, while a third part readied the Thran machine. A loose pile of power crystals was placed on the holder that he had hoped would once again carry the united Weakstone and Mightstone, and his bloodstained hands moved over the glyphs with hurried grace.

The air began to swirl and form its gateway, but it was not yet fully formed when the earth shook beneath his feet. The front of the blast wave was surging up the canyon outside. Gix leapt up the steps to the dais, and looked around. Already parts of the ceiling were beginning to cave in, and the machines were sparking and going dead.

Gix cursed and dived through the small portal, feetfirst. And as he dived, the portal winked shut around him.

There was a scream within the vaults, and then nothing, save for a demon's arm, severed at the elbow, clenching and unclenching at something it could not attain, lying on the floor of the shattered room.

* * * * *

Near the foot of the Ronom Glacier, Feldon and Loran watched as a great dust storm swallowed the foothills far below them. The sand had been drawn from the desert hundreds of miles away and now flayed everything in the lowlands. Even at their height, a hot, dust-ladened wind swept over them, and Loran pulled her cloak tight with her left arm. Beneath the cloak, her right arm was a twisted and mangled remnant.

Feldon surveyed the terrain below them as one valley after another disappeared beneath the blast, leaving only a churned fog of dust and despair that was already trying to climb their mountain. The lower peaks were already vanishing beneath the assault.

"Well," he said at last, "it's over."

Loran said said, "Good."

* * * * *

And there was silence in Terisiare.

EPILOGUES

Diverging Paths

The dreams had called them. From the now-ruined monastery and from the glass-paved lands of Yotia. From the abandoned wreckage of Tomakul and from hidden places within the old coastal kingdoms. They brought with them their inventions, their devices, and their notes on the nature of magic. The dreams beckoned them to the Secret Heart of the Thran, to the caverns of Koilos, and they obeyed.

They dug out the passage where it had caved in. They buried the bodies they found there and made a reliquary for the great demon's arm they found, eternally twitching, at the foot of the dais. They repaired the machines as best as they were able, guided by the old knowledge and by their dreams.

At last they were finished, and they placed the broken and fading power crystals in their holders, touching the glyphs as they had been instructed. The machines hummed and sputtered and came to a slow, flickering life.

Slowly the air pursed and a swirling pool appeared, a gateway into the promised lands beyond. Through that gate came a long mechanical arm, tipped with talons, mate to the one that they had venerated as the arm of Gix.

The arm beckoned to them and withdrew back into its own lands, and a voice rang out from the gate. "Enter, my children," it said, "enter and taste paradise."

Smiling, the priests of the Brotherhood of Gix stepped up to the gateway and entered Phyrexia.

* * * * *

What had once been a verdant coastline was now awash with debris. The flotsam of great trees and the jetsam of huge boulders had been driven miles into shore, creating a blasted region along the shore, devoid of life.

Among the wreckage was a large metal box, seven feet in length, three feet in width and height. It had weathered the destruction and came to rest among the other far-flung remains of what had been Argoth.

Urza stood alongside the box and pressed his hand against the lid.

The box's top slid along its casters, revealing the slumbering form of his former apprentice. Tawnos took a breath, then sat bolt-upright, gasping for air. His face was pale, and he was covered with dead skin that had flaked off but had nowhere to go within his confinement.

Urza waited for Tawnos to regain his composure, standing as patient as a statue. Tawnos took a deep breath, held it, then took a second one. Then he looked around at the devastation that surrounded them.

"It is over," said Urza, sitting on the edge of the box.

Tawnos gulped and looked around. "This was the safest hiding place I could think of," he said. Urza did not reply. Tawnos said, "Your brother?"

"Dead," said Urza. "I . . ." He shook his head. "The demon, the Phyrexian, killed my brother long ago. I never realized it."

"Where are we?" asked Tawnos.

Urza looked around and sighed, deeply. "The southern coast of Yotia."

Tawnos blinked. "It has changed."

"The world has changed," said Urza, "because of what we did. Because of what I did."

Tawnos climbed out of the box, and Urza helped him. Tawnos felt weak from his incarceration and rubbed his arms and legs, both to shake off the dead skin and to restore circulation. It was cold on this shore, colder than Tawnos remembered it as a youth.

"I need one last task from you, my former student," said Urza.

"Name it," said Tawnos.

"I want you to go west. Find the remains of the Union, the scholars of the ivory towers. Tell them what happened here. Tell them what we did, and what we failed to do. See to it that they do not do the same. I trust you to do this."

Tawnos looked at the older man, but it seemed to him that Urza was no longer old. His hair was blond again and his shoulders straight.

But his eyes were old beyond years and pained beyond mortal hurt.

"You can always trust me," said Tawnos. "Where are you going?"

Urza turned from his former pupil. "Away," he said after a short while. "I am going . . . away."

"It looks as if we could use your help here," said Tawnos.

Urza made a noise that Tawnos thought was a nervous laugh. "I don't think the land could survive any more of my help. I need to . . . I need to go away. And think by myself. Where I will not harm others."

Tawnos nodded, and said, "I don't know if there is any place that far away."

Urza shook his head and said, "There are places far beyond the land of Terisiare, far beyond world of Dominaria. When I poured my memories into the sylex, I saw them. I see many things that I had never seen before."

He turned back to Tawnos, and the Master Scholar saw Urza's eyes. They were no longer human eyes, but rather two gemstones, radiating with a cascade of multicolored hues: green, white, red, black, and blue.

Mightstone and Weakstone, reunited at last, within the surviving brother.

The image was only for an instant; then Urza's eyes were normal again. Urza smiled. "I must go away," he repeated.

Tawnos nodded slowly, and the man with human crystalline eyes stood. "You have long been a student," said Urza. "Now go be a teacher."

As he spoke, Urza began to fade from view. Slowly the color drained from him, leaving only outlines; then they too faded. "Teach them of our triumphs and our mistakes," said a distant voice. "And tell Kayla to remember me not . . ."

". . . As you were, but as you tried to be," finished Tawnos, but he was speaking to empty space. Urza had passed from the world into greater worlds that only his crystalline eyes could see.

Tawnos looked around, but there was no sign of life. He struck inland, hoping to get past the worst of the devastation before he had to travel west. He recognized no familiar landmarks, and he had the feeling that he would not for a long time. Tawnos wondered how bad the devastation truly was.

And as Tawnos walked inland, he was greeted by the first flakes of snow drifting down a chill wind.

Tales of Dominaria

LEGIONS

Onslaught Cycle, Book II
J. Robert King

In the blood and sand of the arena,
two foes clash in a titanic battle.

January 2003

EMPEROR'S FIST

Magic Legends Cycle Two, Book II
Scott McGough

War looms above the Edemi Islands, casting the deep
and dread shadow of the Emperor's Fist.

March 2003

SCOURGE

Onslaught Cycle, Book III
J. Robert King

From the fiery battles of the Cabal, a new god has arisen,
one whose presence drives her worshipers to madness.

May 2003

THE MONSTERS OF MAGIC

An anthology edited by J. Robert King

From Dominaria to Phyrexia, monsters fill the multiverse,
and tales of the most popular ones fill these pages.

August 2003

CHAMPION'S TRIAL

Magic Legends Cycle Two, Book III
Scott McGough

To restore his honor, the onetime champion of Madara must
battle his own corrupt empire and the monster on the throne.

November 2003